LOCHANDAR

LOCHANDAR

Margaret Potter

GUILD PUBLISHING
LONDON

Photoset by Input Typesetting Ltd
Printed and bound in Great Britain by
Adlard & Son Ltd, The Garden City Press

This edition published 1988 by
Guild Publishing
by arrangement with W. H. Allen & Co Plc

CONTENTS

BOOK ONE

1909–1924

BOOK TWO

1987

EPILOGUE

1988

Author's note

In the early years of this century, a large number of charitable societies existed for the purpose of sending poor orphans out to the colonies where, it was hopefully believed, they would enjoy happy and healthy new lives. The Orphans' New Life Society is an imaginary organisation which has no connection with any actual charity past or present. Both it and all the characters in this book are fictional.

BOOK ONE

1909 – 1924

PART ONE

CHILDREN OF THE CASTLE

1

The laird of Lochandar was dying. Meg, his collie bitch, knew it and lay all day and night in front of his door with her sharp chin pressed down between her paws. Hamish, the piper, knew it and silently rehearsed in his head the lament which he had last played four years earlier, when the elder son of the house was killed in battle. The servants knew it, and went about their duties in silence. They had no fears for their own positions. The heir to the estate was a child: everything would go on as it had before. But the old man had been laird for fifty years: the moment of his passing would be a sad one for them all.

Ella McEwan had been the first to realise that the end was approaching, and her sadness was genuine. Had he been allowed the choice, the laird would probably not have picked an English girl to be the bride of his elder son, and there was a certain stiffness in his manner when, thirteen years before, the young couple had arrived at Lochandar, still breathless from the haste of their elopement. But ten months later the birth of the first baby – a boy, to continue the line – had healed any hurt that he might have felt at not being consulted about the marriage. For the past twelve years, beneath his brusque manner, he had been as kind to his daughter-in-law as though he were her father. Her true father had cut her off without a penny or a kind word when she ran away at the age of sixteen; now Lochandar was her only home and the McEwans her only family.

It was Ella who warned her two eldest children of what was happening. All three children – even three-year-old Jamie, who was too young yet to be troubled with news of this kind – were by nature matter-of-fact. They might grumble over small troubles, but they shared a stolid acceptance of the larger events which shaped the course of their lives. They were familiar with so many animals – the dogs and ponies, cats and rabbits and mice which were their pets, as well as the deer and grouse and fish which were killed for food – that they had come to understand birth and death and to accept both without sentimentality. Mairi, who was only seven, sometimes wept over the disappearance of a favourite pet, but even she was mature enough to recognise that she was crying for herself, and not for the animal which had died. She did not cry now as she listened to what her mother had to say – although in spite of the beard and whiskers which tickled when he kissed her, she adored the old man whose only granddaughter she was. Grief silenced her. It was left to her twelve-year-old brother, Fergus, to ask a question.

'Will it be soon, Mother?'

'I'm afraid so. I'd like you to sit with him for an hour every day, Fergus. No need for you to talk. Just be there in case he has anything to say to you.'

Fergus nodded. The three children were alike in looks. Each of them had inherited a freckled skin, fair curly hair and clear blue eyes. But in temperament the differences between them became more marked with every year that passed. Mairi needed to love and Jamie to be loved; so Mairi was happiest in the company of animals, and Jamie with Nurse, snug before the nursery fire in the castle tower. In contrast, had Fergus been asked to say what brought him most contentment, he might well have chosen solitude.

He was a sturdy boy, tall for his age, who spoke little and then always the truth. For as long as he could

3

remember he had known that Lochandar would belong to him one day, and his father's death had brought that day much closer. First with the old laird himself and more recently with Robert, the keeper, and Graham, the gillie, he had walked the moors and the mountains and fished the streams and the loch, thereby imprinting on his mind and instincts a map of the land which would soon belong to him. He was too young to understand all that was involved in ownership; but his ancestors had been able to take on the responsibility and so, no doubt, could he.

There had never in the past been any need for the laird to talk of the future with his grandson. It was taken for granted between the old man and the boy. Only now, in the last week of his life, was the subject raised – for the laird, like everyone else on the estate, knew that he was dying and, as phlegmatic as his grandson, did not fight the knowledge. He had had a good run.

'When it's yours,' he said, each sentence short because he lacked breath, 'no need for change. Robert and Graham. Good men. Know what's best. Go on as they are. Till you're full grown.'

Fergus nodded, understanding perfectly the fractured instructions.

'The wee laddie, Jamie,' said his grandfather. 'Your father and your uncle Malcolm. Never good friends, boys or men. But you . . .'

'I'll look after Jamie,' said Fergus.

The laird's blue eyes, once so fierce but now becoming dim and watery, looked hard at his grandson and nodded his approval. 'Tomorrow,' he said. 'Jamie, here tomorrow. With the casket.'

The casket had belonged to the laird himself for seventy years. Neither of his two sons had ever shown any interest in its contents, so he stowed it away in one of the castle's many unused rooms – until the day when he came in from his morning ride to find wee Jamie flicking pebbles at a target in competition with one of the stable lads. The child's podgy thumb lacked strength to bring

4

him success in the game, but his eye was true and he showed a concentration unusual in a three-year-old. The laird gave him the casket as a late birthday present, and lowered his stiff and bulky body to the floor in order to demonstrate the different games which could be played with it.

The box itself was made from a warm brown wood which smelt, when it was opened, sometimes of rose petals and sometimes of spices. On the outside it had been lacquered in black and then decorated with sea shells, which made it prickly to carry. As a general rule, Jamie left it in the nursery cupboard, taking out of it only what he needed for a game.

At the time appointed by his grandfather, though, he clutched it to his chest as his nurse led him from the oldest part of the castle, in which the three children lived with their mother, to the wing which their grandfather had built on for himself fifty years earlier.

'Show me,' said the laird.

Jamie opened the box, the inside of which was divided into sections. In each section was a chamois pouch with a leather thong to close its mouth and act as a carrying strap. The largest pouch held ordinary marbles: the small ones. Their eyes were of different colours – blue, green, yellow, violet, black, and Jamie's own favourite, a rich shade of butterscotch. When he was playing by himself, he divided these marbles into teams, each of one colour, which could compete against each other.

Another pouch contained most of his alleys: the large taws, delicately spiralled with colour, which were used as shooters to win the smaller marbles staked by anyone who could be persuaded to play with him – his brother Fergus, or the stable lads. Margaret, the nursery maid, was usually willing to play, but had no marbles of her own, so that Jamie always had to lend her some before winning them back again.

In a third pouch were the specials, the two great taws which he would never put at risk by using them as stakes. They were very old, and the laird had introduced them to his grandson by name when he made the gift.

5

Connie was the curious one, containing no colour in its centre, but only a pattern of rock crystal in the star-shape of a snowflake. Rialto was the beautiful one. Imprisoned in the middle of Rialto was a yellow butterfly – almost, but not quite, transparent, with thin lines of purple veining the yellow wings. Jamie had never quite been able to decide whether or not it was a real butterfly which had somehow been encased in glass. If the taw were one day to break, would the released butterfly flutter away, or dissolve into dust – or merely collapse into tiny splinters of coloured glass? Any of these would be a tragedy, so Jamie never risked Rialto in a hard battle, but had invented for it a special game of rolling over a rug to rest on particular parts of the pattern.

To the lid of the casket were fastened three targets which could be used with the marbles. As a general rule, of course, all that was needed for a goal was a circle marked out in the dust, with a firing line a small distance away. But the targets made a good game for Jamie when he had to play by himself. One was a wide arch through which a marble should be shot. That was easy. To make it more difficult, there was a portcullis which could be fitted to the arch, dividing it into three much narrower openings, so that an invading marble was likely to bump against a bar and bounce back again.

Hardest of all was the castle. The castle was rather like an upside-down saucer with sloping sides and a small dent in the middle of the top. From the edge of a wide circle marked all around, it was necessary to strike the marble with some force to propel it up the slope – but then, almost always, it was travelling too fast to stop and settle in the dent. Twice since he was given the casket had Jamie succeeded in getting one of his small marbles into place – a success which allowed him to call out in triumph 'I'm Cook of the Castle!' But he had never managed to become Lord of the Castle. For that, he must persuade one of the large alleys to rest on top – and such a feat was almost impossible, for they were too large to settle inside the indentation, but would have to balance on its rim. On the day when he was finally able to shout

'I'm Lord of the Castle!' something tremendously important would take place: he was sure of that. But it didn't seem likely that it would ever happen.

The laird watched as Jamie opened each pouch in turn to display its contents, but his eyes were on the boy rather than on his treasures. A three-year-old with all his life in front of him. What would he do with it? To be a second son was to live with uncertainty. The land around Lochandar Castle was beautiful, but poor. Its tenants, scratching a living, could not be expected to pay more than token rents, which did not at all cover the cost of repairs to their cottages – making them, as much as the castle servants, dependants of the family. Fergus should be able to live off the estate, but Jamie would have to make his own way in the world. Malcolm, the laird's own second son, had never seemed to come to terms with his status. It was to be hoped that Jamie would look at his own situation with clearer eyes.

'Are ye Lord of the Castle yet?' he asked the boy who would never own Lochandar.

Jamie shook his head. He took the castle out of its fastening and set it down on the floor. Choosing Rialto, because there was a rug covering the boards, he tried unsuccessfully to castle it.

'Why is it not "laird"?' he asked his grandfather, as for the fifth time the taw rolled down the further side. 'Laird of the Castle instead of Lord?'

'A laird maun have land. A lord has power; but a laird maun have land.' The old man breathed deeply after a sentence longer than he could easily manage these days. 'Find land for yourself, Jamie.' He could tell that the child didn't know what he was talking about. 'Here,' he said. 'A wee keepsake.'

Set ready on the table beside his bed was a chamois pouch similar to those already in the casket. He had removed it when he first made the gift, thinking that a three-year-old would not understand its value. With a nod of his head he indicated that Jamie should see what was inside.

It was another taw. A round lump of creamy stone, its

surface shining from many years of loving touch by the boy who was now an old man. It was not as beautiful as Rialto or Connie, for there was no pattern in the centre.

'Alabaster,' said the laird. 'The alabaster taw. For you, laddie. To keep. Never stake it. Understand?'

Jamie nodded. Although not disappointed – for he had had no expectations – his bright blue eyes did not at first show any great pleasure in the gift. But clutching it in his hand, he dropped down again on to the rug and began first to roll and then to flick the taw. The stone became alive with colour as it came close to the fire. Jamie picked it up again and held it in front of the flames, turning it over and over in an attempt to see inside. He cradled it in both hands before rolling it again – recognising, as the laird himself had recognised on his own seventh birthday, the harmony of weight and size which would make the taw his most obedient servant. He played for a little while with increasing satisfaction before remembering his manners and standing up to kiss his bewhiskered grandfather in thanks.

With the last of his strength, the laird embraced his youngest grandchild. Then he nodded to Jamie's nurse, who had been sitting quietly by the door, that she could take the boy away.

'Your ain land,' he called after them, angered by the feebleness of his voice. 'Find land for yourself, my wee Jamie.'

Jamie turned his head. He smiled to show that he had heard, but already his thoughts were elsewhere. It was time for his tea. The glowing nursery fire in the round tower of the castle would be forming pictures for him to see, and Margaret the nursery maid would soon carry up a beaker of milk and a plate of oat cakes still hot from the griddle. It was a contented little boy who followed his nurse out of the old laird's bedroom. No one had warned him that he would never see his grandfather again. No one had as yet realised that within a few days the happiness of his childhood was to be brought to a sudden and grim end.

2

'I'm cold.'

Jamie shivered, as though to prove the truth of his complaint. Mairi, sitting beside him on the floor, shivered in sympathy. She was cold as well. They looked longingly at the small red glow which showed that the last two coals in the fireplace were still alight. There were bellows beside the grate which would puff the glow up into a flame. But then the coals would burn too quickly and be gone, and the box beside the hearth was empty.

Outside, the rain beat against the window in erratic fusillades. Their mother, when she returned at last, would be chilled and wet. If there was any warmth to be extracted from those two dull black lumps, it must be saved for her. The younger children grumbled only as a matter of form, knowing that Fergus would not indulge their wishes. Huddled round the fireplace, they listened for the sound of their mother's footsteps. Surely today she would bring good news – news that the last of the necessary documents had been signed, so that they could all leave Edinburgh and go back to the castle.

It was difficult for the children to understand why the world had suddenly become so very cold. Lochandar Castle, after all, was for many months of the year surrounded by the snow which lay on the moors and mountains. But it was somehow a warm snow, which brought colour to their cheeks as they sledged down the hillsides or slid and skated on the frozen loch. The rain was warm there as well – not like this city rain which was so sharp and hard that it could be seen falling in straight lines; but a gentle, friendly mist which filled the air with an almost tender wetness. The three young McEwans were accustomed to spending much of their time out of doors without ever bothering about the weather – knowing that they would return to a cosy nursery or schoolroom in which log or peat fires burned night and day. How different that was from this damp, shivery house in a city pierced by freezing winds.

In the castle, too, it had not been merely a fire which had warmed them. They were loved: it was as simple as that. Gruff though he might sometimes be, their grandfather, the laird, had loved them until the day four months earlier when he died. Nurse had loved them as well. Only Jamie was still young enough to remain part of her kingdom, but the fact that Fergus and Mairi had moved on to the schoolroom made no difference. They came back every day to join their young brother for nursery tea. In that familiar tower room all three children had felt cosy and safe, surrounded by affection as well as comfort.

To say that the outdoor staff loved them might perhaps be an exaggeration, for it was not the custom for men to show more than tolerance to children. But during the laird's last illness, and in the two months which followed his death, the gamekeeper had continued to walk over the moors with the young heir, teaching him to stalk and shoot. The grooms took it in turns to ride with Fergus every morning and the gillie went with him when he had it in mind to fish. They were all silent men, at ease with the silent boy. Fergus was happiest in the open air, with only the ripple of water over rocks or the shiver of the wind in the heather to disturb the silence. That was why he hated Edinburgh, with its noisy, dirty streets, and hoped that their visit might soon end.

At home in the castle, the two younger children had been more boisterous than their elder brother. Mairi talked to the animals – her pony, her puppy, the five dogs of the castle, the kitchen cat, her pet white mice – whilst wee Jamie chattered away to himself in the manner of most little boys. But since coming to Edinburgh they had become as silent as Fergus. Mairi was afraid of their landlady, Mrs Grace, who complained whenever they were noisy; and she was anxious not to upset their mother, who nowadays seemed to be tired all the time. As for Jamie, who had just passed his fourth birthday, he didn't understand what was happening. Bewilderment kept him quiet – as though silence would elicit an explanation, or even a promise that they might soon go back to the castle.

Even Jamie understood about death. His father had died, fighting in another country, before he himself was born. Fergus and Mairi could remember their father, but Jamie had never seen him. To be dead, he had learned, was never to be seen again. So when he was told that the laird was dead, he knew what that meant: he would never see his grandfather again. But he didn't understand – how could he? – why it was that he had had to leave Nurse and Margaret, whom he loved.

To Fergus, Mrs McEwan had given an explanation. Understanding nothing of legal matters, he had not known whether he had become laird automatically as soon as his grandfather died, or whether he must wait until his twenty-first birthday. Something had happened, a few weeks after the old laird's funeral, to make his mother angry, but it had not seemed unreasonable when she told him that she must take the whole family south to Edinburgh in order to settle their affairs. Matters of inheritance, she said, were always complicated. It would be quicker to settle them face to face, rather than in exchanges of letters which might drag on for ever and a day.

By this time in February all the children were aware that the talks with the lawyers were not going well. They did not often have cause to remember that their mother had been born an Englishwoman. As far as they were concerned, she had become a Scot when she married their father. But every day now she sighed over the intricacies of Scottish law – to which her own kind, she implied, was much superior. Nor had she a good word to say for Scottish lawyers, who had to have every little detail spelt out for them and would not believe even the most obvious fact until it could be proved in three different ways. Mairi and Jamie didn't know what she was talking about, and even Fergus took it for granted that it must all come right in the end. So they were not worried about anything except the fact that, after each visit to the lawyer's office, their mother looked even paler

11

and more tired than before. That, and the fact that they were cold all the time.

Even before they heard her footsteps on the stairs, they caught the sound of her coughing. Mrs McEwan had caught a cold from Edinburgh's sharp, icy rain, and for a month now had been coughing to clear her chest and breathing in a wheezy, bubbling way when she failed. If only they could go home again to the castle and be warm! Perhaps today the news would be good.

Fergus gave a tiny puff of the bellows so that a flicker of flame might greet his mother's return, but it was not enough to take the chill off the room. Even before she had taken off her wet cloak and kissed the three of them, Mrs McEwan rang the bell which would call the maid-of-all-work up two flights of stairs.

'More coal,' she said when Jenny appeared at last, looking sulky and none too clean.

'I'm not to be carrying any more up today,' said Jenny.

'Don't be ridiculous, girl. It's barely two o'clock. Do you intend us all to freeze to death up here?'

'I'm sorry, ma'am, to be sure, but Mrs Grace said – '

'Tell Mrs Grace that I wish to speak to her. At once.'

'Very well, ma'am.'

Jenny closed the door and could be heard thumping down the stairs.

'Is your business with the lawyer finished, Mother?' asked Fergus hopefully.

Mrs McEwan shook her head. 'Not yet. But tomorrow, I'll tell him tomorrow. Then we can all go home.'

'Tell him what?'

His mother, sighing as though the effort of speaking had exhausted her, lay back on the sofa. Without being asked, Fergus unfastened her boots, which were losing their neat, expensive appearance in the puddled streets. He lifted her feet on to the sofa, and heard her sigh again and close her eyes.

For most of the past three days she had lain like this, too tired to make any movement except that of coughing; every day she looked more tired than the day before. If she was going to have another quarrel with Mrs Grace in this weak state, then the landlady would certainly win. Fergus took up a position next to the sofa, to make it clear that his mother had a protector, and to speak up for her if necessary. He could not expect any help from his younger brother and sister. Mairi was only a girl and wee four-year-old Jamie was little more than a baby. Already he had hidden himself on the floor behind the sofa, so that Mrs Grace wouldn't know he was there. He didn't like quarrels.

Fergus was not fond of quarrelling himself, but he knew his duty. When the family first arrived in these lodgings, Mrs Grace had been pleasant and friendly. It was only in the past two weeks that she seemed to be cross all the time. Sometimes she spoke sharply to the three children and sometimes she refused to speak to them at all. Fergus didn't mind that for himself, but he wasn't going to let anyone bully his mother.

Mrs Grace took her time about coming, and when she arrived in the room it was without even a tap at the door. She was a tiny woman, always dressed in black, with a sharp nose like the beak of a bird. 'What is it?' she demanded.

Mrs McEwan didn't answer. Her eyes were closed, and each breath she took seemed to be forcing itself out of her body, needing so great an effort that she had no energy left to speak or move. 'Well?' asked Mrs Grace.

Why didn't their mother say something? Jamie, in his hiding place behind the sofa, kept very still; but Mairi glanced anxiously at her elder brother, expecting him to take charge. Fergus, for his part, stared down at his mother for a moment and then looked Mrs Grace straight in the eye.

'Will you call a doctor, if you please, Mrs Grace?' As always, his voice was soft, but he spoke with the firmness of a man rather than of a boy who was only just thirteen.

'A doctor, is it?' Mrs Grace grew shrill with indignation. 'What makes you think that a doctor will come running to a woman who hasn't two pennies to rub together? Let me tell you, Master McEwan, that doctors present bills for their services and expect them to be settled. They're not foolish and soft-hearted like myself, accepting payment in promises.'

'Are you wishing it to be known that your rooms are so cold and damp that to take lodgings here is to invite sickness? Do you not see, Mrs Grace, that my mother is very ill? She must have a doctor – and more coals for the fire – at once.'

The landlady stepped forward to look down at Mrs McEwan's face. What she saw must have alarmed her, for she left the room without speaking and within only a few moments Jenny carried in a bucket from which to refill the brass coalbox.

'Well done, Fergus,' whispered his mother almost before the maid was out of earshot. All three children were surprised to hear her speak, and with such apparent cheerfulness. But while Mairi and Jamie were relieved that she seemed to have recovered, Fergus was disturbed. A truthful boy himself, he always assumed that other people were equally honest, and believed what they told him. It was difficult now not to wonder whether his mother had only been pretending to be ill.

Or was it the cheerfulness which was a pretence? Certainly she made no attempt to move from the sofa and change out of her damp skirts. Instead, her slight body seemed to have collapsed into hollowness through exhaustion. She was not yet thirty, for she had married at sixteen and given birth to her eldest son within a year: but since the death of the laird she had lost her youthful verve and colour, becoming pale and tired and worried. Even if a moment earlier she had pretended to be more ill than she was, her weakness was not all pretence.

Certainly the doctor, when he came, did not complain of being called out without cause. Brisk rather than sympathetic, he sent the children into their bedroom while he made an examination, and then called Fergus back again. Mairi and Jamie stood listening in the doorway.

'She should be in the infirmary,' said the doctor. 'I'll arrange it straightway. Where's your father?'

'Dead, four years since. And my grandfather too, a few months back.'

'Have you any other kin?'

'My uncle Malcolm. But I can look after Mairi and Jamie while she's away.'

'Your uncle had best be told, all the same. I'll send round for your mother within the hour. Keep her warm.'

Fergus put more coals on the fire. The sound disturbed his mother who, without opening her eyes, began to moan softly with each painful breath. The two younger children, alarmed by what was happening, did not dare to move.

'You can be playing with your things,' Fergus told them. 'As long as you make no noise.'

Each of the three children had been allowed to bring one treasured possession to Edinburgh with them – there would not, they were told, be space in their rented rooms for more. All Fergus's treasures belonged to the open air. The streets of Edinburgh were no place for a gun or fishing rod, so he had brought a book, and had read it through three times already. Mairi, too, had been forced to leave behind her new puppy and had chosen instead to carry Bella, the largest of her collection of dolls. She had cheated, in Fergus's opinion, by pushing two tiny peg dolls into Bella's pockets. For Jamie there was no problem of choice. He had carried with him his casket of marbles.

He chose the castle game to play today, because it was quiet and needed neither an opponent nor very much space. He played it with Basta Taw, his grandfather's deathbed gift. Basta Taw was something special. As Jamie fired it now – always straight, and each time adjusting the force of the shot according to whether the previous attempt had fallen short or rolled on too far – he had a queer feeling that he and Basta Taw were partners. It was only a bit of stone, nothing more, but it was learning what he wanted it to do almost as though it were intelligent; like Mairi's puppy realising for the first time what was meant by 'To heel!', or Fergus's pony at last working out how to gather its feet together before a jump. Twice the taw teetered on the edge of the castle's high rim before rolling down again. Jamie flattened himself on the floor and steadied his hand, ready to fire once more.

'This time, Basta Taw,' he whispered. His thumb flicked, and he held his breath. The taw rolled over the carpet and up the slope. Reaching the indentation, it hesitated, and spun itself round before settling securely into position.

'Mother, Mother!' Jamie quite forgot the need to be quiet as he scrambled to his feet. 'Lord of the Castle! I'm Lord of the Castle!' Carefully, so that the taw would not fall, he held the castle up to show her.

'So you are, Jamie,' said his mother, although without looking at it, for she was still lying with her eyes closed. 'So you are.' She was breathing in a different way now. The coughing and the wheezing and the bubbling sounds had all stopped. Instead, each breath emerged heavily, almost as a sigh, as though expelling it brought her comfort. She opened her eyes and smiled at the little boy. Then she gave a sigh more painfully loud than all the rest, which alarmed Fergus and brought him to his feet.

'Fergus,' she said. 'Where are you, Fergus?'

How could she not know, when he was only a few feet away, in the same room? Jamie's triumph turned to unease as his brother came nearer. 'I'm sorry, Fergus,' their mother said. There was a long silence; another sigh. 'Sorry.' Her eyes closed again.

'Sorry for what?' asked Fergus, puzzled; but there was no answer.

3

Fergus was the first to understand the reason why his mother remained silent for so long. Aghast, he took her hand, squeezing and shaking it as though to stir her back into life. Infected by his alarm, Mairi began to cry, and soon Jamie too was wailing, although not yet knowing why. He dropped the castle, forgetting his pride in the achievement of a few moments earlier, and did not notice that the alabaster taw rolled away into a dark corner.

'I can't have such a noise.' The landlady came into the room without being heard above the sound of the children's distress. She was in her cross and complaining mood, checking herself only for a moment as she crossed to the sofa and looked down at the dead woman. 'Could she not have waited –.' she began to grumble.

'*Mrs Grace!*' Fergus was as tall as the landlady and his blue eyes shot daggers of anger at her, whilst the two younger children continued to sob.

'Ach, well.' Mrs Grace smoothed down the front of her skirt with both hands and dipped her head in a gesture of apology. 'It's a bad day for you, and fatherless too. I'm sorry for you.' But she did not waste a great deal of time on her sorrow. 'Who's to care for you now, do you know? Doctor Macdonald was telling me you had an uncle.'

'Yes, but – ' Fergus had seen his uncle only on his occasional Christmas visits to Lochandar, and had no idea where he lived.

'Who did your mother visit when she went out every day?'

'A lawyer.'

'Then he'll know something of your affairs. You'll do well to go there at once and tell him what's happened. If you find his address, I'll set you on the way.'

'I canna leave – '

'Jenny can come up to see that they don't fall into the fire.' Mrs Grace looked sourly at the leaping flames. 'And I'll send for a woman to lay your mother out. You may tell the lawyer, when you see him, that there's money owing.'

Fergus pressed his lips together to restrain his anger, and the effort helped him to keep his grief under control for a few moments. Mrs Grace was hateful and cruel, but part of what she said made sense. Uneasily – because he knew that his mother had regarded the legal documents as private – he opened her handbag and found a letter with a printed heading.

'Blair, Honeyman and Blair. In the Royal Mile.'

'Easy enough, then. You'll see the castle from a good way off, standing high on the rock. The Royal Mile runs from it. You've just to follow the numbers. Have you something to keep off the rain? I'll show you the direction.'

Fergus put his arms round his younger brother and sister. 'I'll not be long away,' he promised them. 'Dinna greet, then.'

But of course they would cry, as Fergus, once he was alone, was also able to cry. He was accustomed to walking long distances, although not on such hard streets, and in any case he had no money in his pocket to pay for any other kind of conveyance, so he strode off into the dirty weather without complaint. As soon as his cheeks were wet from the downpour, he could allow the tears to run. Only when he reached the narrow stone frontage of the lawyer's office did he shake the rain out of his hair and dab his face dry.

Mr Blair was a stout, red-faced man, wearing a formal dark suit. One pale eyebrow rose in surprise as Fergus was shown into his office, but the rest of his face remained expressionless as he waited to discover the reason for the call.

'Dead!' he exclaimed. 'I'm sorry to hear it. Sorry indeed. On her last two or three visits here it seemed to me that she was in poor health, but I never imagined . . . Very sorry.'

'You were acting for her, I think, Mr Blair,' said Fergus.

'Well no, not precisely for her. We act for the McEwan estate. Have done for generations. My father and grand-father before me. Lochandar descends through male heirs. Well, you won't want to be troubled with the details. Your mother had no direct claim on us. But naturally we shall do whatever is needed now. You'd like us, no doubt, to arrange for the funeral. And if there are any debts to be settled . . . ?'

18

'The landlady did mention that.'

'Ask her to deliver a written statement here. To the end of the week, shall we say? And we'll inform your uncle at once of what has happened. We'll take care of everything. No need for you to worry.'

'Thank you, sir. And we would like – Mairi and Jamie and myself – we would like to go back to Lochandar as soon as we can.'

On the other side of the desk Mr Blair stood up.

'Thirteen years old, is it, Master McEwan? Only just thirteen. Not a great age for taking so much responsibility. Your brother and sister. We must see what we can do to help. For today, I must deal with your mother's sad death. There are certificates, formalities. Will you come again tomorrow morning? At eleven o'clock, shall we say? To discuss the future. There will have to be a guardianship arrangement. We'll look in our files; your father may have left instructions to cover this contingency. If not, we must consider what's best. Naturally, we shall do nothing without consulting you. It's a sad time for you. We can't bring your mother back to life, but everything else that can be done, we will do, be sure of that.'

'Thank you very much, sir.' Fergus's voice expressed his relief as he shook hands. Once he was safely back in Lochandar, everything would be all right. Surrounded by men and women who had served his family all their lives, he and his brother and sister would be safe while they were growing up and learning how to deal with the kind of problem which Mr Blair had just taken over. The lawyer had seemed sympathetic and, after all, he must now be Fergus's own lawyer. He had seemed to think that a thirteen-year-old could not understand, but Fergus was perfectly well aware of what was meant by inheritance of male heirs. He could even see how his mother – as the widow of one heir who had not lived to succeed, and the mother of the subsequent heir – might have posed a problem if she was demanding rights for herself. But there could be no possible doubt about Fergus's own

19

rights. Even if a guardian did prove to be necessary, the situation must now be straightforward.

So it was not anxiety which kept Fergus awake that night, but only grief. Within four years he had lost his father, grandfather and mother. He felt very much alone – but from the moment when he awoke next morning he must hide his feelings. Mairi and Jamie would look to him to be strong; and he did not intend to fail them.

The next morning, anxious not to be late, he arrived at Mr Blair's office half an hour before the appointed time, and waited patiently in the clerk's room. When the door of the inner office opened at five to eleven, the client who emerged proved to be Fergus's own uncle, Malcolm McEwan.

Fergus stood up politely. But to his surprise – for after all it was not long since they had last met at the old laird's funeral – his uncle appeared hardly to recognise him. He gave a brief nod, such as he might use to acknowledge the greeting of a casual acquaintance, but expressed no words of sympathy to the newly-orphaned boy. Fergus was still staring after him in bewilderment when Mr Blair appeared at the door of his office to call him in.

'Sit down, Fergus.' The lawyer seemed ill at ease this morning. 'Let us come straight to business. I've news which I fear will come as a shock to you, but I'll not beat about the bush. You said yesterday that you hoped to take your brother and sister back to Lochandar. I have to tell you that this won't be possible.'

'Why not? Lochandar belongs to me now.'

Mr Blair shook his head. 'I fear not. I know that you expected that to be the case. But this is the bad news I have for you. You have no rights in the Lochandar estate. Not to the land, nor the castle, nor to any of your grandfather's property.'

Fergus stood up indignantly. 'That canna be true. My father – '

'Sit down again, laddie. I realise that this will be hard to bear, but we must take it calmly. If your father were still alive, he would naturally have inherited the whole estate. No question about that. If your father had married and left a legitimate heir when he died, that heir would have inherited in turn. But your father did not marry.'

'What nonsense are you saying?' Fergus spluttered with disbelief, and the politeness due to an older man flew out of the window. 'My mother – '

'Your mother claimed to be your father's wife. Every week for the past five weeks I have asked her to bring me the proof of her marriage. A simple request. I am required to make it in every case of this kind. It was not a personal attack on your mother's veracity, although she chose to treat it as such. A certificate of marriage or, if that could not be found, a statement of the date and place of the marriage, so that a search could be made in the records. That was all. I wrote to her at Lochandar Castle as soon as was decent after your grandfather's funeral; and had she supplied the documents or the information that I required, the whole matter would be settled by now. But she did not, and as time went by I realised that it was because she could not.'

'But my grandfather . . .' The old laird had always accepted that Fergus would own the land one day and had said so in so many words when he was dying.

'Your grandfather, I fear, was deceived. When your father arrived at Lochandar with a young English girl whom he said was his wife, your grandfather believed him. Why should he not? A gentleman doesn't demand legal documents so that he may be sure that a young woman is truly his daughter-in-law. It's only lawyers like myself who have to satisfy ourselves that we are handing over property only to those legally entitled to receive it. The story your grandfather was told at the time was that Ella's parents had objected to the proposed marriage – because she was only sixteen years old, and a beauty who might hope for a better match if she waited until she had been presented at court. That part of it was true enough. So they eloped, and were married – they said – by the Scots form on the journey. Your father went back to his regiment not long after he had brought Ella to

21

Lochandar. He was sent overseas, and didn't return for three years. When you were born, at the castle, his name was recorded as being your father – and there's no doubt that you are his son, his spitting image in fact. I remember him as a boy.'

'Well, then?'

'His son; but not his legitimate son.'

'They would have married on the journey north as my mother told you. In a place, no doubt, that she had never visited before. How could she be expected to remember?'

'There are records of such ceremonies. With only a very little information from your mother I could have searched this one out. Indeed, I *have* searched between every date which would fit with your mother's story. I don't like to say this about your mother, but I fear she has told too many lies – to your grandfather and to me. Perhaps by the end she hardly remembered herself what the truth of the matter was.'

'And what could it be? Why should she lie?'

Mr Blair gave a sigh which combined sympathy with an inability to provide a convincing answer.

'My own guess is this: that your parents did indeed go through a form of marriage in the course of their elopement. But that perhaps they used the Scots form while they were still in England. At the age of sixteen, your mother could not legally marry south of the Border without her father's consent, and she certainly did not have that.'

'You make it sound as though – '

'I'm saying nothing against your mother,' Mr Blair assured him. 'She was little more than a child when she ran away from home. Your father was an honourable man. He would have promised her marriage, and I've no doubt, no doubt at all, that they both believed themselves to be contracted. It may have been his very eagerness to regularise the situation at the earliest possible moment that has led to this problem. Your mother has lived as a respectable married woman and has believed herself since your father's death to be a widow. It may well have been that it was only after she received my request for the necessary documents that she discovered the flaws in the ceremony. You've no cause to feel shame in your parentage. But legally, I fear . . .'

He paused, but Fergus could think of nothing to say.

'It gives me no pleasure to tell you all this, Fergus,' the lawyer continued after a moment. 'I've done my best to find some document which would support your claim. If your mother had only . . . She promised yesterday that she would bring the proof today – but she had said that so often before; and each time made some excuse for not keeping the promise. I have to say with sincere regret that your birth was illegitimate, and that as a result you have no legal claim to Lochandar.'

There was a silence even longer than before. Fergus's mind was in a state of turmoil. The lawyer's words churned round and round in his head: he felt as though he were about to be sick. An hour earlier he had been proud to think of himself as the new laird of Lochandar, and now he had to come to terms with the thought that he was only a bastard, landless and penniless. It was almost impossible to believe what he had just been told, and yet it appeared that Mr Blair was speaking sincerely. Why, after all, should he tell anything but the truth?

Even so, Fergus might still have refused to accept the statement had it not been for one short sentence which niggled at his memory. 'I'm sorry, Fergus,' his mother had said. What could that mean except that she had realised that his hopes of inheriting were to be disappointed, and that she recognised the fault as her own?

He looked down at his knees, not wishing to reveal how close he was to tears.

'Then what's to become of us?' he asked. 'Myself and the two wee bairns.'

Mr Blair's manner brightened as he realised that Fergus was attempting to control his distress rather than make a scene.

'Well, now,' he said. 'I've had a long talk with your uncle this morning. Since your own claim fails, your uncle will inherit the estate. He has no obligation in any strict legal sense to support you. But nevertheless, through family feeling . . . He has a generous spirit.'

Remembering the brusque nature of his uncle's greeting half an hour earlier, Fergus did not find comforting the prospect of relying on his generosity. 'I can support myself,' he said. 'And Jamie and Mairi. With a little help in finding employment.'

The lawyer shook his head. 'You're too young yet to take responsibility for two small children,' he said. 'They must be cared for and educated, and it will be a long time before you have the means to provide for them.'

'My grandfather – my *other* grandfather . . .' Fergus knew nothing at all about his mother's family – not even their name. But some maternal relations must surely exist; perhaps they would take an interest.

'Your maternal grandfather disowned and disinherited your mother on the day she eloped. There was no correspondence between them after that, so I have no information on whether he is still alive. It would be unwise, I suggest, to turn down the very generous plan which your uncle offers in order to explore such an unhopeful possibility.'

'So what is his plan?'

Mr Blair looked down at the notes on his desk. 'He will accept responsibility for the education of your younger brother and sister. Since he has no children of his own as yet, he feels that boarding establishments would be the most satisfactory, and has charged me to make enquiries about suitable places. For yourself, he has a suggestion which I would strongly recommend to you. Many of the colonies are anxious to attract more settlers of the right kind, and there is in existence what is called a cadet scheme, under which boys of good family, like yourself, are sent out from Scotland to New Zealand. If you take up a place on the scheme, you would be found a home with a respectable family of Scottish descent. You would work on their farm as though you were a son of the house, not as a servant, and they would give you a wide variety of experience, training you to be a farmer. Your uncle has offered to pay your fare out. Until your sixteenth birthday you would work for your board and a little pocket money. After that you would be paid according to the work you did. And on your twenty-first birthday Mr McEwan has promised to provide you with a sum of money sufficient for you to buy land of your own in New Zealand. He's prepared to sign a statement to that effect, so that you'll know you can rely on the gift. When you have your own farm, you can take over responsibility for Mairi and Jamie.'

Fergus blinked nervously as he tried to take in the implications of the offer. So many new and unwanted possibilities were being thrust at him in such a short time that he felt dazed – and doubtful about his own ability to decide for the best.

'Jamie's only just four,' he said. 'And Mairi not yet eight. I dinna care to leave them with strangers.'

'But what else can you do?'

There was one easy answer to that. They could continue to live at Lochandar Castle, with Nurse to care for Jamie and Miss Scott to give Mairi her lessons as before. But if his uncle was not prepared to offer this, Fergus had no right to suggest it.

'New Zealand is a far way away,' he said instead.

'Very many of its colonists come from Scotland,' Mr Blair told him. 'That's why this scheme is reserved for Scots lads like yourself. They call their towns and homes by Scottish names and I'm told that the mountain scenery has much in common with the Highlands. Your uncle favours this plan because it's in New Zealand that you're most likely to feel at home.'

'May I take time to think about it?'

'What can you think in more time? You've little choice. No one else can offer you as much. There's an acquaintance of Mr McEwan's who is leaving Edinburgh tomorrow to take passage to New Zealand. He's kindly volunteered to look after you and see that you're safely handed over when you arrive there. For a lad such as yourself, who's never been out of Scotland, to make such a journey alone would be difficult; so this is a good solution. Your uncle is making you a very generous offer,

25

Fergus, and he expects you to recognise it and give him a quick answer.'

Tomorrow! Fergus choked on the speed with which his life was changing. He would not even be able to see his mother buried! Yet it seemed to be true that he had no choice. Without his uncle's support, Fergus would be powerless to help his brother and sister.

'As you say, sir, the offer is a generous one,' he said slowly.

'I was astonished myself by the extent of Mr McEwan's goodwill. He acknowledges, of course, that you are his brother's son. Even though you have no legal claim on him, he feels that you should one day be able to live in a style befitting a McEwan. You may not be laird of Lochandar, but with your own land and livestock in a beautiful country you'll be able to build your own castle, so to speak, and rule your own territory. You're a sensible lad to recognise what an opportunity is presented to you. I may take it, then, that you accept your uncle's offer?'

For one more moment Fergus hesitated. Then, swallowing the lump in his throat, he nodded his head.

4

During the years when all three children were living in the castle, Mairi had felt no great need to look after Jamie. It was her younger brother, after all, who had first of all robbed her of Nurse's undivided attention and later had pushed her out of the nursery and into the schoolroom. She didn't hold that against him, knowing that her own arrival in the world must have had the same effect upon Fergus's life, but it certainly would not be true to say that she felt motherly towards him. Nurse gave him all the love he needed.

Mairi, indeed, had often felt herself to be neglected. Fergus – the elder son and grandson, the heir – was the favourite of both his mother and grandfather; whilst Jamie was petted by everyone just because he was the youngest. No one took any particular interest in Mairi except Miss Scott, who was paid to teach her, and the grooms, who were always willing to let her help around the stables. Mairi, who loved her grandfather deeply, was hurt by his apparent indifference, but it was not in her nature to feel resentment or to complain. She took note of the situation and simply looked for love else-where. She loved animals – not only her pets, but all the livestock around the castle – and knew how to remain still, so that even the wild cats would approach and feed from her hand. When she felt the need to talk, it was most likely to be her puppy to whom she confided secrets. It had been a hard parting when she was forced to leave him behind and now Fergus was telling her that she would never see him again, because they were not going back to the castle.

That night, after her elder brother had returned from the lawyer's office with his terrible, unbelievable news, Mairi cried herself to sleep. But when she awoke in the morning, it was with the recognition of a new responsi-bility. Her own distress did not blind her to the fact that Jamie was even more unhappy, and because he was so young, and understood even less than the others about what was happening, bewilderment turned misery into fear. His nurse had been left behind, his mother was dead, and now his brother was deserting him. He didn't understand about New Zealand, any more than Mairi did herself. All that seemed clear to him was that he might never see Fergus again. Mairi had never mothered Jamie before, but she saw that she must do so now.

'I'll write to you,' promised Fergus, almost in tears himself.

'I canna read,' wailed Jamie.

'You'll soon be learning. Mr Blair's going to find an academy for you.'

'What's an academy? Who's Mr Blair?'

Mr Blair arrived at that moment to collect Fergus.

'Can you look after the wee laddie for half an hour,

whilst I take your brother to the railway station?' he asked Mairi. 'Then I'll be back to help the two of you pack up your things. Shall we be away then, Fergus?'

Jamie burst into tears. His brother, never demonstrative, looked undecided how he should say goodbye and for a moment seemed almost on the point of shaking hands. But at the last minute he picked the four-year-old up and hugged him.

'Let's have a smile,' he said. 'You wouldna wish me to remember you like this.'

Jamie, seeing nothing to smile about, shook his head, unforgiving and inconsolable. He rubbed his face into Fergus's shoulder and then, when his brother set him down again on the floor, ran into the bedroom which the three children had shared.

'Look after him,' said Fergus to his sister. 'Till I'm twenty-one. Then the both of you will come to live with me.'

'That's years and years away.' But Mairi knew that nothing could be changed by protesting. 'You'll write a letter, won't you, to tell us where you are?'

'Aye, surely. As soon as I have the address.'

'It will take a little time,' Mr Blair reminded them both. 'It's a long voyage out, with a few weeks afterwards to make arrangements and be sure that Fergus is content with the family; and then the long journey again for the letter.'

Mairi flung herself into Fergus's arms and felt him patting her awkwardly on the back; he was not used to showing affection. Then he picked up his bag and followed Mr Blair out of the room.

In the bedroom, Jamie was howling with grief, but he stopped as soon as his sister came in, perhaps realising that nothing was to be gained by it.

'You're dirty,' she said, too despondent to care, and so stating a simple fact rather than criticising.

Jamie rubbed his tear-stained face with grubby hands. 'Dirty yourself,' he said. The exchange of insults signified only that neither of them wished to speak about Fergus's going nor about their fears of the future; but Jamie's comment was also true. Jenny had not brought up any hot water that morning.

Nor, of course, had there been anyone to tie Mairi's hair into rags on the previous evening, so that her ringlets now drooped in tousled disarray. But why should either of them care what they looked like? They sat without speaking, waiting to find out what was to become of them.

When he returned, Mr Blair brought Jenny up with him to pack a bag for the two children. Their mother had never expected the stay in Edinburgh to be so protracted, so they had brought few possession with them. 'Shall we be going, then?' he asked when all was ready. He had stared at them both hard when he came into the room, but did not suggest, as their mother certainly would have done, that they should clean and tidy themselves before going out.

Mairi felt Jamie tugging at her hand to hold her back, and understood what he wanted. 'May we say goodbye to Mother?' she asked.

Mr Blair hesitated for a moment. Then he nodded and opened the door of the other bedroom so that the two children could go in and see their mother, laid out on the bed. How beautiful she looked! All the worry of her last few weeks had been smoothed away, leaving her face calm and almost smiling. Even though such a short time had passed since her death, it was hard to remember how she had looked when she was able to move and talk. Mairi stared without speaking, whilst tears rolled silently down Jamie's grubby cheeks. But as he turned away, his mood was disturbed by a different thought.

'Basta Taw,' he said.

Mr Blair looked puzzled. Mairi, though, remembered that just before their mother died the little boy had boasted of his success in his game of Lord of the Castle – and then, in the panic which followed, had allowed the precious taw to fall off and roll away.

'He was playing with his marbles,' she explained, and they watched as the little boy turned away from the bed and ran back into the sitting room, scrabbling around on the floor until he found the alabaster taw in the darkest, dustiest corner. If he had been dirty before, he was filthy now, but he took no notice of that in his relief at being able to fit his treasure back into its place. He would carry the casket himself, he told Mr Blair, to make sure that it did not get lost.

Mairi picked up her own treasure. She did not as a rule spend very much time playing with dolls, preferring the wriggling warmth of an animal to the fixed smile on a wooden or waxen face, and had brought Bella only because she was not allowed to have her puppy with her in the city. Bella's body was stuffed, but her head was made of china. She would be safer in her owner's arms than in the bag. Mairi took Jamie by the hand, and they went silently downstairs.

There was a cab waiting at the door and, when they reached the railway station, a train hissing at the platform. Mairi sat in a window seat, opposite Mr Blair, with Bella between herself and Jamie. At first Jamie sat bolt upright in his seat, his legs dangling above the ground. But after an hour or two in which they showed no sign of arriving anywhere, he set his casket down next to Bella, and fell asleep.

Mr Blair had bought sandwiches at the station and produced them half-way through the journey. They were thick and dry, but Mairi accepted one gratefully and took another one for Jamie which he could eat when he woke up. They had had nothing to eat since their breakfast porridge, and did not know when they would be offered food again.

At last the train arrived at its destination, wherever that might be. Jamie clung tightly to Mairi's hand, for the station was crowded. Neither of them had ever seen so many people in such a small area. It was a noisy place, as well: announcements were made and passengers shouted for porters; and although the words used were familiar, the voices which spoke them were strange. 'Where are we?' asked Mairi.

'In England. Have you never been south of the border before?'

Mairi shook her head. England seemed to be a dirty place, as well as being crowded and jostling; but then, Edinburgh had been like that as well. Only in the land around Lochandar Castle had there been clean air to breathe and room to run about and play and the kind of quietness in which small noises could be heard. It seemed unlikely that there were any birds to sing in this noisy city.

Once again Mr Blair found a cab. Their journey, it seemed, was not over yet.

'Here we are at last,' he said as they came to a halt. His voice expressed sympathy for their tiredness. 'This place is called The Refuge. It will be your home for a little while.'

It was too dark to see what kind of building they were entering, except that it seemed to be huge. In front of it was not any kind of garden, but a hard-surfaced yard, surrounded by a high wall. Mairi needed almost to tug Jamie towards the door, not because of any unwillingness on his part, but because he was too tired to lift his feet.

'Mr Chisholm's expecting us,' said Mr Blair to the maid who answered his ring of the bell. He led the children into a small room without needing to be shown the way, as though he had been to this place before.

'Sit here for a moment, Jamie,' he said, lifting the little boy on to a bench: and then, turning to Mairi: 'Come this way.'

'Want to stay with Mairi,' said Jamie, sliding himself down from the bench; but Mr Blair put him back again.

'You have to have your names written in a register,' he explained. 'So I must take you in one at a time. Eldest first. You needn't worry that I'll forget you, Jamie. Wait here for just ten minutes. Then I'll be back to fetch you.'

What he said sounded reasonable enough and Mairi, like Jamie, accepted the words at face value. The thought that she might never see her little brother again did not enter her mind. Still clutching Bella in her arms, she followed Mr Blair out of the room without even turning her head to look back at Jamie.

31

5

To Jamie, left alone in the small, bare room, the wait seemed interminable. Through the door he could hear the sound of voices, although not the words which were spoken, and he knew that Mairi was not far away. But he was so tired that he could hardly hold up his head. The day, containing so many unwelcome experiences, had gone on too long.

At last he heard the sound of a closing door – although not the one he was watching. For a few moments longer the conversation continued in the next room. Then at last Mr Blair opened the door, lifted him down from the bench and led him into a larger room.

'This is Mr Chisholm, Jamie,' he said. 'He'll be in charge of you from now on. You must do whatever he says.'

Mr Chisholm was sitting behind a desk in a chair which swivelled from side to side whenever he moved. Even sitting down he looked very tall. He had a wide black beard and moustache, and black bushy eyebrows, but the top of his head was almost bald. Jamie had never seen a bald man before and found it difficult to understand why Mr Chisholm's hair seemed mainly to be in the wrong places.

'Hello, Jamie.' The black hair parted to reveal a pair of thick pink lips. Mr Chisholm was smiling – but Jamie did not feel any warmth in the welcome. Seeking comfort in an action he had not made for over a year, he put his thumb into his mouth and began to suck it.

'Come now, Jamie, you're not a baby.' Mr Chisholm's voice was suddenly more severe as he considered the little boy's appearance with a critical eye. He turned to speak to Mr Blair: 'As you warned me, I see the child's been neglected. It's some time, I think, since he was last acquainted with soap and water.'

Mr Blair threw both hands up in a sympathetic gesture. 'What can you expect? With both parents gone, he's alone in the world. That's why I'm putting him into your good hands.'

While the two men were speaking, Jamie looked round for Mairi. She was nowhere in the room. Bella, her doll, was lying on a chair, although the two peg dolls which had been in Bella's pockets had disappeared.

'Well,' said Mr Chisholm. 'Let's get on with the formalities, shall we?'

Mr Blair lifted Jamie on to a high stool and stood close behind him. On the other side of the desk, Mr Chisholm picked up a pen and prepared to write in a large book.

'Tell me your name,' he said to Jamie but Mr Blair answered before the little boy could speak.

'James Jamieson. Though he's used to being called Jamie.'

'James Jamieson.' Mr Chisholm was already writing it down when Jamie interrupted indignantly. He might not be able to read or write, but at least he knew what his own name was.

'James *McEwan*,' he said.

'Is that right?' Mr Chisholm inserted a word between the two he had already inscribed. 'McEwan. There we are, then.' He looked at what he had written and then glanced up at the lawyer. 'Is there some family connection with the girl, Mairi McEwan?'

'Yes, of a kind, through the mother. Nothing which need concern you, however.'

Mr Chisholm seemed to hesitate for a moment before looking back to Jamie. 'Do you know when you were born?' he asked.

Once again it was Mr Blair who answered. 'January the twenty-first, 1906.'

'So you're only four years old?'

Jamie nodded, and Mr Chisholm hesitated for a moment. 'As I think you know, Mr Blair, we don't as a rule take boys before their fifth birthday,' he said.

'I would consider it a personal favour.' Mr Blair's tone of voice seemed to demand rather than request.

'Well . . . On condition that the school will admit him. We can't have a boy on his own on the premises all day.

Yes, I should be able to arrange that. Now then, Mr Blair, do you wish him also to be considered for the emigration scheme?'

'I think it would be most suitable. A healthy life. Australia, perhaps, or South Africa.'

Mr Chisholm looked up and stared at Mr Blair. 'All right,' he said after a few seconds' consideration. 'I think that's all, then. Say goodbye to Mr Blair, Jamie.'

Jamie had never seen Mr Blair before that morning, yet his departure provided yet another abandonment. He watched miserably as the lawyer shook hands with Mr Chisholm and left the room.

'I expect you're hungry,' said Mr Chisholm. 'Put your box down here and we'll find you something to eat.'

'Want to keep it.' Jamie hugged his casket close to his chest.

'You can have it back when you leave here. We don't allow more personal possessions than you can keep in a pocket. They get stolen and cause trouble. If there's something small, you can take it out.'

Jamie opened the casket and looked at the chamois pouches. Was he more likely to lose his precious taws if he left them here, out of sight, or took them with him to be stolen? In the end he chose to remove only a handful of ordinary marbles.

All the other boys, he was told, had had their supper and gone to bed. Alone in a huge room which contained six long tables, Jamie dipped a spoon into a bowl of broth, but was too exhausted to lift it to his mouth. His head fell forward and he would have slipped from the bench, fast asleep, had he not been lifted off it and carried upstairs.

Early the next morning, while it was still dark, he awoke to find himself in a strange bed, wearing an unfamiliar and scratchy nightshirt. The mattress was lumpy. Jamie wriggled, trying to make himself comfortable, but without success.

'The new kid's awake.'

Within seconds Jamie's bed was surrounded by a dozen or so boys, all much bigger than himself. Startled, he sat up, rubbing his eyes. Of all the questions which were fired at him at once, the easiest to answer was a demand to know his name. 'Jamie.'

'You aren't half filthy.' It was the tallest of the boys who was looking at him in a disapproving way. 'Better have a scrub. There's inspection before breakfast.'

Jamie did as he was told, although the cold water and the hard bar of carbolic soap did not make it easy to remove the grime. He looked for his clothes, but they were nowhere to be found. Instead, he saw on the end of his bed a pile of much-washed garments which all proved to be too large. He put them on nevertheless, struggling with unfamiliar buttons. It was the first time he had ever had to dress himself without help.

'Cor, look at that rain.' The boy from the next bed, alerted by a puddle forming beneath a leaking window, was staring out at the grey sky. 'Cats and dogs. Going to get soaked going to school again.'

Jamie paused in his struggles to express surprise. 'Is this not school?'

'Nah. Nobody *sleeps* at school, daftie. We go to the elementary. Ten minutes' run.'

It didn't seem to Jamie that his question had been so stupid. He had no first-hand knowledge of school but at home, in the castle, it had always been known that Fergus would go away to school when he was thirteen. He would sleep there during the school terms and only come home in the holidays. Jamie, though, was wise enough not to defend his first question. Instead, he asked another. 'What's this place, then?'

'The Refuge. An orphanage.'

'What's an orphanage?'

'Dump for orphans. Don't know much, do you? Know what an orphan is?'

Jamie shook his head.

'Well, where's your old man? Your father?'

'Dead.'

'And your mother?'

Tears welled up into Jamie's eyes and for a moment he could not speak. 'She's dead too,' he said at last.

'So you're an orphan. Like the rest of us. You'll live here till you're eight or nine. Then they'll pack you off to the colonies. That's what happens to most of us. Can't be worse than this.'

'Deed! Deed!' It took Jamie a moment to realise that the tallest boy, who had come back to see if he was ready for inspection, was mimicking his own pronunciation of 'dead'. 'Where d'you come from then, with that funny voice? Where did you live before you came here?'

'In the castle,' said Jamie hesitantly, not sure whether that was the kind of answer required. Clearly it was a mistake, for all the boys within earshot burst out laughing. One of them lifted him roughly and stood him up in the middle of his bed.

'He's the king of the castle, And we're the dirty rascals,' he shouted. The others took up the chant, dancing round and round and flicking Jamie's bare knees painfully with wet cloths. Jamie cringed back towards the head of the bed, not understanding why the other boys had become hostile so suddenly. In a moment they were going to knock him down: he could tell it from the way they were pressing closer. Not knowing what he had done wrong, he could think of no way to put it right.

'Quiet!' Mr Chisholm, appearing i⁻ ʰe doorway of the long dormitory, brought rescue anu ımmediate silence with his shout. 'Jamieson, get down off that bed this minute.'

Jamie looked around. He was the only one standing on a bed, but his name was not Jamieson.

Mr Chisholm strode down the room. He knocked Jamie off the bed and down to the floor with a hard cuff to one ear, before pulling him to his feet again by the other ear.

'Don't let me ever catch you doing that again, Jamieson,' he said.

'Sir, you've got to be polite to Jamieson, sir,' said the tallest boy. 'Lives in a castle, he does, like the King.' All the boys laughed mockingly, while Jamie, bewildered by their reaction and with his head still ringing from Mr Chisholm's blow, put his hands up to cover his painful ears and tried to become invisible.

36

'Quiet!' ordered Mr Chisholm again. 'Line up for inspection. End of the line, Jamieson.'

Jamie realised that he had somehow become Jamieson, though he didn't understand why. His mind was still full of questions that he wanted to ask. What had happened to Mairi, for example? He wanted to see her again: he wanted her to look after him and be kind. But he was frightened to open his mouth. Only one thing was clear to him at this moment. If he had got to stay in this horrid place, he must never mention the castle again.

PART TWO

THREE BIRTHDAYS

1

Fergus McEwan awoke with the sun on the morning of his eighteenth birthday: the third day of January, 1915. The date was not of any importance to him; this was a day like any other, just as Christmas Day and Hogmanay had been. There would be no celebration, no party, no company – unless five thousand Merino ewes could be reckoned as company.

Before anything else, he must check that the sheep were safe. He stepped out of the hut, whistled up his dogs and strode up to the ridge. Although his sandy, curly hair and freckled complexion had not changed since he was a child, he had grown to be over six feet tall and his long legs covered the rough ground at a steady but speedy pace. As he walked, he breathed in the fresh air with a deep contentment. Later in the summer's day it would be hot; but at sunrise the temperature was perfect.

The air was clear as well as cool. He could see the sheep from a distance, still grazing on the flat which led down to the Rangitata River. All was well. Fergus had a good eye for the size of any mob, and in this part of South Island there were no predators to pick off individual animals. When trouble came, it came on a large scale and so was unmistakable; for if a few sheep were to stray over the boundary into the neighbouring run, or attempt to cross a dangerously flooded river, the whole mob would follow. Nothing of that sort had happened overnight, and Fergus believed in leaving the sheep alone as long as they were happy. Whistling tunelessly to himself, he went back to the hut.

'Hut' was Fergus's word for the shelter in which he spent much of his life. His employer, Mr Sutherland, liked to refer to it as an 'outstation', but in truth it was little more than a steeply pitched roof, its two sides touching the ground without walls. There was room for Fergus to sleep and to store food and a change of clothing; nothing more.

Fergus had no complaint about that. Indeed, he had no complaint about anything. All the promises which Mr Blair had made to him five years earlier had been kept. On the voyage out to New Zealand he had met two other boys who were travelling under the same cadet scheme which had been described to him. They were older, and had made for themselves the decision to emigrate: their excitement about the new life they had chosen was reassuring to the younger boy. He was met and welcomed at Christchurch by Mr Sutherland and taken straight to the homestead.

From that moment on the Sutherlands had treated him like their own son. He had to work hard from the very first day but no harder than Robert, the true son of the house. Since his sixteenth birthday he had been given a little pocket money, and from today he would earn a regular wage. When the last of Mr Blair's promises was fulfilled, in three years' time, and Fergus found himself master of his own land, he would be well qualified to manage it, for he had undertaken every task that was necessary, even to helping a neighbour to build his own homestead.

His life at present was that of a shepherd; a responsible task, for sheep were the lifeblood of the Canterbury community, but also a lonely one. Fergus didn't mind that. He had always enjoyed solitude in open places. If he had any nightmares, they were of being forced to live in a city.

He washed now in the creek and then smiled to

himself. Although his birthday was a working day like any other, he had planned one treat to make it memorable. A pair of paradise ducks had nested not far from the hut. Knowing that they would be too tough to eat, he had left them undisturbed until now, but they would not, he hoped, begrudge him a couple of eggs for his breakfast. He stirred the ashes of the fire into flame, robbed the nest and cooked and ate the eggs.

After he had eaten, he sat back in the seat which he had made out of boulders. Within less than an hour the rising sun had dissipated the coolness of early morning and there was a haze of heat between himself and the distant mountains. Fergus stared at the distorted shapes of rocks and pulled a pencil and notebook from his pocket.

He was not a great reader. His education had stopped dead on the day he left Lochandar Castle, and there was not a single book to be found in the Sutherlands' house except the Bible. But although he lacked reading matter, and hardly noticed the lack, he had a feeling for words. Fergus was a poet.

Or perhaps it was truer to say that he was in love: so overwhelmingly in love that he could express his feelings only in verse. Dorothy Sutherland was barely sixteen; but already, it seemed to him, she was everything that was perfect in a woman. By day she was energetic, hard-working and laughing as she helped her mother with the housework, in the vegetable garden or in the hen-house. In the evening, sitting with her sewing, she was calm and beautiful. Fergus admired her character and worshipped her beauty. Almost every day he wrote a poem to express his feelings; and every day he threw his words on the fire, not daring to let her know that he adored her. He sucked his pencil now and began to write.

'I have built you a castle in my heart.'

Almost at once he stopped, his attention diverted by the word 'castle'. It was the shape of a distant rock formation which had reminded him of the tower of Lochandar Castle: the tower containing the nursery in which he had spent his infancy and the schoolroom above it to which he had graduated at the age of five when Mairi was born.

41

Where was Mairi now, he wondered. He had written to her when first he arrived in New Zealand, giving her his address, and twice a year since then had sent letters to Mr Blair's office for Christmas and her birthday. He had done the same for Jamie, but neither of them had ever replied. They were too young, he supposed, for he still thought of them as they were when he last saw them, aged only four and seven. Or perhaps at boarding school they were allowed no time for letter-writing. Their silence made no difference to Fergus's feelings of responsibility. In three years' time, when he had his own land, he would send for them to live in his homestead. He repeated the promise to them in every letter, so that they should not feel abandoned. Although he trusted Mr Blair to have made as satisfactory an arrangement for the younger children as for Fergus himself, he could guess how lonely they must feel, especially in the school holidays, when perhaps all the other children had parents and a home to which they could return, whilst Mairi and Jamie had to stay at school.

Fergus thought about his brother and sister for a little while and then returned to the poem, staring again into the distance as he searched for words. For a second time, though, his attention was diverted. His hut stood beside a creek, but at a high point from which he could see the Rangitata River into which it flowed. The river bed was a mile wide at this point, although not a mile of water. Instead, the river divided into a dozen or more channels, sometimes meeting to form islands and to become deeper and more powerful before splitting again into narrow strands. It flowed down from the mountains in a gradual, gentle fall, allowing Fergus to look upstream for a considerable distance. What he saw now was a little cloud of dust.

To a stranger, the movement would have meant nothing; but Fergus knew every trick of the weather. He stuffed his notebook into a pocket and stood up. The dust cloud grew larger, blowing towards him down the river bed; it rose higher, obscuring his view of the mountains. It meant that a nor'wester was on the way.

42

The wind would arrive very soon with a violent gustiness, making the day seem unbearably hot and filling his eyes and nostrils with sand. It would be a dry wind at this altitude, but only because it had shed its rain on the mountains and in the gorges from which the river flowed. Within forty-eight hours a fresh could be expected – a flash flood which would swell the river to an impassable depth, trapping any sheep which might have crossed one of the shallow channels to graze on an island. Fergus whistled for his dogs again and set off towards the river.

'Coo-ey.'

Startled, he came to a halt and looked round, to see Robert Sutherland riding towards the hut and waving his hat in greeting. Robert was Fergus's only friend, not because Fergus was unsociable, but because there were no other young men within miles.

'Nor'wester on the way,' he said, tethering his horse near the hut.

Fergus nodded. The two walked together towards the flat on which the sheep were grazing.

'Come to say goodbye.' Robert's announcement startled Fergus for a second time.

'Where are you going, then?'

'To the war.'

Fergus thought about this as he strode forward, his dogs at his heels. He had known, of course, that a war had begun in Europe. But with that news had come a reassurance that it would be over by Christmas – too soon to allow any contribution from New Zealand. In any case, he was still too young to enlist.

'Going badly, they say,' Robert added. 'Need more men. Twenty thousand from the Commonwealth already, but they're asking for more volunteers on top of that.'

'What does your dad say?' With so many sheep to guard, both Robert and Fergus were indispensable, for hired labour was scarce as well as expensive.

'Reckon he don't know what to think. He's kind of proud of having a son to fight for the Old Country. Same time can't rightly do without me. He's gone to the plains to see how old Chauncey's placed.'

Old Chauncey had been the Sutherlands' shepherd when Fergus first arrived from Scotland. Before he retired he had taught both boys his craft.

'Must be getting on seventy,' Fergus considered.

'Could be so. But he don't think much to living with his sister. Reckon he wouldn't mind coming back for a few months.'

By now they had reached the ridge. Looking down, Fergus saw that the normally milky-white glacier water of the river was changing colour, taking on a grey-green hue. That meant that the level must already be rising, swollen by the rains which were too far away to be seen. A group of about three hundred sheep were grazing contentedly in the centre of the river bed. They had stepped across a channel which was still not more than nine inches deep but which might speedily rise to two or three feet.

Fergus was glad of his friend's company. He could have managed alone; but now, while the two dogs patrolled and crouched and growled, Robert shouted and splashed water to discourage the sheep from running downstream. His presence made it unnecessary to encircle the wanderers cautiously before persuading them to step into the deepening water. Instead, Fergus was able to drag a couple of the ewes across the channel and up the high bank by their hind legs, and it was not too long before the rest agreed to follow their leaders and rejoin the main mob. The incident was an ordinary one. As soon as the task had been successfully accomplished, Fergus returned to the subject of their earlier conversation.

'What do your mother and Dorothy think? About you going off to the war.'

'Ma cried. Dotty thinks I'm a hero. Darn it all, I haven't even enlisted yet.'

'They're not supposed to take you till you're nineteen.'

'No one's asking to see birth certificates. As long as you look like a man, not a kid . . .'

44

Fergus was silent as they walked together back to the hut. Only when they were sitting over a cup of tea did he ask the question in his mind.

'What would your father think if I were to come with you?'

'Would you? Well, he'd be glad to know that I had a mate. So would I, I'll tell you straight. But it would be hard on him to lose us both at once. I don't know . . . but he can't stop you, whatever you choose to do. And of course' – Robert grinned cheekily – 'Dotty would reckon *you* a hero as well.' Fergus's infatuation was no secret to his friend, although Dorothy herself might not be aware of it.

'I want to marry her.' Fergus had never put the thought into words before, but it emerged naturally now. 'Would your father . . . ?'

Robert shook his head. 'He'd say she was too young at sixteen. Doesn't mean that he wouldn't like you for a son-in-law, though. After all, you're pretty well part of the family already. Tell you what: he'd let her get engaged. No harm in that. If Dotty said she'd marry you when you got back, you'd have her as firm as if she were your wife. She wouldn't back out on you, not Dotty.'

Once again Fergus fell silent. Did he want to be a soldier? He didn't want to kill or be killed; and that, presumably, was what war was all about. But there was a sense in which his heart was still in Scotland. Like Robert, he felt an urge to defend the Old Country. And once his uncle had provided the money with which he could become a farmer, he might never be able to leave New Zealand again. If he was to see something more of the world, this period before his twenty-first birthday was the time when he must take the chance. A world at war, of course, was not the ideal place in which to travel. But he was Robert's mate. The bond between them was strong. Together, each would know that there was someone at his shoulder; apart, they would both be lonely.

And Dorothy would think him a hero. That very fact might inspire him to speak the words which until now he had only expressed in his poems. If she would have him, he would go to war to prove himself worthy. If she turned him down, he could no longer stay in the homestead, loving her but knowing that she was not for him. He nodded his head casually at Robert.

'Right,' he said. 'I'm with you.'

2

Jamie wore a flat tweed cap and a heavy overcoat which reached almost to his ankles. His grey trousers, equally oversize, were neither long nor short, but stopped just below his knees. Beneath a stout pair of braces, his grey shirt still smelt of the sweat and sickness of the long voyage. Heavy hobnailed boots and knee-length woollen stockings completed an outfit generously supplied from the clothing fund of The Refuge by Mr Chisholm, who had taken note that the group of emigrant boys would be leaving England as winter approached and had not stopped to consider that the January temperature in Australia might be ninety degrees in the shade. Dragging his canvas bag along the ground behind him, Jamie came wearily down the gangplank of the ship which had brought him to Adelaide.

Even now, after so many weeks, the journey was not over.

'Get a move on, Jamieson! The train's not going to wait for you.' Mr Martin, who had been in charge of the party during the voyage out from England, was now anxious to deliver the boys to the Farm School as quickly as possible.

Jamie answered to the name of Jamieson as a matter of course; and indeed, after more than four years in the orphanage, he had forgotten that he ever had any other name. It was used by all his teachers and supervisors; but to the boys he was always known as Wee Jamie. The adjective had attached itself to his name first of all through mockery of his Scottish voice, as well as in recognition that he was the youngest boy to be accepted at The Refuge. In the present group of immigrants he again was younger by eighteen months than any of the others. During the course of the long voyage he had lost track of dates, and even of days of the week: but, although he did not know it, the day of his disembarkation was 21 January 1915, his ninth birthday.

Young he might be, but Jamie was a child only in age. Four and a half years in The Refuge had toughened him in both body and mind. He was a sturdily-built boy with a fighting spirit. Whilst still too small to defeat the bigger bullies of the community, he had developed a defiant toughness which at least removed him from the group of easy victims, and a cheerfulness which eventually made him accepted as a kind of mascot. Nobody made allowances for his size or age, but he was well enough liked by the other boys to escape most of the humiliations which they took pleasure in inflicting on newcomers.

It was less easy to escape the displeasure of the adults who were in control of The Refuge. To the Board of Guardians he was presumably only one name on a list of a hundred and fifty – and such relative anonymity, he quickly realised, was to be valued. But to those who more directly supervised his life he was too easily identifiable. His sandy hair curled cheekily above his freckled face, and the alert intelligence of his bright blue eyes marked him out from his sullen or stupid contemporaries. Individuality was to be slapped down, not encouraged. In his first few months at The Refuge Jamie received more than his share of beatings, until he learned the art of enduring rather than challenging; keeping his mouth shut and making himself invisible by complete conformity. School had taught him to read and write, to add and subtract, divide and multiply; but the orphanage had taught him how to survive. As a little boy he had been a chatterer; but by the age of nine he had learned the wisdom of silence.

Only one enthusiasm of childhood remained unchanged. Free moments were rare in The Refuge, since all domestic chores had to be performed by the boys. But in any time he could steal, Jamie pulled his small bag of marbles from its hiding place beneath his mattress. Sometimes he played with other boys but more often, for the sake of secrecy, by himself. He set himself targets and invented new games, practising various methods of striking, and crouching or lying in different attitudes in order that his eye should be as close as possible to the floor. By the time he left England he could make a marble do almost anything he wanted; and on that last day, to his amazement and delight, his casket had been restored to him.

Jamie had never really believed Mr Chisholm's statement that his treasure was being kept safe until he left The Refuge; but this was one promise that was faithfully kept. The gate and portcullis and castle were still strapped to the lid of the casket, and all the precious, beautiful taws were secure in their chamois bags. He had not risked playing with them on board ship, since, apart from the pitching and tossing of the vessel itself, there were too many holes through which a treasure might disappear for ever. But as he took his seat in the train which would carry him across South Australia to the station nearest to the Farm School, he peeped into his thick canvas bag and reassured himself that the box was still there.

Nobody had ever asked Jamie whether he wished to spend the rest of his life in Australia. After breakfast one morning Mr Chisholm had read out a list of names. These fortunate boys, he announced, were being offered the opportunity of a new life, far from the filth and depravity of the city streets which would inevitably sap their health or tempt them into criminal behaviour if they were to remain in England without friends or family when they were too old for The Refuge. Jamie hadn't understood much of what Mr Chisholm was talking about, so it was one of the older boys who explained afterwards that he would be going to a farm school. As soon as he had learned to make himself useful he would be found a job on a farm and eventually he might hope to become a farmer himself, since there was so much empty land in Australia, and not enough people to cultivate it.

Although Jamie had never spoken of his life in the castle since that first humiliating day in the orphanage when he had at one and the same time been teased for his boasting and disbelieved, he had not quite forgotten it. Every night before he fell asleep he tried to wish himself back into the nursery in the tower. The image of his mother had been quick to disappear from his memory, but Nurse was still a real, solid figure, awaiting his return because, not realising that he might never see her again, he had not said a proper goodbye. Except for Nurse, the other occupants of the castle became more shadowy with each day that passed, but Jamie still recalled his last conversation with his dying grandfather. The laird had made him a present of Basta Taw, and afterwards had issued a final command. 'Find land for yourself, my wee Jamie.'

Now, it appeared, he was being offered land or, at least, the chance of acquiring it one day in the distant future, when he was full grown. To Jamie's uncomplicated view, it seemed obvious that this must be what his grandfather had had in mind. So although he was sorry to leave the elementary school in which a sympathetic lady teacher had taught him his letters and referred to him as her star pupil, he accepted the arrangement made for him without complaint.

There was in any case no one to whom he could complain. He had not seen Mairi since she went before him into Mr Chisholm's office. His first request for a reunion was met with the unyielding statement that the Boys' Side and the Girls' Side were never allowed to meet; subsequent pleas produced the information that she had gone to live in Canada. She had become one of the shadows, as had Fergus, from whom no letter was ever received. However tenaciously Jamie might cling to the dream that Nurse would appear one day to take him home, in his waking life he was well aware that at the age of nine he was alone in the world. He could rely on no one but himself.

49

Brigg's Quarter was a farm of a hundred and sixty acres in the south of Saskatchewan in Canada. Peter Brigg, arriving as an immigrant ten years earlier to take possession of an area of prairie under a homesteading scheme, had cleared the land for wheat and managed it single-handedly with the help only of his horses. From ploughing time to harvest each year he worked from sunrise to sunset, returning home only to eat and sleep.

There was as much work to be done around the farmhouse as on the land. The length and severity of every winter meant that the autumn had to be devoted to preserving food against the days when the dirt track to the nearest small town would be impassable. Fruit had to be bottled, vegetables stored in straw and meat made ready for the first icy days when it would freeze naturally, ready to be packed into the ice houses. The farmhouse had to be kept clean and warm. The farmyard sheltered not only the ploughing horses but also the cows, hens and pigs needed to provide the household with meat, eggs and milk; all these had to be tended. There was no shortage of woman's work on Brigg's Quarter but it was Mairi McEwan, and not her foster-mother, who did most of it.

Mrs Brigg had once had children of her own, but all three had died of the summer sickness when the eldest was only six. It was for that reason that in 1910 she had applied for one of the orphans who were collected each year from the streets and workhouses of England and brought out to start a new and healthier life in Canada. She had promised to treat Mairi as though she were her own daughter, and frequently assured the girl that she was doing so.

Mairi had no reason to doubt this. She noted that Mr Brigg worked hard, and accepted the statement that his wife was a sick woman. There had been a brief period, while she was still attending school, when she had made comparisons with the lives of her classmates and became discontented; but Mrs Brigg resolved that situation by ending her school attendance.

On 18 August 1915, Mairi's working day was as full as usual. She was offered no respite from her tasks merely because it was her thirteenth birthday. She was in the middle of baking the weekly batch of bread when the lady from the Immigrants' Aid Society called. Showing the visitor into the parlour, in which she herself was never invited to sit, Mairi returned to her work in the kitchen. She could hear nothing of what was being discussed. As a general rule Mrs Brigg had a sharp, high-pitched voice which could be heard all over the farm; but today she was speaking softly, almost in a murmur.

Even had eavesdropping been possible, Mairi would not have tried to listen. She was neither curious nor imaginative, perhaps because she had discovered long ago that to indulge these two luxuries of the mind brought nothing but unhappiness. Although she had long left childhood behind her, if childhood was to be defined in terms of love and play and treats and even education, she retained a child's ability to take for granted the way of life which circumstances had imposed on her. Like any other girl, she was often unhappy and occasionally rebellious; but it had never seriously occurred to her that she could do other than accept whatever instructions she was given and stay where she was sent. No one, after all, had ever enquired what her own wishes might be.

So it came as a surprise when, at the end of her conversation with Mrs Brigg, the visitor came into the kitchen.

'Sit down a minute, Mairi,' she said and added, as she saw the girl hesitate, 'Mrs Brigg knows that we're going to have a chat.'

'Having a chat' was an ominous phrase. Mairi wondered what she had done wrong. She washed her hands and sat at the big wooden table, roughened by years of chopping and scraping, which she had scrubbed clean half an hour earlier. Fascinated, she stared at the lady's figure, which was trim enough below the waist but enormous above it. A new tightness in her own skimpy dresses had recently alerted Mairi to two swellings which had matured into small, pointed breasts. Would they, she asked herself now in alarm, continue to grow until she too was weighed down and surely overbalanced by such a deformity? How could a lady of such a shape ever run anywhere or even bend down to fasten her boots? But to stare any longer would be rude. Mairi dropped her gaze and waited to find out what this chat was to be about.

'Remember me?' asked the stranger. 'Mrs Rendall.'

Mairi shook her head.

'I met you, all of you, off the boat when you arrived in Canada, and took you to the hostel in Montreal.'

Mairi tried to think back to the night of their arrival, but that was five years ago. She and the other children had been tired and confused as they left the ship in which they had been so sick. At the age of eight her knowledge of geography was vague, so she had little idea of where in the world she was. And she had remained in the hostel for only three or four days before Mrs Brigg arrived to look her up and down, pronounce the words 'She'll do', and take her off to the farm. It was hardly surprising that Mairi's memories of that time were of travels and discomforts and loneliness rather than of a stranger's face.

Mrs Rendall, it seemed, understood this.

'I don't suppose,' she said, 'that you had much idea about what was happening then, did you? How old were you? Seven? Eight? Now you're old enough to understand, though. Let me explain. Do you remember where you were before you came to Canada?'

'The Refuge. Girls' Side.'

'And what was that?'

'An orphanage.'

'Yes. Now, there are kind, generous gentlemen in England who reckon that an orphanage in a dirty city is no place for children to grow up. Especially as a boy or girl can't expect to earn a living wage the moment he leaves school and might not even find any work at all. A child who has parents will at least have somewhere to live while he looks for work, but it's not so easy for an orphan. Children of that kind find themselves sleeping on the street, dirty, cold, and often tempted to steal.'

Mrs Rendall paused, perhaps for agreement, but Mairi had no comment to make.

'Well, at the same time, these charitable gentlemen know that the colonies are short of people to take up all the opportunities of work which exist in places like Canada. Girls in particular.'

'Why? Why girls?'

'Because a lot of enterprising young men do make their way out here to find a new life for themselves. The very best kind of young men – the ones who are strong and determined to get on in the world. They come alone, because they know things may be tough for the first few years. But after a while they're ready to settle down and look for a wife. And it's not so easy for young women to leave their families in England and come out to the colonies alone.'

Mairi thought it was funny that The Refuge should be shipping out batches of orphans to Canada in order that a lot of unknown young men should be able to get married one day. But the thought did not make her laugh. It was funny peculiar, not funny ha-ha; and after all, she was one of the girls. Somewhere in Canada there might already be living a man who one day would come to Brigg's Quarter, just as Mrs Brigg had come to the hostel, to inspect her and announce, 'She'll do.'

She put that possibility to the back of her mind for the moment, because Mrs Rendall was still explaining.

'So some of these generous gentlemen in England have founded charities to help orphans to emigrate. They pay the boat fares out and buy each child a new set of clothes. There are more than twenty societies which do this sort of thing. The one that sent you out is called the Orphans' New Life Society. That society has set up another charity in Canada called the Immigrants' Aid. We run a hostel for new arrivals, and help to find them foster homes. There are generous people in Canada as well.'

Mairi had had it well dinned into her ever since she arrived at Brigg's Quarter that she was a lucky girl to be so well looked after instead of being left in the gutter. She accepted the statement as true, but had ceased to react to it. If she was curious now, it was only about the reason for Mrs Rendall's visit after so many years.

'Did my brother come here as well?' she asked. 'Here to Canada, I mean.'

'Your brother, dear? I didn't know you had a brother.'

'Wee Jamie,' said Mairi. 'I was supposed to look after him when Mother died. We were taken to The Refuge together. But . . .' The memory still had the power to bring tears to her eyes. So much of what had happened in the year after her mother's death had been confusing and unhappy that she had put most of it out of her memory. But she would never be able to forget her distress when she learned that the boys and the girls in the huge orphanage were never allowed to meet. She had left her little brother sitting patiently in a waiting room, confident that she would return within a few moments to take care of him. She had not set eyes on him since. Bella, her doll, had been kept and returned to her on the day she left The Refuge – although only to be thrown overboard by a spiteful older girl on the second day of the voyage to Canada – but no one had ever been willing to tell her what had happened to her brother.

'He didn't come on the ship with you,' said the Immigrants' Aid lady. 'I'd have remembered. It's very difficult to place a brother and sister together. Your party was all girls, anyway.'

'I know. He'd have been too young, I expect. But later on, when he was eight or nine, he might have come then.'

'Well, dear, I'll see what I can find out when I get back to my office. Jamie, you said.' Mrs Rendall's voice sounded at the same time brisk and doubtful, making it clear that she did not expect the search to be successful. 'Now then, let's talk about you. Have you been well looked after here?'

'All right.' If Mairi's reply was cautious, it was only partly because she had no standard of comparison. It would not do to complain, since all adults were always in league against all children, and Mrs Rendall would certainly sneak on her to Mrs Brigg. Nor would it be wise to appear too contented, in case something better might prove to be on offer.

'How have you got on at school?'

'Haven't been much. Not at all for a year, and not much before that. On account of Auntie being ill.' Mrs Brigg's illness, never precisely defined, but connected by vague allusion to the births and deaths of her babies, prevented her from doing very much work herself, although not from following Mairi around to criticise her efforts. But school had never seemed much more attractive than housework, especially as it involved a two-hour walk at the beginning and end of each day. Mairi could read and write and figure, and saw no advantage to be gained from further attendance.

Mrs Rendall looked as though she were about to make some comment, but bit it back.

'Well,' she said instead, 'you don't need to go any more now if you don't care to. And you don't have to stay with the Briggs either. This is the time you can make some choices, now you're thirteen. You know it's your birthday today, don't you?'

Mairi nodded, although without enthusiasm. There had never been anything special about a birthday.

'Well, now that you're thirteen, the Immigrants' Aid won't be looking after you any more. That means, for one thing, that Mr and Mrs Brigg won't be getting an allowance for being foster-parents any longer.'

'They got *paid?*' Mairi could not conceal her incredulity.

'Well, of course, dear. You wouldn't expect anyone to take a strange child into their house without any benefit to themselves. A few of the families we deal with offer to adopt a child and so take over full responsibility for her as though she were their own. But not everyone can afford to do that. It's an expensive business, bringing up a growing girl. The allowance we made would hardly cover the cost of your food. Now then, two things can happen when this point is reached. Mrs Brigg might say that she can't afford to keep you here any longer. Well, I've had a word with her, and she'll be glad for you to stay. That's nice, isn't it, dear? Shows that the arrangement must have been a happy one.'

Mrs Rendall paused as though she had nothing more to add, so after a few seconds Mairi prompted her. 'There were two things, you said.'

'Yes, dear. Well, the other one is that you might not want to stay here. If you've been unhappy, this is the moment when you could go. But I can see how fond your auntie is of you, and how well she's treated you, so I don't expect . . .'

Mairi was not a complaining girl. Had she been asked outright whether the past five years had been unhappy ones, she would probably have said no. But they had been hard. From the day of her arrival she had been expected to do not just her fair share of the housework, but almost all of it. Because she had made it known to her foster-parents that she loved animals, she had not objected when she was sent to clean out the henhouses and the stables and to milk the cows, but all this had been extra to her work in the house, not instead of it. Her clothes had never been warm enough for the long, cold winters, and her face and hands had become red and rough from the cold water with which she was expected to scrub off the dirt of her daily work. As long as there seemed no avenue of escape, she had made the best of it. But now, it appeared, she was being offered a choice.

'If I left here, what would I do?'

'Well, dear, that's a difficulty. It's all very well for those kind gentlemen in the Orphans' New Life Society to decide that you're grown up and able to fend for yourself on your thirteenth birthday; and, of course, it's easy to see that they have to stop supporting the older ones so that they can look after the young ones who are coming into their Homes. If your uncle and auntie had decided that they couldn't keep you here, I'd have tried to find you work in Toronto. If you got a post as a house servant, you'd have a roof over your head and food in your mouth. You couldn't expect much of a wage, being so young and unskilled; but I do my best when this situation arises to find an employer who'll give you a training, so to speak, so that by the time you're eighteen you can do better for yourself.'

It didn't seem to Mairi that she was particularly young or particularly unskilled. Although she was skinny and had not yet grown to her full height, there were few household tasks for which she lacked the strength. She took her time to think about this new possibility.

The idea of moving into a city, which might have appealed to some girls, did not hold any great attraction for her. She was at ease with cows and horses in a way which she could never be with crowds of people. And it sounded as though the work she might be offered would be exactly the same as at Brigg's Quarter. The only difference would be that her employers would be strangers. They might be kinder than the Briggs but equally they might be harsher. Mr Brigg was a kind man, behaving as though he were a real uncle. When Mairi fell asleep over the mending at night, he would carry her gently to bed instead of shouting at her to wake and finish the task. If he were to spend longer in the farmhouse, her life would be easier, but during most of the year his working day was as long and as hard as her own. Mrs Brigg was lazier, but even she, although she continually scolded and chivvied, rarely raised a hand to Mairi. It would be safer, perhaps, to remain in the life she knew.

That didn't mean, though, that she must necessarily remain on the same terms.

'If you found me a post in Toronto, I'd get wages, you said,' she asked, checking.

'Not very much. You couldn't expect – '

'But something. If I stay here, will I get the same?'

'You can't expect your auntie and uncle to give you money, dear, when they're already providing such a good home, treating you as one of the family.'

'I start work at five in the morning,' said Mairi matter-of-factly. 'And I finish about ten at night. In winter I have to get up in the middle of the night to keep the stove in. If I wasn't here, they'd need another yard hand, as well as a girl to help in the house, Auntie being so poorly. I'm growing out of my clothes, and I only get more when the lady from the church comes round with the cast-offs. When I went to school, almost all the others had a few cents in their pocket each week. Maybe they had to earn it, but I used to earn it as well. Only difference was, I didn't get it.'

This, for Mairi, was a long speech, and Mrs Rendall was taken aback by it for a moment.

'You're saying that you want to be paid to stay here?' she checked.

Mairi nodded. 'The same as I'd get in the city. That's all.'

Mrs Rendall stood up. 'Stay here while I have another word with your auntie,' she said.

She sailed out of the room, her huge bosom preceding her like the bow of a ship. Watching her go, Mairi considered a new thought. Her experience had always been that adults knew what they wanted and exactly how to get it. But she had noticed an odd uncertainty in the visitor's expression, as though she were unsure of something. It was impossible to tell whether the doubts related to the past or to the future, and Mairi herself was interested in neither. She hardly cared at all whether she should stay or go and knew that, in fact, she would stay. The Briggs could not afford to do without her; nor, in a financial sense, could they afford to replace her. She had discovered that she was worth something. Not much, but something. What she had said to Mrs Rendall had been mild enough, but the words nevertheless constituted a small act of rebellion. Mairi recognised what had happened and was elated by her own courage.

This was her thirteenth birthday. The date might have brought disappointment with it, since it was clear that no one would offer her any kind of treat. But far from being disappointed, she gave a small sigh of pleasure. It seemed to her that she had celebrated her birthday with a triumph.

Meanwhile, though, birthday or not, there would be no bread to eat that week unless she applied herself to the task of making it. With all the energy born of satisfaction, she began to slap and knead the dough.

PART THREE

WIDER WORLDS

1

'Ungrateful girl! After all we've done for you!'

Mairi did not have to wait long to learn Mrs Brigg's reaction to her small gesture of independence. Hardly had Mrs Rendall left the farm before the flow of recrimination began. Ingratitude was the most-repeated word, but incovenience also figured strongly in the tirade. The monthly payment from the Immigrants' Aid, which had never been mentioned in Mairi's presence before, was now revealed to be an essential part of the Briggs' income; and because of the war and the consequent dangers of travel across the Atlantic, it appeared that there was a severe shortage of immigrant orphans in Canada.

The warning to Mairi was clear enough, although unspoken: as soon as a substitute, whether paying or merely free, could be found, she herself would have to leave. Why should Mrs Brigg pay out for labour when she could be rewarded for giving it house-room? No doubt Mairi would be expected to make herself dispensable by training some new orphan in her tasks. Meanwhile, there was a more immediate result of her rebellion.

'Haven't we loved you like our own daughter?' demanded Mrs Brigg as, at the end of the first week of the new system, she counted out Mairi's pay coin by coin – but put it away for safe keeping rather than handing it over. 'But you'd rather be a servant than a member of the family. Okay then, if that's the way you want it. End of the month you move into servants' quarters. You can't expect to live like family when you want no part of it.'

'Servants' quarters' proved, when September came, to be a haybed in the cowshed loft. Mr Brigg helped Mairi to move her few clothes and possessions and, finding nowhere to put them, looked round unhappily. He was a silent, practical man, who had left it entirely to his wife to care for their young charge and supervise her duties. This was the first occasion on which he expressed an opinion on her treatment. 'Won't do,' he said.

'It's okay.' Mairi had no objection to the smell. When winter set in, the heat from the hay and the animals might make her new quarters more tolerable than the icy attic in which she had slept since arriving at Brigg's Quarter. She was fond of the cows, and their restless shuffling would provide company in the night. Besides, she would be able to do the morning milking without having to cross the yard first.

'I'll fix you something to keep your stuff.' He returned within half an hour carrying wood and a bag of tools. 'The lady's back,' he said as he began to measure the space. The expansive gesture with which he delineated an imaginary bosom made it clear who the visitor was. 'Wants a word with you.'

Mairi scrambled down the ladder and ran across to the farmhouse.

'I've been dealing with a little problem down in Weyburn,' Mrs Rendall told her. 'One of our orphans isn't strong enough for the life. Since I was so near, I thought I'd call in instead of writing. To make sure that the arrangement you asked for was working.'

She was presumably referring to the question of wages, but Mairi brushed the topic aside in her desire for information.

'That's okay. Did you find out anything about Jamie?'

'I'm sorry, dear. I looked in our records. No Jamie McEwan has been sent out to Canada. Not through the same society as yourself, at least. I told you, didn't I, there are twenty or thirty charities who try to provide a new life for orphans. Jamie might have been helped by one of the others. I'd have no way of knowing that.'

'The Refuge,' said Mairi. 'We were both taken to the same orphanage. Someone must know where he is.' She felt a kind of panic overwhelming her at the thought that she might have lost her little brother. Should she have made more of a fuss at The Refuge and insisted on seeing him? She had asked several times, but each request had been met with a brusque refusal, and high walls made it impossible even to glimpse the boys, much less to visit them without permission. Her stay at The Refuge had been so short that she had not been enrolled at any school, so she had never had an excuse to move outside the grounds of the Girls' Side.

Could she have refused to come to Canada without him? But then, she had not known where she was going until she was actually on board the ship. No one had ever asked her or told her anything. The course of her life had been outside her own control and she was unable to pinpoint any moment at which she could have taken steps to alter that state of affairs.

That did not prevent her now from feeling guilty as well as unhappy. 'Could you write a letter?' she asked.

'It will take time,' Mrs Rendall pointed out. 'The war. Shipping. Some of the emigration societies have closed down. But I'll write to the society which sent you out here and ask it to pass the letter on to the orphanage.'

'Thank you.' Mairi paused, wondering whether she dared ask a second favour. It was the mention of a letter which reminded her that she had another brother.

Fergus had promised that he would write to her. Although such a long time had passed without word from him, Mairi had not worried about his silence until this moment. New Zealand was an unimaginably long way away, so she had not expected to hear very soon. Because she never wrote letters herself, she did not live in the expectation of receiving any. Another of Fergus's promises had been that she and Jamie could join him as soon as he was twenty-one; and, without ever acknowledging the thought to herself, she had perhaps accepted the possibility that he would not bother to make contact until then.

So it came as a new thought that perhaps Fergus had lost her in the same way that she had lost Jamie. She had assumed that some one person was in charge of all three of them and would keep them in touch with each other, but that assumption might be wrong. She told Mrs Rendall about Fergus.

'How would he know where to write?' she asked. 'He thought we were going to school, not to an orphanage. Would anyone tell him?'

That question was too complicated for Mrs Rendall. 'Who took you to the orphanage?' she asked.

'A man.' Mairi was horrified to realise how little, as a seven-year-old, she had understood. Who was the man? Had she ever known his name? If so, she had quite forgotten it.

'Take my advice, dear,' said Mrs Rendall. 'Don't waste time in thinking too much about the past. You've been sent out here to make a new life for yourself. Concentrate on that.'

'But you will, please, you will ask about Jamie?' Mairi spoke with a new urgency. If Mrs Rendall were to fail her, she could think of no other channel of communication.

'I'll do my best, dear. I shall have to come to Weyburn again to bring a replacement for the girl who's sick. But it may not be for a few months. Not till the next ship comes in. If I have any news, I'll call by again then.' Mairi had to be content with that.

Later that night, when she was at last free to go to bed, Mairi found that Mr Brigg had spent the evening working in the hayloft which was to be her bedroom. He straightened himself up as she climbed the ladder, and showed her what he had done and planned to do. At each side of the loft the roof pitched steeply, but there was a straight wall at the end. The farmer had built a low chest against the wall to act as a store for Mairi's possessions, and would return tomorrow evening, he

62

promised, to fasten on a hinged top, strong enough to be used as a bench seat. It would be ungrateful, Mairi realised, to point out that she never had time to sit down. She would be allowed to retreat to her sanctum only when she was too tired to do anything but sleep. Nor did she laugh when he promised to drape some kind of sheet or curtain across the front to give her privacy – although no one was likely to stare at her except the cows. Instead, she thanked him sincerely.

'Don't seem much of a bed,' said Mr Brigg, frowning as he considered it.

'It'll do.' The hay would be too warm in summer, but welcome in the winter, and Mrs Brigg had provided a couple of old blankets so that she would not be scratched by the straw.

'Let's see.' Mr Brigg took hold of her hand and pulled her down so that they lay side by side. 'Comfy?'

'Sure.'

'You're a good kid,' said Mr Brigg. His arm burrowed through the hay to encircle her shoulders and pull her a little closer. 'You work hard. Not much thanks, I know that. I want you to be happy here.' He pulled her closer still and turned on to his side so that his free hand could stroke her cheek. 'No dad or anything. You need someone to care for you. Everyone does. Do myself.'

Mairi was surprised by his unusual talkativeness – and still more surprised when he leaned over to kiss her. For a moment longer he held her in his arms and then gave a heavy sigh. 'Better be going. I'll be back tomorrow to make sure everything's okay. So's you can tell me without her listening, if there's anything . . .'

His kindness helped Mairi to forget her unhappiness about her brothers. As the days passed she looked forward to his bedtime visits. He liked to unplait her long hair and run his fingers through its sandy waves; and when she was especially tired he helped her to take off her dress. His fingers, stroking her skin, were rough but at the same time soothing. 'No dad of your own,' he said often, as if to reassure her that, had she not been an orphan, she could have looked forward to a bedtime snuggle of this kind with her true father every night. Without anything being put into words, Mairi realised that she would be wise never to mention his visits to Mrs Brigg, but provided her own understanding of the reason. Anything that could be regarded as a treat would be forbidden at once.

Mrs Rendall had been right to give warning that no answer to Mairi's enquiry could be expected quickly. Several months passed before she called again at the farm. Mrs Brigg, suspicious, refused to leave Mairi alone with her; but Mairi would not have minded that if only the news could have been good.

'I'm sorry, dear. Your little brother was never placed with the Orphans' New Life Society. And they made enquiries at the orphanage you mentioned, but there was no Jamie McEwan on the register there either.'

'There must be!' exclaimed Mairi. 'We went together. They wanted to see us one at a time. He was told he'd got to wait just while my name was put on the register. Then it would be his turn. He must have gone in straight after me.'

'How old was he, do you remember?'

'Four.'

'That could be the answer, then. Maybe he was too young for The Refuge, and was sent on to somewhere which catered for little children.'

'They must know. Somebody must know. He can't be lost!'

'That's enough,' said Mrs Brigg. 'The lady's got better things to do with her time. Go and bring in the logs.'

Mairi gave one last appealing look at Mrs Rendall, but the visitor could only shake her head helplessly. Numb with unhappiness, Mairi went about her daily tasks. Not until she had cleared and washed up after the last meal of the day was she free to indulge her feelings. Running across the yard to the cowshed, she flung herself down on the hay and began to cry.

She cried because Jamie was lost. She would never see him again. But that was only part of her distress. He was such a *little* boy! To be abandoned at the age of four! And even now, he couldn't be more than ten. Where was he? What was he doing? He must feel himself to be alone in the world – and so he was.

She cried for herself as well. Just as she had lost Jamie, so, almost certainly, had Fergus lost her. There was no way in which she could write to her elder brother; nor did it now seem likely that any letter of his would ever reach her. Fergus had not known that she would be taken to an orphanage. He had talked of a school – and through the distress of what felt like a double bereavement, a strand of resentment began to weave its way. Her grandfather had been, well, perhaps not rich in money, but a landowner, able to live comfortably in a castle full of servants. What had happened to the castle? Perhaps it had been sold after the old laird's death. But then, surely there would have been enough money in the family to provide a home in which the three children could stay together and finish their education?

Had somebody cheated them? Because Mairi knew that she was indeed an orphan, she had never before thought to protest at being treated as one. But not all orphans were poor. There was something wrong somewhere but she could not see clearly enough into the past to understand what it was, and soon she gave up the attempt. Whether or not there had been a good reason for her to be separated from her brothers, she would have to accept that the separation was final. Her tears flowed faster: her sobs became noisier.

Just like Jamie, she was alone in the world.

2

'What's up, then?'

Mairi had been crying too noisily to hear Mr Brigg climb the ladder. Since her banishment to the cowshed she had as a rule looked forward to his evening cuddle, but tonight she shook her head. The misery of her loneli-

65

ness was too deep to be comforted by the company of anyone except her lost brothers.

'C'mon, kid. Tell Uncle.'

He was not her uncle. She had had a real uncle once, seen briefly on Christmas visits. She couldn't remember his name and she didn't know where he lived, but he was real. Could he not have helped his niece and nephews to stay together? Did he know what had happened to them all? If he discovered that his niece was a servant, living in a cowshed, surely he would come to her rescue. Had she been truly alone in the world, not only motherless and fatherless but without any surviving kin at all, perhaps she could have endured it. But to be cut off from everyone who ought to care for her, and from everyone she had loved, when they were still alive somewhere in the world, but out of reach – it was that which was breaking her heart.

Next time Mrs Rendall came, if she ever did come again – but Mairi had no more time to think about her real but barely remembered uncle, because the man she had called by that name for the past five years was sitting down beside her on the mattress and pulling her up and into his arms.

By now her crying was out of control. She was forced to gasp for breath before each new moan, and was left with no strength to protest as the farmer began to undress her. He had often before taken off her frock, but this was the first time that he had also tugged her vest, in which she usually slept, over her head. His hands moved over her skin, touching her breasts and within a matter of seconds he seemed to change before her eyes from the kind but stolid man she knew to a red-faced stranger, excited and rough. He was pulling at her knickers, tearing off his own trousers, pressing her back on to the hay-filled mattress. Her earlier general unhappiness was banished by a pain which was in her body and not in her mind. 'You're hurting!' she exclaimed, doing her best to twist away.

'Sorry. Sorry, sorry, sorry.' With each repetition of the word he thrust down at her, hurting her again as though he were not sorry at all. She wanted to cry out again, but his mouth, wet and slobbery, covered her own to smother the sound.

As suddenly as it had begun, the attack was over. The farmer lay quietly beside her, his face pressed against her shoulder. Mairi would have liked to run away, but was afraid to move. Besides, there was nowhere to go.

'Dirty,' she said, at once indignant and disgusted. She was a farm girl, and had never been shocked by the sight of animals mating. But she was not an animal herself, to be treated in such a way. Her body was sticky and, when she raised her head to look, she saw that she was bleeding.

'Stay there.' Mr Brigg pulled on his clothes and scrambled down the ladder. When he returned, more cautiously, he was carrying a bucket of warm water. Mairi did not object as he began to wash her body. Now that the first shock was over, she felt as though she were watching something happening to a stranger; something which had nothing to do with herself.

When he had cleaned and dried her, the farmer swabbed at the bloodstains on the mattress cover.

'Be best if you don't mention this to Auntie,' he said.

For a moment Mairi thought he was referring only to the stains. There was little danger that they would be discovered, since Mrs Brigg never came to the loft. It was only when Mr Brigg said yet again that he was sorry that she began to understand. She could get Mr Brigg into trouble if she sneaked on him. Although still puzzled and bruised, she was aware that the incident had been triggered by affection rather than by anger or spite. She nodded her head.

A week passed before Mr Brigg came again to the loft at night. Even in the darkness he must have been conscious that it was fear which made her stiffen. The time was past when he could cuddle her as though he were her father, and they both knew it.

'Won't hurt as much this time,' he reassured her. 'Just say stop, and I will. But it'll be all right. You'll see.'

For a little while Mairi remained rigid. But he was

gentler than before, and less heavy. The episode was tolerable, if not enjoyable, and she did not object when he asked if he could come again.

It was at about this time, early in 1916, that Mrs Brigg came out with an unexpected question.

'Have you started yet?'

'Started what?'

'Growing up. Don't you girls at school talk about this sort of thing?'

It was two years since Mairi had last been allowed to go to school. Her bewilderment showed on her face.

'You know,' said Mrs Brigg. 'Bleeding.'

Flushing with guilt, Mairi remembered the bloodstains on the mattress. She had promised not to sneak, but it seemed that her secret had been discovered. Her flush was a clear answer, but to her amazement it did not provoke the expected outburst of fury.

'Thought you might've,' Mrs Brigg said. 'Thirteen and a half. Here you are, then. To keep your knickers clean.' She held out two large safety pins and a handful of cotton rags. 'Wash them out as soon as they're used, or you'll never get the stains out.'

Mairi didn't understand. 'You mean it's going to happen again?' she asked.

'Every month. Hasn't anyone told you?'

Who was there to tell her, except Mrs Brigg herself, and she, it seemed, had exhausted her stock of information. Mairi stored the rags away in the chest which Mr Brigg had built for her in the loft. For a week or two she examined her knickers anxiously every day for signs of this new dirtiness; but as time passed she forgot about the threat. Perhaps, after all, she was not yet quite grown up.

It was Mr Brigg who was the first to realise what had happened. Mairi's years of hard work had made her healthy and she was not afflicted by the sickness of early pregnancy. Nor was it easy, when she was dressed in her working clothes, to notice any change in the look of her body. Although she was a thin girl, her full skirts, gathered on a string at the waist, gave her a dumpy appearance at the best of times, and the apron of sack-cloth which fell from her shoulders still further obscured her shape. But when she lay flat on her back in bed, the farmer, stroking her body at first with pleasure and then in suspicion, began to prod and press his hand down in a way which alarmed her. 'Oh, my God!' he said.

'What's the matter? What's happened?'

'Don't you know? No, how would you, poor kid? You're going to have a baby. But don't worry. We'll get rid of it. I'll fix it.'

'What do you mean?'

'Don't you know about babies? Suppose you never had no mother to tell you.' With his hand still moving over her skin, Mr Brigg gave her some basic information, which Mairi found hard to believe.

'I thought you had to be married,' she said, bewilder-ed. Although Mr Brigg had flung himself on her like an animal on that first night, she had not followed the thought far enough through to think of herself as a sow or bitch which would in due course drop a litter. People, she had imagined, were different.

'But if there's a baby and it's alive' – by now it was her own hand which was pressing down on her abdomen – 'what d'you mean by getting rid of it?'

'You can't have a baby, not here. Auntie'd murder you. Me too.'

'But d'you mean you're going to kill the baby?' Mairi, alarmed, sat up and began to pull on her vest, as though this would afford some protection to the child.

'It's not a baby till it's born. I know someone who looks after this sort of thing. Doctor, kind of. I'll take you along next week, the sooner the better. It'll be all right, you'll see.'

He put his plan into operation two days later. Mairi, cooking and serving breakfast, was able to hear the conversation at the kitchen table.

'I've had an offer of some piglets,' Mr Brigg told his wife. 'Cheap. The sow's dead, so they'll have to be hand-reared. Mairi could look after that. I'll need her to come with me tomorrow to pick them up. Can't manage on my own.'

Mrs Brigg, torn between the wish to protest over the loss of a day's housework and the recognition that Mairi's patience and love of animals would be profitable in the long run, nodded reluctantly. Mr Brigg turned his head towards the kitchen range.

'Soon's you've finished with the cows tomorrow, then,' he said.

Mairi nodded in her turn. But although her face was expressionless, her thoughts were racing. It wasn't right, it *couldn't* be right, to kill a baby. It was alive. Only the previous night she had felt it move.

Nobody could harm the baby unless she let them. For the first time in her life, Mairi realised, she had the power to take a decision about her own future.

The choice she made was founded on emotion rather than practical sense. The baby was hers, her very own. Someone to be looked after and loved; a child who in time would love her and belong to her. She would no longer be alone in the world. There would be two of them, caring about each other. There was really no choice at all. Already she longed for the moment when she would hold her baby in her arms.

That afternoon, while Mrs Brigg was taking her afternoon rest, Mairi cautiously climbed on a stool and reached down a brownstone jar. Right from the start she had needed to remind Mrs Brigg of the arrangement that she was to be paid a wage after her thirteenth birthday, but she had never, in fact, been handed any of the money – for what, the farmer's wife demanded, was there to spend it on, when she was fortunate enough to have all her food provided? But every Saturday evening Mairi would stand silently until a few coins were reluctantly produced and added to the store which was hidden for safety in the jar.

To guard against possible disappointment now, Mairi reminded herself that the money might well have been stolen back again and used for the farm expenses. But no, it seemed that Mrs Brigg, although not generous, was honest. Mairi tied her savings into a cloth and replaced the jar.

The next morning, Mr Brigg drove her in his cart to Weyburn, the nearest small town, and tethered the horse in the station yard. 'Best to go where we're not known,' he said as he led the way towards the booking office.

'May I carry my own ticket?' Mairi was acting a part, making her voice sound childish instead of sly.

'Ain't you never been on a train before?'

'Once in England. And then when I was brought to you and Auntie. But I've never been allowed to hold the ticket.'

'Mind you don't lose it, then. We'll need it for coming back as well.'

Mairi stowed the ticket in her pocket, to be kept as safe as her secret. She stared out of the window as the train sped southward; but her eyes saw nothing, because her mind was busy with its plans. There were so many possibilities, and she must be prepared for any opportunity which presented itself.

It proved easier than she had dared to hope. When they left the train at a station whose name she did not know, Mr Brigg took her to one end of the platform and pointed.

'See that barber shop there? Above that, on the second floor, that's where Doc Mason lives. You ring his bell and when he comes you say, "I've been told you might be able to help me." Then he'll say, "Who told you?" and you say "Lindy Peel." Can you remember that? Lindy Peel.'

'I don't know anyone called that,' said Mairi.

'Don't matter. Sort of code, see. Just so's he knows you're not going to land him in trouble. Then you give him this.' Mr Brigg handed her a sealed envelope.

'What is it?'

'American dollars. He'll look after you well for that. You'll want to lie down for an hour or two when he's done. There's a train back, leaves at two. I'll be at the station ten minutes before. If you need a bit of help from

71

his door, I'll be watching to give you a hand. It'll be all right, kid.'

'So you're not coming with me?'

'Best if I don't. But you can't go wrong. Give me a minute's start and then off you go. Lindy Peel, remember.'

He patted her on the cheek and made his way along the platform and out of the station. Mairi watched through the railings as he turned in the opposite direction from that of the barber's shop and walked off at a brisk pace. On the platform where she was standing, whistles began to blow. It was the simplest thing in the world to jump back on to the train she had just left. If Mr Brigg were watching for her to emerge from the railroad station, he would only discover too late that she had disappeared. In any case, Mairi suspected that he would feel no wish to pursue her. To tell his wife that the ungrateful girl had run away might be the best solution to his part of the problem.

As to Mairi's own problems, she would just have to deal with them one at a time. If her lack of a valid ticket for this journey was discovered, she would put on a show of distress at having gone past her stop. If she waited for a large station at which to alight she could almost certainly, as a child, pass through any barrier as though she were attached to some family. And after that – well, she was used to hard work. Somebody, surely, would employ her.

She should have been frightened, for the cents she had earned and the dollars in the envelope could not support her for very long. Rightly or wrongly, though, she had developed a new confidence in herself. She would manage somehow.

Her true fears were of a different kind. By making it difficult for the Briggs to track her down, she was at the same time making it impossible for Fergus ever to find her, should he try to do so. But after five years without a word, she had to assume that he had already forgotten all about her. She had lost Fergus already, just as she had lost little Jamie. Her only consolation was that this

72

journey, which was carrying her out of reach of every past family tie, was hurrying her also towards a new family. Her own.

3

Mud. Mud was everywhere; the undefeated enemy. From a mud-coloured sky, the rain had been falling throughout the summer and autumn of 1917 on to the mud-coated earth. Every blade of grass was by now trampled in, and the blood of dead and wounded men streaked the ground visibly for only a few seconds before being absorbed into the slime which stank of other submerged bodies and limbs. Two years earlier Fergus had believed that Gallipoli was the nearest place to hell that could exist on earth; but he had met its equal at Passchendaele.

Waiting for the command to move, he stood in the quagmire which was called a trench, with water streaming off his helmet and cape. In this grim half-hour of inaction preceding an attack, all the men had their own routines for keeping fear at bay, routines which quickly became superstitions, bringing bad luck if they were forgotten or interrupted.

Fergus counted sheep. Using all his mental concentration to remove himself back to New Zealand, he counted five thousand Merino ewes across a river; sometimes chivvying them over and sometimes needing to haul them out of the deepening water. But however sternly he promised himself that he would not be distracted by thoughts of his present situation, the moment always came when the sheep began to sink into a quicksand of mud, and not all his tugging or holding steady could save them. General Mud, an opponent even more hateful than Johnny Turk, had conquered his thoughts.

It seemed to Fergus that what the two opposing armies

were doing between them was murdering the land. Before Passchendaele he would not have thought such a thing possible. But he hoped to be a farmer himself one day and he studied his surroundings with a farmer's eyes. Once upon a time Flanders had been a fertile and prosperous area of fields which could be grazed or ploughed. Admittedly, the land was heavy clay which easily became waterlogged; but there had been drainage canals to keep the farm land workable.

Fergus knew that to be true because he had seen it for himself when he first arrived in 1916, after the evacuation of Gallipoli. But since that time he and the rest of the army had trodden down one harvest and made it impossible to sow another. In digging their trenches they had destroyed the canals and so flooded the land, creating unspeakable living conditions for themselves in the process. And the night-long artillery bombardments, which continued for hours at a time, had succeeded in pulverising the earth into a fine powder which bore no relationship to the original heavy soil. The rain played its part as well, helping the two armies to create a sea of slime. Once upon a time, perhaps, the origins of life and the seeds of civilisation had crawled out of such a slime; but now it seemed to Fergus that civilisation was fast slipping back there again.

The thought of all these ruined farms sometimes prompted him to think of the land that would one day be his own. It was a daydream in which he indulged only occasionally, so unlikely did its eventual realisation seem in this setting. In three months' time, on 3 January 1918, he would come of age. His uncle had promised on that day to give him a farm of his own, or at least the money to buy it. Fergus no longer remembered anything at all about his uncle except for that one promise, but he believed it implicitly. Once he was twenty-one – or rather, as soon as the war ended – he would be able to marry Dorothy Sutherland and settle down to the life of a farmer. Then at last he could invite his brother and sister to join him. He had told Dorothy about them, and she, kind-hearted as she was, had not hesitated in her promise of a welcome.

Fergus had not written to Mairi or Jamie since he left New Zealand. He still thought of them as children, who could not be expected to understand about the war. Besides, all his letter-writing time was devoted to Dorothy. But now, reminded that his twenty-first birthday was approaching, he promised himself that he would once again contact that Edinburgh address from which no answer was ever received, with the reassurance that he would look after them as soon as the war was over.

Would such a time ever come? He shook his head wearily, unable to imagine it. Was it good to have something to which he could look forward, or better merely to endure, to survive a day at a time? Flanders had not completely killed his spirit, but had succeeded in bringing it low. Almost forgotten now was the thrill of enlistment, the comradeship of the long voyage, the excitement of a foreign country which their training camp in Egypt had provided. He and Robert had arrived in the Dardanelles in July 1915, too late to take part in the first landing at Gallipoli, but in time for the assault on Chunuk Bair.

That was the moment when disillusion set in. All the Kiwis were convinced that the battle could have been won if the top brass had been less faint-hearted. It was impossible for them to think of the evacuation which followed five months later as anything but an unnecessary humiliation. Nothing had been gained at Gallipoli, and it seemed unlikely that anything could be gained in Flanders. The possibility of losing the war had never occurred to Fergus, but he did not see how it could be won.

Dusk was falling. 'Two minutes,' said Robert; and Fergus, beside him, nodded an acknowledgement. The only splash of cheer in this mud-stained world was the fact that he and Robert Sutherland had not been separated. An outsider, a civilian, would no doubt have regarded as mere superstition Fergus's strong conviction

75

that no harm could come to him whilst he and Robert were together: but it was a conviction shared by Robert. There were many such bonds within the brigade, where it was taken for granted that the loyalty of any two mates to each other served as armour-plating against the dirty tricks of fate.

They would need all the protection they could find today. In the enormity of the Third Battle of Ypres the silencing of a machine-gun post was a mere sideshow, a triviality. In the larger context of a sane civilisation the assault would have been regarded as a suicide mission: but it was a long time since sanity had played much part in Fergus's life. To him, the projected attack on the German pill-box from which a machine gun had been spitting death for the past three days was an ordinary incident in the hell that was Passchendaele. If he and Robert felt any resentment at having been picked for the attack, it was only because the benefit of the section's success – if they did succeed – would be enjoyed not by their own Kiwi comrades but by the Highland brigade on the right which was due to go over the top at dawn. The bloody Highlanders, in their opinion, ought to do their own bloody dirty work. This opinion was not, however, expressed aloud. Before the sun set the next day, a high proportion of those Highlanders would be dead.

The seconds passed. Fergus lifted his feet up and down in the watery mud of the trench like a cat settling itself into a place to sleep, trying to find a foothold on the drowned duckboards from which to push off. As usual, it seemed that nothing could be worse than the nervous period of waiting. And as usual also, the moment of leaving the trench was most certainly far worse. Once outside on the hillside, though, the need for speed left no place for fear. Fergus had no particular quarrel with the aim of the operation, but he had not the slightest intention of obeying the lieutenant's instructions on the approach to the concrete pill-box. Some people, it seemed, had learned nothing since the Crimean War. So instead of running straight up the hill towards the muzzle of a machine-gun, he crouched low as soon as he was out of the trench and made off at speed in a wide sweep which would bring him, if he was lucky, to a point above their objective.

The attitude in which he moved was as individual as the line he took. Although not aware of the fact himself, he ran like a Highlander. His knees were bent and his shoulders thrust forward, allowing his arms to dangle loosely so that they almost touched the ground. This leaning posture, almost parallel to the contours of the hill, made him less likely to slide backwards in the mud, and his own weight provided the momentum to carry him up the steep slope.

There was as much danger in this approach as in the more direct route, for it was impossible in the dusk to distinguish between ordinary mud and the slime which filled shell holes without providing safe passage across them. It was not only bullets and shells which offered death at Passchendaele. Drowning in mud was another way to go.

He was almost level with the pill-box when the rattle of machine-gun fire revealed that some of the others had been observed and were under attack. Fergus flung himself flat on to the muddy ground and began to wriggle along it through the darkness like a snake until he was immediately underneath the protruding muzzle of the machine-gun. Taking the pin from a Mills bomb with his teeth, he forced the bomb through the loophole which the gun was using, dropping back to the ground with his head cradled in his hands as he waited for the explosion. The thick concrete of the pill-box protected him from the force of the blast, which was followed by half an hour of confusion and hand-to-hand fighting. Only after five Germans had been sent down under escort to the line as prisoners and the bodies of eight others hauled outside into the open did Fergus, panting with effort and the relief of tension, have time to look around.

'Rob?' he called. It was impossible in the darkness to distinguish one mud-smeared face from another.

There was a second's stillness; a silence which he was able to interpret at once. There had been times in the past when he too had not wanted to be the one to speak bad news. 'Rob,' he said again, but this time almost under his breath.

'Sorry, Ferg. Rob bought it. Bastards had a look-out up back.'

Fergus began to stumble out into the night but was gripped and held back. 'Better not.' The voice in the darkness was hoarse with sympathy. 'Nothing to be done. I was there. Saw it.'

He shook the hands off. This was too large a matter to take on trust. There must be some miracle which only he could perform. But no miracle, he realised after a ten-minute search, could rebuild the shattered head of his friend. Making his way back to the pill-box, he sat down on the floor without speaking, burying his face in his hands and breathing deeply as he tried to take it in.

Robert was – had been – not just his closest friend, but almost a brother. He was the only son of his parents. How would they be able to bear the news? And Dorothy . . . at the thought that he would have to tell Dorothy, Fergus groaned aloud. In his letters from the front he had written only of his love for her and hopes for the future, doing his best not to mention the hell of battle. What was the point of terrifying civilians who could do nothing but wait for bad news? But the more successful his efforts had been, the greater would be the shock now.

What was the point of it all, Fergus asked himself. For more than two years Robert had lived in danger of snipers and machine-guns and shells. At Gallipoli he had twice come near to death, once from enteric fever and once in the collapse of a tunnel. It was Fergus who on that second occasion had dug him out and pulled him clear, had saved his life, in fact; but for what? So that he could go on fighting. And what were they fighting for? Whatever the original reasons might have been, there was only one answer now. They were fighting for the chance to stop fighting, to get back home again and lead a normal life. But that chance was open only to the survivors; and Robert had not survived.

His mind numbed by grief, Fergus was at first hardly aware that the artillery barrage which preceded any big attack had begun. By midnight, however, it was impossible to ignore. The British guns opened up first, and within an hour the Germans were responding. Earth and sky trembled with the blast of screaming and exploding shells. The seven men in the concrete pillbox had reason to hope that none of the German guns would alter their range to attack such a small target, but their position between the lines doubled the noise they had to endure. They took it in turns to stand guard against any attempt at recapture, but tacitly excluded Fergus from this rota.

At a quarter to six in the morning the Highlanders began their attack. The range of their own guns was lengthened and from time to time between each salvo it was possible to hear the sound of a piper playing his men over the top. Fergus and his companions stood up and collected their equipment together; they were due to be relieved after the attack had swept past them. Although the positioning of the machine-gun slits did not allow their refuge to be used against the Germans, it was important to keep the stronghold out of their hands.

The Kiwi detachment scrambled in, panting out advice about the route back to the trench. As Fergus made his helmet secure, he put Robert out of his mind for the moment, forcing himself to concentrate on the dangers of the next few seconds. When a machine-gunner was the enemy, a zig-zagging course was the safest; but the danger this morning would come from shells which could be neither anticipated nor avoided. Pausing only briefly to choose his line, Fergus ran, slid and jumped straight down the hill.

A German shell screamed overhead, racing him towards the trench; and, winning the race, it exploded a few yards in front of him. Fergus for his part did not scream. He could see that his right arm was wounded, but he felt no pain. Far more unsettling was the curious slow motion with which the blast of the explosion lifted him into the air and hurled him into the crater made by some earlier shell.

The crater, had it been empty, would have been large enough to contain the homestead in which he and Robert had spent six years together. It was not, however, empty, but filled, like every other hole in Flanders, with liquid mud. As he slithered down the side, Fergus flung out his left hand and grasped a protruding post, thorny with barbed wire. His feet flailed and slipped as he tried to walk himself up the side of the crater. He was only five or six feet below its edge, and would be within sight of his own company if only he could haul himself up to the top. With two hands it might have been possible, but his shattered right arm was useless. After a few moments of hopeless effort he was forced to give up.

He was not immediately frightened. The post seemed secure and he could hang on for a little while yet. He would be missed. Someone would look for him. If Robert were alive, he would be there already, lying flat in the mud to stretch down a hand or throw a rope. The picture of Robert matter-of-factly hauling him out was so vivid that for a second Fergus imperceptibly relaxed his grip. His hand slid down the post, which was as slippery as everything else with mud, and pressed painfully against the barbed wire. But he could hang on. Someone would come.

As abruptly as they had opened the barrage twelve hours earlier, the British guns fell silent, suggesting that the Highlanders had reached the enemy lines. The sound of the bagpipes was louder now. Fergus, shouting for help, could hear it whenever he paused to listen for a response, and found it melancholy rather than inspiriting. He had heard something similar once before, many years ago. When his grandfather died, that was it. Hamish the piper had played a lament whilst twelve-year-old Fergus himself – the heir to Lochandar, as he had thought then – stood stiffly to attention. Mairi and Jamie had been thought too young to attend the funeral.

Mairi and Jamie. What would become of them if their

brother were to die now? Only with this thought did Fergus accept the extremity of his danger, with a reaction combining panic and ferocious resistance. He had to stay alive for Dorothy's sake, and for Mairi's and wee Jamie's. His heart began to beat more wildly and he made another effort to press his feet into the side of the crater; but by now they were heavy with the glutinous mud and he was too weak to kick them free. The mud was winning this private battle, sucking him inexorably down. He could feel the strength flowing out of his body with the blood from his useless right arm. If only Robert . . . He gritted his teeth, willing himself to survive. But inch by inch, as the piper played on, Fergus sank into the mud.

4

'Where's that Wee Jamie, then? Set out the bullseye, boy!'

The vigorous shout meant that the shearers had arrived. Jamie tipped the two heavy buckets of pigswill into the trough and hurried back towards the station house, his freckled face beaming with pleasure.

Billy and George and Stripper came to the station punctually on 1 September each year and stayed for three weeks. Jamie had encountered them for the first time only a few weeks after starting his first job two years earlier at the age of eleven and a half.

The work was arduous, for the station manager went out with the sheep for weeks at a time and his wife expected her new hand, in spite of his youth, to tackle all the heavy tasks around the yard.

Still, Jamie was not afraid of hard work. His life since arriving in Australia had not been easy, because the orphans had been expected to cultivate the farm school's own land as well as doing their regular lessons each day. So he had buckled down to his new employment without complaining on that score.

That didn't mean that he had no complaints. He had

been promised that he would be paid wages of fifteen shillings a week, but none had ever been handed over. The first time he asked about them he was reminded that he had grown out of his boots and clothes; where did he think the money had come from to replace them? A second enquiry, six months later, had brought him a beating for impertinence, and he had taken the message to heart.

There was no court of appeal. Even though the friendly shearers might have carried a message for him when he saw them for a second time, he could think of no one who would defend his right to be paid, and certainly no one who could protect him against the whippings which would follow any outside intervention. Jamie didn't waste time worrying about it. He had every intention of making his fortune one day, but it had been clear to him for as long as he could remember that he would have to do it by himself. Until he had grown to his full strength he had better be grateful that he was at least adequately fed and had a roof over his head.

There were, however, two ways of making money open to him. Soon after his arrival at the station he had been taught by Mr Jackson to use a rifle, in case any dingoes came to attack the henhouse. Jamie had a good eye and a steady hand, and discovered with interest after he claimed his first victim that the government paid a bounty of a shilling for every dingo scalp. Mr Jackson, although unwilling to fill his apprentice's pockets with his own money, did not go to the length of stealing the bounty entitlement.

It was a source of income which Jamie was quick to exploit. He was not offered any kind of annual holiday – such an idea did not occur to either his master or himself – but he was occasionally allowed time to ride out to the fence and camp there for a week by himself, killing as many wild animals as he could. This was useful to Mr Jackson, for kangaroos and wild pigs charged the fence and broke it down, wombats burrowed under it and dingoes and rabbits came through the gaps; the dingoes to kill the sheep and the rabbits to graze the grass. Jamie was expected to bring some meat home to his employer, but was allowed to keep for himself whatever cash he could get for the skins and any government bounties on offer: kangaroos as well as dingoes were on the list this year. He was glad of the money and enjoyed the diversion as a change and rest from the heavy work which was his lot when his employer was away from home.

Jamie's matter-of-fact nature helped him to shrug off all the beatings and the physical hardships of his life, but he often felt lonely. After seven years of community life, first in the orphanage and then at the farm school, he missed the company of the other boys and the games they played in their few free moments.

The shearers, hard-working and hard-drinking, had cheered him up in that first September by the sheer vigour with which they lived. Jamie's own contribution to the annual ritual was tiring enough, for he was expected to take each heavy fleece as it fell from the shears and to toss it flat on a table, receiving at the same time non-stop reminders that shearing was thirsty work. The three men themselves, reckoning each to deal with more than a hundred sheep a day, succumbed to a brief exhaustion when they laid down their shears in the evening, but within half an hour were splashing the sweat from their bodies and demanding food and entertainment. Mrs Jackson provided the food, but it was Jamie who had introduced them to a new diversion.

None of them knew how to play marbles; nor had they ever seen a collection as fine as Jamie's. Over seven years he had won almost every marble that the other orphans dared to stake against him. The three shearers had borrowed a dozen each so that they could learn and practise the variety of games which Jamie had invented, but then rapidly lost them all back to the eleven-year-old again. They were strong, skilful men who were amused that a mere kid could so easily outplay them. When they left, that first year, they each bought some of Jamie's stock, promising that on their return he would need to look out for himself.

Stuffed into the mattress with his dingo money, Jamie still possessed the profit of that sale, and he had doubled it the next year by winning his marbles back and selling them again. This time, the men promised in the middle of their roar of greeting that they were ready to show him what was what.

'I've got to chop the firewood,' Jamie told them. 'Be trouble if she finds me playing 'fore that's done.'

'We'll give you a hand afterwards. C'mon.'

Jamie's grin broadened as he nodded acceptance of the offer for which he had hoped. He led the way to a patch of level ground. Picking up a fencing post whose end he had sharpened earlier in the day, he drew the four concentric circles of a bullseye in the dust, with a square around it to provide four firing lines.

'Reckon you're not such a wee Jamie any more, are you?' said Billy. 'Shooting up. How old are you now, then?'

'Thirteen.' Jamie straightened himself and inspected the target before thrusting a hand into his trouser pocket. He carried two or three of his marbles around with him everywhere he went, so that whenever he had a hand free he could rub them together in his palm. And today, knowing that the shearers were expected, he had taken some more from their pouch. Ten each would be needed to play the bullseye game.

Before the contest began, there was the serious matter of opening a book on the result. All the shearers were gambling men and, indeed, found no activity worth pursuing unless it was possible to make a bet on its outcome. Jamie considered the state of his finances carefully as Stripper called the opening odds. He had been holding the money in the mattress in reserve for a special plan: it was his running-away fund. But it didn't take him long to realise that all three shearers, flush with cash from their last job, and in a relaxed and jolly mood, were backing themselves over-optimistically, determined to beat him at last. Perhaps they had been playing each other and were confident of having improved their game.

Jamie was even more confident of his own ability. If

ever there was a time to take a risk, it was now, before they started to play. Once Stripper had been defeated, he was not likely to offer such a good chance again. Jamie backed himself against each of the shearers in turn and staked everything he had left in a variety of side bets on his own total score and the size of the differentials between his score and his opponent's in each round.

The learning which Jamie had acquired at school was of little use to him on the station. He could read and write, but owned no books and was not expected to write letters. He took pleasure in arranging figures quickly and neatly in his mind; but, again, he had little call to put this to practical use. Now, however, he was able to calculate just as quickly as Stripper how much he stood to gain or lose and, even at the speed with which the bets were noted, had taken care not to risk indebtedness if his touch should unexpectedly desert him.

There was to be no fear of that. The four players rolled a marble each to decide the order of play, and the game was on. The quartet provided sharp contrasts in appearance as they took up their positions. George and Billy were both large and burly, whilst Stripper, a leaner man, had been tattooed all over his arms and shoulders, emphasising the strength of his muscles. The thirteen-year-old, although tall and sturdy for his age, appeared pale and slight by comparison. But his eye was true and his balance sure. Dropping on to one knee, with the other foot placed firmly in front of it, he bit his bottom lip in concentration and waited for his turn.

Each circle of the bullseye had a points value. All Jamie's interest was focused on the fifty points which could be scored in the inner ring. Whenever one of the others placed a marble there, he used it as a target, flicking his own with a force sufficient to send the enemy flying right out of the circle whilst itself remaining in the centre.

'Bloody hell!' exclaimed Stripper when the game was over. Jamie had backed himself to score over a thousand points in the three rounds which had been agreed in advance. He had won this bet handsomely, as well as beating each of the three shearers in each round. 'Reckoned we were going to teach you a lesson this time. Been practising, have you?'

Jamie grinned happily as he collected his winnings.

'Try it again,' said George to Stripper. 'I know how to deal with him this time.'

Jamie could guess what he meant. If the three of them ganged up against him, firing him out of the target every time after he had had his turn, one of them was bound to win. He had counted on them not trying that in the first game. 'Time to chop the firewood,' he said.

'You think we're going to help you after you rob us like that? Guess again, mate.'

Jamie shrugged his shoulders, but while he was repeatedly bringing the axe down on the chopping stump, he knew it would not be long before the challenge was repeated.

By the end of the three-week shearing session, Jamie's mattress had developed a satisfactory lumpiness. On the last evening he made a point of suggesting a game whose object was not to score points but to capture opposing marbles.

'*I* can see what you're up to,' said Stripper. 'You calculate that if you clean us out we'll buy them all back off you. Not a hope, mate. We'll take you on at – what's it called? – Plum Pudding.'

As he laid his last bets of the session on the result Jamie smiled. He was aware that he had broken the unwritten code of the gambler by stashing away almost the whole of his winnings and risking only small amounts since the all-or-nothing stake of the first day. Had he been full-grown, he would have come in for criticism from men who took it for granted that gambling winnings should always be re-staked until they were lost. But because he was only a boy, they punished him merely by shortening the odds. In response he changed his tactics and bet on Billy instead of himself, knocking the marbles of Stripper and George out of the circle and then allowing himself to be beaten by Billy.

'Who taught you to be so crafty?' demanded Stripper,

handing over the money. 'And what do you want with a small fortune like this, anyway?'

'Not much of a fortune,' said Jamie ruefully, although it was true that in the past few days he had greatly increased his previous savings. 'But I want to have land of my own one day, 'stead of working for other people.'

'The government's giving land away,' George told him. 'Acres of it, waiting to be cleared. Why pay for it?'

'No one's going to give anything to someone of my age.'

'Why d'you want land anyway?' Stripper asked the question seriously. 'It'll only bring you worry, like. Just look at any farmer you know. Always complaining. The bloody weather, the bloody pests, the cost of fencing, the shortage of bloody labour. Much better to *be* the labour and name your price.'

Jamie didn't know how to answer. Somebody, he couldn't remember who, had told him once to get land of his own. In a life which ever since had been full of people giving him orders, that one instruction had stuck in his mind as a piece of good advice. The speaker, whoever he was, had had his best interests at heart.

Jamie remembered very little of his life before he came to Australia, and nothing at all of the time before he was taken to The Refuge. Certainly nobody in the past nine years had ever offered him love, or shown any special interest in him. But somewhere in the deepest recess of his memory was a recollection of caring warmth; and this was linked to the hunger which he felt for land of his own. 'Dunno why I want it,' he mumbled. 'Just do.'

'You're never going to get enough by playing marbles,' Stripper pointed out.

'Nor as a farm hand,' added Billy.

'I know that.' Jamie hesitated. He had no reason to believe that the shearers would keep his secret; yet he felt a need to confide in someone, and he had no friends at hand. 'But with what I've got now, I reckon I can buy myself a ticket to the goldfields and keep myself alive for a bit till I make a strike.'

'Gold!' exclaimed Stripper. 'Bit late for that, mate. You should have got yourself born fifty years earlier.'

'There's still gold around.'

'Tucker money, maybe. You're not going to find a fortune, though.'

Jamie didn't argue, but his silence was stubborn enough. George, the oldest and largest of the three men, gave a deep laugh and slapped him across the shoulders with a force that nearly knocked him over.

'What's the boy got to lose?' he asked his friends. 'A few years of his life, that's all. Might just as well take a gamble on gold as spend the next five years splitting wood for palings. You follow your nose, matey, and if it leads you to the goldfields, well, the best of British luck to you.'

'Hook on to someone who knows what he's doing.' Billy, following his friend's lead, contributed advice of his own. 'You could waste the hell of a lot of time scrabbling about in the dirt on your own, like. I know what I'm talking about. Tried it myself once, see. Place called Tibooburra. Sits in the middle of a circle of stones. Old volcano, they say. Story used to be that every time it rained, flakes of gold were washed down the main street. Well, that was true, an' all. Only thing was, no one ever found out where they came from. And all the time I was there, it only rained once. Hot as hell the rest of the time.'

'Did you find any gold?' asked Jamie eagerly.

'Enough to pay my slate at the store and make a brooch for my sheila. With the which she ran off three weeks later. But it's a good life. Dang it all, for two pins I'd come with you and have another go.'

'Not in the middle of the shearing season you don't,' said Stripper; and Billy gave a grin of agreement.

'Time we packed up,' he said. 'We'll be off before first light tomorrow.' And indeed it was no later than four o'clock in the morning when Jamie was roused by the sound of horses being watered and loaded. He pulled on his clothes and emerged just as the three shearers were swinging themselves into the saddle.

'See you in a year's time,' shouted Stripper.

'Don't count on it.' Jamie's freckled grin reflected the pleasure he had taken in their company, but he was not prepared to make any promises.

'Think of us, then, when you're rolling gold nuggets instead of marbles into the bullseye. See you.'

Jamie waved a hand in farewell. Then, returning to his bed, he thrust his hand into the mattress and counted his money. It had been a profitable time for him as well as for the shearers. Why should he stay on here to be whipped and ordered about? He could live for several months on what he had now and, when it ran out, well, he was strong and healthy; wherever there was work available, he could do it.

Lining the coins up in neat piles, he made his plans. One more week's shooting along the fence would increase his hoard of cash even more satisfactorily. But the first chance he had after that, he would take himself off. To the goldfields.

5

'You got any idea what prospecting means?' The clerk in the Mines Office, although good-natured, expressed astonishment. 'Before you set off prospecting, lad, you need to get yourself a team of pack-horses, a year's provisions, a tent, a good set of tools, and about ten years' experience in the outback. You can't just "go prospecting".'

Jamie's lips tightened in annoyance. Everyone he had met on the long journey to Tibooburra had pressed advice on him when they learned of his intentions. The most sensible suggestion had been that he should study the mineral maps of the area before getting started, since there would be no point in looking for gold where none existed. So it was humiliating, when he had tried to behave responsibly, to be treated like a child. He was very nearly fourteen years old; tall and strong and well used to looking after himself.

The clerk had time on his hands and a friendly disposition. 'Sit down,' he said. 'No reason why you shouldn't get yourself a dish and go out panning, and good luck to you. You're using the wrong words, see, that's all it is. A prospector's a special kind of man. Explorer. Takes off into the outback in search of country where no one's been before him. But you don't have to start like that, see. Fact, you'd be crazy to try. You want to set out sluicing or crevicing or dry-stacking. Look for the scrapings that no one could be bothered with in the bonanza days. May not seem so exciting, but you'll be surprised what's still lying about in the old workings, and it gives you a feel for the dirt. You've got to know the land as well as a farmer knows his. What the rocks are made of. And not only where the water is now, but where it was a thousand years ago. When you've got that kind of knowledge under your belt, you can go reefing, see. And then, like I said, ten years or so, you'll be ready to start prospecting.'

Jamie was silenced. In his mental picture of the goldfields he had seen himself scrambling up a hill and picking up a nugget of gold the size of an egg. Crevicing, sluicing, dry-stacking: he didn't even know what the words meant, and it didn't seem likely that anyone gave classes in elementary gold-mining. Still, it was worth enquiring.

'What's crevicing?' he asked.

'Well, you find yourself a creek. Anywhere you go round here will have been panned thirty years ago for sure, when the rush was on; but if no one's been back since, you could still be lucky. The old-timers took what came easy, and were glad to have it. Didn't always waste their time on the fiddly bits. So you clean the mud off the bottom of the creek while it's dry, and then you start looking for cracks. You can take a pickaxe to the big ones, but often as not you just scrape away with a bit of wire, see, picking out the mud that's settled hard. When you've got enough, you dish it, and you could find yourself lucky. Only a flake or two at a time, mind, but it adds up.'

Jamie had heard of dishing. It meant swirling water and mud around in some special way so that the dirt came out and the gold stayed. But he didn't know exactly how to do it. Disappointed, and angry with his own ignorance, he bit his bottom lip, trying to decide what to do next.

'Tell you what,' said the clerk. 'You want to hitch yourself on to one of the old-timers. Still some diggers round here who came out in the Eighties. Made a fortune, one or two of them, and spent it and came back to go on digging. Or else never struck lucky but always reckoned that next year would be the year. They're getting on a bit now. Could do with a strong lad to help around. Heavy work, digging.'

'D'you know anyone like that?' Half an hour earlier Jamie would have been indignant at the thought that he could not manage on his own. But beneath the ambition and the day-dreaming which – foolishly, perhaps – had brought him to Tibooburra was a strong layer of common sense. He had always recognised that he would have to work for his living as soon as his small store of cash ran out. To work first, if he could learn the ropes of this new life at the same time, might prove to be the better way round.

'Let's think.' The clerk considered for a few moments. His lips moved, although soundlessly, until at last he clapped his hands. 'Harry the Hat. Came into town six days ago, so he might be sober again by now. He was talking about a new prospect, somewhere up Cooper Creek way. Said he'd be needing a water boy. All salt water out in the desert, see. You go and look for Harry the Hat.'

'Where might he be?'

'Well now, there are thirteen watering holes in this town and none of them prohibits card games. You just stand in each door in turn and give a cooee; you'll find him.'

'What's the rest of his name, after Harry?'

91

'Can't say I know. Never heard him called anything but Harry the Hat.'

'Thanks.' Jamie hoisted on to his shoulder the blanket roll which contained all his possessions and set off down the main street. He did not quite have the nerve to shout in the way suggested, but instead each time asked the person nearest the door. At the third attempt he was rewarded by the jabbing of a thumb in the direction of the bar.

The man who was in the process of carrying four pints of beer across to a table of card players was of a most curious shape. His neck was thick and muscular and his shoulders broad. Down to the waist, he had the build of a powerful man. But his hips were slight and his legs short and bowed, giving him a height of only about five feet. Because of his shortness and the wide brim of the hat which had given rise to his nickname, it was difficult to see much of his face; but from this distance it looked like that of an old man.

For a moment Jamie hesitated. But the older Harry proved to be, the greater would be his need of a helper, and he would have all the more experience to pass on. Jamie walked across to the table at which the cards were being shuffled. 'I'm looking for Harry the Hat,' he said.

Bright eyes looked up at him out of a sun-wrinkled face. 'What do you want with him?'

'I was told you might be looking for a water boy.'

The pack of cards was cut to Harry, who ignored it for the moment. 'How old are you?' He spoke in a way which Jamie found unusual, his lips articulating clearly although his voice seemed to emerge from the back of his throat.

'Fourteen after Christmas.'

'Ride a horse?'

'Yes, sir.'

'Ever used a gun?'

'I'm reckoned to be quite a good shot, sir.'

'Sir!' With a show of broken and discoloured teeth, Harry grinned round the table at his fellow-players.

'When's the last time any of you were called sir? Here's a lad knows quality when he meets it. Name?'

'Jamie Jamieson.'

'Well, Jamie Jamieson, what I need this year is someone to bring me luck as well as water. Stand here behind me, and if I deal myself an ace in this hand, you're hired.' He added more money to the already substantial stake in front of him and touched the table twice with his knuckles before dealing.

The cards flew round the table, Harry picked up his own hand, tapped it into neatness and then fanned it out. He was holding not just one ace, but two. Jamie was aware that the other players were all staring at him, hoping to find in his expression a clue to Harry's play. He stared down at the floor so that nothing should be revealed by the brightness of his eyes.

When the game had been played, and won by Harry, the old man pulled his winnings towards him. 'Should cover your wages for a week or two,' he said, and extracted a sheet of paper from the pocket of his bush jacket. The list handwritten on it was neater than might have been expected from someone whose clothes were so crumpled and sweat-stained. He handed it to Jamie without any further interrogation.

'Take this to Kennedy's store. I'll be along in an hour.'

Pleased that his first errand should be within his capability, Jamie hurried off and watched as everything from nails to tea leaves was weighed and packaged and stacked. 'You Harry's new boy, then?' asked the storekeeper.

'Reckon so. Why's he called Harry the Hat?'

'On account of he never takes his hat off. Ain't no one in Tibooburra could tell you what colour his hair is. Story goes that he's got a map tucked away inside the hat. A claim that's going to make him a millionaire one of these days. Don't reckon that's true, myself. He must be over seventy by now, old Harry. If he thought he could strike it rich, he wouldn't be waiting any longer. But you'd better be warned: try to take a look at that hat when you think he's sleeping and you'll find that he shoots first and says he's sorry afterwards.'

'Is that what happened to his last boy?'

'No. He went off to the war, coupla years ago. Said he'd come back when it was all over, but he never did. Well, maybe he died. Old Harry's been on his own for a bit. Not that he minds that; but you need two pairs of hands in the reefs.'

Jamie would have asked why, but at that moment Harry the Hat arrived. 'I'll call by tomorrow to check this through and settle up,' he said to the storekeeper; and, to Jamie, 'Where are you sleeping?'

'I only came into town this afternoon,' Jamie told him. 'Haven't looked around for anywhere yet.'

'You'd better come out with me, then. Give you a chance to find out whether you can stand my snoring. Sling your swag over the saddle.' He unhitched his mare and led her at walking pace along the main street and past the point where the town abruptly ended. A jagged circle of rocks enclosed the inhabited area like the walls of a ruined castle. Harry wound his way up to the hidden point where he had left his possessions.

'I'm out of the habit of sleeping under a roof,' he said conversationally, in an educated accent inappropriate to his appearance. 'The others, when they come back to trade in their gold, rush off to soft mattresses and hot baths, but I like to see the stars at night. Are you used to sleeping out?'

'Yes, sir. My last place, I used to go out to the fence a week at a time, shooting roos and dingoes.'

'Good. Call me Harry, not sir. Sit down while I brew up. Where do you come from, Jamie? Were you born in Australia?'

Jamie shook his head. 'I came out from an orphanage in England when I was nine.'

'From England, eh? That's where I hail from as well. Not as an orphan, though. I was a remittance man.'

'What's that?' asked Jamie, admiring the speed with which the fire blazed up beneath his new employer's billy.

'Someone who's paid to keep away from his family.' Harry leaned himself comfortably back against a rock and tugged his hat down over his forehead. 'I had five elder brothers when I was a boy. Fine upstanding men; six foot or more, every one of them. Then along comes this little runt, Harry. My father allowed me twenty years to grow to a proper size before declaring that I was no son of his. One doesn't like to cast aspersions on one's own mother, but he may have been right about that. There were one or two other problems as well. On my twenty-first birthday I was given a passage to Sydney, a little money to set myself up, and the promise of a hundred pounds a year as long as I never came back to England. That's what a remittance is. Mine stopped when my mother died, but by that time I was getting a living of sorts out of the goldfields and there was nothing worth going back to England for.'

'Something I wanted to settle before we get started,' said Jamie, who felt no great interest in Harry's family history. 'Talking of goldfields. When we strike gold, what share do I get?'

'Share! You haven't lifted a pickaxe yet and you're asking for shares! I'm hiring you as a water boy and if you stay with me for five years you'll have learned everything I know and then you can go off and make your own strike. Share, indeed!'

Jamie stuck to his guns. 'I'm ready to do anything you ask me, Harry,' he said. 'I'm used to working hard and long. But I came out here to make my fortune. I'm grateful to you for taking me on. But I want to be a partner, not a hired boy. The day I see my first gold, I want to know that some of it's mine.'

'Holy Christmas! The cheek of it! You're pushing your luck, boy, I can tell you that. If I were in the business of making a fortune, I'd box your ears and send you packing.'

'Aren't you?' asked Jamie curiously. 'Trying to make a fortune, I mean.'

Harry the Hat shook his head, laughing at himself as he did so. 'When I first came out here I was as set on being a millionaire as anyone else in the goldfields. Getting on for fifty years ago, that was. Now, well, if I had a million pounds I wouldn't know what to do with it. Don't fancy wearing city clothes or living in a house. Life out here suits me. I have to kid myself that I'm set on finding something big. Wouldn't be any point in looking, otherwise. And the days I make gold, why, I cheer as loud as anyone else would. Just for the moment of seeing it. Weighing it. That kind of thing. But afterwards . . .'

'I'm offering to help you out with your problem,' said Jamie mischievously, suddenly sure that the two of them would get on well, and that his wish was about to be granted.

Harry laughed as though he were never going to stop, pushing his hat up for an inch or two and then tugging it back over his forehead in a gesture that Jamie soon came to recognise as typical of him. 'Tell you what,' he said when he recovered his voice at last. 'Some men are born lucky. You're one of them, all right. Found a soft touch at your first try. So maybe you'll bring me luck in the goldfield.'

'I brought you two aces,' Jamie reminded him.

'All right, then. What I'll do. When we're next back here, with our gold bags bulging, out of what we get I'll take three pounds first of all for each week we've been away. That's because you'll have been eating my tucker and using my tools and learning my lessons. If there's anything left, *you* take three pounds for each week. That's wages. After that, we split. Not fifty-fifty, not while you're a know-nothing lad. But you can take forty per cent. I get the extra ten because without me you aren't going to get as much as a sniff of gold.'

'The extra twenty.' Jamie made the correction to clarify the division, not to challenge it. His elementary school teacher in England had taught him to say his tables and do sums. Lessons at the farm school were more practical, but had included the kind of mathematics needed by boys who might one day own farms of their own and would need to calculate costs and profits. Jamie was at home with percentages and his skill at marbles had left him adept at calculating odds. He recognised that he was being expected to gamble his wages; but forty per cent was a far better share than he had expected. The old man was right. He had fallen on his feet. Jamie grinned as he held out his hand. 'Thanks, partner,' he said.

6

'Don't breathe.' Harry the Hat spoke jokingly, but it was no laughing matter. The bottom of the long ripple box which he and Jamie were studying was covered with black sand, flecked with gold so fine that it seemed likely to float away on the slightest movement of the air. Four years ago, in his first season with Harry, Jamie would have groaned to see such a very small reward for all their weeks of labour. Even now, when he was eighteen and had learned that the odds were always on disappointment, it was hard not to feel let down.

At first sight this had seemed a promising gully: in an arid area, almost desert, but likely to run with water when the storm season came. Test diggings suggested a prospect of gold, so for three months the two of them had dry-stacked the ground: breaking up the bottom with pickaxes, throwing out stones, cutting a race for the hoped-for water, and throwing into it the broken dirt from the bottom. It was heavy labouring work, but they were both strong – and hopeful.

They were ready before the first storm broke; but the first was also the last, and the race ran wet for only two days. Even so, they had made the most of it, using the water and the natural fall of the land to wash the dirt through a series of sapling barriers, matting and, at the end, the two six-foot boxes lined with ripples of basket-work. But all they had to show for their hard work was this powdery dust, too fine to be washed from the sand by any method that Jamie knew.

'Fetch me a potato,' said Harry. 'And blow up the fire while you're there.'

Jamie was too hot to be hungry, but obeyed instructions. By the time he returned to the gully he found that Harry had uncorked the bottle of quicksilver which he always carried and was stirring it into the sand with his fingers.

'Don't you ever do this,' he warned Jamie. 'Rots your fingertips away, so they say. Mine have lasted seventy years, so I don't believe the story but I don't want you to blame me for setting you a bad example.'

Jamie grinned. In their four years together Harry the Hat seemed almost deliberately to have introduced him to all the different ways of looking for gold, as though the breadth of his education was more important than the actual discovery of a fortune.

This season, for example, they had spent some time at the site of an abandoned battery. Its original owners, fifty years earlier, perhaps, must have found gold in such quantity that they hurried off to cash it in, for in a single cracked crucible it was possible to see with the naked eye a streak of what had been left behind. Jamie reckoned that he and Harry could have made more than fifty pounds in cash value by scraping down the whole of the forge and digging the earth around for unnoticed scatterings of gold. But Harry, once he had stowed into his pouch enough to cover their next bill for provisions, moved impatiently on. Gold was an all-or-nothing business, he always said. There was no pleasure in deliberately playing safe. Well, this duffer of a gully had proved to be nearly the nothing.

Jamie watched as the quicksilver amalgamated with the gold dust, drawing it out of the sand to form a ball. 'How are you going to separate them again?' he asked.

For answer, Harry the Hat cut the potato in half and scooped out enough of the centre to contain the amalgam. Tying it tightly together again with wire, he led the way back to the camp fire and pushed it into the hot ashes. 'Might as well boil the billy while we're waiting,' he said: they had trapped enough fresh water at the top of the race to relax their normal rules for rationing the precious liquid.

By the time they had enjoyed their tea, the potato was ready. Harry untwisted the wire and opened it up to reveal a small – sadly small – ball of gold in the centre. He tossed it to Jamie before squeezing the potato hard in his powerful hands. Then, pouring a little water into a dish, he washed the pulp through until beads of quicksilver floated free, ready to be used again.

'How does that happen?' asked Jamie, amazed.

'Didn't they teach you any science at school?'

Jamie shook his head. 'Just reading, writing and arithmetic at my first school. At the farm school, it was more practical, like how to grow crops and build sheds. There was a bit about fertilisers. But nothing about getting gold out of potatoes.'

'Well, now you've seen it done you don't need to know why it works. Did your parents die before you ever started school?' Harry knew that his protégé was an orphan.

'Reckon so. Don't recall that I ever saw my father.' Jamie could not in fact remember his mother either, but he did retain a dim memory that she had been a part of his infancy.

'It's a bad business, when a boy never knows his father. You need someone to take an interest.'

'I've got you.' The simple words were sincere. Harry expected his young helper to work hard and to obey orders, but had never treated him as a mere hired hand. From their first day together his attitude had been that of a friend, a teacher, and almost a father. Jamie acknowledged his own good fortune, and recognised the obligation it imposed on him. Harry was an old man, past his seventieth birthday. His stamina was as yet undiminished, but the day must come when he would be in need of the eighteen-year-old's physical strength. Jamie would be glad then to repay the kindness he had received.

'No point in hanging on here,' Harry growled, stowing the gold away in the pouch which was still far too light after seven months. 'We'll move east tomorrow. How about a shoot-out?'

Jamie beamed as he fished in his swag pack for his bag of marbles. On the day of their first meeting Harry had made him spread out all his possessions, approving only the barest minimum to be carried into the bush. The casket was rejected on grounds of weight, and had to be left with the storekeeper, Mick Kennedy, whose services included the provision of deposit space. But Harry had conceded that a fourteen-year-old must be allowed some amusement during what would be a long and lonely trip, and a selection of marbles had travelled with them ever since.

Harry, like the three shearers whose contributions had started Jamie on his way to the goldfields, thought nothing worth doing unless he could place a bet on it. After considering the sporting and gambling possibilities of marbles, he had announced that he would not think of trying to fleece his new young partner but that instead, during the length of each prospecting trip, they would play for points; the overall winner to buy the first drink on their return to civilisation. Jamie, although not prepared to accept the assumption that he must inevitably be the loser, recognised the good sense of keeping their games friendly.

As part of the routine with which each game started, Jamie wandered a few yards away from the camp site and picked up two stones of roughly equal size. His excuse was always that these should be rolled to determine who should start the game but he had never managed to deceive Harry into believing this. What Jamie hoped for every day was to find that one of his randomly-selected stones was a nugget of gold. Everyone knew that there was no rhyme or reason to nuggets. Even the most experienced prospector could not look at a site and recognise it as 'Nuggety Corner'. Everyone also knew that where there was one nugget there might be hundreds. Other men had made their fortunes by stumbling on a single golden stone. Jamie laughed at his own hopes while continuing to indulge them. But on this occasion the stones were just stones; as usual.

'Time we had a bit of the luck you were supposed to bring with you,' said Harry next morning. 'We'll cut over the desert while we've got water.' He jabbed at the map with a finger, although not accurately enough for Jamie to have any clear idea where they were; and then pointed to a distant ridge. 'Make for that. Looks promising, wouldn't you say?' Harry was always an optimist.

For two days they trudged eastwards. On long treks like this the horses were used to carry the equipment and water rather than for riding. The recent storm, although brief in duration, had been sufficient to tint patches of scrubland with green, and even to speckle the tenacious tufts of grass with flowers. Within a day or two, no doubt, the unblinking stare of the sun would parch the brilliant colours back into a desert drabness; but for the moment, in Jamie's eyes at least, it was beautiful.

After five hours on the move on the third day they arrived at the ridge a little before noon. Although rising as a steep cliff on the side from which they had approached, it proved to be the edge of a plateau which sloped more gently down to the east. Jamie's first task was to find shade, if any, for the horses, whilst Harry set to work at once with his pick to test the ground.

'Sandstone,' he said with disgust as Jamie rejoined him. 'I thought there might be quartz here, the way the sun was striking it.' His bright eyes fixed on Jamie's hands. 'What've you got there?'

Jamie's freckled cheeks flushed. Pursuing his dream of gold nuggets, he had picked up a couple of stones from the place where he left the horses. But a quick scrape with his knife had revealed no trace of gold. The only reason why he had not thrown them away was because he liked the feel of marbles or stones in his hand. He opened his palm flat to show what he was clutching.

Harry the Hat frowned to himself as he took one of the stones in his fingers and stared at it. It was a dirty grey colour, looking neither valuable nor beautiful; but the old man set it down and took his small pick to it,

101

cracking it with a sound like breaking glass. He held up the pieces to show Jamie, pointing to a tiny speck of green in the centre. 'Potch,' he said.

'What's potch?'

'I suppose you could call it a baby opal. Not worth anything. Needs to grow for another million years or so. But . . .' He tossed the broken pieces of stone thoughtfully in his hand for a few minutes. 'But where there's potch, there could be opal. Down below.' Once again he paused to consider. 'What do you think?' he asked. 'I've never gone for opal myself. Too chancey. You can't work out in any reasonable way where you're going to find it. You can only hope to speck it by accident, like this. And even here, even if we find potch lying all along the ridge, the opal may not run for more than a few feet. You can break your heart looking for opal. Dig for months and pass within an inch of it and never know.'

He seemed genuinely to be asking for his young partner's opinion, so Jamie gave it. 'There's water here,' he said. 'A pool filled by the storm. What have we got to lose except time? It's not as though there's gold shouting out to be found anywhere around. You asked me to lay on a bit of my good luck for you, and I've found you potch, even if I didn't know what it was. So it's my lucky day. So we shall find opal as well.'

Any claim on luck could count on a quick response from Harry the Hat. 'I'll hold you to that,' he said. 'Right. Roll me one of those marbles of yours from the top of the ridge; down the slope, not over the cliff. Wherever it stops, we'll shaft down. Opal doesn't cling to a bottom, like gold: it clusters under a cap. You have to go down through the bottom and then drive forward, looking up. May need more timber than we've got, if it's too deep. Still. Right, we'll give it until we're down to two days' water. Go and find your best marble.'

Jamie scrambled down the cliff and unstrapped the pack which he had already unloaded from the saddle of his horse. His treasured pouch contained twenty small glass marbles, with eyes of different colours, and two large ones. It made most sense now to pick out one of the small marbles, in case it should be lost, but Jamie found his hand reaching instinctively for his most precious alley. He still called it by the name he had given it in childhood, Basta Taw, but by now he knew it to be alabaster. It was not a sensible choice for this purpose, because it picked up the colour of its surroundings and might become invisible on the sandstone. And yet he felt compelled to use it. Of all his stones it was the one which, when he held it, seemed to become a part of himself: the one which, surely, would bring them luck.

By the time he reached the top of the ridge again, Harry had moved lower down the slope, ready to watch out for the resting place of the marble. Jamie stood upright on the highest point, feeling a curious exultation, as though everything in sight belonged to him. Then, scraping a circle into flatness with his boot, he looked at his treasure. 'Go and find it, Basta Taw,' he said aloud and, moving his palms sharply in opposite directions, spun the alley out on to the ground.

For a moment the speed of its spinning held it within the circle. Only as it slowed did it begin to trickle down the slope; tentatively at first, but soon picking up speed. Jamie ran behind it, anxious to keep it within view; whilst Harry, on the lower ground, moved rapidly across to cover the direction in which it was moving. The two men were less than six yards apart when the alabaster taw disappeared.

Jamie sucked in his breath with dismay as he realised that the crack through which it had fallen was a deep one: but Harry, not realising how precious a possession had been put at risk, nodded with satisfaction as he hurried up and drove his pick into the spot as a marker.

'Half an hour for some tucker,' he said. 'Then we'll see what we've got.'

Jamie was hungry, and thirsty as well, but in spite of that he found himself reluctant to move away. Fear that he might have lost Basta Taw forever had killed his earlier excitement. He told himself that it could not have fallen far, and that they were bound to find it as soon as they started to dig. But whereas a few moments earlier he had felt confident that fortune was with him that day, now he was overcome by unease. Was Basta Taw leading them to good luck, or bad?

7

'It's a ruddy cathedral!' exclaimed Harry with something very much like awe in his voice. Jamie had never been inside a cathedral, but presumed that the comment referred to the pillars of earth and rock which had been left in place to support the roof whilst a huge cavern was hollowed out around them. Six feet down from the surface, the shaft dug by the two new arrivals had broken through the top of an old working.

'They must have come in from the other side.' Harry, talking aloud to himself, held up the lantern so that the shadows swayed. Jamie was anxious to look for Basta Taw, but recognised the value of listening to the old man's opinion.

'Air's fresh, so part of the entrance may still be open. But no light, so they must have turned a corner. Suggests that they'd found colour and were following it. Went on digging after they were out of timber. That's why they had to leave these supports. They must have had reason to think it would be worth their while pressing on as far as this. Chances are good that they were finding opal in the dirt they shifted. Chances are not too bad that we'll find it in the dirt they left. That marble of yours knew where it was going, all right.' He began to claw with his smaller pick at one of the pillars.

'Won't it bring the roof down if you cut that away?' asked Jamie cautiously.

'I'm only testing. If it seems promising, we'll bring our own props down and make a job of it. Stand near me a minute and keep your ears open. Opal makes a different sound from anything you'll have heard before. More like glass. If you hear me yell for a find, remember the sound you picked up just before. Then when you get to work yourself, you'll know what to listen for. This isn't like gold, where the dirt has to be broken up. If you smash an opal, it stays smashed. But there's likely to be another one next to it.'

For a little while he gouged away, occasionally pausing to scrape a piece of rock with his knife and hold it to the light; but each time he shook his head.

'Find yourself another pillar,' he said to Jamie. 'No point standing around when nothing's happening. Take off large pieces from the top and pile them in a basket. We'll have a good look at them in the daylight.'

Jamie nodded and fitted a candle into his wire spider, lighting it from the lantern. Although the sandstone roof of the cavern was hard enough, and unlikely to collapse, it seemed sensible to choose a pillar some way away from Harry's. Approaching the end of the working, he needed to stoop, although a little man like Harry might still have been able to stand upright. He stuck the wire which held his candle into a pillar, swung his pick to gouge out a lump of rock – and then drew in his breath as he saw the candle's light reflected back out of a dark corner.

'Basta Taw!' he shouted with such enthusiasm that Harry came over to see what the excitement was about.

'What have you found?' But even as he asked the question he appeared to be answering himself by bending to pick up a pebble which had broken away from the rock dislodged by Jamie.

'No, not that,' Jamie said. 'The alabaster taw that fell through the crack. I thought for certain that it would have been covered by the dirt when we were driving the shaft. But it must have fallen right through and rolled down the slope.' He took a step towards it, but was checked by Harry's silence. 'What have *you* found?'

'Give me a minute.' Harry was snipping gently at the pebble he had picked up. 'Come here, Jamie,' he said at last. 'Take a look at this.'

The outside of the pebble was as dirty and undistinguished as the lump of potch which Jamie had picked up earlier. But in the groove made by the snipper a

105

narrow streak of a familiar colour glinted in the candlelight.

'Gold!' exclaimed Jamie.

Harry the Hat shook his head. 'Black opal,' he said. He gave a high-pitched laugh. 'Black opal! As good as gold.'

'Thought it was supposed to be unlucky.' Jamie took a second curious look.

'May be unlucky to wear. Wouldn't know about that. But to find and sell luck doesn't come much higher. This one's only a titchy little thing. But there's never only one black opal by itself. Unless it's been cleaned out already, somewhere round here there has to be a pocket of nobbies. Go and get the props, Jamie. This is where we're going to make our fortunes.'

'Yoo-hoo!' Jamie's shout of triumph echoed round the cavernous workings. 'Well done, Basta Taw.' Leaning down, he stretched his hand into the dark corner to retrieve his treasure – but then staggered back again with an even louder roar. This time it was one of pain.

'What?' But Harry did not need to ask, for the black snake which Jamie had disturbed emerged briefly into the candlelight before gliding with extraordinary speed into another patch of darkness. 'Where? Show me.'

Panting with the effort not to groan, Jamie held out his left arm, which his right hand was instinctively clutching in an attempt to numb the agony. In a single quick gesture Harry slashed across the purple marks of the bite with a knife so sharp that this second wound could not be felt, and raised the bleeding cut to his lips, sucking and spitting. He paused only briefly to tie a tourniquet above the bite before once more sucking out the venom.

'Got to get you out of here while your head's clear,' he said. 'Think you can hold on to the rope while I haul up with the windlass?'

'I can climb,' said Jamie, gritting his teeth. 'Got two good legs and an arm.' Staggering slightly, he made for the shaft. The ascent, although successful, was a struggle. He found it hard to understand why all his strength should have drained away with the loss of only a little blood, but found himself standing still in a bemused manner whilst Harry brought the horses round.

'I'll be all right. Thanks for sucking it out. A night's sleep, and I'll be fine.'

'You're not going to sleep,' Harry told him. 'You're not going to close your eyes until you get to a hospital. We can make Noccundra in twelve hours, if the horses are up to it. You keep talking all the way. Stop talking, and I slap your face. Come on, up you get.'

Jamie's muscles seemed to have escaped so much from his control that he almost shot right over the horse to land on the other side. But Harry settled him into the saddle, checked that the water bags were full, and gathered both sets of reins into his own hands. 'Start talking,' he said, kicking his own horse into movement.

'Nothing to say.'

'Right. Listen to me, then. Repeat this after me, one line at a time. Breathes there the man with soul so dead.'

'What you talking about?'

'Say it! Breathes there the man with soul so dead.'

'Breathes there the man with soul so dead.'

'Who never to himself hath said.'

'Who never to himself hath said.'

'This is my own, my native land.'

'What native land?' asked Jamie.

'In his case, Scotland. Sir Walter Scott. A poem I learned when I was at school. The only one I can call to mind at this moment. Come on. Whose heart hath ne'er within him burned.'

Jamie began to laugh as he jogged up and down in the saddle. What was he, a boy who had no knowledge of even the name of his own birthplace, doing riding across Australia and reciting poetry about Scotland which had been memorised in an English school? But because it was so funny, he did as he was told, repeating the same lines over and over again until he knew them by heart. He was still muttering them when, collapsed over the horse's neck, he at last arrived in a hospital compound. 'Whose heart hath ne'er within him burned/As home his foot-steps he hath turned/From wandering on a foreign

107

strand.' He heard a doctor talking about delirium and tried to explain that it was supposed to be poetry. But then a needle pricked his arm and he was, at last, allowed to fall asleep.

How many days passed while the serum did its work? Jamie had no way of telling. Even after he became drowsily conscious that he was clean and comfortable in a bed, it was some time before he found the strength to open his eyes. The other three patients in the room with him were all, he learned then, suffering from broken limbs. Jamie, too weak and dizzy at first even to sit up, watched as they practised hobbling about in their splints. None of them seemed to feel ill, and their visiting hours were rowdy affairs. Jamie would have liked a visitor of his own, but Harry did not appear. Probably he had gone back to pick up all the equipment which had to be left behind in order that the horses might be ridden. Probably, too, when he was back at the workings he had found himself unable to resist another look for black opal. Jamie hoped he would remember that the snake might still be there.

Thinking that he knew the reason for Harry's non-appearance, he asked no questions. So it came as a shock when the nurse, telling him that he could at last get out of bed, asked whether he would like to see his grandfather.

'Grandfather?'

'Wasn't that who brought you in?'

'That was my mate, Harry. I've been waiting for him to come.'

'We've put him in a room by himself. I'll show you.'

'Hold on,' said Jamie. 'You mean he's been here in the hospital all the time?'

'Didn't anyone tell you?'

'No. What's up with him?'

'Same as you. Snake poison.'

'He didn't get bitten.'

'He sucked the venom out, apparently.'

'But he spat it out.' Anxiety made Jamie's voice vehement. 'I saw him.' Harry, who had so much practical knowledge in so many different fields, had been as competent to deal with snake bite as to recognise opal.

'Yes. He told us that. But his teeth are in bad shape, you see. Rotten gums. The poison got into his bloodstream through the gums. By the time he collapsed, it had been circulating through his body for a day or two. Got to the heart. And he's an old man.'

'What are you saying?' asked Jamie, aghast.

'I'm saying that the chances aren't too good. We treated him the same as you, as soon as we realised, but he doesn't seem to be picking up. He knows it himself. He's been asking to see you.'

Jamie followed the nurse in silence along a short corridor. She opened a door for him to pass through, but remained outside when she closed it.

Jamie looked down at the stranger who lay with closed eyes in the bed. A white sheet, tucked up to Harry's chin, made him seem even smaller than usual by revealing the shortness of his legs whilst at the same time concealing his powerful arms and shoulders. His face, closely shaved, seemed in a curious way to have smoothed itself out, shedding all the leathery creases of a lifetime spent in the sun. But the most extraordinary sight of all was the pale egg-shaped dome of baldness which changed the proportions of his head, making the lower half seem longer and more dignified even though the top was so absurd. For more than four years Jamie had wondered what Harry would look like without his hat. The fact that he could see the answer now made his spirits sink even lower. If Harry the Hat had abandoned the fight to sleep with his head covered, he must indeed be in a bad way.

Harry's eyes opened suddenly, as though he had been awake all the time and was merely allowing Jamie time to absorb the shock. 'Get the hat,' he whispered.

Jamie looked round the small room and then stepped outside and found the nurse. 'Harry wants his hat.'

'That filthy old thing! We try to keep our patients clean.'

'I'll tell him he can't wear it, if you want me to. But just to look at. It would cheer him up.'

The nurse shrugged her shoulders and pointed to a locker in the corridor. 'All his personal things are there.'

Jamie scooped everything out and carried the bundle into Harry's room, holding up the hat to show his success.

'Good. Cut out the lining.'

Using the sheath knife from Harry's own belt, Jamie did as he was told. At any other time he would have felt excited about the prospect of solving the mystery about which so many people had speculated for so long; but the fact that Harry the Hat was prepared to reveal his secret suggested that he was turning his back on life. Only by bending his head low over the task of cutting the stitches could Jamie conceal the tears which were flooding into his eyes.

The hoarse whisper came again: 'No need to be finicky. Shan't wear it any more. It's yours now. Just slash it through.'

With as much anger as though he were stabbing into the neck of the black snake, Jamie jabbed the knife into the gap he had made and ripped out the lining.

'Should be a bit of paper there,' Harry said. 'Show me.'

What had been concealed in the hiding place was not, as everyone had assumed, a map, but a small piece of paper stained by sweat and dirt to the same colour as the hat itself. Jamie held it up in front of the dying man's eyes.

'Good,' said Harry for a second time. 'Now then, Jamie, listen to me.'

8

Jamie Jamieson stood six feet three inches tall in his desert boots, with a sturdy build appropriate to his height. Above his crumpled clothes and freckled face, the tight curls of his sandy hair shone like the lantern of

110

a lighthouse, attracting the attention of the passers-by in whose path he stood. For more than four years his blue eyes had been narrowed against the bright desert sun; but on Wednesday, 16 July 1924, they were wide open with amazement at the noise and bustle of the city, and with concentration as he looked down at the envelope he held in his hand, checked the address on it with the door outside which he was standing, and looked down once more to make sure.

Nothing in his life had prepared him for the crowded confusion of Sydney. He had thought of Tibooburra, with its single wide street, as a town. But here the roads crossed each other, and each was made dangerous by trams and motor cars which greeted any pedestrian's natural hesitation with an impatient hooting; whilst more people had jostled past him during the past half hour than would visit Tibooburra in the course of a whole year. Jamie ignored them all as he satisfied himself that he had arrived at the right place and knew what he was going to say.

In spite of all his rehearsals, he seemed unable to speak when he found himself confronting a young woman across a desk in a reception office. His envelope was addressed to a gentleman. Had he come to the wrong place after all? For a moment he stood awkwardly, fidgeting the envelope between his fingers, before silently holding it out for her to see. She frowned over the name inscribed on it and, without speaking, stood up and disappeared through a door which she closed behind her.

Jamie waited, ill at ease. In this city that was so full of noise, did nobody talk? But the young man in his early twenties who finally emerged through the same door was smiling as he held out a hand to be shaken.

'Good afternoon. I'm afraid Mr Marriott's deceased. Some years ago, in fact. Your business with him must have its roots way back. Perhaps I can help you. My name's Fred Johns.'

'You're a lawyer?' Thawed by the friendliness of the greeting, Jamie found his voice at last.

'Right. This is still the same firm as in Mr Marriott's day. Partners come and go. Have a seat through here. Now then, what can I do for you?'

'It's all in the envelope.' Jamie was afraid that if he tried to explain, he would get the details wrong – because the whole affair was so mysterious that he hardly understood it at all. He watched as Mr Johns opened the envelope and drew out three pieces of paper. One of them was so greatly darkened with sweat and dirt that the lawyer made only a brief attempt to read it before passing on to the other two. Of these, Jamie recognised the first as Harry's death certificate. The other he had not had a chance to read before it was sealed up, but could now see to contain two sentences, written in two different hands, and two signatures.

Mr Johns, having studied these, picked up the yellowed sheet of paper for a second time and crossed to the window so that he could hold it up to the light. When he turned back to face Jamie, his eyes were wide with what looked like excitement and for a moment it seemed that he was about to burst out with some comment. Controlling whatever he had been tempted to say, however, he sat down again at the desk and pulled a pad of paper towards him.

'Would you be kind enough to tell me your name?'

'Jamie Jamieson.'

'Do you have any proof of identity on you?'

'Such as what?'

'Well, a birth certificate, for example.'

'Never had such a thing,' said Jamie. He thought for a moment and then pulled some scraps of paper from the pocket of his bush jacket and studied them before extracting two and handing them across. 'That's the assay office paying Jamie Jamieson for six ounces of gold,' he said. 'And that's to say that Jamie Jamieson's account has been settled at Kennedy's store. Ain't no one but Jamie Jamieson likely to do that.'

Mr Johns struggled with an inclination to grin as strong as his earlier signs of excitement. 'Well,' he said, 'we may have to search for something more formal before our business together is settled, but for the moment we'll assume that you are who you say you are.'

'Thanks very much!' Jamie's nervousness vanished in an exclamation of such astonishment that Mr Johns could restrain his laughter no longer.

'You must forgive me,' he said. 'This is a big moment for me. I'm trying to be businesslike and do everything right. Otherwise one of the others will snatch you away from me.'

Jamie waited to be told what he was talking about, but instead was faced with another question. 'Can you tell me the name of the owner of this piece of paper?' Mr Johns was talking about the sweat-stained sheet which for so many years had been sewn into the lining of Harry's hat.

'Harry the Hat.'

'You don't know any more, shall we say, *formal* name?'

Standing beside Harry's deathbed, Jamie had learned that his teacher and partner and friend had been christ-ened Henry Pierce Fortescue. He recited those three words now.

'Good. And how much do you know about the contents of this envelope, and its significance, Mr Jamieson?'

No one had ever called Jamie Mr Jamieson before, but he swallowed his surprise in order to answer. 'It says that Harry's dead. And the doctor told me that he'd left me his claim.'

'His claim?'

'Well, that's what I supposed it to be. Everyone always reckoned it was a map of a goldfield that Harry carried round in his hat. When it turned out to be just your address, and some number, I took it that he left the map here with you.'

'You're partly right, Mr Jamieson, but only partly. There *is* a map, but not of a goldfield. Does that disap-point you?'

Jamie shook his head. 'All the way travelling here I've been telling myself not to set my hopes on anything. I've disappointed myself in advance, you could say. I often

113

asked Harry; we used to talk about his paper, laughing, see, because everyone knew he had it and he didn't mind me teasing him: I used to ask him why he didn't take it up, if it was a good claim, and I'd help him dig it out. What he always said was that a man needs to have something to look forward to, something he has faith in, and something that can't disappoint because it's never tested. First of all, when I was only a boy, I believed that straight. It made a lot of sense. But afterwards I thought, probably he didn't really believe there was gold there at all, and that was why he wasn't ever going to test it out. He liked having the idea of it, but he knew it had no bottom. So, no, I didn't set my heart on finding myself in Nuggety Corner. All the same, he was a good mate of mine, Harry. He wouldn't have sent me all the way here for nothing at all.'

'What a sensible chap you are, Mr Jamieson. Well, let me go and pull out the right file. It's thirty-odd years since Mr Fortescue was last in this office, as far as I'm aware, so his affairs aren't exactly handled as current business. If you want to study the papers you've carried here, go ahead.'

Jamie accepted the invitation while he was left alone. He had been told by Harry himself, as he lay in hospital, to go to the address which had been concealed in the hat; and he had also seen the death certificate. The only document new to him was the sheet of paper on which was written in Harry's surprisingly neat hand: 'Deliver with full title to my sole heir Jamie Jamieson.' Below his signature Harry had printed the name Henry Pierce Fortescue, and below that again one of the hospital doctors had attested to the fact that he was a witness to Harry's signature. But except for a number written beneath the lawyers' address on the hidden paper, there was no indication of what a sole heir might expect to inherit.

'I've got a question to ask of you,' said Jamie when young Mr Johns returned to his office, bearing a single slim folder. 'You said it was thirty years since Harry was here. You couldn't have been here yourself then, and Mr

Marriott's dead, you said. But you seemed to know what this was all about as soon as I came in.'

'So I did. A lawyer's office can be a dull place, Mr Jamieson. We need to have an occasional little fantasy, a fairy story which may or may not have a happy ending, the odd extraordinary character. Mr Fortescue was such a character. I don't expect I have to tell you that. There are four of us here. From time to time we get together and gossip. The story is passed down, even to new arrivals like myself. How old must Mr Fortescue be by now? Is he still alive? When is the next seven-year-letter due? Who will turn up in the end: our client in person, immensely aged? Or some rough larrikins who's managed to rob him of everything except his most secret possession: his name? You could have come here, Mr Jamieson, carrying that number and swearing on your soul that you were Harry's devoted friend, which I believe to be the truth, or even, if your imagination had run wild, that you were his most dearly-beloved son or grandson. But without that password of his full name' – Mr Johns tapped the writing on his desk – 'we should have shaken our heads sadly and sent you away empty-handed.'

'I don't understand all this. What do you mean by the seven-year-letter?'

'Let me begin again at the beginning.' Mr Johns smiled happily as he leaned back in his chair. 'Mr Fortescue was a gambling man. Before he was half-way through university in England, he'd gambled away everything he owned and a good deal that he didn't. So his family shipped him out here, where they needn't know what was going on. There was an arrangement made with our Mr Marriott that an annual allowance would be sent to our offices for Mr Fortescue to draw on, so that he would never starve. Arrangements of that kind were quite usual.'

Jamie nodded. Harry had told him about the allowance, although he had given a different reason for his exile; and it was true that gambling had been in his blood.

'So Mr Fortescue arrived in Sydney about fifty years

ago with a little money in his pocket, thanks to a soft-hearted mother and several profitable card sessions on board ship. First night ashore, he fell into a game. There was an Irishman in the game, Magee, one of the 1852 gold rush diggers, who'd never made it. He was going to buy passages back to Ireland the next day for himself and his family. Had the money in his pocket but Mr Fortescue cleaned him out and took a hefty IOU off him into the bargain. Next morning Magee turns up with a wife and two kids in tow and asks for his passage money back and promises that he'll drown himself if he doesn't get it. He's got a few last possessions to offer, but no time to sell them before the shipping office opens, and in any case, Mr Fortescue holds his paper for any money he raises on them.'

'So Harry gave him the cost of his tickets? He always used to say he was a sucker for a sob story.'

'He bought Magee's stuff up for the cost of the passages – without knowing much about what he was getting. A field, he was told, with a tent pitched on it, and a horse grazing and a set of gold mining tools. He'd already decided he was going to make his own fortune that way, so the horse and tools would come in useful. Besides, everyone knew that to carry cash to the goldfields was asking to be robbed, so he could think of this as a safe deposit for some of his ready money. He went along to see that the horse was all right, and took a look at the field while he was there. Then he came to call on our Mr Marriott. To fix how he should draw on his allowance; that kind of thing. He'd got the original purchase papers of the field in his pocket, so he handed them over for safe keeping.'

'And is that what – ?'

'Yes,' said Mr Johns. 'That's what.'

9

Silence filled the lawyer's office whilst Jamie struggled with his confused reactions. He had managed to persuade himself in advance that any claim he inherited would probably be worthless, but he must have expected that there would still be some kind of a claim. Something on which he could take the gamble which Harry the Hat himself had never risked. Something which *might* bring him a fortune, even if the odds were a million to one against.

Well, there was to be no gold. He nodded his head in realistic acceptance of the fact. 'What happened next?'

'The next thing that happened, sometime in the 1890s, was that his allowance stopped coming. He didn't seem to notice it for a couple of years, because he had a good strike about that time. But,' – Mr Johns looked down at the file on his desk – 'in 1895 he called here for a second time, to find out what was going on. He was told then that any time he was short of money he could raise a tidy sum by selling the field. You quoted him, Mr Jamieson, as saying that he liked to have something to look forward to. He made much the same remark here. About treating the field as a place of last resort.'

'That's different,' said Jamie, although he could not have explained the difference.

Mr Johns considered the point and nodded, almost in surprise. 'I see what you mean. Well, anyway, Mr Marriott – he was still alive then – felt that the arrangement ought to become a little more formal, more lawyer-like. You can't exactly leave land lying around. People trespass on it, or stretch their fences a few feet at a time and before you know where you are they're claiming that they've been there so many years that it belongs to them. Besides, Mr Fortescue might die out in the bush without us knowing of his death or his friends knowing of the land. So this arrangement was made: that he would write to us every seven years – to say he was still alive, really – and that we would then set foot on the field in his name and check that the fencing was sound and that his title was not infringed. If more than eight years passed – the seven years, plus twelve months' grace – without any communication from himself or his heir, we were empowered to give the field to a charity for fatherless boys.'

Jamie gave a startled gasp at this statement. 'I'm a fatherless boy,' he said. He couldn't help laughing at the idea that he might be standing in for a charity.

'I think we can assume that you were left the land in your own right, as Mr Fortescue's friend. The system under which he proposed to make any ultimate bequest was also laid down at the time of his last visit here. He was well aware that he might be robbed of anything known to be valuable. But nobody except ourselves knew his full name. He could reveal that at a time and to a person of his own choosing. The plan had its disadvantages, of course. If he had died suddenly, without the chance to alert his chosen heir to the conditions . . . You're a lucky man, Mr Jamieson.'

Jamie's blue eyes were troubled as he stared across the desk. What sort of luck was it that depended on the death of a friend? To his surprise, Mr Johns seemed to understand what he was thinking.

'He was over seventy years old, and he must have had a hard life. Men like that often don't want any extra years in which to grow old and feeble. I should think that during his last illness it must have afforded him pleasure to think that he was giving you a good start in life. Would you like to look at the field now?'

'You mean it's near here?' asked Jamie in surprise. His walk from the station to the office had given him the impression that the blocks of buildings and streets extended for many miles.

'Very near. It fronts on George Street.' As he announced this, Mr Johns tilted his head to one side and looked intently at Jamie, as though expecting some reaction. But the name of the street meant nothing to the country boy, and the lawyer grinned once again as he opened the door of his office.

'When Mr Kendall is next free,' he said to the young woman who had first received Jamie, 'would you tell him that the presumed heir to Fortescue's Field has arrived and that I've taken him out to see his inheritance.' Leading the way from the building, he turned to explain to Jamie. 'Mr Kendall's the senior partner. Would have expected to deal with the matter himself. He'll be sick as mud that he happened to have a client with him when you turned up. Come on, then.'

A short walk brought them to a crossroads, and they turned right into a street even busier than the route which Jamie had taken from the station, and flanked with more imposing buildings.

'This is George Street we're in now,' said Mr Johns. 'Harbour straight ahead.' He was almost running in his eagerness to arrive; but Jamie, with his long stride, was able to match his pace until the moment when they came to an abrupt halt. 'Here we are, then. Fortescue's Field.'

Jamie inspected it in silence. It was not easy at the first glimpse to feel excitement. The field was overgrown with an untidy scrub which made it unsuitable even for grazing. It went back a good way, but its frontage was little more than twice the width of any one of the banks or stores which lined the busy street. An area just about this size had been used by the Jacksons to grow vegetables and provide a run for the hens. They had always referred to it as 'the patch', because that was all it was compared to the acreage of the rest of the station. This field, too, was only a patch.

It was fenced off from the street with palings and wire. How many hundreds or even thousands of such palings had Jamie split during his boyhood to enclose Mr Jackson's land or that of the farm school! *Other people's land*. Whatever flicker of disappointment he had felt was now stifled by the excitement of possession. The next paling he chopped and tied would be his own. With one hand on the end post, he vaulted the fence. Mr Johns, out of respect for his own tighter trousers, remained on the outside.

'Let me explain the possibilities,' he said. 'On your

119

right is a store which until a year or two ago claimed to be the largest in Sydney, and would dearly love to renew the claim. On your left is another store which a year or two ago added an extra storey and now claims to be the largest store in Australia. The claim isn't necessarily true, but the owners would like it to be. Sit yourself down here with a chair and a table tomorrow and you could enjoy the sight of two store owners fighting for the privilege of making your fortune in order that one of them could expand and not the other. And the noise they made would attract a line of other buyers. I know at least one bank which is desperate to set up in this area. And the ferry company is looking for a site for a fancy new head office. You own the best undeveloped business address in the whole of New South Wales. On top of that, you could reserve a piece of land at the back and sell it off separately. It's my great pleasure to tell you, Mr Jamieson, that – always provided you *are* Mr Jamieson – you have struck gold.'

The sparkle with which the lawyer's eyes revealed sincere enjoyment of a stranger's good fortune warmed Jamie's heart. He said nothing for the moment, but turned to walk slowly first of all right round the field and then into its centre, his thornproof boots trampling down the scrub. Tugging out a tuft of grass, he sat down to study the earth beneath it, crumbling a handful through his fingers as he had so often watched Harry the Hat do.

There was a routine he had been taught at the farm school – for most of the boys who went there hoped eventually to qualify for a government loan and land allocation in order to set themselves up in a small way. Water was always the first requisite, since only a fool would try to tame the desert single-handed. After that, a would-be farmer must study the soil to see what it was fit for, and visit the neighbours in order to learn which of their early hopes had been fulfilled, and which disappointed. For any crop or stock there was a right place and a wrong place.

Fortescue's Field was too small to sustain any kind of

120

farming operation. And the grains of earth which he tossed now on the palm of his hand promised nothing in themselves. This was not opal dirt or gold dirt. Nevertheless, Jamie understood perfectly the value of his inheritance. It was land in the right place, and Mr Johns was undoubtedly correct in describing the profit he could expect from it.

That was easily accepted. What needed more thought was the method by which the profit should be extracted. Harry the Hat, who had never cared a fig for money itself, but only for the pleasure of gaining it, would not have intended merely to fill his young friend's pocket. To use the lawyer's phrase of half an hour earlier, he had offered Jamie a start in life; a foundation on which he ought to build.

Jamie's education had been brief and its range was limited, but it had given him the chance to prove himself a quick learner. He was intelligent enough to know that he *was* intelligent, while at the same time being aware how much he needed to know. He marshalled his thoughts now with a slow care which might have made a casual onlooker dismiss him as a mere country lad; strong and healthy, and perhaps possessing all the necessary skills for survival in the outback, but lacking the quick reactions of a city-dweller. Yet, in spite of the fact that he had arrived in Sydney that morning with no idea at all of what the day had to offer, by the time he stood up and returned to the fence he was quite sure what he wanted to do.

He held out his hand to Mr Johns above the palings. 'Thank you for bringing me here. Now that Harry's dead, will you be a lawyer for me instead? Not just your firm, I mean, but you.'

'My very great pleasure.' Mr Johns' handshake was firm and enthusiastic. 'I suppose you'd like us to handle the sale for you. An auction would probably be the best plan.'

Jamie shook his head. 'I'm not going to sell. But there's something I'd like you to do for me right away. I want you to find me a partner. Someone who knows about business things. Someone who has money, but who needs land. Someone who won't cheat me while I'm finding my feet in the city. I don't know anything at all about business. I can learn – but I'd have to rely on you to find someone I can trust while I'm learning. I want to be able to go fifty-fifty without wondering all the time whether I'm being rooked. And I'd need a lot of other advice from you to start with. About the value of the land that I'd be putting into the partnership, and the best thing to build on it.'

Doubt and amazement struggled to rule Mr Johns' expression. 'Are you quite sure that you don't want simply to sell?' he asked. 'Perhaps you should give it more thought. There's no risk involved in just picking up the money.'

'A gambler like Harry wouldn't think much of someone who couldn't take a risk. Yes, I'm sure.' Jamie jumped the fence again.

Before leaving the site, he turned to look back. It was something more than his feeling for what Harry would have wanted which made him reluctant to part with this unexpected inheritance. There was a memory almost completely buried by time: a memory from a far-away childhood. *'Find land for yourself, my wee Jamie,'* someone had said to him. *'Your ain land.'*

He had never heard that word, *ain*, spoken since that day, but as it came back to his mind now he knew instinctively what it meant. He couldn't remember who the speaker was, or what was the occasion. But the gruff voice had been that of someone who loved him. *'Find land for yourself, Jamie.'*

Well, he had found it.

BOOK TWO

1987

PART ONE

WEE JAMIE

1

Wee Jamie Jamieson stood on the upper green of Sydney's City Bowling Club and studied the head. Of his opponent's four bowls, one was only a few inches from the back ditch, but the other three clustered around the jack in a neat triangle. It was a game lie, for the Masters' Tournament would be won by the first of the two finalists to score twenty-one shots, and Wee Jamie was 16–18 down.

He was not finished yet. He still had one more bowl, and he had been presented with a good target. For a moment longer he studied angles and considered possibilities. Then, without speaking, he revealed by a grunting noise in his throat that he had made up his mind.

His face as he walked back to the mat gave no clue to his intentions. Wee Jamie was renowned for his impassive behaviour in playing the game at which he had been a champion for so long. Off the green he was sociable and friendly. But from the moment a match began he refused to chat or to acknowledge any comment from his opponent. Apart from any necessary questions to the marker, or agreement about the number of shots, he kept his mouth shut.

Everyone knew him as Wee Jamie, although nobody knew the reason why the adjective had attached itself so inextricably to his name. It was a very long time indeed since he had been the youngest boy in an orphanage, the youngest again in a party of immigrants and at a farm school. Newer acquaintances assumed the description to be ironical, because Wee Jamie was huge – over six feet tall and weighing eighteen stone. Once a year his doctor told him that his weight would kill him one day; and once a year Wee Jamie retorted that it was taking so long to do so that he didn't propose to worry. He had already passed his eighty-first birthday. Not much to complain about there.

With his back to the pavilion he picked up his last bowl and jiggled it up and down in his hand as though trying to estimate its weight. His eyes stared at the clouds scudding like yachts across the blue sky; above the centrepoint tower, with its wasp-waist corset of cables; above the nearer twin towers of St Mary's Cathedral and, further away, the skyscrapers of downtown Sydney. He did not see any of these buildings. Immediately across the road from the club, a children's festival was in full swing in Hyde Park. Bands were playing, roundabouts turning to the sound of fairground organs and children shrieking with delight. But Wee Jamie did not hear any of this either. He was withdrawing into himself so that he could concentrate totally on what – if it failed – might be his final shot of the match. He settled his feet firmly on the mat, swayed for a moment to test his balance, and then slowly raised his head.

On the open roof above the verandah of the pavilion a buzz of excitement spread through the spectators. 'Wee Jamie's firing.' Bowlers themselves, every one of them included the firing shot amongst his repertory of deliveries, but Wee Jamie's style was special. This was what had kept him amongst the champions right into his old age. There were a good many bowlers who were better than he was at drawing to the jack, or trailing it, or constructing a good head. The reason why they so often had to accept second place was simple: when Wee Jamie saw that he could not win an end by skill or subtlety, he always used force. If possible, he would drive the jack back into the far ditch, with his own bowl resting beside it in a winning position. But if there seemed no chance of success in that manoeuvre, his aim would be to send the jack flying instead across the strings which marked the boundary of the rink, so that the end was dead and would have to be played again. This was not necessarily a way to win, but it was the best possible way of not losing.

Naturally enough his style of playing had its critics. Every opponent who had ever lost to him came away feeling robbed. There was a general unease at the facility with which a player superior in every other department of the game could be blasted off the green. But at heart even those whom he frustrated shared with him the belief that the point of playing competitively was to win; recognising, if they were honest with themselves, that they objected more to his success than to his weapon.

Because this was the nub of the matter: Wee Jamie's firing shot never missed. Using the natural bias of the bowl to approach the jack by a curving route, he was no more accurate than any other top-class player. But as soon as he added the speed and weight which allowed the bowl no time to show its bias, he could be relied on not only to hit the target but to propel it in whatever direction he chose. On this occasion, in view of his opponent's foresight in placing a back wood near to the ditch, he would undoubtedly be trying for a 'no end'. The players on the two neighbouring rinks took their minds off their own game for a moment in order to guard their ankles against flying missiles.

Wee Jamie was almost ready to play. He bent both knees slightly, to check that they were ready for movement. Over the last few years, as he became older and heavier and stiffer, he had been forced to change his normal delivery when merely drawing to the jack, because he could no longer crouch close to the ground. But he had not been prepared to interfere with his firing routine. Now he raised his right hand, holding the bowl straight out in front of him. His eyes fixed themselves not just on the jack but on the exact point of its surface which he intended to strike. He took his arm back as far as it would go, to give himself the maximum swing. As it came forward again, he stepped out on to his left foot and sank almost on to his right knee, so that his hand shaved the grass as he propelled the bowl straight towards the jack.

It was part of the routine that he should not lift his head, nor be quick to straighten himself. He remained frozen, his right arm stretched in front of him and his right leg extended behind. He heard the crash as the bowl found its target, and the applause of the spectators. Now he could stand up and study the effect of the shot.

No, he could not. Something was wrong. A movement which should have come naturally, if perhaps requiring a certain effort, refused to take place at all. It was as though he needed to manipulate certain muscles by pulling strings, like those of a puppet, but could not discover which to pull first. And while he struggled, trying at the same time to maintain his balance, he was conscious of a new and sinister development. A shutter came down behind his eyes: he was not blind, and yet he could not see. Something which felt like a circle of steel inside his skull began to tighten around his brain. It brought with it an almost unbearable pain; and yet when he tried to cry out, no sound emerged. His sense of balance disappeared and, at the same time, all his muscles dissolved into water. He was still in his stretched position when his left knee collapsed beneath his weight and, with a single groan, Wee Jamie fell face downwards on to the green.

He was not unconscious. He could hear the sharp intake of breath from the spectators, the hurried footsteps of his opponent, to whom he would now have to cede the match and the championship. There were shouts; a worried consultation above his head. Doctor. Ambulance. Stretcher. Jock.

Jock was in Western Australia, competing for the right to defend Australia's possession of the America's Cup. As his face was lifted and turned from the turf into which it had been pressing, Wee Jamie tried to say that his son must not be brought home or even disturbed by bad news. But his speech was as much out of control as his muscles. His eyes rolled in an effort to communicate, but no one understood. By now, though, the president of the club had arrived to take charge, moving back the circle of worried onlookers and assuring them that a medical member of the club was playing on the lower green and would be on the spot within seconds.

'Family,' he said, thinking aloud. 'Jock's in Fremantle. But Bev must be somewhere around. Matt, track her down, will you? Then hold her on the line until we can say where he's been taken. Give him air, the rest of you.'

The faces above his moved away. Though still unable to move, Wee Jamie was conscious that the band of steel around his head was relaxing its hold very slightly. And Beverley would look after him. In just a little while, everything would be all right.

2

Wee Jamie lay in bed, propped up by pillows so that he could stare out of the window. The nurse, at his request, had turned off all the lights in his room in order that he might enjoy the view. As soon as his speech returned after the stroke he had demanded to be brought home from hospital to his penthouse at the top of The Castle.

The skyscraper was the newest of three hotels which had been built in succession on Harry the Hat's block of land. The first, four-storey, building was called The Castle Hotel, but both its original replacement and the present tower were known simply as The Castle. Wee Jamie had from the start intended the penthouse for his own use. His wife had died just too early to see her only son married, and the house on Darling Point was too large for a man living alone. He had given it to Jock as a wedding present and for the past twenty-five years had lived in one or other of his hotel suites. Here he could expect good service and was able, before his illness, to wander without warning through the public rooms below, unobtrusively checking that all was well.

The true reason for his choice of home, though, was the view it provided. That was why he had asked for his bed to be moved close to the huge window. Talking tired him, but he could never grow tired of looking.

Beverley was at the opera. Wee Jamie himself had little interest in music, but pride in his adopted city had made him one of the most generous patrons of the Opera House. He had insisted that his granddaughter should leave his bedside in order to attend the performance and the party for benefactors which was to follow it.

He could see the Opera House from his bed, the curves of its roof made even more dramatic than in daylight by the deep shadows between the segments. Often, staring at the delicate illumination of its tiled surface, he wondered whether that Taj Mahal in India which Jock had once described to him had anything on the Opera House, even by moonlight. But he had never been curious enough to go and see. He had never been curious about anything outside Australia, in fact. Except perhaps the castle. The *first* castle. The castle of his dreams and, very dimly, of his memory. It was odd that as he grew older he found himself more and more often trying to build up a complete picture from what was only the roughest of sketches in his mind.

He shook the subject away now and stared again from the window. Between the black night sky and the black water of the harbour the speckled lights of North Sydney stretched like a galaxy of distant stars towards the Pacific. Nearer to The Castle, a pale green glow lit up the arch of the Harbour Bridge. Above it a red light flashed, guiding planes towards the airport and ships from the ocean into safe harbour. Two rows of bright lights illuminated the carriageway itself, and between them surged the never-ending procession of cars. The ferries, too, moving islands of light, continued to glide in and out of their moorings at the quays, sinking into darkness as they rounded a point. At any hour of the day or night people

129

were on the move. It was restful to watch them, knowing that he would not be going anywhere again.

Wee Jamie had no doubts about that. His doctors were jollying him along, assuring him that he would soon be as right as rain. He didn't believe a word of it. He could speak and see and move one hand and foot, but part of his mind and body was dead. Dead for ever, not temporarily stunned as they were trying to make him believe. He knew his own body and what it could and couldn't do. What was the point of fighting, when any victory could be only for a short time? Eighty-one years of life was enough for any man. He would like to hang on until Jock sailed into harbour; but that was the extent of his fighting spirit.

A flurry of taxi activity outside the Opera House suggested that the evening's entertainment had come to an end. Wee Jamie closed his eyes as he lay back on the pillows, waiting. Beverley had moved into the penthouse to be with him as soon as he left hospital and tonight had promised that, however late it might be, she would come to see whether he was awake. It was not long before he heard the door being cautiously opened.

'Gramps?' It was the faintest of whispers, but enough to charge him with energy.

'Put the light on, Bev. Come and tell me all about it.' But as she bent down to kiss him, he abandoned all pretence of being interested in the opera or its singers. 'Let's have another look at you.'

Beverley Jamieson, at the age of twenty-two, was an attractive example of gilded youth. She was intelligent, and had just completed a university degree course with honours; but there was nothing in her appearance to suggest the bluestocking. Like Jock, her father, she spent her spare time sailing, allowing the sun to tan her slim, athletic body and to bleach still whiter her naturally blonde hair. The circle of society in which she lived, although wealthy, did not expect its younger members to look elegant; but even when casually dressed she drew the eye by the healthy grace with which she moved: long-legged, straight-backed and with head held high.

Wee Jamie considered her to be the most beautiful girl in Sydney; but it was not often that he had the chance to admire her appearance 'dressed overall', as she had put it before she left.

Beverley rarely wore jewellery, but tonight the black opal pendant which he had given her for her eighteenth birthday hung from a gold chain round her neck, stirring memories in her grandfather's mind. He had kept only one stone from the cluster he discovered on his return to the workings where a snake had bitten him and done for Harry the Hat. All the rest were sold to help finance his ambitious plans to build a chain of hotels. But this, the most beautiful of the opals, he had reserved as a gift for Fred Johns' younger sister, who was to become his wife; and after her death he had put it aside until his only granddaughter should be old enough for it.

She wore it now above an evening gown which was cut low and straight to reveal her slender neck and shoulders. As a rule she avoided hairdressers. Tonight, though, because she was representing her grandfather, she had allowed her long blonde hair to be spun into a formal crown. Nor did she often use make-up, but it seemed to her grandfather – unless his sight was fading – that her freckles had temporarily vanished and there was a subtle impression of green and brown around her eyes. 'My, but you're a beauty!' he exclaimed.

Beverley kissed him again. 'Nonsense. I've got a generous grandfather, that's all. This dress – '

Wee Jamie tried to shake his head, but it was one of the movements which he had not recovered after the stroke. He interrupted her instead.

'Beauty comes from inside,' he said. Pausing, he considered his own good fortune. 'Lucky,' he said. 'Not much family. But you and Jock, just what I wanted. Right on.'

Beverley, pulling a chair to the side of the bed, changed the course of the conversation with a firmness which made clear her refusal to listen to her own praises.

'Didn't you ever have any other family, Gramps?' she

131

asked. 'I know you were an orphan, but even orphans can have uncles and aunts and cousins.'

'I was trying to think. Just today. About the castle.' He saw the puzzled frown on Beverley's face. To her, of course, The Castle was the building in which she was now sitting. 'The other castle. Where I was small.'

'What do you mean? Are you trying to say that you *lived* in a castle?'

'Think so. No, sure I did. Born there, I think. All I really remember is a tower. A round room – a nursery – with a fire. Nurse brought hot oatcakes for tea.' He laughed to himself, wondering how he could be so sure about that when he didn't even know what an oatcake was. 'Reckon there was a girl there as well. A sister? I'm not sure about that. But the oatcakes in the tower, I do remember those.'

As he spoke, he tried to focus his mind on the sister, but no face or name materialised. Instead, there was another picture, of a doll that had fallen sideways on a chair and his own infant voice calling in vain for M . . . M . . . Was it May, Mary, Margaret? He had never seen her again and until very recently had not even thought about her. Old men remember. He was beginning to remember now. A little more with each effort of will. Mary. 'Mary,' he said.

But the incredulity on Beverley's face was not directed towards the sudden resurrection of his sister, her great-aunt. 'For twenty-two years,' she said in a voice which would have been bullying if she had not been laughing, 'I've been asking you to explain your obsession with castles. Castle House. Castle Hotel. The Castle. The whole of Sydney has wanted to know. Have you ever done more than shrug your shoulders at the question? No, you have not. And now, without warning, you're pulling a castle out of a hat and claiming that you were *born* there! Come off it, Gramps. You'll be telling me next that it was Windsor Castle and that by rights you should be sitting on the throne of England.'

Wee Jamie laughed as strongly as he was able, but the laughter faded as another memory sprang to his mind.

'I told people once. They laughed. Hit me, I think, for boasting or telling lies. I promised myself then that I was never going to talk about it again. And as time went on, I really did forget. It's just that lying here, with nothing to do, it gets clearer every minute.'

There was another picture. Just as Beverley was sitting now beside a dying man, he, Wee Jamie, had been present at a deathbed. The unexpected revelation came to him with an almost physical pain, so that he cried out aloud and Beverley, alarmed, sprang to her feet. With his one good hand he waved her back to her chair. A shutter in his mind had sprung back. He could remember it all, as though the scene were being played at this moment.

'My mother,' he said. 'My mother was dying. I was on the floor, playing marbles. She said . . .' What was it she had said? She had said to someone else that she was sorry; that part of the conversation was difficult to place. But a moment earlier Wee Jamie himself had shouted with excitement that he was Lord of the Castle. He had meant only that for the first time he had succeeded in lodging his alabaster taw at the top of a toy which he called the castle, but his mother had not understood that. 'So you are, Jamie,' she had said, and she had not been talking about marbles. Slowly now the old man repeated her words. 'She said that I was Lord of the Castle. And she meant, I think, the castle in which I was born. But then she died, and I was never there again.'

His voice was changing. He was conscious of its different accent; he was not altering it deliberately nor was he able to control the change. Was that how he had spoken at the age of three or four, with a Scots accent? Was it a Scottish castle? His memory, which for a few seconds had been so clear, was clouding again. Tiredness swept over him. He was ready to sleep.

'You mean . . .' Beverley's voice, far from tired, was still puzzled. 'Do you mean that your mother had some kind of premonition? That one day you'd own a building like this?'

Once again Wee Jamie tried and failed to shake his head.

'I believe she was telling the truth, the literal truth. There was a castle, and I should have possessed it.' He let his breath out with a heavy sigh. He had been Lord of the Castle for most of his adult life, in a sense; but it was a different castle. 'I was too small to do anything about that.'

'If it's true, though' – Beverley's puzzlement was turning to indignation – 'it must mean that somebody diddled you out of it.'

'What if they did? I've had a good life. I ought to be grateful.'

'A good life! You've *made* a good life for yourself, sure. But when you were a boy – the orphanage, and all that.' Although she had never before heard any mention of the castle, Beverley was well acquainted with the story of her grandfather's early years. Recognising, perhaps, that it was not for her to feel anger on behalf of someone who showed no resentment on his own part, she asked curiously, 'Haven't you ever wanted to find out? To go and look for the original castle, if it exists?'

'No. I remember once, when I was still a boy. Harry the Hat.' He saw the smile on Beverley's face. Harry the Hat was another familiar part of the family history. 'He had a theory. Philosophy, almost. Good to keep a treat in reserve, he always said. Everyone needs to have some pleasure that he can look forward to one day, one of these days, when he gets round to it. It's a happy man who never in the end feels the need to get round to it. I'm a happy man. Remember that, Bev, afterwards.' He could feel himself receding from her. It would not be long now. He summoned the last burst of energy. 'You, though. You could go and look for the castle if it amused you. The tower. Nursery. Tired now.'

His eyes were closed, but he could hear Beverley leaving the room. She returned in a moment with the nurse, and together the two women pulled away some of the pillows and eased his heavy body into a sleeping position. ''Night, girl,' he said drowsily, without opening

134

his eyes. For what was to be the last time he felt her cool kiss on his cheek. She was wearing some kind of perfume which for a few moments after she had gone continued to scent the air around his nostrils. Then it faded, to be replaced by the aroma of a smouldering fire and a plate of oatcakes, hot from the griddle. There was no need to keep himself awake any longer. Not so much drifting into sleep as letting go of consciousness he felt himself falling in darkness from the top of The Castle.

PART TWO

BEVERLEY'S QUEST

1

Beverley Jamieson was sailing in Sydney Harbour. Or rather, she was sitting in her *Flying Dutchman*, allowing its sails to flap idly while she dabbled her fingers in the luminous green water of The Basin. It was mid-March – officially the first day of winter, but still hot enough for her to feel comfortable in a bikini top and brief pair of shorts.

She sighed with pleasure at the beauty of her surroundings. Although a headland cut off any view of the graceful harbour bridge or the billowing sails of the Opera House, the distant backdrop of towering skyscrapers did not spoil the outlook; instead, it enhanced the unspoiled peace of the nearby bays and the cheerful activity on the water. Other small yachts pressed purposefully towards marker buoys in race formation, their brightly-coloured spinnakers filled with wind. But Beverley was not going anywhere – at least, not for the moment. It was her imminent journey to England which was under discussion.

'Grey skies. Rain. Ugly towns. Stuffy Poms. I must be mad to think of leaving.' She sighed again. 'This has to be the most beautiful place in the world.'

'You *are* mad,' agreed her father affectionately, stretching himself out in the boat which seemed too small to contain him. Like his father, who had died five weeks before, Jock Jamieson was a big man. Most of his sailing was done in an ocean-going twelve-metre yacht, more appropriate to his bulk. But this would be Beverley's last day in Sydney for several months: he had wanted to keep her company. There was no trace in his manner now of the forcefulness which he displayed when he was racing or in the chairman's office of the business inherited from Wee Jamie. In the company of his beloved daughter Jock was always relaxed. 'Does it mean so much to you, this academic stuff?' he asked her.

It was not a question which Beverley found easy to answer. After graduating in history at the end of the year, she had decided to take a Master's degree; it was the research necessary for her thesis which would be taking her to England. Her subject was not particularly original – indeed, with the preparations for Australia's bi-centennial in full swing it had become over-fashionable. She proposed to study the home backgrounds of the first arrivals in Sydney and had persuaded herself that this was worth a few months of her time: yet in her heart she shared her father's doubts.

'I don't really know what I want to do with myself,' she confessed.

'You don't have to *do* anything.'

'I know I don't.' Wee Jamie had left all his business interests to his son, but had bequeathed a share of his personal fortune directly to his only grand-daughter. Beverley was a wealthy young woman now, no longer dependent on her father's generous allowance and her grandfather's equally lavish presents. 'But I feel I should.'

'I can give you a job anywhere in the world where we own a hotel.'

'I know that too. Somehow that makes it more difficult, not less. Everything's always been made too easy for me. You know how it was with Gramps. I only had to hint at something I wanted and there it was.'

'You could have said no.'

'Oh yes? I remember when he gave you your first twelve-metre yacht as a surprise for your fortieth birthday.' It was Beverley's turn now to laugh affectionately. 'I could almost *hear* your jaw drop. You didn't really want it, did you? I wondered then – I was only a kid – why you didn't turn it down. But when I thought about it, I understood.'

'Understood what?'

'How much it meant to Gramps having you and me as family – and *only* us. I mean, being an orphan himself and having that terrible childhood. The only presents ever given to him were those marbles.'

'Don't forget Harry the Hat,' said Jock, laughing. Harry the Hat's dirty scrap of paper, from which Wee Jamie's hotel empire had grown, was part of the history of Sydney.

'That too. But that was all. It seemed to me . . . I mean, when you look around, you see rich men going one of two ways. Either they're as mean as hell or else as generous as Santa Claus. Gramps was one of the generous ones, wasn't he? Nothing in the world offered him more pleasure than giving things away – and especially to his family, just because he didn't have any family at all when he was a kid. Well, I don't need to tell you.'

'All that may be true,' agreed Jock. 'But it doesn't logically explain why you've chosen the life of a bluestocking.'

Recognising the truth of what he said, Beverley shrugged her shoulders and flicked at the water with her fingers.

'I lack ambition,' she admitted simply. 'Can't blame that entirely on money. Gramps was a tiger on the bowling green long after he became a millionaire. And I'm sure you'd have cut a few throats if that would have helped you to win the America's Cup. But me, I don't seem to have any competitive spirit. One thing about going to university was that Gramps couldn't hand me my degree as a gift. I had to do all the work and pass all the exams myself. The same with this research. It's fine having the money to fly off and do it, but it will only be any good if I do it well.' Beverley burst out laughing.

'I'm killing time, Dad. That's all it is. Until I find out what I *really* want to do with my life.'

She had not expected to spend these last hours on the water discussing anything as serious as her own future, and was glad of an interruption. From behind the nearest headland appeared a speedboat, making towards the yacht with a directness which would have been threatening had Beverley not recognised its occupant. Just when a collision seemed inevitable the noisy engine was silenced and the boat, turning sharply, glided to a smooth halt beside the *Flying Dutchman*.

The driver of the speedboat put out a hand to hold on to the yacht and keep his own craft steady beside it. He was a tall, muscular young man of exactly Beverley's age. At this moment he wore only swimming trunks, but from the gradations of the tan on his legs, arms and neck it was possible to deduce that he spent most of his time in the sun dressed in a tee-shirt and shorts.

'Hi, Ken.' Beverley smiled with pleasure at the encounter; whilst her father laughingly added, 'You look like an ad for a body-building gym.'

'Oh, I am, I am.' Ken used his free arm to demonstrate the rippling of his muscles. 'I only flew in this morning,' he told Beverley. 'And when I called Ma to say I was home she mentioned you were flying out tomorrow. So I'm here to say hello and goodbye. Ships that pass in the afternoon.'

Beverley's smile widened as they chatted, with Ken bringing her up to date on his recent travels and successes. She was aware of her father listening with interest to the conversation, but without interrupting it.

'Well,' said Ken at last, 'have a good trip. But come back, right? Sydney won't be the same without you.' He blew her a kiss before releasing his hold on the yacht and roaring away in the speedboat.

'Nice kid,' commented Jock, watching him go. He stared at his daughter intently with eyes as blue as her own. 'When you talk about what you want to do with your life, Bev, does Ken come into it at all? I know he's playing the field a bit now. But it could be that he feels he should make his own million before he asks someone like you to marry him – and he seems to be well on the way.'

'Playing the field, as you call it, has become a risky business since AIDS hit the headlines. But anyway – ' Beverley struggled for a few moments to consider her feelings about Ken.

She had known Ken Murray all her life, for she was only a baby when her mother died and Ken's mother was employed to act as housekeeper. Mrs Murray brought her own baby with her, and the two children grew up together.

It was Beverley who, at the age of seven, had first shown talent with a tennis racquet. She had never lacked for anything money could buy. Her father found her the best coach in Sydney and built a practice wall in his grounds. There was already a court laid out in the garden. Here Beverley needed an opponent and Ken, of course, was always to hand. As soon as Jock Jamieson realised that his housekeeper's son seemed likely to prove an even stronger player than his daughter, he arranged for Ken to be included in the coaching. Later, he ensured that the boy should always have the right clothes and equipment and the money necessary to cover tournament expenses.

Beverley did not remain serious about tennis for long. She was a good player who enjoyed a friendly game, but her favourite outdoor pastime was sailing. Ken, by contrast, was fiercely competitive and ambitious, and had progressed through state tournaments to win both the Australian and Wimbledon junior championships: as a senior he had climbed his way up the ladder of tournament points until he stood at number five in Australia and number seventeen in the world. As Jock had suggested, he was well on the way to making his fortune.

'No,' said Beverley now in answer to her father's probing. 'I'm not interested in him in that way. We're best friends. I hope we always will be. But . . . It's the same problem we were talking about before, in a different form. I mean, suppose we were to get married. Ken probably reckons to have ten more years on the tennis circuit. How does his wife spend those ten years? Sitting at home and seeing him for Christmas? Or trailing round the world, moving to a different hotel every three weeks, and feeling that she's just a kind of appendage? A complication, even. Not for me. If I marry, I shall want to feel that I'm sharing my life with someone. And before I can do that, I need to feel that I've got a special kind of life to share. See what I mean?

'Nope. When I married your mother, I expected her to share *my* life.'

'That was because you're a great big bullying Jamieson. But perhaps I'm a great big bullying Jamieson as well. It's just that I haven't discovered my proper sphere of bullying yet.'

'Can't think that you're going to find it in Public Record Offices,' growled Jock. 'Sounds deadly dull to me.'

'Could be you're right. But . . .' Beverley hesitated. She had not planned to mention her latest idea to her father, yet it concerned him as much as herself, and it was a way of changing the subject of the conversation away from Ken. 'While I'm in England, I thought I'd look for the castle. Might relieve the dullness a bit.'

'The castle?'

'You remember. I told you what Gramps said the night he died.'

'I wouldn't waste much time on that, Bev. An old man, half-delirious.'

'I don't think he was. He couldn't remember much, but that's different. I don't believe he was inventing anything. There must have been a castle.'

'Probably turn out to be a pub.'

'Then I'll find the pub. It's only a bit of fun. But it'll make a change from the rest of the slog. The quest for the castle.' She sighed with the need to bring a happy day to a close. 'Time to get back. Come on, crew, let's see a bit of work out of you.'

'Cheeky.' Jock Jamieson acted as his own helmsman on his ocean-racing yacht and was used to seeing other people jump to his commands. But he hauled obediently on the sheet as his daughter turned the yacht close to the wind. Then, sitting side by side, they threw their weight back until their shoulders were only a few feet above the water.

'You must come to Newport,' shouted Jock above the sound of the wind and water. 'I'll be there in July for the racing. I'm renting a cottage for the crew. Plenty of room for you. And you'll be on the doorstep.'

'Pretty wide doorstep, the Atlantic.' But Beverley was pleased by the invitation. 'I'd love to come, Dad. Thanks.'

The exhilaration of the dash for home silenced them both for a while; but as they rounded the last of the big headlands and turned into Rushcutters Bay for the approach to Darling Point, Beverley burst out laughing.

'Castle House!' she exclaimed. 'And you're trying to make me believe that Gramps was delirious on that last night? There must have been something tucked away in his memory all those years. I mean, he never left Australia after he first arrived as a kid. He can't ever have seen a real castle, except in pictures. And yet he commissioned an architect to build a house looking like this!'

The building which commanded the end of the point – the mansion which Wee Jamie had handed over to his son as a wedding present and in which Beverley had been born and brought up – was a Scottish baronial castle. Beverley's mother, before her death, had surrounded it with hibiscus and frangipani which by now had grown lush enough to soften the bleakness of its design at ground level; but nothing could mask its battlements and turrets.

The house was not as wholly impractical as it appeared at first sight, for when Sydney sizzled in a heatwave the thick walls and small windows provided a welcome coolness inside, and the size of the fireplace in which logs burned in winter provided a conversation point as well as a deliciously smoky smell. But there was no denying that, compared to all its neighbours, it was not only striking but odd.

143

'You could have a point,' agreed Jock. 'Okay, then. Since you're going to be in England, you can have a look round for Wee Jamie's castle if you like.'

Beverley brought the *Flying Dutchman* smoothly to rest beside the landing pier, and grinned at her father as he jumped ashore and tied the boat up.

'Thanks for your kind permission,' she said. 'I was going to anyway.'

2

Thirty-six hours later, Beverley flew into England. It was the first time in her life that she had needed to organise her own living arrangements, but she had inherited her grandfather's instinct for a good location and her father's decisive efficiency in concluding a bargain. Her newly-inherited fortune would not tempt her to an extravagant style of living or dressing, but she was sensible enough to use it for her own convenience. Instead of searching the Little Australia area around Earl's Court for a place in a chummery she rented a furnished flat which would provide her with a private and comfortable *pied à terre* in London. Then she bought a car.

It was a fast, expensive car with a roof which opened at the touch of a button. As much on land as on the water Beverley liked speed and the feel of the wind in her hair. Whilst she was in Britain she would need to travel widely, often to remote villages untouched by any form of public transport. The Ferrari could be regarded as a tool of her research.

The subjects of her study would not be merely the convicts who were brought to Botany Bay at the end of the eighteenth century. A great deal had been written about them already. Her net would be cast more widely. Administrators, soldiers on escort duty, sailors deserting ship, camp followers, penniless immigrants, remittance men – the names of almost all the first settlers were on record and in many cases their careers in New South Wales were chronicled. What interested Beverley was their background, the lives and homes they had abandoned, whether voluntarily or under arrest, and the reasons for either their choices or their misdeeds, often hardly deserving to be called crimes.

Before leaving Sydney she had studied archives and made extensive notes, so that she arrived in England with a list of names and home towns. To this list she had added the subject of her more personal search: Wee Jamie's birthplace. From the records of the farm school to which he was delivered at the age of nine it had proved possible to discover the name of the organisation which had sent him there. The Orphans' New Life Society. Knowing something of the hardships he had suffered during his early years, it was difficult not to regard the name with some cynicism. And yet, no doubt, its officers had at the time believed genuinely, perhaps even correctly, that the forlorn children they shipped across the world would have found life even harsher had they remained in England. Until the conversation with her dying grandfather, Beverley would certainly have been prepared to give the Society the benefit of the doubt. But mention of the castle had sown suspicion in her mind. She intended to track down the truth.

It took her a little while after she settled down in London to find out where the records of charities for orphans were to be seen, and the length of the list was daunting. In the early years of the century, she discovered, no fewer than twenty-eight societies existed for the specific purpose of stocking the British Empire with fatherless children. The Orphans' New Life Society was listed amongst them, but a footnote told her that it had ceased to submit reports in 1916. Several other societies had closed their books at about the same time, perhaps because of the dangers of sea travel during the war, so there seemed nothing sinister about this sudden break in the record. However, it did not make a researcher's task any easier.

Would anyone know what had happened to the

Society's organising secretary if she visited his last known address? Seventy years was a very long time, but she made the journey anyway, and found herself staring at a huge comprehensive school; a sprawling rabbit warren of halls and classrooms and covered walkways. At a guess, it had been built about thirty years earlier.

Beverley was not easily daunted. She strode in through the nearest door just as two thousand children were pouring out. Three questions and two referrals later, she found the person she needed: the head of the history department, who over a cup of tea in the staffroom expressed delight at her interest.

'It was one of my first ideas after I was appointed here,' he told her, 'to make every child in his first term do a project on The Refuge. That's what the building which used to be on this site was called. I felt it would give the kids an instant sense of history, show them a little of what historians have to do to get at the facts, and possibly suggest to them that, however rotten they reckon their own lives to be now, their great-grandfathers had it harder.'

'What exactly was The Refuge?'

'The best description of it would be a dumping ground for unwanted kids. The man who ran it was in the business of child emigration.'

'I know a bit about that side of it,' Beverley told him. 'That's why I'm here.'

'Well, there were rules and regulations. You can imagine. The parishes were willing to pay to keep homeless children out of their own workhouses, but the colonies demanded a clean bill of health with every young immigrant they accepted. So The Refuge was a kind of holding post; you might almost think of it as a quarantine station. It accepted children off the streets covered in dirt and lice and fleas and ringworm, gave them a good scrub and a new set of clothes and a taste of education and sent them on their way. A short-term orphanage, you could say.'

'So you reckon it as a genuine organisation? Genuine, I mean, in trying to do its best for the kids.'

146

Mr Sharp, the history master, hesitated.

'I wouldn't want to go overboard on that one. The man who started it originally was a philanthropist, no doubt about that, taking children into his own home. By the time it moved to this site and became established, it was being run by a paid organiser and supervised rather remotely by a board of guardians. I wouldn't like to claim that life as an orphan here was all honey and roses. I'm not sure that the chappie – Chisholm, his name was – always looked too closely at the homes to which he sent the children. And by our standards he was ruthless in splitting up families. He sent out batches of girls, batches of boys, all about the same age. I suppose it would have bugged the system to keep brothers and sisters in the same party, or even the same continent. I'm not saying he was a villain. But insensitive, yes, that.'

'Have you got the records here for your pupils to study?' asked Beverley.

Mr Sharp gave a rueful laugh. 'Far from it. Big problem. More tea? No, Chisholm hung on to all his old records after the Society folded. Fair enough, I suppose. He left them to his daughter. And will she give access? No, she damn well won't. I was allowed just a couple of hours in the shrine; she's got a room in her house furnished like her father's old study. Maybe it actually *is* his old study. I had to sit on one side of the desk with her on the other, watching like an eagle to see that I didn't nick anything.'

'So the project for your classes?'

'Never worked out the way I planned it. A good subject, all the same. I never expected, of course, that she'd let a hundred and eighty eleven-year-olds rampage through her papers every year. All I wanted was permission to make some photocopies: registers, assessments, the letters that the kids wrote back. A few specimens of each. But no dice. So we do it the other way round. Imagination. The result's nearer to creative writing than to history, I'm afraid. I give them a talk. We have discussions. Then they turn themselves into orphans. Choose new names. Each of them writes a piece

147

about his imaginary life. Life as a guttersnipe, life in The Refuge, on the voyage out, in Australia, Canada, South Africa. They collect pictures, or paint them, and we make up a scrapbook. So they get the social history part of it. Not the lesson in historical research, though. Pity.'

'My grandfather was one of those boys,' Beverley told him.

'Really! From The Refuge?' Mr Sharp looked at her with new interest. 'How did he get on?'

'He was sent out to Australia. He did well in the end, but not through anything the Society did for him. He had to run away before he made his fortune.'

'Will you come and give a talk here in October? We do the project in the first term of the new intake. It would bring everything to life: a real boy. Anything you knew about his background, and then what he became.'

'It's because I don't know anything about his background that I came here to ask questions. If I discover anything – and if I'm still around in October – I'll certainly tell you about it. Could you give me the address of Mr Chisholm's daughter?'

'Mrs Dancy. She lives in North Oxford. One of those huge houses built to take twelve children and twelve servants.' He looked up the address and wrote it down for her. 'She'll say no to anything you ask. So you might find it better not to give her the chance. Just turn up, I mean, and hope to charm her.'

'Thanks for the hint. And the information.'

Mr Sharp's expression became wistful as they stood up.

'I envy you,' he said. 'Searching for the past. Finding a real person behind a name, or behind a paragraph in a history book; or in your case, a real young person behind a real old person. When I remember how I once wanted to be a historian, a proper historian . . . Ah well.' He sighed, and then smiled. 'I hope you manage to crash the barrier.'

'Thanks.' As she shook hands and made her way out of the school, Beverley felt a new kind of exhilaration bubbling within her. Her research into the backgrounds of the earliest colonists was interesting, even fascinating. But to track down the secrets of her grandfather's past – as the history master had said, to discover a real child – that indeed could offer her a different and more intense excitement: the thrill of the hunt.

3

Oxford was littered with bicycles: bicycles padlocked to lampposts, bicycles leaning three-deep against walls, bicycles being propelled with either fierce earnestness or swerving nonchalance by riders clutching tennis racquets or cricket bats: books and lecture notes seemed less in evidence on this sunny May afternoon. The summer term, although the University of Oxford did not call it that, was in full swing by the time Beverley arrived in the city for her confrontation with Mrs Dancy.

Mrs Dancy's house was as enormous as all its North Oxford neighbours but, to judge by the single bell, it was neither divided into flats nor converted into student lodgings. Outside, a painted notice sternly announced that any bicycle propped against the fence would be removed. Perhaps in the past this warning had been translated into positive action for, as Beverley brought her Ferrari to a halt, only one battered machine littered the section of pavement outside the house, and even that was just on the point of departure. Its undergraduate owner, stooping to unlock it, raised his head at the sound of the braking car, and stared in astonishment.

'You're not!' he said as Beverley walked towards the gate. 'You can't be! The historian?'

After some thought Beverley had taken only part of Mr Sharp's advice. Rather than arrive completely without warning, she had written to tell Mrs Dancy of her interest in Mr Chisholm's papers and to mention that she would be passing through Oxford on Saturday; but her letter made it clear that she was on the move and that no prohibition would catch her up. It would appear that the young man had been informed of her visit.

Beverley nodded her acceptance of his identification. 'Mrs Dancy lives here, right?'

'A blonde in a red Ferrari! Why aren't there any historians in Oxford like that? You should see my tutors. Mrs Dancy, yes. I'll show you in.'

'You live here?'

'I'm Luke Dancy, I lodge here. How d'you do. I'm in my second year at Oxford and since I'm too broke to pay rent to anyone and my grandmother is terrified of burglars, a concordat of mutual convenience has been struck. I was proposing to go out to tea rather than listen to an argument which I've heard too often before, but now I've changed my mind.'

'I wouldn't want you to alter your plans for my sake.' Beverley, though, was grinning as broadly as Luke.

'Yes, you would. Without me you won't get past the front door. But since I have a key, you're at least into the drawing room before the shutters come down.'

'Is it as bad as that?'

'You'll see.' Luke, as he had promised, unlocked the door and led the way inside. 'Miss Jamieson's here, Granny,' he called.

'Granny' seemed too cosy a word for the irate old lady who appeared at the door of her drawing room. 'I told you,' she began.

'I know you did. But Miss Jamieson's come all the way from Australia. The least we can offer her is a slice of your delicious fruit cake. Come and sit down, Miss Jamieson. You know, you hardly talk like an Australian at all.'

Beverley might have retorted that she had been expensively educated, that she had hardly had a chance to open her mouth, or that in fact she was proud to be an Australian and not disposed to take his remark as a compliment; any of these comments would have been true. But for the moment it seemed profitable to regard Luke as a useful ally, so instead she smiled without speaking.

150

Mrs Dancy, accepting the need to endure the visit, took its course back into her own hands.

'I'll show you my father's study,' she said. Choosing a key from the bunch at her waist she unlocked a heavy mahogany door. After opening it, she continued to hold on to the handle as though at any moment it might be necessary to slam the door shut again.

Beverley looked curiously round the room. It was a gentleman's library rather than the kind of businessman's office she had expected. A huge leather-topped desk was still furnished with ink pots and pens to dip in them. A large globe stood in one corner beside windows draped with heavy red curtains. Two of the walls were lined with bookshelves whose contents were protected by a fine wire mesh. The only incongruous element was provided by a row of wooden filing cabinets along a third wall. Beverley looked at them hopefully, but made her approach with caution.

'Is this the room to which the children would have come in the first place?' she asked. 'Before any plans had been made for them.'

'Oh, dear me, no. Naturally my father had an office in The Refuge, before it was closed down. It was only after the Society ceased to exist that he moved here. He worked in this room for the last twenty years of his life. He lived for those boys, you know. Not the girls so much, because he'd had a female assistant to run the girls' side. But for twenty years, without a penny in salary, he answered all the boys' letters. He was a father to them because not one of them had a father of his own. He followed their careers, helped them with advice. He was a saint. Some of the letters would move you to tears.'

'Were there any from my grandfather?' In her preliminary approach Beverley had mentioned the reason for her interest in the society.

'No.' The curtness of the reply suggested that wee Jamie Jamieson had shown himself by silence to be ungrateful, and so could not expect his name to be met with approval.

'May I see any papers that you have relating to him?'

'I'm afraid not. Confidential.' With a brisk and unexpected action Mrs Dancy swung the door back into the closed position so forcefully that Beverley had to step backwards if she was not to be hit in the face by it.

'Confidential to whom? I'm here as my grandfather's representative.'

'So you say. If you had a letter . . .'

'Yes, I have.' In the interest of her other, less personal, research, Beverley's university supervisor had provided her with a document to establish her bona fides as a scholar and ensure her access to the archives she would need to search. But Mrs Dancy gave it only the most cursory glance.

'From your grandfather, I mean. Only the boys themselves are allowed to see their records. Or someone like yourself bringing direct authorisation.'

'My grandfather asked me personally – '

'Ask him to write a letter,' said Mrs Dancy.

'I can't. He's dead.'

For the first time, the old lady's eyes flickered with interest. 'I'll be glad to know the date of death,' she said. 'So that I can close the file.'

It was only with great difficulty that Beverley controlled her double anger: anger at the lack of sympathy and anger at the assumption that someone who offered no information herself yet had a right to receive it. 'I'd be delighted to give you full information about his life, as well as his death,' she said. 'So that you can bring the file right up to date. All I'm asking is the chance to see – '

'I'm sorry,' said Mrs Dancy with a marked lack of sorrow. 'Would you care for a cup of tea before you go? My grandson will entertain you while I put the kettle on.'

Beverley did not often lose her temper, but she was about to explode now. As she drew breath, she was aware of Luke's hand on her arm, propelling her towards the drawing room.

'Keep your cool,' he murmured as his grandmother disappeared down a corridor towards the back of the house. 'I know you're seething, but all may yet be well. Trust me – and wait just round the corner when you leave.'

'I'm leaving now. If she thinks I'm going to sit and sip tea while she tells me again that her father was a saint – '

'Okay. Round the corner, then. Five minutes.'

He arrived, strolling in an ostentatiously casual manner, before that time was up. 'May I sit in your beautiful Ferrari? Now then, first of all let me apologise on behalf of the family.'

'What right does she think she has?' demanded Beverley. 'The Orphans' New Life Society was a charity, not her father's private hobby.'

'Everything you're saying and thinking is true. But – '

'You don't know what I'm thinking. What I'm thinking is that I need a lawyer. I reckon that there may have been some funny business. A long time ago, of course, nothing to do with your grandmother. But her father. It seems to me – '

Beverley's grandfather himself had not seemed greatly bothered by the possibility that he might have been defrauded of his rightful inheritance, but Beverley herself was prepared to be indignant and even vindictive on his behalf. 'For all I know – since I'm not to be allowed to check the facts – Mr Chisholm may have been operating some kind of child slave racket.'

'You don't *really* think that.' Luke's voice was soothing. 'You're just cross, and quite rightly too. I can promise you that there was nothing sinister about the Society. It did what it purported to do. I've read some of the letters. A few of them still trickle in today, although naturally most of the boys are dead by now. I suppose it's only the grateful ones who write, but even so . . . I've tried to make my grandmother see reason on the subject. Unfortunately, though, she got mixed up in a nasty case fifty years ago, and it seems to have affected her for life. Not long after her father died, someone turned up, saying he was one of the boys. Well, I suppose he was. She answered all his questions and showed him the register and helped him to find out who his mother was; he was illegitimate, like a lot of the so-called orphans. She thought she was being helpful. But what happened was that he went off to tell his mother what he thought about being abandoned. It broke up her marriage, because she'd never told her husband about her secret past; and as a result she went off her rocker and killed her son. All good headline material for the gutter press. Granny blamed herself and said Never Again. There's no logic to her position. But she can't be budged.'

'Can't she so!' Beverley was a determined young woman, used to getting what she wanted.

'No need to fight. I'm here to issue an invitation. Come back here at five past eleven tomorrow morning. Definitely no earlier, and not much later. Don't bring the Ferrari. Too conspicuous. I can get you into the study, and open a few drawers.'

'Why should you?' asked Beverley curiously.

'Because you're a beautiful blonde and you've swept me off my feet. Because if I can make you grateful you'll let me drive you off to lunch afterwards in your Ferrari. Because to me, although not to people like you, my grandmother's actually quite a decent old biddy and I don't want her to start getting lawyers' letters. I do recognise the steely look in your eyes. It's my ambition to replace it with a smile of adoring gratitude.'

Beverley laughed. She couldn't help it. 'Okay,' she agreed. 'Five past eleven.'

4

'The thing is this,' said Luke, punctually at five past eleven the next morning. 'The one unalterable engagement in Granny's diary is morning service in the cathedral. I suspect her of having a crush on the dean. Even allowing for the very shortest of sermons, we have an hour. Come on.'

'But how?'

'I had the key copied,' said Luke, using it to open the study door. 'As a matter of fact, although Granny won't let anyone else loose here, she did once allow me to prowl around. Years ago. I was spending a couple of weeks here while my parents were on holiday, and she hadn't the foggiest idea how to amuse a fourteen-year-old on a wet day. She started telling me all about the orphans, and I, well, I sort of got hooked. Could be what started me on the history lark. Anyway, she must have realised that I wasn't likely to raise any scandals, so she gave me the run of the room for a week, on condition I left everything as I found it – just as you're going to do now. I could guess that Bluebeard's secret room would be firmly locked before I came again, so I took the necessary steps. You know what boys are like about getting in to forbidden places.'

He locked the door behind them again and went straight across to unfasten the window. 'Now then. First rule of burglary. Always secure your escape route. There's one chance in a million, I suppose, that Granny might be taken ill and have to be brought home. If that happens, you whizz out of here and disappear. So. What do you want to know?'

'My grandfather's name was Jamie Jamieson,' Beverley told him. 'He arrived in Australia in 1915. That's the only certain date I have so far. He reckoned he'd been in the orphanage over here for four or five years before that. I'd like to get the dates straight and to find out where he came from – you know, who his parents were, what happened to them, who took charge of him after they died.'

'Right.' Luke fiddled for a moment or two with a drawer of the heavy desk. Beverley was not close enough to see what tool he was using to open it, but within a few seconds he held up a bunch of small keys. 'File card for Jamieson first. That will give the date of admission. Then we go to the register.'

Jamie had not been one of the grateful boys who wrote to Mr Chisholm as though he were a father. A single page was enough to record the boy's registration, illnesses, school attendance, acceptance for emigration, arrival at farm school and first employment. The last line consisted only of the laconic statement: Ran away. Mrs Dancy, it seemed, had not yet had time to add the information that the subject of the file was dead.

Beverley made a note of all the dates mentioned, although the only useful one was likely to be the date of birth. Assuming that her grandfather's birth had been officially registered at the time, it should be possible to discover the area in which it took place. Meanwhile, Luke was opening the register at the appropriate year.

'Here we are,' he said, pulling out the chair for her and standing behind so that he could read over her shoulder. 'James Jamieson. Only four years old, poor little chap.'

'James *McEwan* Jamieson. Look, the McEwan was put in afterwards.' Beverley frowned to herself in surprise. Her grandfather had never admitted to having a middle name. But the addition seemed of little significance compared with her next discovery. 'And I wonder . . . Just before he died, he began to remember that he had a sister called Mary. And there on the line above there's a Mairi McEwan. They were both brought to the orphanage on the same day. It does seem likely that the two children were related.' The difference of surname was a puzzle, but the fact that Jamie's middle name was the same as Mairi's surname pointed strongly to a link. 'Perhaps she was a half-sister.'

She continued to study the page. The columns headed 'Father', 'Mother' and 'Previous address' had been left tantalisingly blank in the case of both Mairi and Jamie. But under 'Introduction' the same name was inscribed on each line: Mr G. Blair. 'Who would he be?' she asked herself aloud, puzzled. 'Why is there so little information?'

'A lot of the kids were literally picked up off the streets,' Luke reminded her. 'No welfare state then. A boy could certainly shiver and possibly starve without anyone noticing. This Mr Blair could be a Doctor Barnardo kind of man, someone who walked the streets looking for waifs and bringing them to shelter. He probably didn't have any connection with them except what was prompted by kindness.'

Reluctantly Beverley nodded her agreement. 'Let's see what happened to Mairi,' she suggested.

Mairi's file was little more revealing than Wee Jamie's, but at least Beverley was able to copy down two addresses. One was of the charity's reception hostel in Canada, whilst the second was of a Saskatchewan farmhouse to which the little girl had been sent for fostering. The last line of the record was the same as that of Jamie's: Ran away.

'A footloose family,' commented Luke; but Beverley was upset by the coincidence.

'More likely it means that they were equally unhappy. Fancy separating them like that! You'd think they could at least have been kept on the same continent. Is there any way, do you imagine, of tracking down this Mr Blair? Is there a separate file for Introducers?'

'Let's think.' But while he was considering, an unexpected sound – that of the front door opening and closing – made him lift his head in surprise. 'Out!' he commanded, moving at speed to push up the sash window. 'Round to the right. Keep close to the wall. Then back to where we met before. Wait for me.'

Beverley obeyed his instructions with such athletic speed that it was only after she had reached the pavement unobserved that some of the previous day's indignation returned. Why should she have to behave like an intruder, and even feel ashamed of the intrusion, when she had a perfect right to inspect the documents of her family history? But it would not be fair to take out her annoyance on Luke, who was putting himself to some trouble on her behalf.

When he rejoined her fifteen minutes later, however, he was as nonchalant as ever.

'Did she catch you red-handed?' Beverley asked.

Luke shook his head. 'If she goes into the study now, she won't notice anything amiss. Everything's stowed away and locked up except for the window catch, since

I used the same exit as you. She's not likely to check that, and I'll deal with it during her afternoon nap.'

'Was she taken ill?'

'No. Overcome with fury rather than faintness. When the time came for the sermon to be preached, who should appear in the pulpit but a *woman*. It was bad enough that she was American, but to be female as well! Granny walked out on her. Ostentatiously, no doubt. The ordination of women is a fighting issue in the Church of England at the moment, and there's no doubt which side Granny is on. I'm truly sorry you were interrupted. But now I know what you're looking for, I'll have a scout through the other files myself and see if I can come up with anything. We'll make a rendezvous for tomorrow afternoon. In the morning I have a tutorial. And that means that this evening I have a crisis. But tomorrow, at four o'clock. At the Cherwell boathouse.' He pointed down a side street. 'Anyone will tell you.'

'Thanks a lot.' But Beverley sighed as she remembered how little there was to work on. No father's name, no mother's name. The only possible lead was the man who had handed over the two small children. 'Mr Blair,' she said. 'Anything you can find out about Mr Blair.'

5

Beverley was familiar with most varieties of small boat, but she had never before found herself in a punt.

'What an extraordinary method of propulsion!' she exclaimed as Luke, showing off, tossed the long pole hand over hand into the air before thrusting it down into the river bed and using it to steer the flat vessel as well as to move it forward.

'Well, we're not trying to circumnavigate the globe or anything ambitious like that,' he pointed out unnecessarily. 'The journey, not the arrival, matters, as you might say. We'll just meander a little way up the

Cherwell, pause, and come back again. So there's no need to be in a hurry.'

It was just as well, thought Beverley, laughing aloud as she sat back on the cushions and trailed her fingers in the water of a narrow, placid river overhung by willows. Other punts, less expertly steered, pursued an erratic, meandering course, contrasting with the businesslike vigour of an occasional canoe; but Luke pressed steadily on.

True to his promise, he did not travel far before pulling into the bank, plunging the pole down into the mud, and mooring the punt to it.

'Now then,' he said, sitting down on the cushions to face her and pulling a sheet of paper from his pocket. 'Your Mr Blair. Nothing in the register was of any help. But he bobbed up in the correspondence file.'

'Go on.' Beverley's eyes brightened with hope.

'It may not be relevant. There doesn't appear to be any connection between this letter and your grandfather. Only the name of the addressee. It's a handwritten copy of a letter written by my great-grandfather, Mr Chisholm, to Mr Gordon Blair of Blair, Honeyman and Blair. A firm of lawyers in Edinburgh. That's in Scotland,' he added helpfully, as though ignorance must be presumed in an Australian visitor.

'I know that, for heaven's sake. What does the letter say?'

' "Dear Mr Blair, I acknowledge with thanks the gift of five hundred pounds made to the Orphans' New Life Society, to be put towards the running expenses of The Refuge. I appreciate the fact that although the donation is taken from the estate of your deceased client, the specific choice of the charity to receive the money was left to your discretion. Naturally I am delighted that you should have chosen our cause to receive such a generous benefit. I can promise you that it will be well spent in the interests of the unfortunate children whose futures are in the hands of the Society. If there is ever any way in which I can show my appreciation, please do not hesitate to call on me." It's dated a month or two before young Jamie Jamieson was admitted to The Refuge, so it's difficult to see any link.'

'Unless . . . unless taking the two children into the orphanage was asked for as the gesture of appreciation which the letter offered. I mean . . . suppose this Mr Blair was actually their father, but not married to their mother. When she died . . .' Wee Jamie had never doubted that he was in truth an orphan when he arrived at the orphanage, but he had no memory of a father. In his last conversation with Beverley, it was only about his mother's death that he was clear. 'When she died, he needed to get rid of them for some reason, and called in his debt of gratitude from Mr Chisholm.'

'Sounds a bit melodramatic to me,' said Luke doubtfully. 'A father wouldn't shunt his children off like that, surely. I mean to say, I'm sure the Orphans' New Life Society did its best for the kids, but even so . . . No. I don't really see the connection. Only the name.'

'I'll be going up to Scotland within the next week or two,' Beverley said. 'I can check out the address then.'

'What fun!' exclaimed Luke. 'What fun to be doing *real* historical research. I mean to say, every week my tutor here gives me a subject to investigate and write up in an essay. Mostly I have to get the facts out of secondary sources – history books written by historians who all have their own axes to grind. Sometimes, just sometimes, I can get my hands on original sources. Diaries, chronicles, despatches, laws. Not in their original forms, as a rule. Printed and edited and annotated, but all the same, something that was written actually at the time. Even then, though, I haven't a hope in hell of discovering anything new. The ground's far too well sieved for that. Well, I suppose a mere undergraduate can't expect to make discoveries. But even professional historians seem to spend their lives slogging away at the minutest of subjects. Land tenure in East Suffolk before the Conquest. That's what one of my tutors got his doctorate for after five years' hard slog. Sometimes I think that I'd like to be a professional historian, but the prospect of all that grind – yuck! But what you're doing is detective work, not research. You're looking for real people; and when you find them, your discoveries will be important.'

'Only to me,' suggested Beverley.

'That's all that matters. I envy you, I really do. To have such a subject: your own grandfather.'

Beverley looked curiously at Luke. From the moment of their first meeting he had done his best to give the impression of being a good-natured fool. But she already suspected that he was intelligent – after all, he would hardly have got a place at Oxford otherwise – and now it seemed to her that beneath his banter was a fundamental seriousness.

'You're an idiot,' she said mildly. 'If you decided to make history your career, you could find a subject on your own doorstep that wouldn't be a grind at all.'

'And what's that?'

'The same as mine, of course. I'm only investigating the life of one child – or perhaps two,' she added, remembering that the career of Mairi McEwan might also be of interest. 'But you could see what became of the whole group. Every child who passed through your great-grandfather's hands. A fascinating piece of social history. And if your grandmother has treated every would-be researcher in the way she's treated me, you'd be treading virgin territory.'

There was a very long silence. Luke twisted the piece of paper between his fingers before looking up to stare at Beverley.

'It's odd,' he said at last. 'Five minutes ago I didn't have the foggiest idea what I wanted to do with myself. Then you throw out a casual suggestion and I realise that that's what I've been wanting to do all my life. Well, ever since I was fourteen, at least.'

Luke being serious was a completely different person from Luke the light-hearted. Beverley found his gaze disconcerting. Her suggestion had not been entirely casual, but rather was prompted by an insight into his character. It was her turn to put on an act of light-heartedness.

'I owed you one,' she said, smiling. 'Gesture of

appreciation of favour received, as Mr Chisholm might have said. And when you're a professor of history and publishing your big book I shall expect a dedication.'

Luke held out the paper on which he had copied the letter to Mr Blair. 'Will you write down your address and phone number in London?' he asked. 'Granny threw your letter away in disgust before you arrived. I'd like to know how to get in touch.'

'So that I can tell you where Wee Jamie came from, if I ever find out?' she asked teasingly.

'That would be interesting. But mostly so that I can look you up, if I may. I'll be getting some kind of a job in the long vacation. In London, it could be.' The look he gave her made it obvious why London had suddenly become attractive. 'You really are quite something, you know. I mean – '

'Talking of London, I have to get back there tonight.' Beverley interrupted him vigorously. 'And since this extraordinary vessel doesn't exactly move at the speed of light . . .'

'Sure. Right.' Luke stood up and untied the punt. As he propelled it back to the boathouse with surprising speed, he chattered in his earlier bantering manner. Only when the time came to say goodbye did he hesitate in a way which Beverley had no difficulty in interpreting. He was wondering whether he might kiss her.

She answered the unspoken question with a business-like move into the Ferrari; but as she drove out of Oxford she smiled to herself at the encounter. Since her arrival in England she had applied herself conscientiously to her main research. There had been plenty of conversation – with librarians, archivists, oldest inhabitants, parish clergy – but no true social contacts. Luke was the first person of approximately her own age to show any interest in her as a young woman since her departure from Sydney, and it was impossible not to feel warmed by it. From the moment when she first set eyes on him she had enjoyed his cheery grin; and the hint of some-thing more serious beneath deepened her interest. If he did look her up in London . . .

162

As to that, she would have to wait and see. She turned her thoughts instead to what she had discovered with Luke's help. Her smile faded as she considered the inadequacy of her grandfather's registration and Mrs Dancy's secretiveness. If Wee Jamie had indeed been a destitute guttersnipe, as Luke assumed, the lack of information was perhaps not surprising. But such a background didn't square with the memory of a castle. His mother had told him that he was lord of the castle. Whether or not that was a true memory and whether or not there was ever a real castle, somewhere or other there must be hidden the reason for his certainty. And perhaps not hidden only by the dusty overlay of time, but concealed deliberately by someone who, all those years ago, might have stood to gain from a little boy's disappearance.

Beverley tutted to herself as she reached the motorway and put her foot down on the accelerator. She was being melodramatic again, blowing up her suspicions of the long-dead head of an orphanage merely because his daughter proved unhelpful. It was important to stick to facts, and in that respect her visit had been a success. She had a date of birth. She had that inserted name, McEwan, to puzzle over. And she had the mystery of Mairi McEwan – who might or might not be her own great-aunt – to consider. Mairi might even still be alive. Even if she were not, by following her forward through her life, it might in the end be possible to track her back. There were two chances now, not one, of finding a way through the maze which surrounded the castle.

6

The time of Beverley's visit to Newport, Rhode Island, was approaching. Her father had confirmed the invitation and the date, and Beverley herself worked out an itinerary which would allow her to fly from Scotland after spending some time there on her research. Taking her

163

car from London to Inverness on the Motorail, she drove gradually south towards Edinburgh, pausing whenever she reached the home of one of the immigrants on her list. Her grandfather's history, although naturally of most personal interest, was one of many to be investigated and she took it in its turn rather than making any special expedition.

So it was in July, several weeks after her visit to Oxford, that she walked up Edinburgh's Royal Mile and came to a halt outside a tall building whose forbidding black stone was relieved by only the smallest of windows. A hundred years of polishing had rendered the brass plate beside the door illegibly smooth and shining. Abandoning the attempt to decipher the letters, she went up the steps and rang the bell.

Inside the reception office a middle-aged secretary confirmed that these were still the premises of Blair, Honeyman and Blair. Beverley, aware of the tenacity with which legal firms all over the world held on to names whose owners had long since departed, was not unduly surprised at this. Less to be expected was the discovery that there was still a Mr Blair amongst the four current partners.

'I'd like to see him, please,' said Beverley.

The simple request caused a considerable amount of dither. For someone to come in off the street near the end of the working day, without an appointment, without any previous contact or even a letter outlining the problem to be considered: it would seem that such a thing had never happened before. But when Beverley, pressing the point with polite firmness, suggested that Mr Blair might be asked to decide for himself whether he was willing to make time for her, the secretary reluctantly disappeared upstairs. Although the quill pen had given way to the typewriter, it appeared that an internal telephone system must smack too much of over-mechanisation.

For form's sake, perhaps, since no other client left the building during the period, Beverley was kept waiting for twenty minutes. When the secretary at last reappeared, clutching a bundle of signed letters and forms, the invitation to go upstairs was accompanied by ostentatious glances at the clock on the wall. No words were necessary to make clear her opinion that the unscheduled caller should be off the premises before five o'clock: six minutes away.

Mr Ian Blair, in contrast, appeared to have all the time in the world. Irrationally, Beverley expected all lawyers to be elderly, or at least middle-aged; and in this case she had subconsciously, against all reason, been hoping to meet an immensely aged Gordon Blair who had once delivered her grandfather to an orphanage. Reminding herself that the idea of such an encounter was ridiculous, she shook hands with a young man who could not be more than thirty.

Even his polite smile did not greatly animate the gravity of his expression. He had a soft, serious face, with steady grey eyes and thick, wavy fair hair. Like a doctor, he waited for her to explain the reason for her call.

Beverley had had time by now to learn that archivists and librarians, registrars and parish clerks were all impressed by pieces of paper rather than oral explanations. So she carried with her everywhere a folder containing the names of those early immigrants whose backgrounds she was studying, together with photocopies of some of the information she had so far gained. To the cover were clipped letters from her supervisor and the university librarian, intended to act as references. None of this, of course, had the slightest connection with her quest for her own family background; but on the assumption that a lawyer, too, might be reassured by indications of scholarship, she opened her folder on his desk as she began to explain her mission.

'Gordon Blair was my grandfather,' the young man said. 'But that's all the information I'm able to give you without looking through our files.' He glanced at his watch, although in a manner less ostentatiously aggressive than the receptionist. 'Mrs Fraser will be putting on her coat by now. If I ask her to stay, you're likely to get a speedy response that nothing is on record. So you might care to come back tomorrow afternoon, when we've had time to make a thorough search. Or, if you're in a hurry to be away from Edinburgh, you could come up to the muniment room with me now, and we'll see what we can find.'

'I'm not so much in a hurry to go as impatient for information,' Beverley confessed. 'If you're willing . . . I'd be very grateful. I've no right – '

'It's a pleasure,' said Mr Blair. 'Almost everyone who comes through that door has some tricky legal problem for me to solve. And, I don't know why it should happen, almost everyone who comes through that door is over fifty. To be confronted by an elegant young lady requesting nothing more than a little information is a treat to be prolonged.' His expression remained as grave as when she had first entered the room and, before Beverley had time to decide whether she was being teased, he stood up and stretched himself as though to expand his body after a day bent over a desk. 'I'm going to ask that you should call me Ian, in spite of the briefness of our acquaintance,' he said. 'Mr Blair would be obliged to set that clock contraption ticking and charge you by the minute. Ian, however, can do what he likes out of office hours.'

Beverley was about to agree with a smile when she was startled to see that he was removing his jacket. Were they alone in the building? Mrs Fraser, presumably, had departed. Did he have partners on the premises? Or . . . But even as the lurid possibilities raced through her mind, she was forced to stop and laugh at herself. Hanging the jacket over the back of his chair, he took from a cupboard a straight cotton coat of the type worn by warehousemen.

'Experience teaches that eighty-year-old files defend themselves against disturbance by bombarding any attacker with dust,' he told her. 'May I offer you similar protection?'

Dressed in the same shrouded fashion, Beverley followed the lawyer up two flights of stairs, each narrower than the one before, into an attic under a pitched roof.

'Anything between fifty and a hundred years old should be in here,' Ian told her. 'Assuming, that is, that it was ever one of our cases, and that it has been considered to be closed. Now then, Jamieson, you said.'

It took him a surprisingly short time to find the rack he needed and to search through the almost identical parcels of papers, enclosed in brown folders and tied with ribbon. Regretfully he shook his head. 'We seem never to have had a client of that name at all. I'll look downstairs as well, of course, in the current cases, but it hardly seems likely.'

'Would it be under your grandfather's own name?' suggested Beverley. 'If he took an active part in making the arrangements . . .'

'Whatever he did, it would only be on behalf of someone else, and would be filed that way. Unless, of course, you're suggesting that the boy was some personal connection of his own.'

Beverley flushed slightly, since she had wondered exactly that. Taking the flush as an answer, Ian moved to another rack, but once again shook his head after only a short time. 'His will is here, and copies of some property deeds. Nothing of significance. He didn't, for example, leave his fortune to any young Jamieson.'

'Obviously not. I didn't – ' Beverley saw that there was no need to protest and paused for a moment in disappointment. Only now did she realise how greatly she had pinned her hopes on making a significant discovery here. The lawyer waited politely for her to bring the investigation to a close.

'McEwan,' she said suddenly. 'I won't ask you for any more files after this, but might you have one for McEwan?'

7

So startled did Ian Blair appear to be by Beverley's abrupt request that he looked at her with a kind of doubt: not doubt about whether he might have such a file, but about whether he should answer her question. 'Why should you suddenly produce such a name?'

'Your grandfather took a little girl called Mairi McEwan to the same orphanage on the same day,' she explained. 'And when I looked in the register a little while ago, I found that on the next line to hers, someone had written the name James Jamieson and then inserted a word in the middle to make it James McEwan Jamieson. Yet my grandfather didn't seem to know he'd ever had a middle name. And it seems odd that a surname should be used as a forename. It's something that rich people do, to show that they claim descent from two good families. But not destitute guttersnipes.'

'The suggestion would be that it might be his mother's family name, you mean?'

'Yes. Or it could be the other way round. Suppose he was illegitimate. He might only have been entitled to use his mother's surname. But she could have added his father's when he was christened, out of, well, out of a kind of pride, perhaps.'

'I see you're a brave researcher. Not afraid of any truth that may tumble out.'

'The worse his background, the greater his triumph in escaping from it,' said Beverley. But it was fact, not speculation, in which she was interested. 'We're talking about McEwan. You know the name, don't you?' From his reaction to the first mention of it, she was sure of that.

'Well, of course. It's quite a common name in Scotland.'

'But you know more than that. You had a client.'

'I must be a little careful now. The need returns for confidentiality over a client's affairs. Perhaps after all Ian will have to withdraw and allow Mr Blair to take his place.'

'But it's almost eighty years ago!' exclaimed Beverley. 'Your client can't possibly be alive still. There must be some kind of statute of limitations, some moment when living law cases become dead history.'

'Does history ever die? As lawyers, we have a continuing relationship with a family. Generations of McEwans, generations of Blairs. For more than a hundred and fifty years. Not necessarily, of course, the McEwans in whom you may be interested. But should there prove to be a connection, loyalty, I fear, must override even the delight of being in your company.'

'But you could look,' pleaded Beverley. 'You're only recognising a name, right? I mean, you don't *know* what's in your files. Especially seventy, eighty years ago. I'll stay out of the room if you like. Or anyway, I'll promise not to peep over your shoulder. You could judge for yourself what needs to be kept secret, but tell me if there's anything relevant.' 'Relevant' was a word which Beverley had never had much cause to use in Australia, but in England it had frequently proved vital in extracting information.

There was a very long pause. At the end of it, the lawyer brushed down his coat and held open the door of the attic.

Beverley looked at him anxiously, not knowing what new argument she could put forward. Her reward was the slightest of flushes on Ian's serious face.

'A different set of files,' he said. 'Everything up here refers to business that is finished. There's another room downstairs. I'll ask you to wait in my office this time, if you don't mind. I shall have to use my discretion as to what I'm able to tell you.'

'Of course.' For a moment Beverley allowed her anxiety to show in making one last appeal. 'But it means such a lot to me. And it was so long ago.'

'I'll see what I can do.' His manner, which had so surprisingly unbent when she first arrived, was stiff again. He followed her down to his office and left her there, closing the door behind him.

How odd it was that everyone should be so secretive! But no, Beverley told herself, all lawyers would undoubtedly behave with the same caution. Mrs Dancy's jealous guarding of documents was unforgivable, but it was right that Ian Blair should first discover what information he might or might not possess before deciding whether to share it with her. She had come without warning, to ask about events occurring long before he was born. It would be ridiculous to think that he was trying to cover up any kind of misdeed on his grandfather's part. If only, though, he would not be so long.

When at last he reappeared, her heart leapt with hope as she saw that he was carrying a bundle of papers. His expression was puzzled and doubtful at the same time.

'Tell me again the names of the two children – your grandfather and the little girl.'

'Jamie and Mairi. Mairi spelt in an odd way.'

'M-a-i-r-i? Not so odd in this part of the world.' He set down on the desk the papers he was holding and put on his jacket before sitting once more in the chair behind his desk. Beverley was unable to control her impatience.

'You've found something, right? What is it?'

'I've found something, yes. What its significance is, I can't guess. And for that reason I ought to investigate a little more before . . . but on the other hand, as you said yourself, it was a long time ago and the principals are dead.' He was talking to himself, trying to persuade himself to a course of action which half of his mind knew to be unwise. Beverley kept very quiet until at last he sighed.

'The file is that of a young man called Fergus McEwan,' he said with a new briskness. 'A boy, to start with. He went out to New Zealand under a farming cadet scheme. From the little I've had time to read, he seems to have been very happy there. Twice a year he wrote letters to this address. They were sent to my grandfather, with the request that they should be forwarded to Jamie and Mairi. It's quite clear from the context that he was their elder brother. He seems to have intended them to join him in New Zealand when he was twenty-one: he had the promise of a farm of his own there. Before that time, though, he joined the Anzac expeditionary force. He died at Passchendaele.'

'How come you still have the letters here? Why weren't they forwarded?'

'I don't know,' confessed Ian. 'Presumably because my grandfather didn't know where the two children were.'

'But he took them to the orphanage himself!'

'He might have lost touch after that. If they were sent abroad, and no good records kept; or if they ran away.'

Beverley remembered that they had indeed both run away. It was to be presumed that they, unlike Fergus, had been unhappy. But that had not happened straight away; and in any case it failed to explain why the letters had not even been passed on to Mr Chisholm at the orphanage. Nor, it seemed, had Fergus been allowed to learn that contact with the two younger children had been lost. She could feel herself becoming angry, as she had been angry in Oxford, at the thought that there had been some hanky-panky somewhere in her grandfather's life. It was frustrating that she could not quite put her finger on it. For the time being, she must remind herself that Ian could not be held to blame for anything that had happened.

'If Jamie was Fergus McEwan's brother,' she said slowly, 'then he must have been a McEwan himself, and not a Jamieson at all.'

'Not necessarily.'

'Why not?'

Ian didn't answer at once. 'I think you'll have to leave this one with me,' he said at last. 'I need to study the case before I can deal with questions on it. I'm not trying to brush you off. I'll be happy to reopen the discussion later, when I know the ground.'

'So Mr Blair has taken over from Ian.' Beverley sighed with a rueful smile. 'Well, you've been very helpful. Thanks a lot.' She paused, before chancing her luck yet again. 'Just one last question. A check for me. Will you

171

tell me Fergus's home address, before he went to New Zealand? If it confirms what my grandfather told me, then I shall know we're on the right track.' If she was giving the impression of greater knowledge than she in fact possessed, it was no more than Ian Blair's excessive caution deserved.

He hesitated again. After waiting for a moment, she shrugged her shoulders.

'Forget it, then. I can check direct with the McEwans. All of them, if necessary, until I track down your lot.'

As she had expected, he was horrified by the suggestion, but realised that the only way to stop her carrying out her threat was to supply the information she needed.

'Fergus McEwan was born and brought up in Lochandar Castle. It would, of course, be quite improper for you to contact the family with any suggestion that I had given you an introduction.'

Lochandar Castle! A castle! Beverley hardly heard what Ian was saying. So triumphantly sure was she that she was on the right track that her only anxiety now was to get away.

'It checks,' she said. 'Right on.' It was tempting to clap her hands in delight. 'You've been very kind, Mr Blair . . . Ian. Sparing me your time and interest.' She stood up, unable to conceal her smile of success.

'Just a minute, before you go.' Ian also leapt to his feet. 'Will you give me your address? And telephone number?'

'Yes, of course. In case you find yourself able to pass on any more information, you mean?' She bent over the desk to write down her address.

'Well, that, yes, naturally. But it would be nice . . . I come to London once a month for a committee. If I might get in touch . . . Perhaps we could have dinner?'

Beverleywas surprised by his interest – but pleased as well. It was not so long since Luke Dancy had made the same kind of request, and she recognised a compliment in each case. There was more than a minor social success, however, to send her humming with satisfaction along the Royal Mile. She was on her way to her grandfather's birthplace. Everything else was mysterious, but of this one fact she felt sure. The castle was real – and soon she would be inside it.

8

Beverley drove to Lochandar as a tourist. Sussing it out, she thought to herself, and laughed at the idea. As though she were some kind of detective! And yet that was how she was beginning to see herself. At the beginning of her investigation she had been concerned only to track down the castle which had provided Wee Jamie Jamieson with his lifelong obsession, and it was possible that she was just about to succeed in this. But each stage of the enquiry was increasing her suspicions about the events of the past. Why should that helpful Ian have so suddenly reverted to being cagey Mr Blair? What was he trying to conceal?

It was natural, she told herself, that a lawyer should be cautious when it came to revealing the affairs of his clients, long dead though they might be. And perhaps it was equally understandable that an old woman, revering her father almost as a saint, should keep his study as a shrine which was not to be desecrated by vulgar curiosity. But each encounter had reinforced Beverley's feeling that there was something not straightforward about this period of her grandfather's life. Until she knew what it was, she was not prepared to introduce herself to the owner of the castle as a possible relation.

Lochandar Castle was marked on her road map in the coloured ink which denoted a place of historic or artistic interest, open to the public. But so remote was its position north-west of Perth that, as she drove across the moors and towards the mountains, she feared that she might, conspicuously, be its only visitor that day. And if it attracted few tourists, it was possible that the work of guiding or guarding the rooms might be undertaken by

173

the family. When the building came into sight, Beverley braked the Ferrari to a halt in order to plan the best approach. Might she be putting herself in a false position by appearing once as a stranger and perhaps soon afterwards as a possible member of the family?

At the point where she had stopped, the road ran beside a loch. No wind stirred its dark, peaty water, so that it provided a mirror reflection of the castle which was built on an escarpment of natural stone above its further bank. It would be exaggerating to describe the building as beautiful, because it consisted of two distinct elements which fought rather than blended with each other: an old stone castle to which a more recent wing had been added. But striking, yes, it could certainly be called striking.

Even the early section was not all of a piece. Intrigued by her grandfather's memories, Beverley had bought and read books on castle architecture since her arrival in Britain, and she viewed this one now with a historian's eye. With some confidence she identified as sixteenth-century the sheer stone walls which had been built to the shape of a triangle, their formidable battlements and machicolations testifying to the practical necessity of keeping enemies at bay. But at one corner of the triangle a round tower, higher than the rest of the structure and very much plainer in design, was perhaps as much as two hundred years older.

Here, however, Beverley's interest in architectural history was swept away by the memory of her last conversation with her grandfather. The tower! If Lochandar Castle were indeed his birthplace, then this must be the tower whose memory had haunted the whole of his adult life, inspiring the design of Beverley's own home as well as the name of the family business.

The sight of the tower swept away her hesitation. She had to see it, to step inside it, to climb the stairs to the nursery in which Wee Jamie had once upon a time eaten hot oatcakes in front of a peat fire. She drove on round the loch and was relieved to discover that at the foot of the steep and rocky incline which led up to the castle from the landward side there were parked two tourist coaches as well as a handful of private cars. In such a crowd she could be anonymous.

The passengers from one of the coaches were waiting in the Great Hall for the tour in progress to come to an end. To judge from their accents and topics of conversation, they had travelled in a party from the United States in order to tour Scotland. Beverley bought a guide to the castle as well as an entrance ticket, and sat down to study it while she waited.

Of most immediate interest was the genealogical tree at the back of the booklet. With occasional dotted lines to indicate gaps in the records, it traced the male descent of the lairds of Lochandar since the fourteenth century. Beverley, whose interest was in the past eighty years, began at the bottom.

The present laird, she learned, was David McEwan, who had been born in 1956 and already had a young son to ensure that the line would continue unbroken. His father, Robert, had been born in 1928, and his grandfather, Malcolm, in 1880. Malcolm had been a second son, his elder brother, Donald, having died without issue in 1905. There was no mention of Jamie, whose birthdate Beverley had now confirmed as being in 1906; nor did the names Fergus or Mairi appear.

Looking more closely, Beverley saw that no women's names were included at all. At any other time she might have felt indignant at the omission, but now it prompted another deduction. Donald and Malcolm were of the right generation to have fathered a boy of Wee Jamie's age; but more likely was the possibility that they had had a sister, not mentioned here, a McEwan daughter who had married a Jamieson. Never entitled to inherit Lochandar herself, she would have been left out of this simplified family tree because the male line had continued to bear heirs, with the consequence that her children would never inherit either.

That solution, if it represented the truth of the case, would be such a simple one that for a moment Beverley wondered why she had allowed herself to become so indignant about the suspicion that her grandfather had been cheated of his heritage in some way. Perhaps it was only because of the difficulties she had encountered in eliciting straightforward answers to her questions. But no, she told herself, the doubts could not be explained away as easily as that. Fergus and Mairi had the McEwan surname, although Jamie did not. Since Fergus believed Jamie to be his brother, that discrepancy itself was odd. Besides, would a laird of Lochandar have allowed his nephew and niece, if that was what they were, to be shipped abroad as destitute emigrants? Surely family pride would have ensured that orphaned relations would be provided with a home.

There was something else as well. Wee Jamie's upbringing in Lochandar Castle – if in the end this did prove to have been his home – would have been natural enough if his mother was a McEwan, perhaps widowed when young. But his suspicion, which he had expressed almost as a certainty, that he should have inherited the castle could not be so easily explained away.

Beverley reminded herself that small boys dream dreams and invent fantasies. If she could not completely convince herself, she did at least succeed in pursuing her quest with a mind more open than before as the guide to the castle's treasures called the new group together and began the tour.

Even before she entered the Great Hall, the starkness of the castle's stone walls and the bleakness of the land around it had suggested to Beverley that its owners might have inherited a long pedigree but not much wealth. She was not expecting to be shown great works of art, and there were to be no surprises.

Those parts of the old castle, the triangle of stone, which were on the public tour, were not furnished as a family home but decked out as an exhibition for tourists. The walls were covered either with tapestries or with hunting and fishing trophies: huge salmon were suspended in glass cases and the antlers of once-majestic stags spread across the walls as their stuffed heads looked down with curling lips at the admiring or disapproving

176

trippers. Suits of armour and a collection of clan tartans were presented as displays, without any pretence of family connection. In a large banqueting hall, though, a long and roughly-hewn table was scarred in a manner which suggested that convivial feasts over many centuries had ended with the hurling of dirks into the wood as though it were a dart-board; whilst, on a higher floor, the heavy draperies of tester beds indicated that they had been chosen for their efficiency in guarding against draughts. In each room there was a huge stone fireplace: but the castle must always, Beverley felt, have been unbearably cold.

She waited eagerly to reach the tower. This was the last part of the old castle to be visited in the tour. A round guard-room at ground level had been decorated with shields and weapons arranged in geometric patterns. The artistry with which the daggers and pikes, swords and muskets were grouped in circles and segments had all the satisfying symmetry of a rose window.

Beverley looked hopefully for a staircase; but if any door existed, it must have been hidden behind one of four long banners which hung from ceiling to floor, and the tour guide made no mention of upper rooms. Wee Jamie's nursery, if it was somewhere above her head, was not on public display.

The group moved on to the Victorian extension. This had been built on lower ground; and although the guide referred to it as 'the new wing', it was virtually a separate building, with only a covered staircase linking its ground floor to that of the old castle. The difference in atmosphere prompted one of the Americans to ask immediately the question which had been on the tip of Beverley's own tongue.

'Does the family still live at Lochandar?'

'Och, aye.' The guide, a plump lady whose kilt gave her a square appearance, had from the start spoken with an accent which Beverley suspected was as contrived as the exhibition of clan tartans, broad enough to convey a satisfyingly ethnic impression, but at the same time clearly enough enunciated to aid comprehension. 'The laird and wee Rabbie are in residence in the old castle. But his father and grandfather and great-grandfather all lived in this new wing; it was his great-grandfather who built it, and it's not been greatly changed since.'

Beverley found that easy to believe as she moved with the rest of the group through the dark-panelled rooms. The Victorian laird who planned this extension had perhaps effected an increase in his own comfort, but without giving thought to light or beauty. While the stone castle was chilly, this new wing was stuffy. Large windows in such an exposed spot would have let in the cold; so the openings were small and almost completely obscured with heavy curtains. The pictures on the walls, with the exception of a pair of chieftains in colourful plaids, were large and yellow with varnish, depicting stags or horses or dogs or dead game birds hanging from hooks. For three generations, it would appear, the lairds of Lochandar had been content to live in this gloom. Beverley wondered whether the present laird, in the old castle, had done better or worse for himself.

Once the tour was over she considered what her next step was to be. There was no town or village nearby in which she might hope to find some ninety-year-old inhabitant with a memory of young children playing in the castle at the turn of the century. Her best hope would seem to lie back in Edinburgh in the General Register Office. But would she have time to call there before setting off for Prestwick and her trans-Atlantic flight? What a fool she had been not to go straight to Edinburgh from Oxford instead of keeping rigidly to an itinerary worked out before she had ever heard of Blair, Honeyman and Blair. The discovery of Lochandar made her determined to solve the mystery of why her grand-father's name did not appear in the family tree.

There would just be time next morning, she decided, to check the records. Working backwards from the time at which she had to report for her flight, she reckoned she could allow herself thirty minutes in the General Register Office from the moment it opened its doors. If everything went smoothly, that should be long enough to find details of Wee Jamie's birth, and perhaps Fergus's as well.

Her first task when she arrived next morning was to discover the district in which Lochandar Castle was situated and fill in the request for the appropriate register. It seemed to Beverley that this had only taken her a few moments, but on putting in her application she was told that she was too late. Someone else was already studying the same register behind the closed doors of the search room.

'Could I ask him or her, whoever it is, to let me have just ten minutes?' Beverley pleaded. 'I have to catch a plane; I may not be back in Edinburgh for weeks.'

'I'm sorry.' The answer, although sympathetic, was definite. 'Searchers who have paid their fees have the right to remain undisturbed.'

'Of all the records you must have here, that just this one should be unavailable!' But Beverley could see that there was no point in arguing.

'We can do the search for you, if you have sufficient information, and post you the result.' The registry officer pushed a printed scale of fees across the counter, while Beverley scribbled down all the information she possessed about her grandfather.

How unconvincing it looked when seen as the guideline for a search. Wee Jamie's birth had been recorded in the register of the Orphans' New Life Society, but could she trust either the man who had supplied the information or the man who had written it down? She must assume his birthplace to be Lochandar Castle, but it was only a guess. She could not be sure of his surname, and so had to offer Jamieson and McEwan as alternatives. If it was McEwan, his father might, or might not, have been either Donald or Malcolm. If it was Jamieson, his mother might possibly be a McEwan by birth. Beverley herself, given time, had sufficient motivation to search widely until she found the answer, but she knew that the fee she was paying would cover only a limited number of years and areas. Still, it was the best that could be done for the moment, and perhaps she would be lucky.

It was only later that day, as the plane took off, that she realised the explanation for what had seemed an extraordinary coincidence. It was not that Edinburgh was full of people who were trying to trace their ancestors from the area round Lochandar. Ian Blair had said that he would need to study the case, and his studies would have taken him straight to the old registers. He would be looking for records not just of Jamie but of Fergus as well, and no doubt of their parents.

Beverley felt a moment's uneasiness as she realised that at this very moment he might be discovering something that she needed to know. Would he pass his discoveries on to her? There was no reason why he should conceal anything, and yet Beverley was becoming so suspicious about the past that she found it difficult to trust anybody. At least he could not alter the registers. Could he? No, of course not. Her own requested search would be made as soon as he had finished his. It would be interesting to compare the two versions.

9

The smell of the sea! Beverley opened the window of the cab which was driving her from the airport and breathed deeply, her spirits rising with every mile which brought her nearer to Newport. For three months, since her arrival in Britain, she had been land-locked. She knew better than to hope that her father would allow her to crew for any of his races, for, unlike her own *Flying Dutchman*, a twelve-metre yacht demanded a strong team of men to manage it with a precision drilled into them by months of practice. But she was approaching one of the great yachting centres of the world, and just to feel an ocean breeze slapping against her cheeks and lifting her hair would be a delight.

Her father had spoken of renting a cottage. So when the cab turned off Bellevue Avenue through a pair of gilded wrought-iron gates, skirted round a circular marble pool in which a fountain was playing and came to a standstill in front of what appeared to be a palace, she made no move to get out.

'Here y'are,' said the driver; but Beverley shook her head.

'It's the cottage I want,' she said. 'Is it somewhere in the grounds?'

The taxi driver laughed in the manner of a man who had enjoyed the same joke often before. 'This *is* the cottage,' he assured her. 'May look like a palace to you'n me. But the folk who built these places so's they could get out of New York in the hot summers, they kidded themselves they were coming here to live the simple life. Gang of Aussies renting the place now. You one of them?'

'I suppose so,' said Beverley, continuing to stare at the massive white building. Double rows of pillars supported a portico in front of its main section. This alone was larger than the house in which Beverley had been brought up, but was flanked by two wings of almost equal size. An ornamental balustrade edged the flat roof and every window was fringed by an elaborate fretwork of stone. Statues stood in arched niches, whilst the terrace wrapped by the three sections of the house was divided by avenues of white stone urns, bright with flowers. Cottage, indeed! What *did* her father think he was doing?

Beverley picked up the single bag which she had packed for what she expected to be a few days of casual living and walked towards the mansion and through its open front door. The portico dwarfed her and the entrance hall, with its curved double staircase and wide expanse of immaculate red carpet, made her feel ill-groomed. The first door she opened at random led to a ballroom in which crystal chandeliers hung from a painted ceiling. It was the largest room she had ever seen in a private house.

'Brought your balldress?' The sound of her father's

voice startled her. 'Lovely to see you, Bev. Come and get a drink.'

It came as little surprise to find that her father's crew had congregated in the kitchen of the mansion rather than in any of the grand entertaining rooms. After the first exuberant greetings were over, she sat quietly in a corner, sipping her drink and listening to the discussion of the day's practice and the tactics to be pursued next morning. The sound of Australian voices made her feel homesick. England and Scotland had, on the whole, been friendly towards her during the past few weeks, but still she was a stranger there, a foreigner. Here, for a moment, even in such extraordinary surroundings, she felt at home.

'Breath of air, Bev?'

Beverley smiled at her father and walked out with him to a terrace at the rear of the mansion. An avenue of statues led them to a summerhouse in the shape of a temple. Father and daughter sat down together and listened in silence to the ocean at the foot of the cliff. Every few seconds they could hear a wave gathering itself together to rear upwards before rolling in to break on the rocky shore, and then to be sucked back with a rattle of pebbles just as the next wave began to swell. The sound was soothing in its repetitiveness; a lullaby for a jet-lagged traveller.

'The landlubber's idea of what the ocean sounds like.' Jock Jamieson's voice held a touch of regret. 'Bit different from life out there, isn't it? The hard slapping of the waves, and the drenching spray, and the wind. I shall miss the wind. The best opponent I ever had; and the best friend.'

'Miss it?' queried Beverley, startled.

'One of the reasons I'm glad you've come over. Better than the telephone, talking like this. I'm selling the *Jocasta*.'

'And buying another yacht?'

'Nope. Something I realised at Fremantle. In the big league nowadays – challenging for the America's Cup, that sort of thing – the day of the owner-helmsman is

182

over. Costs are too high. Only a syndicate can bear them, and a syndicate wants a professional to look after its investment.'

'You're better than any professional.'

'Uh-uh. I'm one of the best of the second best. Doing it for fun isn't a winning recipe any more. Mind you, this week's races we *have* to win, to get a good price. But after that – anyway, I haven't the time. Your grandfather's death made a difference.'

'You mean you've got to spend more time on the business?'

'Haven't got to, but I'm going to. Suited us both while Dad was alive that I shouldn't spend too much time in the office; and there are good managers. But now . . . I ought to give it more attention. I've got ideas for new projects, too. I'll enjoy it okay.'

'You won't be able to keep away from the water,' Beverley predicted. 'You'd better buy yourself a twelve-footer to replace *Jocasta* and I'll race you out to the Heads every Sunday.'

'Might take you up on that. Except that I've got something else to tell you. Goes with the change of lifestyle. I'm getting married again.'

'I'm glad.' Beverley's exclamation was sincere, and she kissed her father enthusiastically. She had felt for a long time that a succession of glamorous female friends did little to save him from loneliness. 'Do I know her?'

'Jan Macaulay. Saw a lot of her twelve years ago. Then she went off to Cambridge as a professor's wife. Came back a few months ago without the professor. We're planning a wedding in the summer. October or November.'

'I'll be there.'

'How about yourself, Bev? Still fancy-free?'

'Of course. What should have changed?'

'I wondered if you'd seen anything of Ken before you flew over here? At Wimbledon?'

'Wimbledon!' Beverley gasped with amazement. 'I didn't even realise . . . Just shows how hard I've been working!' Since leaving her London flat for Scotland she had neither watched television nor bought a newspaper and, unfamiliar with the programme of sporting events in England, had not realised what she was missing. 'How did he get on?'

'Went out to Becker in the third round. He's been rating a few gossip paragraphs as well as tennis reports. I thought you might have noticed.'

'No. Tell me.'

'Some young girl who's just defected from behind the Iron Curtain. Ken seems to have appointed himself as protector and coach and mixed-doubles partner.'

'I imagine the gossip writer suggested another role as well. No skin off my nose. I told you before.'

'Good.' Jock slipped his arm round Beverley's waist and hugged her affectionately. 'Now then, what about all this work you're pretending to do?'

'Pretending! Dad, you won't believe it, but I've found Gramps's castle. I've been there.'

'Go on!'

'Yes. And there's something not quite straight about it. I haven't sorted it out yet, but he should never have been sent to Australia. It could have been just a muddle, but I think there was some dirty business. I'm going to get to the bottom of it.'

'You mean that he really ought to have owned the castle, like he thought?'

'No, not that, because he had an elder brother. But that's part of the dirty work; that he had family, but was snatched away from everyone who might have looked after him. There seems to have been a sister, for example, who was sent to Canada. While I'm over here I want to see if I can track her down.' Beverley gave her father the details of what she had learned.

'Go off tomorrow then, or the day after, to make sure that you're back in time.'

'In time for what?'

'The ball. If we win this week, and sell the boat, we shall lay on a celebration to make the Newport Four Hundred think they've never known what a proper party was. I was only joking about the balldress, though. I know better than to think I could get that gang in there into penguin suits. We shall have a bi-centennial fancy dress do. Come as a convict. You'll look smashing wearing just a very few rags.'

'It's a date.' Suddenly tired after her day on the move, Beverley stood up. 'I'll skip supper. I was stuffed with food on the plane. An early night. Goodnight, Dad.' She hugged him as they kissed. 'Congratulations about Jan. And thanks for asking me here.'

Tired though she was, she lay awake for a little while after going to bed, thinking about Ken. It sounded as though this affair might be more serious than any earlier ones. Did she care? She allowed herself to visualise his tall, sun-tanned body, the fair hairs on his freckled legs, the hard muscles of his playing arm, the close-cropped hair which grew straight up from his scalp, and the easy grin which changed to tight-lipped determination whenever he was on the tennis court. Had she secretly hoped that one day, when he had won enough championships and made his fortune, Ken would return to see whether she had waited for him?

The answer was reassuring. What she had told her father in Sydney Harbour three months earlier was the truth. However exciting Ken might be as a lover, she was not prepared to hang on to the coat-tails of his talent. When she was ready to marry, she would look for a husband whose career would mesh with her own way of life; but she was not looking yet. Drowsy with satisfaction, she slipped into sleep.

Next morning she awoke before anyone else was stirring. Her bedroom was a corner one; a light lemon froth of a room whose four-poster bed was frilled with gauze. Briefly she remembered the beds, similar in size and shape, which she had seen in Lochandar Castle. Everything about the castle had been heavy, designed to cushion the owner against cold and damp. Here, by contrast, in the perfect climate of a summer resort, decorative beauty could be used for its own sake: luxury need have no function other than to delight the eye.

The thought of Lochandar reminded her how fortunate

185

she was. When so many people in the world were hungry or unhappy or merely bored, she, without having done anything to deserve it, enjoyed the greatest gift that money could buy: the freedom to choose how she would spend her life.

How different it must have been for those two small children, Mairi and Jamie. Shipped half-way round the world without ever being consulted or reassured and without hope of ever returning home, they must have experienced not just misery but despair. *Ran away.* The laconic note at the bottom of Mr Chisholm's file cards stabbed at her heart. Poor little Mairi. Her passage across the Atlantic would have been far longer and far less comfortable than Beverley's. There was no loving father to greet her, no comfortable bed and hot bath, but only the unhappiness from which in the end she had tried to escape. Ran away. Where had she gone? Was she as successful as Jamie in making a good life for herself? Before the end of the week Beverley hoped to find out.

10

The first stage of Beverley's quest for Mairi McEwan was simpler than she had expected. The committee which was originally set up to find homes for immigrant orphans, and to keep an eye on their subsequent well-being, had not dissolved itself as the flow of children dried up but instead widened its scope. Until 1939 it continued as a reception organisation for immigrants of all ages, and even after that undertook the emergency wartime task of helping young British evacuees. Its records were not jealously guarded by a private individual but efficiently stored and catalogued in a public record office. Beverley had learned from Mr Chisholm's records the address to which Mairi had been sent as a foster-child, and was quickly able to confirm this.

Someone called Emily Rendall had been the committee

member responsible for Mairi, meeting her on arrival in Canada and handing her over soon afterwards to Mr and Mrs Brigg, who took her off to their farm in Saskatchewan. It seemed from the annual reports on her progress, which consisted mainly of questionnaires filled in by the Briggs, that she had not been visited for some years.

When Mrs Rendall at last met the child again, on her thirteenth birthday, she reported her as being hardworking but restless. An independence of nature, which had prompted her to ask for wages rather than to continue living as a daughter of the house, might well, in the opinion of the visitor, develop before long into rebellion; she did not expect the new arrangement to continue for more than a year or two. In the meantime, she noted, Mairi had expressed anxiety about her two brothers, and especially the younger one, Jamie. Attached to the report was a copy of a letter written to Mr Chisholm of the Orphans' New Life Society in England to request information. It appeared to have received no answer.

It was only a few months after the date of this report that Mairi was recorded as having run away. At first Mrs Brigg had accused her of theft; but later, under pressure, had agreed that the only money taken from the house was Mairi's accrued wages, which were being saved for her. The girl had committed no crime and so there was no need to track her down. She had simply disappeared and was never heard of again.

Beverley sat thoughtfully at the desk to which the papers had been brought. She had learned nothing new. The facts in front of her confirmed that Mairi was her own great-aunt, but she had felt sure of that even before arriving in Canada. Could she hope to learn anything by visiting the farm? It seemed unlikely. Mr and Mrs Brigg themselves must be dead by now, as she knew Mrs Rendall to be, and there had been no other child on the isolated farm who might have been entrusted with the runaway's secrets.

'How would I get to Saskatchewan?' she asked the desk clerk as she returned the papers to him.

'Hell of a way.' He found a map and showed her. 'And hell of a big place when you get there. Wilderness or prairie. Not what you'd call cosy. Which bit you thinking about?'

'Sounds as though it's in the middle of nowhere. The nearest place is called Weyburn.'

It took a little finding, but at last he jabbed his finger down on the southern part of the state. 'There you are; near the border.'

The map showed railway lines but not airports. Beverley considered the distance involved, and the likely complications of reaching the remote township. With so small a chance of discovering anything by a visit, it wasn't worth the journey. It was, after all, Jamie rather than his sister whose life she was investigating. Her present trip had brought her along a genuine trail, but now seemed to have reached a dead end.

'I suppose the farm would be on the telephone,' she said, talking almost to herself. The clerk, who had taken the file back from her, was clipping to it a card which he had removed before handing the folder over. Apparently it contained further information, because her helper, after studying it, shook his head.

'Doesn't exist,' he told her. 'Lot of these small homesteads were pulled down when the land was merged into bigger units.

'Oh.' That seemed to be that. There was, though, one practical step which she could usefully take. 'May I add something to the file?' she asked. 'My address and a note of my interest? Suppose the girl who was the subject of these notes suddenly bobs up to see what's on record about her, she might get in touch with me.'

She made the suggestion without any real hope. Mairi McEwan was hardly likely to start ferreting around after seventy years. Still, it couldn't do any harm. She tore a page from her notebook and wrote down her name and the address both of the temporary London flat and of her home in Sydney. Beneath them, picking her words

188

carefully, she added: 'Family connection. Able to provide further facts about Mairi McEwan and interested in learning more.'

'Sure, I can put that in.' But the clerk was still studying the card which Beverley had not been allowed to see. 'Seems there's been one enquiry on this case already,' he said. 'Not recent. Ten years ago. Another family connection.'

Beverley's eyes sparkled with excitement. 'That's exactly the sort of thing I wanted to know. Why wasn't it in the file?'

'Yellow card like this means reserved information. What you've seen is open access. Anyone can dig around. Reporters and such. Could be that someone doesn't want it known that he's related to an immigrant orphan.'

'Well, he won't mind me, because I'm related to her as well. Can you give me his name and address?'

'Sorry. He's marked it as confidential.'

'Oh, come on!' exclaimed Beverley. 'What was the point of leaving the details with you if no one was ever to know them?'

'Guess he hoped someone like you might turn up one day. But he wants to be in control of any contact. What I can do, with your say-so, is send this note you've left to the address we've got for him. Ten years old, mind you. Then he can get in touch with you if he wants to.'

'I shall be the other side of the Atlantic by then,' protested Beverley. 'I'm only in Canada for the day. Look, will you call him for me?'

'Could try, I suppose.' Still holding the file, the clerk disappeared into an office, returning ten minutes later.

'Not available,' he reported. 'It was an office number he left. I spoke to his secretary. He's on vacation in Europe. He calls her every two days, she says, so she'll tell him about you. He's on the move, touring, so she couldn't give you an address anyway.'

If this secretive gentleman was in Europe, it would be easy for him to make contact if he chose. And surely he would be curious. Beverley had to be content with that hope. There was nothing more to be done in Canada.

As she returned to Newport, Beverley shrugged off the mystery of the disappearing sister. It was Wee Jamie's childhood which she wanted to explore. Until a week ago she had been allowing the research needed for her thesis to determine where her travels should carry her; the background of her own grandfather had taken second place to that. But her priority had been changed by the visit to Ian Blair's office, and the sight of the castle. Jamie Jamieson's history had aroused her passionate interest, and from now on that would come first.

11

Beverley returned to England from her Rhode Island holiday refreshed in both body and spirit. Because little of the ocean racing could be seen from the land, her father had hired a small yacht from which she could watch at least the starts and finishes at close quarters. Wind and exercise had brought colour to her cheeks and an invigorating feeling of fitness. *Jocasta* won her class, and the ball which celebrated the event was voted the social success of the regatta.

That evening, in its magnificent setting, had provided the most memorable single occasion of the week; but just as enjoyable for Beverley had been the camaraderie of the Australian group. The raucous sing-song of their last evening together was still ringing in her ears as she unlocked her London front door and was brought back to earth by the silence of a flat which had been empty for the past month.

She dumped her bag in the hall and wandered around opening windows, although the heavy atmosphere of a city heatwave did little to freshen the air. The sight of the study made her laugh aloud. It contained a shelf filled with reference books which she had bought since arriving in England. A pile of folders containing notes on individuals. A less tidy pile of photo-copied pages of records, waiting to be sorted out. An assortment of notebooks, and two boxes of file cards containing facts that she was almost ready to feed into a computer. What did she think she was doing? The whole scene was out of character.

'Admit it,' she said aloud. 'You're not really a scholar. Acting the part of one, that's all.'

There was nothing bogus about her interest, and yet it hardly seemed compatible with what she thought of as real life. At home in Sydney she had a choice of activities and escorts every night. How extraordinary it was that she should not have felt lonely in England.

It was the week of cheerful company and the sound of Australian voices which made her conscious of her lack of social life in London. She went to plays and films and concerts, but always alone. It was partly because her research kept her on the move: partly, but not entirely. Although she had no close friends of her own in England, she was well-stocked with the names and addresses of friends of friends. A single telephone call would have been enough to introduce her to the network of expatriate Australians. Why had she never troubled to make such a call?

Putting this question to herself as she unpacked, she was startled by the sudden buzzing of her entryphone. Who could be calling on her at nine o'clock in the evening without notice? Indeed, who knew she was here?

There was an easy answer to the second question. Both Luke Dancy and Ian Blair had asked for her address. Beverley smiled with pleasure at the thought of seeing one of them again. Which one would it be? Which one did she hope it would be? Luke with his thread of seriousness beneath the froth? Or grave Ian with his shy smile of humour beneath the solemnity? Well, if she didn't answer the second, longer, buzz, she would never find out.

'You don't know me, Miss Jamieson.' The American voice which crackled through the speaker disappointed whichever hope she might have entertained. The system was not intended for long conversations but only for brief introduction. 'Name of Matt Schwartz. Grandson of Mairi McEwan.'

'Come on up.' As Beverley pressed the release and waited for her unexpected visitor to climb the stairs to her door, her eyes sparkled with excitement. To guard against disappointment, she had persuaded herself that a man so secretive about his own interest in Mairi McEwan would be unlikely to contribute to her search. But he had come, and he was the grandson of Jamie's sister. Surely now some new facts would emerge.

Matt Schwartz was a man in his mid-fifties, with a high colour and hair as black as his name; a short, solid figure, overweight rather than muscular to judge by the signs of breathlessness with which he arrived at her door.

'Come in.' Beverley put out a hand to be shaken. 'Coffee? A drink?'

'If you have any Scotch . . .' Matt glanced round the living room but, no doubt recognising it as rented, showed no interest in it. 'I called my office from Paris coupla days ago,' he said as he sat down. 'My secretary gave me your address and what it was about.'

'The people who keep the records wouldn't help me to get in touch with you directly,' Beverley explained. 'I had to hope – it's great to hear from you so quickly.'

'I've always wanted to find out more about my grand-mother. Went along to that office ten years or so ago. What I was looking for was the low-down on the family who fostered Gran when she was a kid. You didn't say what your connection with her is.'

'I'm not completely sure myself. Mairi McEwan and my grandfather were taken to an orphanage by the same person and on the same day. They had different surnames, but my grandfather did have McEwan as a middle name. And he told me once that he had a sister when he was very small, though he could hardly remember anything about her. Perhaps she was a half-sister. It's all very confusing, but it does seem likely that your grandmother was my great-aunt.'

'Say, then, we must be kinda cousins.' Matt leapt to his feet with the clear intention of embracing Beverley in a cousinly way; but she, more cautious about welcoming unknown relations, turned away – not too obviously, she hoped – to pour a drink for herself as well. Only when she was sitting down at a safe distance did she ask the all-important question.

'Is your grandmother still alive, Mr Schwartz?'

'Hey, call me Matt. Cousins, after all. No, she died, must be twelve years ago now.'

Beverley grimaced with disappointment. 'That note I left, with my address, was in my own interest,' she explained. 'I haven't got much to tell. I hoped that if I could find Mairi McEwan, she'd be able to tell me things. About her family background. I'm trying to find out about my grandfather, you see, but he was only three or four when his mother died. Mairi was older. She might have remembered more. Did she ever talk to you about her childhood, Matt?'

'Hardly a bit until the year before she died. It was a tough time, that was all she'd ever said before. But at the end, when she got ill, it began to come out. Guess it had been on her conscience, manner of speaking. She'd always let everyone believe it was rape, see.'

'Rape?' Beverley allowed her surprise to show. 'I don't know anything about Mairi's life,' she explained. 'Except that she was sent to Canada as an orphan and spent four or five years as a foster-child on a farm called Brigg's Quarter before running away.'

If she had hoped that Matt would start at the beginning of his grandmother's story and follow it through to the end, she was to be disappointed.

'She had a baby when she was only fourteen,' he told her. 'That was my mother. Born more or less on the street. The two of them were picked up and taken to a hospital for the destitute. No one ever found out how she came to be in North Dakota at all. Turned off a train, she said, a few months before the baby arrived. Anyways, found herself in a God-fearing Lutheran community. The pastor looked for a home for her and the baby. Home, I say, but she was a servant, working for their keep. A hard life, my grandmother's, to the end of her days.'

'You said she was raped,' Beverley reminded him.

'Right. Well, the folk who took her in, decent church-going people, they wouldn't have let her through their doors if they thought she was a loose girl. But what they saw when they looked at her must have been a frightened child. They took it for granted that she'd been forced, and she never told them anything different. Tell you the truth, she may not even have known what rape meant, she was so young. By the time she found out, she was stuck with the story. Only odd thing, in the eyes of that community, was that she wouldn't ever put a name to the man. Never said where she'd been living before. There'd have been some rough justice if they'd found out, interfering with a child. Well, maybe not across the border; I wouldn't know about that. She never even let on that she'd come from Canada.'

Was Matt ever going to come to the point of his first comment about his grandmother's conscience? Beverley waited patiently, and was at last rewarded.

'My mother never knew who her father was. She died without knowing, when I was just a kid. It was my grandmother who brought me up. She told me in that last year, when she knew she was dying. A man called Mr Brigg, she said. Didn't even know his first name. I suppose I said something like the brute, the swine, and that was when it all came out. No, she said, he was a lovely man. The only man who'd ever loved her, she said. Comforted her. Cuddled her. That was the word she used: cuddled. Having no mother or father to kiss her or hug her, she'd been glad of it. Didn't even realise she was doing wrong until he tried to make her get rid of the baby. That was why she wouldn't ever sneak on him. That was why she was ashamed all her life that she never had the courage to say out loud that her baby was conceived in love.'

'She told you the address of the farm, did she?'

'Nope. Guess she thought I'd be off there with a

194

handgun to take a late revenge on my grandmother's honour. But she did tell me that it was a charity handling immigrant orphans which found the foster home for her. After she died, I looked it up, so's I could visit the farm. No one called Brigg there now. No homesteads at all, just one huge prairie farm. I didn't go into it too far. Brigg himself would have been dead by then, for sure.'

'And did your grandmother ever talk about her life before she arrived in Canada?' asked Beverley. 'That's the bit that interests me. Did she mention her brothers, for example?'

'Just the once. She was angry that she'd been separated from them. Even if they all had to go to different places for some reason, she thought they ought to have been allowed to keep in touch by writing. She did try once to find out where they were, through the charity, but didn't get anywhere. She was an angry old lady, my grandmother, but I guess she had a lot to be angry about.'

'Right,' agreed Beverley. She began to pace up and down the room, angry herself on her great-aunt's behalf. Mr Chisholm had held in the files of The Refuge enough information to tell Mairi where Jamie had been sent. What motive could he have had for refusing to release the information? Why had he registered Jamie under an invented name? Was it only an accident that the two children had been despatched to different continents? Or had Mr Chisholm been instructed to divide them? If so, the instructions could only have come from the lawyer who brought them to the orphanage: Mr Gordon Blair.

Mairi's enquiry could have been forwarded to Mr Blair's office if Mr Chisholm was reluctant to answer it himself and then the link with the other brother, Fergus, would also have been revealed. There might perhaps have been an innocent explanation – simple inefficiency, perhaps, or a letter never delivered – for the silence on one point. But on two, no! Beverley wasn't going to swallow anything like that. Someone had taken a deliberate decision that the three children should be parted, and had gone to some trouble to ensure that they should never meet or even correspond again. Mr Chisholm had

195

a lot to answer for, and his daughter's secretiveness suggested that she knew it. As for Mr Gordon Blair, his behaviour was even more sinister. In this case, though, it did seem that his descendant, Ian, might be beginning to suspect this himself. It would be interesting to find out whether he would be as open about any discoveries he might make as Luke Dancy had been.

Calming herself down, Beverley returned to her chair to repay Matt's information with some of her own. It seemed best not to make too much of her grandfather's ultimate good fortune in Australia, since in even the short space of his visit she had recognised that Matt's emotions were on a short fuse. He had described his grandmother as angry, and he was likely to become angry himself if he discovered that, at least during the last years of her life, she had had a brother living who was rich enough to provide her with comfort. So Beverley spoke only of those of Wee Jamie's experiences which paralleled his sister's: the years in the orphanage, the farm school, his first job. Leaving the story there, she described the early stage of her own research into the children's background. The curious business of her grandfather's changed name, and of the letters from his elder brother which were never forwarded, could wait until Ian had made his promised report on his discoveries.

As she had expected, even the briefest mention of Mrs Dancy's obstructiveness was enough to arouse her cousin's temper. Beverley stood up again to bring the visit to a close.

'Leave it to me,' she said. 'I've got several leads and I'm following them all up. Give me an address, and naturally I'll let you know whatever I find out.'

'I'm on vacation.' Matt reminded her. 'On the move. Best if I call you from time to time, if that's okay with you.'

'Right.' Beverley gave him her telephone number. 'And if you think of anything, anything that your grandmother ever remembered about her early years . . .'

'She wouldn't ever talk about them. I used to ask her

straight out, but she'd only shake her head. Never knew if that meant she didn't remember or didn't want to remember.' Matt, who had been taking the hint and moving towards the door, turned back again. 'But there was one thing. Animals. Gran always had a way with animals. Even stray dogs that were half way wild. She'd bring them in off the street, talk to them. I warned her once. And she said . . .' Matt furrowed his brows as he tried to remember her actual words. 'She said, "I was brought up from the cradle with dogs and horses. First friend I ever had was a staghound." Then she looked kinda puzzled, as though she didn't understand what she meant herself. "I don't know what a staghound is," she said. "But this was a dog called Chieftain. I was too small to say it right, so I called him Cheffy. But my grandfather said, No, I must always give a dog his full dignity. Chieftain. He was bigger than I was." When she'd come out with all that, she went on looking puzzled for a time, as though she hadn't known she knew it.'

Beverley nodded in understanding. 'My grandfather talked in just the same way about hot oatcakes, and I'm not sure that he knew what *they* were. If you think of anything else like that, do please tell me. Thanks for coming.'

She opened the door and pressed the switch to light up the staircase. As she waited for him to reach the outside door and close it behind him, she could feel her eyes brightening with excitement. Beverley didn't know what a staghound looked like any more than her great-aunt had done. But it was not too hard to guess that a staghound sniffed out the trail of a stag; and if she were to ask herself where in Great Britain she might hope to find stags, one answer would surely, certainly, be the mountains of Lochandar.

197

12

In the excitement of Matt Schwartz's visit, Beverley had forgotten her intention of collecting any letters from the ground-floor mailbox after she had unpacked. She made that her first task the next morning and smiled as she recognised the crest of the Scottish General Register Office on one of the many envelopes which had arrived during her absence. Tearing it open while she was still running up the stairs, she sat down at once in her study to find out the result of the search.

There was no record of the birth of James McEwan Jamieson in the district and within five years of the date she had specified. However, on that exact date a baby boy christened James McEwan had been born in Lochandar Castle. His father was recorded as being Donald McEwan of Lochandar, younger, whose profession was that of an army officer. The mother was Ella McEwan, *née* Vernede. The birth was reported to the registrar by Alistair McEwan, laird of Lochandar, the baby's grandfather.

The clarity of the statement almost took Beverley's breath away. It must be her grandfather, it must! The later addition of an invented surname carried no weight against Wee Jamie's birthdate and his conviction that he had spent his earliest years in a castle. The memory might have surfaced only late in his life, but there was a sense in which he had devoted the whole of his business career to searching for it.

So his connection with the family and the castle was not after all through the female line. By now Beverley had spent long enough in genealogical research to know the significance of the word 'younger' in a Scottish register. It signified here that Donald McEwan, Wee Jamie's father, was recognised as the heir of his own father, the laird.

Wee Jamie, then, had been in the direct line of descent and must have had a claim to the estate – and to the lairdship – superior to that of his uncle Malcolm. It would not, however, override the claim of his elder brother,

Fergus. According to Ian Blair, Fergus had died in battle in 1917, so only after that date would Wee Jamie have been entitled to claim his inheritance, and of course he could not have had any knowledge of the change in his situation. Yet he had believed that the castle ought to be his. How could that be explained? If Beverley had ever been inclined to dismiss the old man's distant memories as representing only childhood fantasies, the paper in front of her now would have changed her opinion.

All the same, memories could be mistaken. It would not be difficult to forget the very existence of a brother last seen seventy-six years earlier and never mentioned since. Beverley strained her own memory to recall the actual words which her grandfather had used, and reached for a pen and paper to write them down.

'I'm Lord of the Castle.' Jamie had said that himself. But he was not then talking about any real castle: not about Lochandar. It was something to do with a game of marbles he was playing.

'So you are, Jamie.' That was his mother speaking. Perhaps she had been talking about marbles as well, congratulating him on a small success. Jamie himself must surely have taken the remark in that sense at the time. But later he had given it a wider meaning, assuming it to cover the building from which by that time he had been removed and which he would never see again. Why? What had happened to make him feel so sure, or at least suspicious?

There was something else. His mother had said she was sorry, although not to himself, Jamie thought. Sorry for what? Just that she was dying and must leave her children unprotected?

Beverley puzzled over the question for a little while and then set the letter to one side. Very often, she had found that a problem would solve itself if it was pushed to the back of her mind for a time. She made herself a cup of breakfast coffee and settled to the task of sorting out and filing all the information she had acquired in Scotland for her Master's thesis. The hours passed quickly while she was absorbed in the work, and not until six o'clock that evening did she reach for the Jamieson file again. But before she had time to open it, the telephone rang.

It was Ian Blair, his voice soft and hesitant as he hoped he was not disturbing her. He had just arrived in London, to be ready for a committee meeting early the next morning, and wondered if he might take her out to dinner.

Beverley accepted the invitation promptly. Her enthusiasm for the meeting was fired – or so she told herself – by the presumption that Ian must be ready to report to her what she had, unknown to him, already learned for herself about her ancestors. Perhaps in addition he would now be prepared to reveal some of the secrets which at their first meeting he had protected. But it was not solely the excitement of research which hurried her to wash her hair and bathe before dressing more smartly than she ever thought necessary for days of burrowing in libraries. The visit to Newport had revived her interest in a social life. At the end of a silent day, an evening out with a young man was just what she needed. She had only met Ian Blair once, but she liked him. She liked him very much.

Her memory was of the humour in his eyes and his diffident but infectious smile. At that first encounter his thick fair hair had been tousled, as though he had spent the day running his fingers through it whilst he struggled with legal problems. And then, before long, he had donned an overall which was sensible wear, but hardly smart.

This evening, however, his hair lay in neat, shining waves and he wore a well-cut and neatly-pressed dark suit. The explanation that this was his 'uniform' for the next day's meeting was made with an apologetic air which did not deceive Beverley at all. He had dressed up to impress her and she could read in his eyes an admiring appreciation of her own well-groomed appearance. All this added to her pleasure in the evening.

Throughout the meal Ian chatted more easily than she might have expected from his hesitant manner in his own office. He described the charity on whose committee he sat as a Scottish representative, and he expressed such interest in the research which had brought her to England that for a time she wondered whether he was trying to check up on her. Was he suggesting that she was using the early immigrants only as a cover for other enquiries?

Later in the evening another explanation occurred to her. By now his questions had taken another turn, and were about her life in Sydney. He was controlling the conversation, she realised, in order to keep out of it the one thing she wanted to discuss: her family history. Because she was enjoying his company, she waited until the coffee before asking him straight out.

'What did you find out?'

'About what?'

'Come off it, Ian.' She was sufficiently at ease with him to tease. 'You've been searching the registers, just as I have. I've made an unexpected discovery, and you must have as well. Has it persuaded you that there's a lot of explaining to do about the way my grandfather was dumped in an orphanage, and about all those letters from Fergus which were never forwarded to him?'

Ian paused before answering, and his answer was not what she wanted to hear.

'This isn't the time or place,' he said. 'I can't start spreading birth certificates out on the table here.'

'Why not?' Beverley outstared her host until he dropped his eyes, laughing in defeat.

'I'd hoped that if I could keep all that in reserve, I might have the pleasure of your company again tomorrow.'

'If you don't tell me what I need to know, you'll never have the pleasure of my company ever again.' Beverley riposted; and, as she had expected, his laughter indicated surrender.

'Clearly I can't risk that. Very well, then. I have it all with me. Shall we go back to your flat? I can lay it all out there.'

Beverley was sufficiently sophisticated both to realise the implications of allowing Ian to accompany her home and to reckon that she could handle them. 'Right,' she said.

13

Unlike Matt Schwartz, Ian Blair arrived at the door of Beverley's flat without showing any signs of breathlessness. He also reacted differently, looking around with curiosity, even surprise, at the well-furnished but characterless rented sitting room to which she led him.

'I don't work in here,' she explained. 'There's a separate study. Means I never have to tidy up – just close the door on the mess.'

'May I see?'

It seemed an odd request, but Beverley shrugged her shoulders and opened the door of the smaller room. As she had warned him, the desk was covered with papers, although most of them were stacked in neat enough piles. She pointed to a map of the British Isles, fastened to a cork wall-board and studded with pins of different colours.

'Distribution of subjects by birthplace,' she said briskly. 'Red for soldiers, black for male convicts, blue for female ones, that sort of thing. Only to mark the people I'm investigating in depth. Obviously I couldn't hope to look at all the thousands who went out. I'm doing a statistical analysis of the whole list and then extracting a balanced sample to study in detail.' She picked up a folder which was near to hand and looked inside. 'This is a girl from Peebles who went out as lady's maid to the commandant's wife. She didn't intend to settle; expected to come back when their tour of duty ended. But she married a soldier who was discharged unfit, and she set up as a dressmaker. Did very well for herself. There weren't too many people around at that time who were able to provide the pins and needles of a civilised social life. She was one of the people whose address took me to Scotland just before I called on you.'

'I see,' said Ian; and Beverley burst out laughing at the expression on his face.

'You haven't been believing anything I've told you about my work, have you?' she said accusingly. 'You think I'm making it all up. But what possible reason could I have for that?'

'Oh dear.' Ian turned back into the sitting room and sat down on a sofa. 'What can I say that won't put me straight into court as a sexist? It's very difficult to look at a beautiful woman and recognise a scholar. I don't know why that should be so. There's no logic to it. I have to accept, since you say it, that you see yourself as a researcher. But I see you as someone so packed with energy that you could do anything in the world, anything at all, if you chose to. And it seems odd that what you've chosen is the history of a lady's maid from Peebles.'

'I lack ambition,' said Beverley lightly. She had used the same words to her father on the afternoon before she left Sydney, and nothing had happened since to make them untrue. 'Energy, yes, I have that; you're quite right. But no direction in which to channel it. No driving urge. So perhaps I'm marking time. Just as you are wasting time. You promised you'd tell me . . .'

Ian pulled a folded sheet of paper from his pocket and smoothed it out on a coffee table. 'Assuming that everything you've told me is correct,' he said, 'your grandfather was the son of Donald McEwan, whose father, at the time of Jamie's birth, was laird of Lochandar. Donald had two other children, Fergus and Mairi, both older than Jamie.'

None of this was any longer news to Beverley, who made no comment on it, but waited for him to continue.

'Donald was an army officer who was killed in action whilst his father was still alive. When the old laird died in 1909, his younger son, Malcolm, inherited the estate and became laird.'

'Why?' asked Beverley. 'The title would automatically go to the eldest son of the eldest son. And surely the land would be entailed with the title.'

' "Laird" isn't a title in the sense that "baron" is, or "earl",' Ian reminded her. 'You might call it a style, indicating the ownership of land granted by the Crown. So yes, the style and the land go together by definition. But as for where it went in this case . . .' There was another pause, as he appeared to be struggling to come to a decision. 'This is difficult for me,' he said at last. 'I told you in Edinburgh, my firm still represents the family. Even though the events we're discussing took place so long ago, we're still obliged . . .'

'But I am the family!' cried Beverley. 'Don't you see? After the death of the old laird, the line passes through Donald to his elder son Fergus. If Fergus had no children before he died, then my grandfather was his heir, and my father after him. You're not representing the family at all, because if you were you'd be looking after the interests of my father and myself.' She checked herself, not wishing to give the impression that she was in fact trying to press any kind of claim; but she was unable nevertheless to conceal the passionate indignation she felt. 'The client whose secrets you're protecting is a man who has no right to hold Lochandar. And if your grandfather believed he was loyal to the McEwan family, it was Fergus, not Malcolm, whose interests he should have represented.'

'Hey, hey!' Ian put up a hand as if to protect himself from her attack. 'None of this old history, you know, has anything to do with me.'

'But you're covering it up, and I don't understand why. Heavens, I'm not fortune hunting. I'm just trying to get at the truth.'

'The truth is that Fergus and Mairi and Jamie were illegitimate. Their parents were never legally married.'

The clarity of this statement reduced Beverley to silence and even seemed to have startled Ian himself, as though he were not used to such plain speaking.

'How do you know?'

'That is the explanation for everything that happened. When the old laird died in 1909, my grandfather, as the family lawyer, expected to recognise Fergus as the heir. As a matter of routine he would need to inspect Donald McEwan's death certificate; and there was no problem about that. Equally as a matter of routine, he asked Ella, Fergus's mother, to produce her marriage certificate. From his point of view it was a simple formality. But it appears, from the notes made at the time, that she couldn't do it. So he asked her for details of the ceremony, because he could have made a copy from the register; and she told him a series of lies. He checked out everything she said, and it was always wrong. In the end, he had to issue a kind of ultimatum. If she didn't tell him the correct date and place where the wedding took place, he'd have to proceed on the assumption that she'd never been married at all. She never did produce the information.'

'She died.' Beverley spoke slowly, still considering what Ian had just said.

'She died in the end, yes. But she had plenty of time before that to put a simple fact on record, if she could. You must understand that my grandfather had no personal interest in the outcome of the affair at all: no advantage to gain from one conclusion rather than another. His only concern was to establish the legal facts. It appears from his notes that he went to a good deal of trouble on Ella's behalf, searching the records. He sets it down as an undoubted fact that no wedding took place on the date she claimed, or, indeed, within two years of it. So you see, after that he had no choice but to recognise Malcolm as the only legal heir.'

'My grandfather was born in Lochandar Castle,' said Beverley, still puzzled. 'And since his father was over-seas, it was the old laird himself who notified the regis-trar of the birth. He wouldn't have done that, surely, if there'd been any doubt . . .'

'Why should he have known of a doubt?' Ian chal-lenged her. 'If your son turns up with a young woman and claims that she's his wife, you may feel put out that you weren't invited to the wedding, but you don't normally ask to see proof that a wedding took place.'

'If your son claims to be married, it's usually because he *is* married,' Beverley riposted. 'Why on earth should he have not have done what he said he'd done?'

'The most likely reason is that there was some impedi-ment to the marriage. For example, if one of the parties was already married. There may have been some secret which Donald or Ella didn't dare to confess to anyone except each other. The old laird wouldn't have known anything about that. When the children arrived, they were undoubtedly his grandchildren. I'm sure he loved them as any grandfather would do, and if he'd been an ordinary chap with just a few odds and ends to bequeath, he'd have made a will which specified by name who should inherit what. But he didn't have that kind of control over the estate. It had to go to the legal heir.'

Beverley considered all this in silence. It made sense in a kind of way, but she had the feeling that something was missing, something which would make intelligible the behaviour which seemed from this distance to be irrational.

'None of this explains – ' she began; but Ian spoke at exactly the same moment.

'How did you know that your grandfather was born in Lochandar Castle?' he asked curiously. 'You weren't aware of that when you came to see me.'

'You're not the only one who knows how to look things up.' She was tempted to refer back to his ridiculous comment that she didn't look like a researcher; but this did not seem the moment for joking.

Instead, she continued to express her doubts. 'What you've said doesn't explain the way the three children were treated,' she said. 'Okay, your grandfather felt that he had to act for Malcolm but that doesn't excuse him for throwing the children away, almost. No one seems to be disputing that they were Malcolm's nephews by blood. Someone ought to have felt a responsibility. The head of the family. I know a lot about my grandfather's child-hood, and I've recently learned something about Mairi's. They had a terrible time, terrible. And the worst thing was the feeling that nobody cared. They weren't even allowed to keep in touch with each other.'

'Fergus was told the truth,' Ian said. 'He was old enough to understand, I suppose, in a way that Mairi and Jamie weren't. His uncle paid generously to set him up, and everything I've read suggests that Fergus was very happy with the arrangements that were made.'

'And the other two? It was your grandfather who dumped them in an orphanage and kept their brother's letters from them. How could a man with any feelings treat two small children like that?'

An uneasiness in Ian's voice suggested that he felt little enthusiasm for the defence which he formally offered. 'He was presumably acting on the instructions of his client.'

'That's not good enough.' Beverley stood up, surprising herself by the force of her anger. 'A man who knows that he's committing a crime can't excuse himself by saying that he was asked to do it. Not even a lawyer.'

'No. I agree. Though "crime" may be too strong a word.' Ian looked up at her, his expression at first grave and then attempting a smile. 'Now you see why I wasn't prepared to talk about this over dinner. All I can say is, please remember that it's my grandfather whom you're putting on trial, not myself.'

Beverley expelled her anger in a single deep breath. 'Right. Sorry.'

'Really sorry?' Ian stood up to face her. 'Can I ask you to prove it? By coming to the theatre with me tomorrow?'

'I'm not sure . . .'

'I asked you out tonight because I knew you wanted to talk to me, to see what I'd found out. It was a business meeting, in a sense, and I didn't expect to enjoy the business part of it if you were half as quick off the mark as I expected you to be. I would have liked to have been able to look forward to a purely social evening with you. And now that I've given you the chance to express your feelings about my family and firm, I do feel that I deserve a reward. An evening that we could enjoy together with no mention of the McEwan family passing either of our lips. It will be a month before I'm in London again, and I can't . . . well. This is Ian asking you, not Mr Blair of Blair, Honeyman and Blair. Please.'

Beverley hesitated a moment longer. But everything he had said was true. Whatever the truth about her grandfather's behaviour, Ian had no responsibility for it. He was being honest with her; she must give him credit for

207

that. Besides, she might well need his help again if she was to pursue her investigation. She managed to smile as she accepted the invitation.

It was easy to tell, as she showed him to the door, that he wanted to kiss her goodbye. But he was too diffident to push himself forward without some indication that she would welcome the gesture, and she gave him no encouragement.

After he had left, though, she asked herself why she had held back. He was an attractive, interesting, intelligent man, whose very shyness increased his appeal. It would be the easiest thing in the world to fall in love with him. All that stopped her was an obscure incident of family history. Absurd, really.

She began to turn off the lights before going to bed, but paused to sit for a moment at the study desk, staring down at the sentences she had written down earlier in the day. 'I'm Lord of the Castle.' 'So you are, Jamie.' And then, to someone not Jamie, 'I'm sorry.' Such flimsy clues; and yet, as Beverley's tired eyes stared at the words, a possible explanation flooded her mind with light.

Ella had said she was sorry to *Fergus*. Because some action – or non-action – of hers had deprived her elder son of his rights. By hedging and delaying she had tried to protect Fergus's right to succeed his grandfather; but with that apology she was admitting her failure and acknowledging that her younger son could claim those rights instead.

Beverley gasped with the simplicity of a theory which would explain everything she had learned so far. Ella had married Donald McEwan not in the year when she claimed to have done so, but later. Fergus was indeed illegitimate, as Gordon Blair had claimed. But Jamie was not.

PART THREE

REVENGE AT LOCHANDAR

1

On the morning after Ian's visit, Beverley arose early. So intense was her excitement over the mental leap forward of the previous evening that she regarded it as a revelation rather than a guess. It had to be right. It was the only reasonable explanation. She pushed her academic notes to the side of her desk and out of her mind. The search for her grandfather's past was true research: the discovery of historical facts which *mattered*. That the truth seemed to have been deliberately concealed was not a discouragement but a spur. After breakfast, she began to list the enquiries which must be made, but had not yet chosen a starting point when the telephone rang.

'It is I.' Luke Dancy's cheerfully identifiable voice brought an immediate smile to Beverley's lips. 'Any civilised Englishwoman would slap the phone down on a seven-thirty caller, but I said to myself that Beverley Jamieson looks like a bright-and-early girl. Besides, I've been ringing your number ever since the end of term, but you're never there. This is my effort to catch you before you disappear into some library or other.'

'I've been in America. And in Scotland before that.'

'Ah. On the trail of the mysterious Mr Blair of Edinburgh? How are you getting on? But don't answer that question now, because hearing all about it is my excuse for wanting to see you. Can we meet? In St James's Park?'

'Why there particularly?'

'I could say that it's the prettiest park in London, which it is. Or I could say that I have a passion for pelicans, which I haven't. But the truth is that I'm working in the cafeteria there and I have to clock in at eleven.'

'What are you doing that for?'

'Because I'm destitute, of course. Have you forgotten what it's like being a student? My grandmother may give me bed and board in term and a paternal government pays my university fees; but it expects my mother to come up with any actual cash that I need and, poor dear, she can hardly keep herself afloat. So the long vacation is devoted to self-help. My money is going to run out on this call soon. Will you come? Ten o'clock on the bridge. I shall provide the stale bread.'

'Why?' began Beverley; but Luke's money had indeed run out, and her only answer was an impersonal buzzing. Since he had allowed her no time to refuse the invitation, she would have to go. She laughed at herself for needing an excuse; but it was true that, while it would be pleasant to see Luke again, she was even more impatient to set her new enquiries in train.

They were not necessarily alternatives, she realised, as – early rather than merely punctual – she leaned over the parapet of the bridge and laughed aloud to see the ducks surging towards her, recognising the first tourist of the day. A scattering of crumbs tossed over her shoulder announced Luke's silent arrival. She turned, smiling, to greet him; and at once found herself being kissed.

'Cheeky,' agreed Luke, recognising that he had startled her. 'But I'm younger than you by at least two years. Think of me as a child. Your favourite nephew, perhaps.'

'Idiot. Let me have some of that bread.' She held her hand out flat so that sparrows could feed from her palm before tossing larger pieces into the air for gulls to catch. 'What do you earn?'

'That's a very direct question. Gentlemen never divulge their incomes.'

'Favourite nephews do, if they have expectations.'

'I have no expectations. However. I earn two pounds

an hour plus my meals and any tips which I can manage to conceal before they're swept into something which is called the staff pool but which never comes anywhere near the temporary staff.'

'I'll pay you two pounds-fifty an hour,' said Beverley briskly. 'Plus expenses. Guaranteed for one forty-hour week even if you finish the work within the first five minutes.'

Luke's eyes opened in exaggerated amazement. 'Beautiful historians may be rare birds, but beautiful *rich* historians are extinct. I accept, naturally. What's the job?'

'Research assistant. Delving around in old registers. Child's play to a history student like yourself. Could be boring, though. A lot of digging before you hit pay dirt.'

'Leave it to me. What am I looking for?' He tipped the rest of his bag of bread into the water and together they began to stroll round the lake.

'The record of Donald McEwan's marriage. Probably, but not necessarily, in Scotland.' She brought Luke up to date on everything she had discovered so far, including her theory about what might have happened. 'Gordon Blair appears to have searched the period before the first child, Fergus, was born. That's what he claimed, anyway. It needs checking, but it's likely to be true. My guess is that we shall find the marriage some time between 1897 and 1906, after Fergus's birth and before Jamie's. But of course it would have been highly secret. Donald and Ella certainly wouldn't have gone through a ceremony anywhere near Lochandar. That's why it's going to be such a chore. It could have been anywhere, and there's no central register in Scotland. You'll have to take it district by district.'

'There would be army records as well.' All Luke's flippancy had fallen away and the sparkle in his eyes showed his interest in the hunt. 'They might have been married by a regimental chaplain. On the other hand, to cut the possible times down, there must have been periods when they couldn't have got married because they weren't together – when he was overseas with his

211

regiment and she was at home with the baby. Oh yes, I shall enjoy this.'

'How soon can you start?'

'Tomorrow. Someone less scrupulous than myself might walk out on the spot and leave the hungry masses to be waited on by an army of slaves even more overworked than usual. But a man of my integrity – '

'Okay, okay.' Beverley laughed as she sat down on the grass and pulled a notebook out of her shoulder bag. 'I've written down everything I know here. Names, dates, places. It doesn't add up to much. Black ink means something certain, red ink is a guess. Call me every morning between eight and nine to say how you're getting on.' She took out her cheque book and, before opening it, began to scribble calculations on the cover. 'Wages. Search fees. Phone calls. Hotel. Train fare.'

Luke cocked his head to study the total. 'I shall bed down with a friend,' he said. 'And I have a student railcard. The whole economy of this country is based on the principle that any young man who comes to rest for a moment should be encouraged to move somewhere else at minimum cost.'

'Any profit you make is your business.' Beverley wrote the cheque without allowing further argument. She was ready to move on; but Luke, sprawling beside her, looked at her seriously.

'Last time we met, you put an idea into my head. A subject for research. I've been thinking about it. Making the idea more specific. Not just emigrant orphans in general. I'd like to write a biography of your grandfather. What would you think about that?'

Beverley, startled, was not sure how to answer. 'He wasn't anyone famous,' she said slowly. 'No one in England – hardly anyone outside New South Wales – has ever heard of him.'

'The interest is in the life, not the fame. It's fairly extraordinary, after all, to start as a destitute orphan and finish up as a millionaire. And if on top of that we find that he ought never to have been a destitute orphan after all – well, that would be quite a story!'

Beverley looked curiously at her companion. 'How did you know he was a millionaire?' she asked.

'Research. The word of the moment. You inspired me. I told you.'

'What I was suggesting was the use of all your great-grandfather's records. A general survey.'

'I know. Sitting at a desk in my grandmother's house. Might be all right. But a biography . . . I'd have to go out to Australia. I'd need to pick your brains, learn all you could tell me about him.'

'That's the attraction, is it?' laughed Beverley; but Luke's face was unusually serious.

'Of course it is. I mean to say, you'll finish your work here and go back home and I shall never see you again.' He turned over to lie face downward and began to pick blades of grass and eat them. 'It's very hard, you know, to meet the right woman too soon. When you're too young to have anything to offer: no money, no job, no anything. All I can hope to do is to keep in touch, close enough to frighten off your other suitors.' He rolled over again and gave a rueful grin. 'Sorry. Perhaps I'm embarrassing you. But you must be used to hearing lovesick swains saying that they adore you. I expect you've got a system for dealing with it.'

'I don't as a rule find myself being regarded primarily as a historical source,' Beverley said lightly.

'But that's only an excuse,' Luke protested.

'That's your answer, then.' Beverley was not joking now. 'It's not a good enough reason for devoting months, years of your life to writing a particular book. I can't stop you, of course. But I'm not going to encourage you. Besides – ' She stopped to consider whether what she was about to say was true, so unexpectedly had the thought flashed into her mind. 'I might want to write the book myself.'

'Yes, of course. I do keep forgetting that you're a historian. Well. Can I offer you a snack? The food is lousy, but I could promise you the very best service.'

Beverley shook her head, but walked with him towards the restaurant. He paused outside the staff entrance for a second, but then grinned and waved a casual hand before turning to go inside. Earlier that morning he had been able to greet her with a kiss, because he could pretend then that it didn't mean anything. It was because he couldn't pretend any longer that he was not repeating the gesture.

Beverley wondered whether she had been unkind. But for the moment she had no interest in either flirtations or friendships with young men. All her emotional energy was focused on the one aim of establishing the truth about her grandfather's childhood.

'Good hunting,' she said.

2

'Eureka!' cried Luke, triumphant over the telephone, then thoughtfully translated the word in case his employer's classical education was inadequate. 'I have found it! On 3 September 1901 Donald McEwan married Ella Vernede in Oban, both parties having been resident for the period required by law. Your guess was absolutely right. They must have discovered something faulty about the first ceremony. So Donald comes back from the Boer War, tells his father he wants a second honeymoon, and takes Ella off to the west coast to put everything right. Are you still there?'

'I'm still here,' confirmed Beverley. 'Struggling with the implications.'

'Your guess about the implications was right as well. Fergus was born out of wedlock, but Mairi and Jamie were legitimate. Ella must have had a certificate from that second wedding or at least knew how to get hold of one. Why d'you think she kept quiet about it? Or could it have been the lawyer who suppressed it?'

Beverley considered the question in silence. 'No, not the lawyer, I shouldn't think,' she decided at last. 'It's more likely, isn't it, that she couldn't bear to disappoint her elder son. He'd been brought up to believe that he was certain to inherit, and suddenly she'd got to tell him that his younger brother was going to scoop the pool, and all through a mistake on his parents' part. She'd do everything she could to look for some other solution, hope she could bluff through the earlier wedding date. She can't have intended that both boys would lose out, so I suppose she would have confessed to the Oban ceremony in the end.'

'But died first.'

'Yes.' Beverley was chilled by the realisation of what that death had cost the three children in comfort and happiness. The greatest penalty of all had been their separation. With a surge of anger, she remembered how deliberately they had been prevented from supporting each other. A moment earlier she had been on the point of accepting the events of 1910 as the result of an accident, a human mistake. But the way in which the children had been treated was not accidental. It was deliberate cruelty. Why should anyone have treated them in such a way?

'I'm learning a lot about Scottish law.' Luke, less personally affected by what he had discovered, chattered lightly on. 'I'd thought that the old Gretna Green system was in force until quite recently. But Lord Brougham seems to have put a stop in 1856 to the old elopement scenario – you know, young English couple galloping over the border with girl's father in hot pursuit, and shaking hands over the blacksmith's forge, so it's snooks to you, Daddy dear. It could be that that's what caught Ella Vernede out. Romantic young girl, her head full of stories, she probably thought at the time it was all above board.'

'And it wasn't?'

'Not in 1896. But it still went on, you see. Gretna Green continued to do a roaring trade, especially with sixteen-year-olds who couldn't legally marry in England without their fathers' consent.'

'You mean that Scotland is full of people who think they're married but aren't?'

'Not now, I don't suppose. But then, yes. Fifty years ago there were over a thousand irregular marriages a year being registered at the Sheriff Court in Edinburgh, all presumably of people who thought they'd done it properly the first time.'

'Hold on,' said Beverley. 'Are you saying that there was some system for changing an irregular marriage into a regular one?'

'Well, yes and no. Yes, as long as the marriage would have been legal if it hadn't been irregular.'

'I'm not with you.'

'Just one example, then, and it may well have been the one which got this couple into trouble. Under Lord Brougham's Act, one of the parties to a marriage had to have been living in Scotland for the twenty-one days immediately before the ceremony. If that condition wasn't fulfilled – and in the Gretna Green type of case it usually wasn't – registration would be refused, whether it was applied for at the time or later. So that puts you back to where you started, with Ella and Donald not being legally married in 1896.'

'You've been very helpful,' said Beverley. 'I must come back to Scotland. Will you get hold of a certified copy of the Oban ceremony for me?'

'Already done.'

'Good. We'll meet in Edinburgh. Come to the Royal Caledonian for lunch tomorrow.'

'Ay-ay, ma'am.'

'And thanks a lot, Luke. Thanks a lot.'

Hardly had she replaced the receiver when the telephone rang again. Matt Schwartz was calling to ask whether she had discovered anything more about their common family history.

'Dirty work, I reckon.' Had Beverley stopped to think, she might have chosen to be discreet, but the treatment of the three McEwan orphans made her emotions churn with indignation every time she thought about it. She didn't exactly know who it was who had condemned her grandfather and Matt's grandmother to poverty, but there was a villain somewhere in the story. She poured

216

out the details of what she had learned so far, and heard Matt spluttering with fury on the other end of the line.

'Who gains?' he exploded. 'That's what you have to ask yourself in any case like this. Who gains? Not much problem answering that, is there, hey? Who's sitting in that castle now, living in stolen property?'

'He couldn't be expected to know . . .'

'Not him, perhaps. But his father. Or grandfather. A crime's no less a crime because a few years have passed. Christ, when I think of that poor old lady . . . Someone's going to pay for this, I tell you; someone's going to pay.'

'Matt!' Alarmed by the reaction she had produced, Beverley prepared to calm him down by emphasising the part which accident and Ella McEwan's evasiveness had played in these old events but he had already hung up. She stared uneasily at the telephone, but had no means of contacting her choleric cousin. Mentally shrugging her shoulders, she began to pack for her trip to Scotland.

There was an unexpected problem in the shape of the Edinburgh Festival. Earlier in the summer a spur-of-the-moment trip had presented no difficulties. But after the overnight journey she arrived to discover that the capital was now bursting at the seams with visitors and performers. All the hotels, and even the private houses which offered beds, were full.

'Where are you staying?' she asked Luke over lunch.

'On the floor of a university hall of residence. Some Oxford friends of mine are putting on a revue. Part of the Fringe. All comers welcome at the dosshouse. Bring your own sleeping bag. Unless, of course,' he added hopefully, 'you'd like to share mine.'

'Thanks for the invitation, but I'll start driving north. Find a bed-and-breakfast place between here and Lochandar.'

'So you're going to do your own research from now on? You won't need me any more?'

Beverley pulled an apologetic face. 'Heavens, what have I done! Persuaded you to give up a regular job; and now I'm throwing you back amongst the three million unemployed.'

'Half of the three million are unemployed because they won't consider any career except fashion designing or brain surgery,' Luke told her cheerfully. 'For anyone who doesn't care where he goes or what he does, the unemployment problem doesn't exist. You've paid me handsomely and given me a holiday trip into the bargain. I was only checking. I'm not going to see you again, am I?'

He directed the question straight at her eyes; and, staring back into his, she understood what he was asking.

'You've been tremendously helpful, Luke,' she said. 'Not only this week. If you hadn't started me off with your grandfather's records, I should never have got anywhere at all. But no, we shan't meet again. Unless you ever find yourself in Australia. Then you must come and look me up.'

'Take that back!' Luke held up his hand with the palm facing her, as though to block the passage of the words. 'It's only a formal politeness, a kind thought, what people say. I know that really. But remembering your voice saying it, come and look me up, I might, I might . . .' Surprisingly for such a cheerful young man, his voice thickened with emotion. 'I might forget that you didn't mean it seriously, that if I did turn up you probably wouldn't remember even who I was. When you're back in your own life, amongst your own friends, all this will be nothing but a holiday memory. I know all that, but you could confuse me with kindness. I'd rather, really, that you said straight out that I'm too young and too poor and that it's been nice knowing me but that it's time to say goodbye, full stop.'

'It *has* been nice knowing you,' said Beverley sincerely. She could not add anything else. It didn't matter in the slightest that he was short of money, but the age difference – so very small when counted in years – was curiously important. Or perhaps, she thought, it was a matter of status: the difference between an undergraduate and someone who had graduated into the real world. A twenty-year-old who had left school four years earlier and earned his living ever since might be her own equal in maturity. But a twenty-year-old undergraduate, she felt, could be taken seriously only by another undergraduate. Since there was no way of saying that without being patronising, she accepted his instructions. 'And it will, I'm afraid, be time to say goodbye, full stop, in about fifty minutes. I have an appointment with the lawyer at three o'clock.'

Luke nodded his head, accepting the verdict he had himself spelled out. There was a moment of silence as he came to terms with it. Then he grinned at her, and the disappointment in his eyes was replaced by the bright intelligence which he had brought to her affairs.

'There isn't much doubt, is there,' he said seriously, 'that your grandfather ought to have inherited the Lochandar estate? Are you going to try and establish a claim?'

'It would be for my father to do that if he chose, not me.' Beverley was silent for a moment, wondering what his attitude would be. Regarded as a property, Lochandar was certainly not something he needed. But it might amuse him to think of himself as a laird. She shrugged her shoulders. 'I don't know anything about the law. Probably there's some cut-out time, isn't there? A statute of limitations, or whatever it's called. If anyone could go back indefinitely to upset the established order, confusion would reign.'

'It could be that in a case of deliberate fraud, the time would only start running from when the fraud was discovered. Scottish law is completely different from English law, so I can admit that I haven't the foggiest idea what the position would be here without having to let on that I'd be equally ignorant in England. Anyway, since you've got a lawyer . . .'

Have I got a lawyer? Beverley wondered as the rest of the meal passed in the light-hearted chatter which was Luke's speciality. She had an appointment, certainly. She needed to talk to Ian Blair, because the files in his office might contain the answers to the new line of enquiry opened up by Luke's discovery. But when it came to a show-down, Ian would be on the opposite side. If what she needed was impartial legal advice, she was going to the wrong address.

3

As she climbed the stairs to Ian Blair's office, Beverley was surprised to find that she was feeling nervous, just as though she had a case to defend rather than an accusation to make. And Ian was nervous as well. Because their previous meeting had been a social one, he was unsure whether he could treat her as a friend and, if not, whether she was to be regarded as a client or an adversary.

First of all she gave him time to produce any new discoveries that he might have made; but it seemed that he had nothing to report. Only then did she hand across the desk the marriage certificate which Luke had produced. He read it gravely before giving a sigh.

'What a deal of trouble would have been saved had Ella McEwan shown this to my grandfather before she died.'

Beverley put forward the explanation which seemed to her most likely. 'I presume that she didn't want to see Fergus deprived of his inheritance.'

'There would have been no reason for that to happen. The subsequent marriage of Donald and Ella McEwan would have had the effect, under Scots law, of legitimising even a child born before the marriage. There were, and still are, many differences between the Scottish and English legal codes. That was one of them.'

'Are you telling me – ?' Beverley felt as though her breath had been snatched away by Ian's matter-of-fact statement. 'Then why didn't she simply produce her certificate?'

'As an Englishwoman,' suggested the lawyer, 'Ella may have been unaware of these legal differences.'

'She should have been told! Your grandfather ought to

220

have been representing Fergus's interests: the interests of the elder son of the elder son.'

'How could my grandfather have known of this second marriage if it was never mentioned to him?' Ian asked the question softly in an attempt to smooth over the tension building between them.

'Ella McEwan came to Edinburgh to fight an inheritance claim.' Beverley's voice, by contrast, was briskly cold. 'She would have brought with her all the legal documents she possessed. Even though she made the mistake of not producing them all at once – and then suffered the misfortune of dying before the matter was settled – you're never going to convince me that the original of this marriage certificate wasn't somewhere accessible to your grandfather, either in Donald McEwan's effects or else in Ella's handbag, or whatever women carried around with them in those days, something that he must have had the chance to examine after her death.'

Ian shrugged his shoulders with a grimace of helplessness. 'I don't know what happened in 1910,' he said. 'If you're saying that my grandfather was inefficient, I've no information with which to defend him. I can only ask – '

'Inefficient!' Beverley sprang to her feet, her blue eyes blazing. 'I'm not saying that he was inefficient. I'm saying that he was part of a deliberate plot to rob three children of their home. A *wicked* plot. To take a four-year-old boy all the way to an orphanage in England and to change his name in the hope that he couldn't be traced: that's not inefficient. It's a highly efficient form of devilry. When I think of that little boy – ' And then, to her great chagrin, Beverley burst into tears.

'Please.' Ian moved quickly round from his side of the desk. 'Please don't cry. I can see why you're upset, and you're quite right.' Beverley felt his arms embrace her, pressing her close so that she could weep on his shoulder, and for a moment or two she found herself soothed by his closeness. But he made the mistake of continuing to talk. 'What happened to the children was certainly terrible and I don't understand why – '

'Don't you?' Beverley pulled away from him and dabbed her eyes dry. 'Shouldn't have thought it would present much difficulty to a keen legal brain to understand why. Someone who thought he'd like to inherit Lochandar himself made it worth your grandfather's while to remove anyone with a better claim. Oh, I don't know, any more than you do, if what you mean by that is having proof. But I *do* know, all the same, I'm sure. You're sure as well. You just haven't got the guts to admit it. I suppose lawyers are brought up never to admit anything. And you're still representing the laird of Lochandar. The *de facto* laird of Lochandar. What's Wee Jamie Jamieson to you?'

'What I was trying to say – ' He needed to struggle with the words. 'If you should wish to bring a charge of impropriety against my grandfather in his capacity as a lawyer, then the firm of Blair, Honeyman and Blair is still in existence, as you've discovered, and could be required to defend itself. After seventy-seven years, of course . . . but it's not my intention to be legalistic. You could undoubtedly bring us some very unpleasant publicity if you were in the mood for revenge. All I'm trying to say is that I, Ian Blair, an individual, born in 1956, I am not personally to blame for anything that happened. I wasn't alive. I haven't benefited from it. Nothing that took place in 1910 was my fault.'

'Of course not.'

'No, but – ' Ian took her both hands, trying to pull her back towards him. 'It means so much to me that you should realise . . . It's not enough for you just to say in words that I can't be blamed. I need to believe that you truly mean it.'

Beverley stared at him without replying at once. It was not very long since Luke Dancy had claimed to be head over heels in love with her. He did his best to make a joke of it, but she had been sensitive to realise that beneath the self-deprecating banter his feeling for her was sincere. She felt equally certain at this moment that Ian Blair also was trying to tell her that he loved her, although he was using restraint rather than chatter to guard against rebuff.

She ought to be kind; but the effort demanded more strength than she could summon. 'I'm sorry,' she said, freeing her hands. The brief outburst of tears had left her feeling weak, and there was a sense in which she felt a need to be comforted. But Ian Blair was not the man from whom comfort could be accepted at this moment. Her emotions were focused not on the possibility of a love affair but on the feelings of a four-year-old boy, abandoned in an orphanage. 'I accept that nothing was your fault. But words are all I can manage.' Even basic politeness required an effort.

The lawyer bit his lips, taking a grip on his own emotions. He managed to phrase his next question not passionately but as a superficial social invitation.

'After you phoned to make the appointment, I managed to get hold of a couple of seats for the Military Tattoo. Tickets are like gold dust, you know. Will you . . . ?'

Beverley shook her head. 'Thanks a lot. But I didn't manage to find a room in Edinburgh, so I'm moving on straightaway. I made a call this morning to the laird of Lochandar. Introduced myself as a cousin remote in both geography and generations. He seems to have a hospitable nature. Invited me to stay.'

'As a personal guest?'

'What else?'

'Well, he does, as a matter of fact, take paying guests from time to time.'

'You mean that Lochandar Castle is a kind of bed-and-breakfast place?'

'Some people will pay a lot for that sort of thing. Stags' heads and log fires in the baronial hall, with the laird himself handing round the whisky. And he needs all the income he can raise. The upkeep of the house . . . Why do you want to go there?'

'Isn't it the most natural thing in the world?' Beverley was genuinely surprised by the sharpness of the question. 'If everything had turned out as it should, I would have been born in Lochandar Castle. Spent my infancy in a nursery in a tower, like the one my grandfather remembered. Wouldn't you be curious in such circumstances?'

'I just wondered . . .' Ian seemed to be uncomfortable in his wonderings, making it easy for Beverley to interpret them.

'You don't imagine, I hope, that I'm playing out a Monte Cristo act, searching down a list of villains on whom I hope to take revenge?'

'I certainly hope not.'

'Nor am I a blackmailer, in case that idea – '

'Good heavens, no!' The lawyer looked horrified, not at the thought that she might be hoping to come away with a portion of the estate, but at the insinuation that any such suspicion was in his mind. Beverley could not help laughing at his expression, melting a little of the icy barrier which had been raised between them.

'You told me at our first meeting that you found me "different",' she reminded him. 'All that means is that I'm Australian. You probably haven't had much contact with the species before. But I can promise you, every Australian reckons to lead a better life than anyone in the old country. There's nothing I want for myself out of Scotland except the truth. If I seemed edgy earlier on, it's because someone has gone to a lot of trouble to bury the truth deep. But you were right to remind me that it wasn't you. Sorry.'

It was not much of an apology, but that was because she was still in a fighting rather than an apologetic mood. She turned away, ready to leave.

'But – ' Ian's face expressed distress. 'We shall meet again, I hope. Beverley, I love – '

Beverley interrupted quickly. 'It's no good, Ian. I'm sorry. It's simply not a runner.'

'You said you didn't blame me. All we need is a little time. So that you can get to know me better. It means so much to me.'

'I may not blame you, but I can't simply push the facts that I'm discovering out of my memory. It's a crime for which no one has ever been punished. It would always come between us.'

'You mean that you're using me to take revenge on my grandfather. On my family.'

Was that true? Perhaps it was, because with anyone else, surely, she would have been kinder. Still, if she was saying no, she might as well say it decisively, using the words which Luke had put into her mouth.

'You seem to be taking it for granted that I'm looking for someone to fall in love with. But I'm only here for a visit, remember? My life, my home, my friends are in Australia. I shall be going back there soon. There's no point . . .' She shrugged her shoulders. 'If you discover anything else, you know where to find me. If not . . .' She held out her hand. 'Goodbye,' she said.

4

So charming was David McEwan, and so hospitable, that Beverley felt guilty about the ease with which she deceived him. She was by nature straightforward, but could see that to introduce herself truthfully on this occasion would be to invite a frosty reception indeed.

On the telephone she had been able to speak honestly at least about the general nature of her historical research; and from there it was a simple matter to claim that in the course of it she had tracked down a remote ancestor of her own to Lochandar. Her kinsman accepted the story without asking questions, and invited her to stay in a manner suggesting that any McEwan was entitled to a bed in the family home at any time.

Now, as she parked her car just outside the castle wall, he came out, casually dressed in a pale blue sweater and jeans, to greet her with a smile and a handshake.

'My Australian cousin! What a great pleasure to meet you.'

'My pleasure to be here. It's very kind of you to invite

such a distant connection. Did you know that you had relatives in Australia?'

'Not to name names, no,' said David. 'But for several centuries the British Empire was kept running by the younger sons of Scottish families. A special breed. Self-reliant, practical, level-headed. But poor. Because there was nothing for them to come home for, they stayed where they'd settled. So I wasn't necessarily surprised. Delighted, though, now that I see you. None of our family portraits gives any hint of such beauty waiting to emerge.'

He bowed slightly towards her as he paid the compliment; and Beverley, accepting it, took the opportunity of searching his face for any resemblance to her grandfather or father. David McEwan had darker hair than any of the Jamiesons, and was slighter in build than either of the men. He was as tall as they were, but it was a lanky rather than a sturdy height. One resemblance, though, was startingly close: the blue eyes which smiled at Beverley now were as bright as her own.

'Come along in,' he said, picking up her suitcase. She noted the matter-of-fact gesture with interest. Ian Blair had explained to her that 'laird' was not a title, but a word denoting only the ownership of land and carrying with it more duties than privileges. Nevertheless, she must subconsciously have expected the laird of Loch-andar to live in some style – to call for a servant, for example, rather than to do a job himself. She reminded herself that this was no time to indulge in Australian egalitarian prejudice. She might believe – she *did* believe – that her host had no right to the estate to which he had invited her; but it would be unfair to think of him as a stuck-up aristocrat.

'Do you think – ?' she began, putting out a hand as if to hold him back. 'After so much driving, I'd love to stretch my legs for a few minutes.'

'Surely.' David set the suitcase down again and glanced at her footwear, approving it as sensible. 'I'll take you to my favourite place on the loch.'

The way down to the water was steep but safe, for the

solid rock on which the castle was built extended in strata as firm as a flight of steps. Round the edge of the loch itself a well-trodden path served a scattering of small wooden platforms.

'These are for the paying rods.' David interpreted Beverley's questioning glance. 'We let out fishing rights by the day or week – or season, it could be, but no one stays so long.'

'Salmon?'

'Not here. This is a trout loch. There are salmon in the river.' He gestured towards the head of the glen. 'The salmon fishing's good as a rule, but this year it was a disaster. A fungus disease.'

The view of the mountains which his gesture had indicated prompted another question. Mairi McEwan, according to her grandson, had talked of a staghound. 'Do you go stag-hunting here?' Beverley asked.

'Stalking.' The correction was only on her choice of word. They were walking side by side, and David turned his head to look at her as though considering whether the question was a hostile one. Certainly his answer, when it came, took the form of a defence.

'This is a primitive part of the world in some respects,' he said. 'Look at Lochandar on the map, and you see a huge estate. But the land is very poor. Beautiful, indeed, but almost worthless. We have no cash crop, except for the wool, and the grazing supports fewer sheep than you might expect. Whatever natural resources we have, we must use. I fish for the pot and I shoot for the pot. We have a few grouse on the moor – not enough for a commercial shoot, so I keep them for myself. For three days every year there are duck on the loch. Lochandar, I believe, took its name from their annual passing. It's continued for centuries, and every laird in turn has extracted his fee for their landing rights. As for the deer . . . I use my gun to keep the household in venison. And it's necessary to cull the old stags, to prevent them breeding with their own daughters. I see that that's done as well.'

'You mean you don't do it yourself?'

'I said we had no cash crop,' said David, laughing. 'Not quite true. We have tourists and sportsmen. If someone will pay me two hundred pounds for the pleasure of stalking a twelve-pointer, I take his money. My stalker knows every stag on the land. He makes sure that only the beast he nominates is killed and that it's a clean kill. Shall we pause here? This is where I like to sit.'

'Why this place in particular?' Beverley lowered herself on to the grass beside him.

'Look over to the castle. What do you see?'

'Well, the castle.' It was the view which had been reproduced on the cover of the brochure – but of course she could not mention that she had seen that. 'It's beautiful.' The stone walls were not of a grim dark grey, but sparkled with flecks of lighter colours. 'And the reflection . . .' It was while looking at the reflection that she guessed why David had chosen this viewing point. From the place on the road where she had first glimpsed Lochandar, the proportions of the old castle were spoiled by the wing which had been added more recently at the side. But from here that extension was invisible. This also was something which she could not admit to knowing.

'That's right. The castle – as it *ougi .   ,* look. Unfortunately, there's another part of the building which you can't see from here but which attacks the eye from every other angle. A monstrosity. I like to sit here and pretend it doesn't exist.' He glanced at his watch. 'But since if does exist, you might like to take a look at it. We have to open it to tourists in the summer – part of our cash crop. The last public tour of the day will be finishing soon. We could nip in before the new wing is locked up for the night. I try to avoid tampering with the time switch on the alarm if I can help it. The insurance company insisted that we should install a system, but it's fiendishly complicated.'

Beverley accepted the suggestion without revealing that she had already taken the tour. Together they strolled back around the loch and, by a more gentle slope this time, approached the front door of the Victorian wing.

'I see what you mean,' began Beverley; but just as she spoke, the last party of the day emerged into the open and immediately David checked both himself and his guest, not precisely hiding, but flattening himself against a wall as unobtrusively as possible.

'It'll cost me half an hour in autographs if they see me,' he murmured.

Beverley smiled her understanding but then she too froze. She had recognised – hadn't she? – one member of the group which was straggling towards the car park. He turned to look back at the castle, as though wanting to study it as a whole; and then Beverley was sure.

What was Matt Schwartz doing at Lochandar?

5

Beverley was disconcerted by the sight of her cousin. She tried to persuade herself that he was merely sight-seeing, out of natural curiosity; but could not make herself believe it. A single meeting had been enough to tell her that Matt Schwartz had allowed his grandmother's anger at her ill-treatment to breed an even fiercer anger in himself. What was his purpose in visiting Lochandar? Should she step forward to let him see her – or, to put it more crudely, to warn him off her patch? But while she was still trying to decide, he turned away and hurried off towards the coach and David was moving forward again, reclaiming her attention.

It was not easy, going round the Victorian wing for a second time, to feel or express any enthusiasm for its contents – especially as her host, unlike the paid guide, made no secret of his scorn. 'Hideous!' he muttered as he opened each door in turn until at last Beverley asked him directly, 'Why do you hate it so much?'

Coming to a halt in the billiards room, he offered a

reasoned answer. 'It's a question of suitability,' he said. 'All this might perhaps be delightful somewhere else. But here! Did you notice the original round tower of the castle? That was built for a specific purpose. It was a watch tower to look out for raiders and a defensive position for when they arrived. It was the right shape for its purpose and built in precisely the right place. Then the rest of the old castle was added, and that was appropriate as well. An enclosed courtyard, more comfortable living quarters, but still in the right place and for a necessary purpose and, above all, built of the right materials. The castle stands on stone. It's surrounded by stone. It's absolutely right that it should be built of stone. But then round about 1860, along comes some ancestor of mine. He's thinking of getting married and his bride must have nothing but the best. So he imports bricks – *bricks*, for heaven's sake – and tacks on this monstrosity. I suspect that the design was scribbled on the back on an old envelope, since it includes such nice touches as the flat roof which holds the snow and provides every top bedroom with an individual waterfall.'

David checked himself in mid-flow and laughed apologetically. 'I'm sorry,' he said. 'I do go on about this rather.' He led the way into the dining room. 'The problem is that it costs the earth to keep this sort of place up. I lie awake at night worrying about how to pay the next bill. I seem to spend my whole life running in order to stand still – and it feels like the waste of a life, when it's all to preserve something which isn't worthy of preservation. I'm only talking about the monstrosity when I say that. The old castle, where I live, is magnificent. Full of history, and a beautiful object in itself.'

'Can't you just pull the newer part down?' suggested Beverley.

'If only it were as easy as that! No, I can't. No doubt Australia is enlightened in these matters. But over here you can be informed by the same post that you are obliged to maintain a building because it's an important part of the national heritage, and that you can't have a grant to maintain it with because it isn't a sufficiently important part of the national heritage.' He paused, recognising an exaggeration. 'Well, I do get a small grant. That's why we have to let the day trippers in – it's one of the conditions. But it's not enough to make much difference.' They moved on to the drawing room.

'You said you lived in the old part,' commented Beverley. 'But this . . .' She gestured towards the shabbily comfortable chairs, the well-worn carpet, the books chosen for content rather than appearance: a lived-in room.

'Let me explain.' David glanced at the grandfather clock which was ticking steadily next to the door. It must have told him that he still had time in hand before falling foul of the alarm system, for he indicated that she should sit down. 'My father and grandfather and great-grandfather each lived on this side while he was laird. The old castle was reserved in their day for the heir who was waiting to inherit. And a very uncomfortable wait it must have been in the past. When I got married, my wife, Wanda, gave one shiver at the prospect she was expected to endure and invested what money she had of her own in heating and plumbing and carpets and – well, you'll see in a moment. She turned the castle, all but the exhibition rooms, into a comfortable home. So when my father died I decided to stay there and to use the monstrosity as a kind of hotel. For anyone who wanted to fish or stalk or walk, outside the summer day-tripper season.'

'Sounds a good idea.'

'In theory. Not in practice. The costs gallop ahead of the receipts. Although there are eighteen bedrooms here, there are only three bathrooms. That sort of detail would cramp the style even of a professional hotelier, and I'm far from being that. Of course, I could always borrow some huge sum and modernise the place, but my over-draft gives me nightmares already, and I don't believe that Lochandar would attract enough extra guests even to service the loan.'

'Could you sell one or two paintings, instead of

borrowing?' Beverley suggested. 'If the insurance company thinks they're so valuable . . .'

'That's another of the great jokes of the situation. I'm compelled to insure for a high sum just because some clerk at head office has heard the name Landseer or Raeburn or whatever. If they came to take a look . . . well, there are one or two decent portraits, but the rest! Dead birds hanging upside down. Nobody's buying that sort of picture these days.'

'You obviously need to interest a burglar in them.' Beverley smiled as she spoke and was surprised by his look of startled disapproval of what she had intended as a joke.

'Even a burglar would turn up his nose at this lot,' he said. 'I did send a couple of pictures to auction last year. They came back again unsold and having *cost* me money. The only ones which might interest a buyer are the paintings of the castle itself and some of the old lairds' – he gestured towards two full-length portraits hanging on either side of the fireplace – 'and of course those are just the ones I wouldn't want to part with.'

He tutted to himself and smiled at her. She had noticed when they first met that his smile was curiously lop-sided as though he felt the need to fight his own amusement or pleasure. One end of his mouth turned up while the other was pulled down. Earlier the smile had expressed welcome. Now, equally clearly, it was apologetic. 'Nothing more boring than listening to other people's financial woes,' he said. 'Unforgivable of me to talk like this when you've only known me an hour. Becomes a bit of an obsession, I'm afraid. I'm determined not to hand over to my son the sort of mess and worry that I inherited.'

'How old is your son?'

The laird burst out laughing. 'Rabbie's only three. Plenty of time to get things straight, you might think. Let's hope so. I ought to mention, in case you're wondering, that my wife is dead. In an accident two years ago.'

'I'm so sorry.' Beverley did her best to express surprise as well as sympathy.

'An avalanche in the Cairngorms. We were both mad about ski-ing. I've given it up now. It wouldn't be fair to Rabbie . . .' He stood up, looking once more at the clock. 'We'd better be moving. The place locks itself up. Out of hours, the combination systems on the doors can't be operated even if you know the right numbers. Anyway, you must be panting for a wash and a drink.'

'You've no guests staying here now, then?' commented Beverley as she followed her host out.

'No. We can't mix the paying guests with the day-trippers. We keep the house open until the end of the Edinburgh Festival. The visits would tail off after that in any case. Tomorrow is the last day for public opening. We allow ourselves five days to clean up and rearrange the furniture. That fits in well with the stalking, which will be at its best from the end of next week until the season ends on 20 October. Let's go this way now.' He indicated the covered flight of steps which linked the old castle, on its platform of rock, and the extension. As Beverley went past him and started to climb the stairs, he pulled across a heavy metal door. 'That's a fire door as well as a security barrier. Now – ' They had reached the old part of the castle. 'I'll show you to your room. When you're ready, come down one floor. Drinks will be waiting.'

David's wife had used her money well, thought Beverley as she soaked herself in hot water in a bathroom not merely modern but strikingly well designed. It did sound, though, as if he would have done well to marry an even richer woman. She found it difficult not to be amused when she considered all his money worries in the context of her theory that he had no right to own Lochandar. She could do him a favour, from one point of view, by demanding that the property which caused him so much anxiety should be handed over to her father, who could so easily afford to keep it up. But David would probably be too sentimental, and Jock

Jamieson too much lacking in sentimentality, for such a solution to appeal to either man.

That she should even consider David McEwan's position from such a point of view suggested that his charm of manner was having an effect on her. But any softening in her attitude was abruptly halted when, at the end of the evening, she stood up to go to bed.

'Shall I be able to meet Rabbie in the morning?' she asked.

'Not tomorrow. He's staying with Wanda's parents by the sea while his nurse has a holiday. But he'll be back on Friday. I shall be taking him to our local Highland Gathering on Saturday. I hope very much that you'll still be here for that. One of the annual highlights of our life. While Rabbie's still away, let me show you his nursery. Wanda painted it herself.'

The drawing room in which this conversation took place was in one of the three long sides of the castle. Beverley had worked out, from her memory of the tour, that it must be over the banqueting hall. Now David led her along a corridor and opened the door into a room which was completely round. The walls had been plastered and then decorated with a mural. It depicted the battlements of a fairy-tale castle through which peeped various nursery story characters, with others climbing up the wall or dangling over on ropes.

Beverley's eyes took in the details of the painting, but in her heart she was conscious only of the room's roundness. She took one step in and could go no further. 'The tower – ?' she began.

'Yes, this is part of the original old tower. It's been used as children's quarters for the past century or so. This was my own nursery once. There's a schoolroom just above. Beverley, are you feeling all right?'

Beverley, swaying, willed herself not to faint. This nursery, she reminded herself, belonged to a little boy called Rabbie, who was staying with his grandparents. But what she saw, more clearly than anything that was actually in the room, was another little boy called Jamie, eating hot oatcakes by the light of a log fire. Smiling happily at his loving nurse and confident that his life would continue in this safe, comfortable way for ever. Beverley was determined that she was not going to burst into tears again, as she had in Ian Blair's office; but the self-control required brought her close to collapse.

'It's beautifully done,' she said, forcing herself into a politeness which must have disappointed her host by its lack of enthusiasm. She was tired, she told him then, and went gratefully to bed. The tiredness was genuine enough, but for a long time she could not sleep. And it was not, she realised at last, sympathy for her grandfather which kept her awake, but anger. Anger about both the events of the past and their consequences. Three-year-old Rabbie was an innocent child. Almost certainly she would find him lovable when she met him. But he had no right to be in that nursery. It did not belong to him.

6

On the morning of the Highland Gathering the Lochandar household rose early. Beverley was still in her bedroom when she heard the sound of David's voice below. Looking down through the narrow window, she could see that a variety of vehicles had been brought round to the side of the castle, and a small crowd was assembling around them. The kitchen staff, already dressed in their best clothes, were carrying out hampers of food and drink to be stowed in the lockers of two old shooting brakes.

By the time Beverley made her way down, one of the smaller cars appeared almost ready to leave. A piper was carefully arranging his bagpipes in the boot, whilst four dancers argued about who should sit where. So splendid were their costumes of velvet jacket and lace jabot above tartan kilt and hose that David, in his Highland day dress, seemed soberly clad by contrast. He wore a tweed jacket over an ordinary shirt and tie, and his knee-length stockings were an unobtrusive shade of lovat green. But, ordinary as this might seem, his kilt, with its doeskin sporran, gave him an unexpected grace and dignity. He was the laird of Lochandar; a different person from the man, casually dressed in jeans and anorak, who had taken her to walk in the mountains on the previous day.

All the same, she couldn't resist teasing him. 'Why aren't you so gorgeous?' she asked, indicating the wearers of the velvet jackets.

'These are competing in the games. That's why they must be away now. It's a fair distance to the Gathering, and the piping and dancing competitions will be judged first. You and I needn't leave until eight. The shepherds will be down from the hills by then.'

'Is *everybody* going?' asked Beverley. 'Even the shepherds?'

'Surely. Tom Pirie, the head shepherd, is our strongest man with the caber. This is a great local occasion, the Gathering of the Three Glens. The one time in the year when everyone can be merry together. There's no one who would offer to stay at home on such a day, and I wouldn't ask it of them. The weather is good and the sheep will come to no harm. The only danger is that we may lose a deer. But Johnny Dundas, who thinks of himself as official poacher to the estate, is a fast man over rough ground. I've offered a prize for a hill race today, and I'm hoping he'll value the chance of it above venison. Now then, you must take a good hot breakfast. It will be a long day. Have you tried the Arbroath smokies? And you mustn't turn up your nose at our porridge.'

He held the door open for Beverley to go inside to the dining room, and she helped herself from the silver dishes in which food was kept warm by a reservoir of hot water.

'All those people outside,' she said as she took her plate from the sideboard to the table. 'Do they all work for you?'

David gave her a sideways looks. 'You're thinking that

a man who complains so loudly about the cost of running his home ought not to employ so many servants?'

'Well . . .'

'What would you have me do? There's no other employment within miles. Some of the young ones go to the towns, but the others have been here for generations. This is their home. And they're proud people. If I were to tell them that I couldn't afford their wages any longer but that the state would pay them to do nothing – well, I very much think that they'd go on working just as before, to my shame. This is not quite a family, not quite a charity, but whatever it is, the people are part of the land. I couldn't change the system if I wanted to, and I don't want to. I may fume about the cost of a damp course, but not about the pension I pay to our old water-bailiff. Ah, Rabbie, are you ready for our picnic, then?'

He opened his arms to his son, who climbed up on to his father's lap and compared the pattern of their two kilts, the large and the small. Rabbie smiled shyly at Beverley. On meeting her for the first time the previous day, he had run to be picked up and cuddled by her, withdrawing only when he was told her name. He was a little boy who was looking for a mother: a child made vulnerable by the realisation that something was missing from his life, in spite of the loving care which surrounded him.

The drive to the Gathering took two hours, although any of the eagles which hovered overhead could have covered the distance in a far shorter time: there was a steep-sided hill in the way, as David pointed out. He took Beverley, Rabbie and Jean, the nurse, in his car. They were the last to leave, for just as they seemed ready to go, David returned to the castle to search out a shooting stick for Beverley; but they overtook the two heavy shooting brakes on the road.

A piper was playing as the party arrived and, whilst David was instructing Rabbie to hold tight to his or Jean's hand all day because of the dangers of the heavy throwing events, Beverley looked round at the lively scene. There was not a pair of trousers in sight, for all

237

the men were wearing the kilt. Some of them were perhaps only present as spectators but, except for Beverley herself, there were no outsiders. David explained to his guest that this was only a small, local festivity. Tourists who wanted to gawp at a colourful occasion would make their way to somewhere like Braemar, whose Games were famous all over the world.

Everyone – again, except for Beverley – knew everyone else. Indeed, hardly had they begun to move away from the car when there was a roar of greeting. 'Lochandar!' The speaker was an elderly bearded man. 'Our usual wager on the caber, Lochandar?'

'Aye.' A Range Rover had just pulled up beside David's car, and he shouted across to one of the men who climbed out of it. 'Tom! Is it today that you'll toss the Three Glens caber? Kirkcumrie has laid a silver flask of his best malt against you, and it's yours if you can earn it.' He turned to Beverley, laughing, and his voice, which since their arrival at the Gathering had unexpectedly developed a Highland accent, reverted to normal. 'He won't manage it, of course. This wager's been running for years between our two families, and no one's claimed the stake yet.'

'What are you talking about?' asked Beverley.

'I'll show you.' He led the way across the field, looking back to make sure that Rabbie was safe with his nurse. 'Later this afternoon there'll be the competition to toss the caber. You see this log here.' He indicated something which seemed to Beverley to be a tree trunk rather than a log. 'This will be used for the competition. A man like Tom, and maybe some of the others, should be able to handle this. If no one succeeds, a little will be sawn off the end and they'll try again. But over there' – he pointed to a longer trunk which was standing upright in a cairn of stones – 'That's the Three Glens caber. It's nineteen feet long and it's never cut. It was tossed and turned just once, thirty years ago, so it can be done. It will be brought out after the competition for anyone who wants to try. That's when Tom will try to win the wager.'

'Do you have to see how far you can throw it?'

'No, it's more complicated than that. You hold it by the thinner end and throw it straight up, vertically, so that it turns in the air and the thicker end hits the ground first.'

'What an extraordinary thing to have a competition in!'

'Strong men like to show off their strength. And poor people in past centuries had to make their games with what came to hand: hammers, pieces of masonry, tree trunks.' He showed her the throwing hammers and heavy stones which were also awaiting their turn to be used later in the day. 'It's no more foolish than hitting a ball with a cricket bat.'

'It certainly does seem to breed strong men.' Everywhere Beverley looked she saw giants, men who were over six feet tall and as sturdy as the cabers which they apparently tossed around with such ease. It occurred to her that her grandfather had had just such a build but she made no mention of this to her host. It was an odd aspect of her visit that he had shown little interest in the nature of the family connection which had brought her to Lochandar, and she was not volunteering any information.

For the whole of a fascinating morning she wandered around with David, watching the dancing and the jumping and the pole vaulting. When it was time for lunch the Lochandar group, laird and servants, sat down together. David congratulated the competitors who had won their events and the cook on the excellence of her game pie. 'Is Johnny Dundas here?' he asked his stalker. Beverley remembered the name as being that of a poacher.

'I've no set eyes on him. I'm thinking we'll be a beastie short the nicht.'

Tom the shepherd stood up and stretched himself, ready to take part in his event. 'Johnny Dundas, was it?' he said. 'Here's himself coming as ye speak the name.'

Beverley turned her head to look where he was pointing and was in time to see a small, wiry man running into the crowd, wearing old and mud-splashed clothing. 'He looks as though he's just finished a hill race

239

rather than coming to start one,' she said; but before anyone could comment on this, the bearded laird of Kirkcumrie came striding over the ground towards them.

'Lochandar! Lochandar, take yourself home. Your castle's afire.'

7

Startled by the announcement, David half rose to his feet – but then, to Beverley's astonishment, settled himself back on the ground and smiled round at the members of his household before replying to his neighbour. 'Are ye so afeared of losing your wager, Kirkcumrie?' he said, his Highland accent returning. 'Ye'll hae me take Tom awa afore the first toss, is it?'

'It's nae jest, Lochandar. Johnny Dundas has seen the smoke and come running over the mountain.'

Any hesitation which David still felt was banished by an announcement over the loudspeaker, calling him to come to the organiser's tent and any firemen present to report to their station. He hurried off and was gone for ten minutes, returning with a worried expression.

'Which way was the wind when we left this morning?' he asked the stalker.

'North-west.'

'Thank God for that. The fire was in the new wing, Johnny says. It should be blowing away from the old castle, then.' He accepted an invitation for Rabbie and his nurse to stay with the laird of Kirkcumrie and then began to give a bustle of instructions. Beverley kept quiet and out of the way, but was amazed to see that as well as leaving all the women and children to enjoy their outing, he sent Tom Pirie off to take part in the cabertossing as though nothing were amiss; and a young lad with hopes of a running victory was also encouraged to stay.

'Won't you need everyone you can get to fight the

240

fire?' she asked when at last David was able to extract his car from the parking area and set off for home.

'It's a good two hours since Johnny saw the fire, and it must have taken hold by then for him to notice it from a distance. It will be another two hours before anyone can reach it. Either it will be out of control by then or else it will have burned itself out. Either way, one more man with a bucket of water won't be much use. This is Tom's big day. Let him enjoy it.' He said nothing more, concentrating on his driving and on his own thoughts. When the car at last pulled off the road and came to a halt, it was in the place from which Beverley had first glimpsed Lochandar Castle on her earlier visit. Without speaking, they both left the car and stared across the loch.

The fire was still burning at the extreme end of the new wing. Flames had broken through the roof and were roaring upwards in a narrow shaft, as though confined in an invisible chimney. Except that 'roaring' was not the right word, thought Beverley, for she could hear no sound. Once, in Australia, she had seen a bush fire and would never forget the horror of the speed and noise with which it devoured the forest, jumping from treetop to treetop and at the same time surging along the ground as though following a fuse trail of gunpowder. The knowledge that the flames could not be checked and that in the heart of the inferno people were losing their homes and perhaps their lives had brought terror even to the onlookers who knew their watching place to be safe. Compared with that, this self-limiting fire was almost a cosy one.

That, however, was not a comment she could make to a man who was watching the destruction of his property. Beverley had travelled to Lochandar prepared to hate the grandson of the man who must have condemned three young children to exile for his own advantage – and was not even sure that she had spoken the truth in telling Ian that she had no wish to take some kind of revenge on her grandfather's behalf. Hatred, though, was a cold emotion. Part of her reason for staying on longer than

241

the brief visit she had first planned was the wish to calm her feelings, to control the anger. If she could see David McEwan as an honest man who held no responsibility for the sins of his forefathers, then she would be able to return to Australia remembering only that her grandfather had made a good life for himself from an unpromising beginning. That, after all, had been Wee Jamie's own attitude. And so she was allowing herself to feel a friendliness towards the laird of Lochandar, and sympathy in his present loss.

'The wind's turning,' David noticed. The pillar of fire was bending back towards the black and smoking ruin of what it had already consumed.

'It's made its own firebreak.' The part of the building nearest to the old castle was already burned out.

'Yes. And there'll be rain this evening.' David watched the clouds in the sky for a moment and then raised his binoculars to his eyes. Was he studying the castle, or merely trying to conceal how upset he was?

'David, I'm really sorry,' Beverley said. 'To see your home destroyed like this. All your family memories as well as your possessions. It's tragic.'

David lowered the binoculars and turned to look at her. 'Only half a tragedy,' he suggested. 'The old castle seems to be untouched, thank God.'

His expression was suitably grave, but there was something wrong about his mouth. Was it just that oddly lopsided way in which its corners turned up and down which seemed to be in conflict with his tone of voice. Puzzled, and still searching for some suitable comment of her own, Beverley studied his face for clues, and suddenly understood. He was not upset at all by the destruction of the wing which he regarded as so hideous and which cost him so much to maintain. He was glad.

The approach of a fire engine saved her from any need to speak. David let it go past and then followed in his own car, parking well away from any danger of flying sparks and from the pumps and hoses which would be used to draw water from the loch.

'Will you let yourself into the castle and stay there?'

242

he said to Beverley, giving her the keys. 'I want to be sure that you're safe.'

'You be careful yourself, then.' She recognised that there was nothing she could usefully do. Once inside, though, it seemed sensible to walk right through the building. Although from a distance it had seemed untouched, there must be a danger that the hours of intense heat or an explosion of sparks might have started a smouldering which would sooner or later burst into flames.

She began at the top. Because the castle was built round an open courtyard, the smell of burning had penetrated most of the rooms before she opened their doors, making it useless to sniff for any newer trace. Instead, she kept her ears open for the crackle of fire, and pressed her hand against each wall and floor to test for excessive heat. But David's confidence was justified. The two parts of the building had been joined only by the single covered flight of steps which, as she had seen, was closed by an efficient fire door. The stone walls of the old castle were very thick and the outside windows very narrow; as good a defence against fire as against seventeenth-century weapons.

Naturally she included in her inspection the ground floor rooms which in the summer were open to the public. The various exhibitions had a closed-up look now. Showcases were covered with dustcloths, furniture was stacked together to allow for more thorough floor-cleaning than perhaps was possible during the season, and in the room devoted to tartans half a dozen pictures were propped against a wall, waiting to be rehung. Except for one painting of Lochandar Castle itself and another of a stag posed against a mountain sunset, the pictures were all portraits of fierce-looking gentlemen in plaids or kilts of the same McEwan tartan which David was wearing at this moment. Beverley recollected that she had noticed one or two of them before, in different rooms. It was a sensible idea to use them as illustrations in the exhibition. She tested the wall against which they were leaning; this too was stone-cold.

243

Satisfied that no danger lurked in the structure, she settled down to wait. Some considerable time passed before David came to look for her. His face was tired and his clothes were dirty and smelt of smoke but Beverley saw with relief that he was also very wet.

'Yes,' he said. 'The rain has arrived. The fire's out.'

'Can I come out and see?'

'Surely. Keep away from the building. The walls aren't safe. I'm just going to offer the men a dram.'

He joined her outside a few moments later, carrying some bottles of whisky, and the task of packing away the fire-fighting equipment was interrupted for a while. The rain was falling as a warm mist, so that Beverley did not notice how wet she was becoming.

'Do you have any idea how this could have started?' asked the fire captain.

David shook his head. 'It's a mystery. If there'd been workmen in the house . . . but it was completely empty.'

'You weren't expecting visitors?'

'No. Why do you ask?'

'Another wee mystery. We had the first warning from Johnny Dundas, as you'll know. But within five minutes there was a call to make the same report. Someone else who'd seen the fire but needed to drive an hour before he found a telephone. He rang off without giving his name. It sounded like an American, I was told.'

David looked puzzled for a moment, but then thought of an explanation. 'Lochandar Castle was open to the public until two days ago. This will have been a tourist who didn't check the dates.'

'A long way to come by mistake,' commented the fire chief; but he appeared to accept the explanation. Only Beverley could think of another possibility.

'Matt Schwartz!' she exclaimed.

'Who is Matt Schwartz?' Both men had turned to look at Beverley, but it was David who asked the question.

Beverley didn't answer at once. The moment she heard herself speak the words she knew that she should have kept quiet, for it must surely be an over-vivid imagination which had startled her into speech. Matt Schwartz had

244

come once to Lochandar as a tourist, just as she herself had at first. Might he not have decided – again, just like Beverley – to return and make himself known to the laird whom he regarded as an usurper? He would have found the castle empty; at his mercy. He was a quick-tempered man. 'Who gains?' he had demanded to know when talking about the banishment of his grandmother, and had made no attempt to conceal the rage he felt against Malcolm and his descendants. 'Someone ought to pay.' How likely it was that the urge to take a late revenge would have overcome him when an opportunity like this presented itself.

Nevertheless, she ought not to have mentioned his name. Her suspicions could be nothing but speculation; and she was talking about a criminal offence. She hurried to correct the impression she had produced.

'An American tourist. You thought it might be a tourist, didn't you? I found myself chatting to this one a few days ago and mentioned that I was coming to Lochandar. He made some remark about it sounding interesting. But when I think about it now, he was probably just hoping that I'd offer him a lift. I don't think he had any transport of his own.'

'Well, whoever it was who made the call, he was trying to be helpful,' David said. 'There'd be nothing more he could do. It was all a most terrible accident. An act of God.'

He pulled a hand wearily across his soot-smeared face. Had he questioned her more intently about Matt, it would have been difficult to justify her sudden mention of the name. But to her relief he was obviously satisfied that the fire must have been accidental. She need not tell any further lies.

8

Rain was still falling on the Monday after the fire, but it was such a misty rain, gentle and warm, that Beverley agreed without hesitation when David suggested another walk. The smell of smoke and of damp burnt wood permeated the castle, and she was glad to escape from it to the fresh air of the moor. They would not have time today to drive to the start of a mountain walk, David told her, because he would need to be back before the insurance adjuster left the premises.

Together they set off across the heather and beside one of the many rocky burns which splashed their way into the glen. She found no difficulty in keeping up with David's stride, so it surprised her when, after little more than an hour, he came to a halt as though expecting her to be tired. Or was there some different thought in his mind? He was staring at her with an expression hard to understand. She looked back, waiting for him to start moving again. Instead, he asked an unexpected question.

'A lot of people who are used to living in towns or villages find it hard to come to terms with all this open space,' he said. 'The feeling that there are no neighbours, that if you walk over the nearest mountains you will see only other mountains, with nothing stirring but sheep or deer or an eagle in the sky. People can get quite frightened by the emptiness. But it doesn't bother you, does it?'

'I have to keep reminding you that I'm Australian,' said Beverley, laughing. 'One thing we have in Australia is open space. When I was a little girl my grandfather used to take me camping in the bush. And when I was older my father took me ocean sailing. I can tell you, there's nothing in the world as empty as an ocean. And that's a hostile environment. This one is positively friendly.'

'That's what I'm thinking, that you see it as friendly. I'm wondering whether you might feel that you could live in it? Make your home with me in Lochandar?' He came to stand closer to her, although not quite so close as to touch.

Beverley found it impossible to disguise her amazement. Was he suggesting that she should marry him? Yes, she could tell from the expression on his face that he was. 'But David, you've only known me a week!' she gasped.

'When something is right, absolutely right, you can tell it in the first second. I watched you drive up to the castle, with your hair blowing in the wind. You got out of the car and looked up at the walls and before I'd spoken a word to you I felt sure that you were the right person to be the lady of Lochandar. I saw Rabbie run into your arms a day or two later and I knew that you were the right mother for him. He knew it as well. And when I stood beside you on the bank of the loch, watching the fire on Saturday, I was certain that you were the woman I wanted for my wife.'

Disconcerted by the intensity with which he spoke, Beverley took a step backwards. 'I'm not so impulsive. I can't possibly say . . . The thought hadn't even occurred to me.'

'I realise that. That's why I had to speak. Otherwise you might go away without knowing how I felt. I want you to look at Lochandar and consider whether you could see it as your home. To look at Rabbie and myself in a different way from before. I want to be able to talk to you about my own future. It will all be quite different, you see, now that the burden of keeping up the monstrosity is no longer round my neck. I shall be able to pay off all my debts and have money left over to turn the whole of the old castle into a comfortable home, or a hotel, or whatever seems best. And without so much anxiety I can plan out a way of life which isn't simply that of a property owner. I want to discuss it all with you.'

He moved forward and took her in his arms, kissing her passionately. Uncertain of her own feelings, Beverley did not attempt to pull away from his embrace, but nor did she respond to it with any warmth. And when at last he released her, she began to walk on ahead of him, without speaking.

She should have been considering her own feelings, but instead asked herself silent questions about David. Did he, she wondered, know how rich she was? Since her arrival to stay at Lochandar there had been plenty of time for conversation. He had seemed genuinely intrigued by the research which she had described to him, and interested also in Australia. Why had he shown so little curiosity about her family which was, after all, the link between them? Was it considered rude over here to ask direct personal questions? Or had he not needed to ask because he had enquired into her background just as Luke Dancy had done? Luke had seen her wealth as an obstacle, but David would not share that view.

It might have been enough for him to rely on his own observations. She had told him, without going into details, that her grandfather had founded his own business. She had made her appearance at Lochandar driving an expensive car. She had probably also mentioned that her father owned an ocean-racing yacht – hardly a poor man's hobby. She was well aware that in financial terms she was regarded as a catch, and for all his optimism about the way in which the insurance pay-out would solve his problems, the thought must have crossed his mind that a wealthy wife would be an asset.

It was easy to see where her thoughts were leading her. Did she believe that he was sincere in his reasons for wanting to marry her? No, she didn't. He hoped that she would fall in love with him, but why should she contemplate such a step? Had he but known it, she had jumped a giant hurdle already in thinking of him not as merely the grandson of the evil Malcolm McEwan but as himself, a generous and charming host.

With nothing to say that he would want to hear, she was unable to introduce any other topic of conversation, so that their walk continued in silence. Only as they were approaching the castle at the end of the afternoon did he reach out a hand to hold her back for a moment. 'You'll think about what I said?'

'Yes, of course.' Beverley found herself looking at the castle in a new way, as though obeying his instructions to see herself as its mistress. Lady of Lochandar. That was the phrase he had used for the wife of the laird. She couldn't help smiling to herself at the sound of it, but then she was distracted by the sight of a man walking towards them from the burned-out ruin, leaving two others still poking around amongst the fallen roof timbers.

'This will be the adjuster from the insurance company,' said David, and called out to him as he approached. 'Have you seen everything you need?'

The adjuster nodded. 'If we could have a few words?'

David led the way into the castle. All three of them took off their boots and waterproofs before climbing the stairs to his private quarters. Beverley sat down on one of the sofas and picked up a newspaper, but concentrated her attention on the conversation rather than the news. The adjuster unzipped his waterproof bag and produced several bundles of paper.

'All this relates to the contents insurance,' he explained. 'The inventory of articles of individual special value for which valuations were provided. It seems to have been divided into two groups, which will save us a deal of trouble. This is the list of the contents of the old castle, in which we are now. Am I right in believing that no damage at all was sustained to any article in this building?'

'Quite right.'

'So we're concerned only with what is called here the new wing. The fabric of the building was insured, and that has been completely destroyed. As far as the contents are concerned, anything within the new wing at the time of the fire has also been destroyed. What I must ask you to do at this time is to check through the inventory and mark any items which had been removed from the new wing since the list was made. I have two copies here, if you'd be kind enough to make your alterations on both.'

'It won't take long.' David took the lists over to a

bureau. 'We move the table silver over here for safety during the public opening season. It was due to go back today. So luckily that's safe.' He found the place and crossed through several lines. 'That's all.'

'If you'd be good enough to read through the whole list carefully, all the same,' the adjustor requested. 'It's three years since the inventory was last checked. You might have made changes and forgotten about them.'

'If you wish.' There was a long silence as David turned over each page. 'No. No other changes.'

'Then if you'd sign both copies, and the claim forms, and keep one of each for yourself.'

David did as he was asked. 'Can I now make a start on getting the debris cleared? It's dangerous as well as unsightly, and I have a small son. You know how hard it is to stop children from exploring.'

'Well, there's one other matter to be investigated first. One or two details which I noticed when I was making my preliminary notes suggested that I should have a word on the telephone with the officer who attended the fire on Saturday. And as a result of that conversation he and a police officer are having a look round at this moment. Perhaps you'd like to come outside and discuss the matter with them.'

'Police?' David exploded with surprise, even indignation. 'What have the police to do with this, an accidental fire?'

'I'll leave the experts to speak for themselves,' said the adjustor. 'I wouldn't want to go further than to say that, judging by my own observations, the possibility of arson can't be entirely ruled out.'

'Arson!' This second shock appeared to render the laird speechless. He moved towards the door, in company with the insurance representative, without making any further comment.

Beverley stayed where she was. She had no wish to get wet again, nor to intrude into a situation which was upsetting her host. Besides, she had some thinking to do. Saturday's dramatic events had prompted her unwisely to mention the name of Matt Schwartz. David,

250

accepting the fire as an accident, was not then looking for a criminal. But if he returned from the scene of the fire in a few moments' time convinced by police evidence that the blaze had been started deliberately, he was certain to repeat his earlier question, 'Who is Matt Schwartz?'

So she must decide quickly what to say. She began to pace up and down the long drawing room. There was no doubt in her mind that the telephone call of warning had been made by Matt, following a second visit at which he had hoped for a confrontation with the laird. She couldn't prove it, but she believed it. With less confidence she could imagine that his frustration at finding no one to whom he could express his anger might have led him to make a gesture of some sort. Moving into the realm of fantasy, she envisaged the possibility that he might have lit a fire, intending it only to be a small one, and became quickly frightened by the speed with which it spread. That could explain why he telephoned an alarm, a curious thing for a man seeking revenge to do.

If she did believe all or any of this, was she going to sneak on him? After two more pacings of the room, Beverley came to her conclusion. No, she was not. It was her duty as a citizen to pass on everything she knew or suspected to the police and allow them to do the investigating; but she did not propose to do her duty. She had too much sympathy with the reactions of her cousin.

And no one had been hurt. It was ironic that the man whom Matt – if he were the culprit – would have intended to harm should actually have profited from the action. The laird of Lochandar was not upset but pleased that he would have money in his pocket in place of a building which he disliked and could not afford to maintain.

Beverley stopped pacing and stood still in the middle of the room. One of the phrases which she had just used in her thoughts had a familiar ring. It was only two days ago that she had recalled Matt's angry question. 'Who

251

gains?' Let her ask it about this new crime. 'Who gains?' There was not much doubt about the answer. Matt Schwartz would gain nothing from the burning of Lochandar except satisfaction at the righting of an old wrong. But David McEwan . . .

Who gains? The police would ask that question themselves but might not arrive at the same answer. In their presence David no doubt would be more discreet about the crippling cost of keeping up the Victorian wing and the fact that he had been refused permission to demolish it. But even if they found traces of arson, even if their suspicions pointed them towards a motive, they would need proof of a link between the owner of the building and its destruction; and probably none existed.

Or was there perhaps something? It seemed to Beverley that, if she thought a little harder, she might recall some detail which at the time had not seemed important enough to store in her memory. What was it? She stood where she was, concentrating. Then she crossed over to the bureau at which David had checked the inventory and sat down to read through the long list of items.

9

Beverley was once again seated on the sofa with a newspaper in her hands when David returned to the drawing room. Looking up with a questioning smile, she saw that he was edgy; near to anger, but finding it wise to control himself.

'They seem to think the fire was started deliberately,' he said. 'I can't say I follow the details, but I suppose they know what they're talking about. I've suggested they should bring along a more senior officer, a specialist. But they have to investigate it as a suspected crime, apparently. They're scraping around for questions to ask. And one thing occurred to me. On Saturday, when someone mentioned the American voice on the telephone, you appeared to know who that might have been.'

He paused, but Beverley gave him no help.

'Something like Schwartz, was that the name? Matt Schwartz?'

'That was a crazy thing for me to say. As though there were only one American in the whole of Scotland.'

'But he was interested in Lochandar,' David insisted. 'It may not be much of a connection, but it would be a starting point. I told the sergeant that you might be able to give him some useful information. I mean, I can imagine, can't you . . . He drives out here without checking the opening times, gets annoyed when he realises he's wasted his time, sees that there's no one around and decides it would do no harm to get inside and give himself the public tour.'

'And then starts a fire to destroy his fingerprints?'

'A carelessly-dropped cigarette would be enough.' But David must have realised that this suggestion hardly fitted with any evidence of arson which the police might have discovered.

'I can't start involving some perfectly innocent holiday-maker – ' began Beverley, but David interrupted her with a show of reasonableness.

'If he was nowhere near the place, he'll be able to prove it. If he did accidentally start something, he'll explain that instead, and an accident's an accident. No one expects you to produce a theory which would solve the whole mystery. Just his name and some details of your conversation, that's all. Let the sergeant ask his questions, and tell him the truth.'

'Tell him the truth.' Beverley gave a half-sigh and stood up. 'Right. Where do I find him?'

'Downstairs in the armaments room. I'll show you.'

'I know the way, thanks.' Beverley had no intention of answering questions in David's presence. In addition, she proposed to make a short detour before presenting herself to the policeman.

A few minutes later she closed the door of the circular

253

armaments room behind her and accepted the offer of the only chair there.

'I'll not keep you long,' promised the sergeant, whose grimy hands and boots made it clear why he had not been invited upstairs. 'If you'd be kind enough to tell me anything you know which could have a bearing on the fire.'

'That won't be much,' Beverley said. 'On Saturday I left the castle at eight in the morning, in the company of the laird. I didn't notice anything unusual. We were together from that time onwards at the Gathering, where we first heard the news. And we drove back together. By the time we arrived, the new wing was almost totally destroyed.'

'Do you recall who was the last to leave here for the Gathering?'

'I think that probably we were, the laird and myself. The competitors certainly moved off earlier, and so did the slower vehicles. We were in the fastest car. But I didn't take any particular notice.'

'Why should you, indeed? It was unfortunate that this was the one day in the whole year, or so I'm told, that there would be no one about at all; not even a caretaker.'

He paused as though waiting for some comment, but Beverley could only shrug her shoulders. 'I'm only a visitor here,' she reminded him. 'I don't know anything about the usual arrangements.'

'No. Now then, in the course of the day there were two warnings given about the fire. We needn't waste too much time wondering why Johnny Dundas should be in the neighbourhood. He'd have had his eyes on one of Lochandar's beasts. It wouldn't have been in his interests to draw attention to himself by throwing down matches and indeed, he could well have kept quiet about what he saw. The other warning was from some American gentleman. The laird was suggesting that you might be able to put a name to him.'

'I don't think so.'

'He remembered a name himself.' The sergeant

254

glanced at his notes. 'A Mr Schwartz. But I understood that the first mention came from yourself.'

'Right. I spoke without thinking, though. He didn't have a car. He couldn't have been anywhere near.'

'But he expressed interest in Lochandar Castle?'

'I was talking about it first.' That was true, although her next sentence was more imaginative. 'He may have been hoping that I'd offer him a lift but of course I was planning to stay for a few days, so I couldn't give him the day trip he would have wanted. I told him that some coach tours took in Lochandar Castle, so he was going to look for one.' That must also be true, since Beverley had seen him climbing aboard a coach. 'The tour operators might have the names of people who book with them. But of course they'd know the date on which the season ended. If he came here at all, it must have been earlier than Saturday.'

'Can you suggest any way in which we could confirm that with him?'

Beverley shook her head. 'He was on vacation. Moving round all the time. But anyhow, I really don't think . . .'

'It's the only lead we have. Unless, of course, you can suggest any other line which we might follow up.'

Beverley stared for a moment at the sergeant, who looked steadily back as though he were sure that she held the key to the mystery. Uncertain of what she wanted to say or do, she stood up and began to wander from one side of the room to another. She had accepted David's warm hospitality. She was his guest. There were obligations . . . but even as she tried to silence herself she became aware that she was pacing round and round the room. The circular room, at the base of the ancient tower. Only just above her head was the nursery from which her grandfather had been snatched away at the age of four.

Wee Jamie Jamieson had been happy with his life, thinking himself lucky. He would never have wanted his granddaughter to settle the score for his childhood ill-treatment on his own account. She must be clear to herself about that. What she was going to do now could only be described as spiteful. Speaking to Ian Blair she had laughed away any suggestion that she was seeking a revenge which must, because of the passage of time, be unfair as well as belated: but if he had doubted her, it was with good reason. She had tried to think of herself as a scholar, an impartial searcher for the truth. Now she had to recognise that she had been following this particular trail more in the fashion of an avenging Fury.

The opportunity to take revenge had been offered to her by its victim. David had invited her to tell the truth. Standing beneath Wee Jamie's nursery, and remembering all the lies which had been told on the orders of Malcolm McEwan, Beverley prepared to do what Malcolm's grandson had asked.

'I don't know exactly what's been happening,' she said slowly. 'But is the man from the insurance company still on the premises?'

'Indeed he is.'

'He wasn't going to trouble with checking the contents of the old castle, because there was no damage here and no claim made against this half of the inventory. But if he did decide to take a quick look round on this floor . . . It might prove to be only a formality. Or he might find, when he looked in the exhibition room devoted to tartans, that some pictures have arrived there within the last few days which are still listed on the inventory of the new wing. There's a painting of the castle, and some old chieftains, and a Landseer of a stag. A week ago they were hanging in the drawing room that's been burned down. I expect there's some reason – or perhaps I've made a muddle of it – but . . .' There was nothing more she could say. Any direct accusation must come from the loss adjuster, not from herself.

'I'll make that suggestion at once. If you'd be kind enough to wait here for just a moment, Miss Jamieson.'

It was a long moment. Almost certainly he had gone to inspect the pictures himself. But his face, when he returned, revealed nothing.

'Thank you for your help, Miss Jamieson. We'll be getting a report on the insurance aspect in the morning.

I'll be wishing to have another word with you after that. You'll be here?'

'No,' said Beverley. How could she possibly remain as a guest of the man she had betrayed? 'No, I'm just about to leave.'

'Not tonight, I'm thinking. It's a long way to anywhere from here, and the driving would be difficult once the sun's down. If you'd be kind enough to come to the police station at eleven o'clock tomorrow.' He pulled out a map and showed her where it was. 'It's on your way south, so you can drive straight on from there.'

'Why should you need to see me?'

'It depends on the insurance report. But we may need to have your signed statement about the date and place where you previously saw the pictures in question. At eleven o'clock, then.'

After he had left, Beverley became aware that she was still wearing her damp walking clothes. A hot bath seemed advisable, and would give her time to prepare for what would be an uncomfortable meeting with her host.

When, however, she appeared in the drawing room, clean and changed, David seemed as pleasant as ever although a little distracted. Over a drink and dinner they chatted about Scottish history and customs; it was only as the meal was ending that David threw out a casual question. 'You had your interview with the stolid sergeant?'

'Yes. I have to go to the police station at eleven tomorrow to sign a statement.'

'I'll drive you in. They want to see me as well, at twelve, and it will give me the chance to pick Rabbie up and bring him home.'

'Thanks for the offer, but I'll drive myself and then keep going. It's time I got back to work. And I imagine that you'll need my bedroom. You're expecting your first paying stagstalkers soon, aren't you?'

'That's no problem. There were only three bathrooms in the monstrosity, so we never booked in more than three couples at a time. I hoped you could stay longer.

Still . . . You told the sergeant about the American, did you?'

'I told him that Matt Schwartz is a tourist on vacation, with no address at which he can be contacted – and that in any case I didn't reckon him to be a fire-raiser. Why are you so anxious to involve an innocent man, David?'

'Why are you so anxious to protect a suspicious character?' His voice was still easy on the surface, but there was a hardness beneath it which she had not heard before. 'Is he some kind of a relation of yours? Someone else who considers that he has a right to Lochandar?'

Beverley stared at him without speaking. How long had he known? 'I suppose Ian Blair . . .' she began slowly.

'He phoned me up after you first called on him to say that you'd pressed him into confirming my address. The impression he gave was that you knew it already. I'm not sure that I believe that – in fact, it's probably because it wasn't true that he felt he ought to confess to me that you knew where to find me. At that time he didn't know what your interest was. After you got in touch with me, I decided that I needed a little more information. Which I must say he was remarkably reluctant to give. I didn't get anything like the full story, even when I reminded him that he was supposed to be my family lawyer. After all, you might have been some kind of confidence trickster.'

'Is that what you thought when we were talking on the moors this afternoon – that I was a con girl?'

'What I thought this afternoon was that you were the most beautiful, delightful, desirable young woman it has ever been my good fortune to meet. The possibility that Lochandar might be part of your heritage as well as mine made the thought of a marriage seem even more right.'

'And something has happened since then to change your view?'

'While you were downstairs with the sergeant, I had a third conversation with Ian Blair. There are various points on which I shall need advice – amending the details of the listed building, considering what

258

permissions I may need for making more use of the old castle, that kind of thing. And he can deal with the insurance claim for me. That's bound to be a tedious process. I've asked him to meet me at the police station tomorrow. I don't know precisely what they want to ask me about then, but it can't do any harm to have a lawyer at hand.'

He paused as though he had completed what he meant to say, and then remembered her question. 'I learned from Ian that when you left him to come here you were angry. Very angry, he said. I asked whether he meant that you might be in the mood to take some sort of revenge for the rather nebulous events of the past which he'd mentioned. He presumed that I couldn't possibly be asking such a far-fetched question seriously. From which I deduced that he was reluctant to give a serious answer. So I told him of the police suspicion that the fire here was caused by an arsonist. And of my own suspicion that the arsonist might have been you.'

'Me! You must be – ' But no: he was not joking and he was not crazy. Underneath the charm, the present laird of Lochandar was as ruthless as his grandfather had been. 'Ian Blair was quite right to say that I was angry. Angry with Malcolm McEwan, because he was a wicked man. I reckon you've inherited more from him than just a parcel of land.'

She walked out of the room without looking back, and went upstairs to pack.

10

At half-past eleven the next morning Beverley emerged from her interview and stood for a moment outside the police station, filling her lungs deeply with the warm autumnal air. It was the end of an episode in her life, or so she had expected. But it seemed that there was one scene still to be played. Ian Blair was standing beside her car.

He walked towards her with the smile of a man uncertain of his welcome. 'I'd hoped to catch you before you went inside,' he said. 'But I was held up on the road and arrived too late.'

'What is there left for us to talk about?'

'Shall we be a little more private?' Ian suggested. He opened the door of his own car and, after a brief hesitation, Beverley took a seat in it. 'I was going to offer my services to you,' he continued when they were both settled. 'And I'll still do so, if you feel I could be useful.'

'Your services as a lawyer? Why should I need a lawyer?' She knew the answer to that question, of course, and mischief sparkled in her eyes as she asked it. By now she had thrown off the sombre mood of the previous day, when she had been appalled by her own spitefulness without being able to control it.

'I was speaking on the telephone last night to David McEwan, and he mentioned the possiblity – '

'He told you that when he saw the police this morning he intended to accuse me of arson. Supporting the accusation with information which could only have been supplied by a certain Mr Blair.'

'Yes, I never dreamt, of course . . . I'm sorry. I felt I owed it to my client to keep him in touch with the facts of the situation.'

'Naturally.' There was no trace of resentment in Beverley's smile. 'Blairs are always loyal to McEwans. I should know that, if anyone does. So how come that a Blair, if I understand you rightly, is offering to defend me against an accusation made by a McEwan?'

Ian turned in his seat to meet her eyes steadily. 'It's true that the Blairs have represented the legal interests of the McEwans for many generations,' he agreed. 'But even a long-standing arrangement can be brought to an end. People forget that the highest loyalty of any lawyer should be to justice. I see the possibility here of a grave injustice being done. I'm not saying that I know how to protect you. But if you would like me to try, you have only to ask and I'll do my best.'

'So Mr Blair the lawyer is prepared to change sides! If only Gordon Blair had had the same courage and integrity!' She held out her hand and smiled as he gripped it with both of his own. 'Thanks, Ian. That gives me a good feeling.' She couldn't help laughing, though. 'Aren't you going to ask me whether I did burn half of Lochandar Castle down?'

'Of course you didn't.'

'Right. Of course I didn't. But I don't believe I need a lawyer to persuade the police of that. David was unwise enough to alert me last night to what he proposed to say, so I brought the subject up myself half an hour ago. I reminded the police that there was an elaborate security system to protect the new wing. I wouldn't have had the faintest idea how to get inside and start a fire, nor am I competent to set up something which will only burst into flames after a delay. I also told them that I'd only met the laird for the first time a few days earlier, and suggested that I could have no possible motive for attacking the property of a virtual stranger.'

'But David could say – '

'Yes, he could. He could drag out all his family's dirty linen and say that I was trying to take some kind of revenge on Malcolm McEwan's descendant. But that theory rather collapses when I point out that the destruction of the new wing was what the laird wanted. If I'd burned it down, I'd have been doing him a favour, not playing him a dirty trick – and I was well aware of the fact. He'd told me that he'd tried and failed to get permission to demolish it legally. The police have already discovered that, so the moment they found out that I knew as well, the revenge theory flies out of the window, doesn't it?'

Ian, still holding her hand, began to laugh. 'And I believed you were in need of a lawyer!'

Happily relaxed, Beverley joined in the laughter. 'Just for good measure – and because I don't want to be hauled all the way back for questioning – I volunteered a brief statement of my personal financial position. It isn't of any actual relevance that I'm the daughter of a millionaire and have a healthy bank balance in my own right, but it does make it that little bit less likely that I'm skulking round the countryside perpetrating sordid little crimes.'

Ian let go of her hand. 'Are you the daughter of a millionaire?' he asked.

'Only a weak-dollar millionaire. But on the other hand, there may be more than one million. Didn't you know?'

'How should I? You were the one who was investigating your family pedigree, not myself. And your description of your grandfather, cut off from his family, sent to a home for penniless orphans . . . well, you told me that he had a hard life, and I assumed . . .'

'He made good in the end,' Beverley said. 'I suppose I ought to have made that clear. And that's why – since I reckon I don't need any legal help myself, thank you very much – I'm going to tell you how best to defend David McEwan. Your client.'

'Defend him? Against what?'

'Didn't he tell you?'

'He wants me to deal with various claims and permissions for him. There are bound to be complications.'

'There are indeed. And one of the complications is that he's open to a charge of attempting to defraud his insurance company. By claiming the value of some paintings which he said had been destroyed but which in fact he'd moved from their original positions a day or two earlier. And because he claimed for them falsely after moving them deliberately, suggesting that he knew in advance there was going to be a fire, he could also be charged with arson. If I were you, I shouldn't ask him whether he's guilty, because I'm sure that he is. If a lawyer is supposed to be loyal to the idea of justice, it might put too great a strain on your principles to know the truth.'

'You're teasing me again,' protested Ian; but his expression was troubled. 'You mentioned a possible defence.'

'I've done my best for him,' said Beverley. 'The police asked me about various details, and I could see where the questions were leading. I told them that the insurance inventory and claim form had been put in front of the laird to be signed on the spot. He might have felt hustled, or thought it was simply a formality; he might genuinely have forgotten about moving the pictures. That's what I suggested, anyway. Although three of them – a Landseer and a couple of Raeburns – are valuable, the choice of pictures to be moved does seem to have been based on their family associations, on which ones were most suitable to include in an exhibition.'

'And so?'

'And so he may get a second chance. When he turns up for his interview he won't know – or rather, the police will think that he doesn't know – that the removal of the pictures has been discovered. He'll be asked to go through the inventory again and answer a few questions about current values. If he should take the opportunity to exclaim that he made a mistake which he's only just realised, and would like to amend the claim – if that seems to come spontaneously, it might help him to escape the charge of fraud. And that in turn would slightly weaken the case for accusing him of arson. I mean, is it a crime to burn down your own house if nobody is hurt?'

'The insurance company is hurt, if he makes any claim at all,' Ian pointed out. He looked at her curiously. 'Why are you telling me this to help him? I'd have thought you'd be pleased to see him in trouble.'

Beverley was not prepared to give more than a partial answer to that question. No one was likely to trace her part in building the case against David McEwan, because the insurance adjuster had been quick to take sole credit for discovering the discrepancy in the inventories. Nevertheless, she was not proud of her own behaviour on the previous evening. It was true that she had done no more than reveal the truth in the interests of justice, but her motives were not as high-minded as that would suggest.

263

She was trying now to make amends for a petty act of revenge; and was ashamed to say so.

There was, however, another reason for her new attitude. 'There's Rabbie, you see,' she explained. 'When I first went into the nursery which was once my grandfather's, I was so upset.' She paused, re-living the emotions which had overwhelmed her there. 'I wouldn't have lifted a finger to help David McEwan then. But I've had time to think. My grandfather is dead now. And Rabbie is very nearly the same age as Wee Jamie was when he was taken from his nurse and nursery. He has no mother. I wouldn't want him to lose his father – and it seems to me that there's a risk of imprisonment. I'm not prepared to tell any lies myself. But I shan't come back to challenge any that the laird may tell on his own account.' She allowed her voice to reveal the scorn that she felt for him. Then her mood changed as she smiled at Ian.

'I shan't forget that you offered to desert him for me,' she said. 'A friendly act. Thank you, Ian.'

'So may I hope that we can meet again?' he asked. 'With no business affairs to come between us?'

'If I were staying over here, I'd like that. But I'm not. I'm going home.' Although she had not known of the decision until she heard herself speak the words, she was sure at once that this was the right thing to do. 'My father will be getting married again in a few weeks' time. I want to be there.'

'But you'll come back again? Your research – '

'Is hardly worth the paper it's written on. I might write the story of the lady's maid from Peebles as my contribution to all the bicentennial junketings, but for the rest . . . I think I've been using an interest in the past to cover for the fact that I didn't know what to do with myself in the present. My grandfather never made that kind of mistake.' She opened the door and got out. David McEwan would be arriving soon for his appointment with the police, and would need his lawyer's undivided attention.   Ian moved quickly round the car to stand beside her. 'So what are you going to do with yourself in the present?' he asked.

Beverley was not ready to answer that question. As she lay awake on the previous night, preparing herself for the interview with the police, her mind had been invaded by a jumble of ideas. She had considered three-year-old Rabbie, motherless and in danger of losing his father for a while. She had remembered Wee Jamie, alone in an orphanage, alone in Australia. Into this train of thought had intruded Ken Murray, who had once been her tennis partner. Harry the Hat, her grandfather's benefactor, had forced himself on her attention as well, although for a long time she could not put her finger on any connecting link. From a confusion of images the germ of an idea had begun to sprout, an idea which might provide an answer to Ian's query. But it needed a great deal more consideration before she could put it forward as a plan.

'I need to work on my tan,' she said lightly. 'Thanks again, Ian, for all your help. Goodbye.'

She made herself comfortable in the Ferrari, and was just reversing out of her parking space when David McEwan arrived. In the rear mirror, as she drove away, she could see the two men standing side by side as they watched her go, but she did not wave or look back. The laird could sleep safely in his castle, as far as she was concerned. She would never return to Lochandar.

EPILOGUE

1988

1

'What's all this?' asked Jock Jamieson. 'An appointment in office hours? I'd have given you dinner.'

'I know you would. But this is a business matter.' Beverley smiled at him affectionately. After her return from Europe, she had spent Christmas in her old home, but soon afterwards moved out to a place of her own. The new Mrs Jamieson would not want to have a stepdaughter around all the time. The move, though, had not affected the closeness of her relationship with her father. 'I've come to ask for money.'

Jock, who was his daughter's unpaid business consultant and knew the size of her independent fortune to the last cent, raised his eyebrows but made no comment.

'I want to start a charity,' Beverley told him. 'I shall put some of my own money into it to start things off. But if it proves useful, it will need a lot more. I know that most companies make charitable donations. What I'm asking is that my charity should be put on your list. Well,' she added honestly, 'put at the top of your list.'

'There are plenty of charities around,' her father pointed out. 'No need to start your own. All you have to do is choose the one you like and write a cheque.'

'I aim to do a lot more than that. I want to choose the individual recipients, and organise different ways of benefiting them. But if it gets around that I'm giving away money person to person, I shall be swamped with begging letters. So it needs to go through a fund. And I shall run it myself. It's going to be my job.'

Even before returning to Australia she had decided to abandon her research and the idea of taking a Master's degree. It seemed wrong to do nothing but enjoy herself: sailing, dancing or playing tennis, but, on the other hand, it would be ridiculous for someone who already had a sufficient income to sacrifice her days to the discipline of a paid job unless the work really interested her. A seed of the idea which she was about to explain had begun to germinate while she was still in Scotland. She had allowed it time to grow before producing it for her father's approval.

'What kind of charity?' Jock asked.

'A suitable one for Jamieson money. Harry the Hat's idea.'

Jock awaited further enlightenment. Naturally he knew all about Harry the Hat's place in their family history, but did not immediately see its connection with his daughter's proposal.

'You remember what Gramps was told by Great-Uncle Fred?' Some years after his arrival in Sydney Wee Jamie had married his lawyer's younger sister, bringing Fred Johns into the family. 'If no one had turned up to claim Harry the Hat's land, the proceeds of selling it would have been given to a charity for fatherless boys. The boys didn't get the money then, because Gramps had it instead; so in a way we owe it to them now.'

'You're proposing to set up a fund for fatherless boys?'

'And girls too. Yes. That's what Gramps was himself, a fatherless boy. So it seems appropriate. That time I spent tracking down his early days made me realise how terrible it must be to be young and have no one you can ask for help when you need something special. No one who cares.'

'Hell, Bev, there must be hundreds of charities for orphans and half-orphans. Why go to the trouble – '

'I want to take a particular slant. To help deserving kids in the same way you helped Ken Murray.'

'Ken?' said Jock, puzzled. 'I didn't do anything special for him. He lived with us because his mother was working for us. If you mean that I let him use the tennis court after he'd shown that he had an eye for hitting the ball, that was for your benefit. It was good for you, having a strong opponent always on hand.'

Beverley shook her head, laughing. 'You can't have forgotten,' she said. 'You paid for him to join the tennis club. You paid for him to be coached with me. You paid for all his tennis gear. You paid his entry fees for tournaments, and his travel expenses to get to them. What you did for him was what a prosperous father would have tried to do for a talented son – and you did it so matter-of-factly that Ken may not even have realised how lucky he was. But if you hadn't done it, he would have had no one to ask.'

'His mother was a widow. I was glad to help out with a few treats for the boy. But most kids who are fatherless nowadays have some silly bitch of a mother who simply doesn't believe in marriage.'

'It's not the children's fault. I'm not thinking in terms of orphanages or big grants, Dad.' She leaned forward earnestly as she explained. 'The ones I want to help are those who have some talent or ambition, like Ken, and who've done something about it for themselves, but who can't get any further on their own.'

'Example?'

Beverley had carried a folder into her father's office. She laid it on the desk now and opened it, pulling her chair closer.

'There was a story in the paper three months ago, in May, about a girl who got to the last six of the Young Musician of the Year competition. All the judges said how good she was, although she didn't win. It turned out that the only place she could practise was at school and the caretaker was always kicking her off the premises so that he could lock up. She needed a good piano of her own; and she deserved it. I've been cutting out stories like that ever since Christmas, trying to decide how I'd have dealt with them. And my friends keep mentioning cases. For example, Ken came across this brilliant nine-year-old – '

'Okay, okay.' No doubt Jock could see from the thickness of the folder that the rest of his afternoon schedule was at risk. 'I get the idea.'

'I reckon there are a lot of tears shed on the pillow by children who've worked hard to take the first step towards some ambition but who need a helping hand if they're ever to take a second step. That's what I'd call the charity: The Helping Hand.'

'Are you sure you realise what you'd be taking on? You'd have to publicise what you're offering, sieve the applications, investigate some of them, find the right people to advise on the right help and provide it. You'd have to manage the money – which would mean investing some of it as well as spending it – keep proper accounts and have them audited, fill in legal returns, claim tax exemptions. You'd have to work out from scratch a filing and forecasting system to keep track of each case. And you'd probably have to go fund-raising as well: however much you start with, there's never enough. You could find yourself as much a slave to the luxury of giving money away as most people are to the necessity of earning it. And summer's coming!'

'I'd have a voluntary committee to help with the advice part. And an office with a secretary and a fund manager.'

'Which is going to cost you.'

'Which is why I'm suggesting to my dearly beloved father that his company might like to make a generous donation – perhaps in memory of his own fatherless father.' She waited, holding her breath in hope, for the decision.

Jock stood up and walked across to the window, looking down at the harbour. As a rule he sat with his back to it, perhaps in order that the sight of yachts gliding in should not make him regret his own sailing days.

'You seem to have been thinking along the same lines as your grandfather,' he said at last. 'He never forgot

271

Harry the Hat either, nor the fatherless boys. You wouldn't know about this – he kept very quiet about it – but he built up a trust fund out of the company profits. The annual income has to be distributed to charitable institutions for the benefit of children. I'm the chairman of the trustees. Every year I sign over large sums to be administered by various reputable charities. It would be possible – it would be appropriate, even – for some of that to come your way.' He turned back to face her. 'You understand, Bev, that your affairs will have to be whiter than white, your accounts more strictly kept than the state bank's. I don't want any suspicion that I'm syphoning money off to my own family. But if you promise me that everything you do will stand up to hostile scrutiny – why, sure I'll put you on the list as soon as you have legal recognition.'

'Dad!' Beverley ran to the window to kiss him.

'We'll find you a room somewhere here for an office,' he offered. 'To keep your running costs down till you get going.' He returned to his desk and began to scribble memos on a pad. 'D'you remember Lena, who was my secretary until two years ago? She left to have a baby and now she's shrieking with boredom and longing for part-time work. Just the person to start your filing system off well. I've got a good bloke in Accounts who'll give you some hints and keep an eye on you. And once you've accumulated enough data to show how you're going to operate, I'll get someone to write a program which you can use on the computer. The most important thing will be the choice of manager, of course. He needs to be not only efficient but so honest that you never need feel even a flicker of doubt. I'll ask – '

'No, Dad.' Beverley interrupted before he could go any further. 'Everything else you've offered will be great. More than I could have hoped. Thanks a lot. But I'm going to be working so close to the manager, poaching on his territory half the time, that I'd rather pick him myself, to be sure that we'll get on.'

'Right.' Jock drew a line under his notes. 'Now, you've

asked your questions. I've got one for you. That lawyer chap you met in Edinburgh.'

'Ian Blair? You're not suggesting I should bring *him* out from Scotland to run The Helping Hand?'

'No. Change of subject. I found a letter from him waiting when I got back.' Jock had returned only a few days earlier from an exhaustive tour of all the Castle Hotels in Australia and the South Pacific. 'Has he been in touch with you as well?'

Beverley felt herself flushing. The letter which had arrived from Edinburgh two months earlier had been warm and emotional, full of regrets that circumstances had divided them and of wishes that it might yet be possible for them to meet again. Ian, so reserved in conversation, had revealed himself as unihibited in writing. To ignore the letter would have been unkind, but she acknowledged it only with a postcard, making it clear that she did not propose to embark on a romantic correspondence.

'Yes,' she said. 'He wrote to tell me that the laird of Lochandar had been declared bankrupt. Apparently he'd run up a mountain of debt, always intending to pay it off when he got his hands on the insurance money. As things turned out, he wasn't able to put in any claim at all, not even for the fabric of the building. Reading between the lines, it sounds like a trade-off, as though the insurance company and the police decided not to proceed with a prosecution provided David made no claim on his insurance policy. Otherwise he'd be charged with arson.'

'I can see that would suit the insurers nicely.'

'Yes. And I suppose that if they were happy enough with the solution not to press any charge of fraud, the police might have trouble linking David to whatever evidence they had of arson.' She suspected, too, that traces of feudal respect might still linger in Scotland, to make the idea of putting a laird behind bars seem distasteful; and the unsolved mystery of the American tourist could have provided an excuse for inaction.

'Writing between the lines seems to be Mr Blair's

speciality,' growled Jock. 'What he wanted to find out from me was whether I'd be interested in the Lochandar estate. I've read the letter three times and I still don't gather whether I'm expected to buy it, or to hire him to pursue a legal claim. Of course, if it's rightly ours, perhaps *I* could claim on the insurance!' He grinned at the idea.

'What are you going to do about it?'

'Nothing. Zero. Nix. What's the point? I'm not interested in killing things. Who wants a weekend cottage that's twenty-four hours' flying time away and where it's always raining when you get there?'

'You could develop the castle as a hotel.'

'Not worth the hassle for anything under a hundred beds. Maybe I'd have felt sentimental about it if it had been my own birthplace, but . . . the answer's no, unless you've fallen for the place yourself. You can have it if you want it.' He waited for his daughter's reaction, but Beverley shook her head. Memories of her grandfather had made Lochandar a sad place for her.

'Doesn't mean that I can't be sentimental in other ways, though,' Jock went on. 'I'll show you one of these days. Well, good luck with your charity. I'll let you know as soon as there's an office ready for you.'

'Thanks again, Dad.' Beverley's eyes danced with pleasure as she made her way home. She was still humming happily to the tune of *This is my Lucky Day* when she opened her front door and bent to pick up a note from the mat.

It was headed with the date and the time – the same time as the appointment with her father – and continued:

'I arrived in Sydney an hour ago and am just about to sleep off my jet lag. I shall phone you at eight o'clock tomorrow morning, to invite you to lunch or dine with me. Please be ready to say yes.

Luke Dancy

'Of course I will,' said Beverley aloud, as cheerfully as if he were listening. Eleven months had passed since they said goodbye, but the afternoon when Luke had

274

burbled nonsense at her, whilst propelling a punt along what pretended to be a river in Oxford, was one of the most delightful memories of her time in England. What was he doing in Australia, she wondered. Going straight to the telephone, she booked a table for lunch the next day.

2

'Why aren't you in Oxford?' asked Beverley, smiling with the pleasure of seeing Luke again as she ordered their drinks. To make it clear that he was her guest, she had arranged to meet him at her club.

'Because I'm a grown-up person now,' he told her. 'No longer *in statu pupillaris*. The Oxford academic year ends in June.'

'Of course. I forgot. How did you get on?'

'Modesty forbids me to say.'

'A First? Congratulations, Luke.' She lifted her glass to toast him before leading the way from the bar to a pair of comfortable chairs. 'So why, with the world your oyster, have you come to Australia?'

'An Australian ought to take it for granted that, with the world my oyster, I would go for the pearl. Well, the answer is, I've come across the world in order to have lunch with you.'

'Of course. Naturally. How could I imagine there'd be any other reason?' Beverley grinned cheerfully, but Luke did not smile back.

'I'm not joking.' Leaning forward in his chair, he reached across to take hold of her hand. 'I won't push this at you after today, but I need to say it straight out just once.' He spent a moment searching for words, which then emerged in a rush. 'When you were in England I told you that I loved you. Or at least, I think I did. It's so easy to run a dialogue through your mind over and over again until it comes out the way you want it, and then you honestly believe that 's the way it happened.'

He looked at her in a questioning way, as though hoping for confirmation, but Beverley did not speak. The smile had faded from her own face as well. She was not sure that she knew how to deal with this conversation; but the length of his journey had earned him the right to have his say.

'Anyway, whether I said it or not, you knew. But I couldn't expect you to give me another thought. Someone you were never going to see again. Someone you only met by accident. When I remember how easily I might have missed the chance of knowing you! If I'd cycled off from my grandmother's house just half a minute earlier! It was fate which decided we should meet that first time. But if there was ever to be another meeting, it seemed to me that fate needed to be given a helping hand. That if I loved you as much as I thought I did, I'd got to prove it to myself as well as to you by taking some kind of second step. Burning my boats. Turning down the prospect of immense wealth as a merchant banker in order – ' He stopped in mid-speech to ask, in a lighter tone of voice, 'Why are you staring at me in what literary folk call wide-eyed astonishment?'

'Sorry. It was just that you used a phrase . . . A helping hand, you said.'

'Is there something odd about that?'

'No. Only a coincidence. I've been thinking recently about a charity for fatherless children, and – '

'I don't know how we've got on to the subject of charities,' said Luke. 'But I'm a fatherless boy. Does your charity dish out beautiful brides to deserving cases?'

'Are you really? Fatherless, I mean.'

'Have been for fifteen years. What was the coincidence you mentioned?'

'The Helping Hand. That's the name of the charity.'

'Good old fate!' said Luke. 'Picking up its cue.' His moment of earnestness had passed. But as he returned to the bantering style of speech which she had found so engaging in England, Beverley found herself moving in

276

an opposite direction, towards seriousness. Yes, it did seem like fate.

'You said you'd turned down a job back home?' she checked.

'Not just a job. A career. Greater love hath no man than to turn his back on bullion markets and multi-national conglomerates.'

'In favour of what? I mean, what are you going to do in Australia? Have you got a job?'

'It depends who's asking the question. I can tell you, getting an Australian visa which allows one to work for one's living here is just as hard as getting a First at Oxford. But I managed to find the right kind of sponsor. A good friend of my tutor, willing to certify his need to employ me as a research assistant. The tricky part is that since I can't hope to live on what he has promised to pay me – and he can't afford to pay it anyway – it's silently understood between us that I should become self-supporting as soon as possible. There shouldn't be any problem about that. I'm extremely employable and not at all fussy.'

'Could you run a small office?' asked Beverley.

'Of course I could. If I'd chosen to go into the Civil Service I'd have been running the whole of the United Kingdom in thirty years. Beverley, you're not inter-viewing me for a *job* are you? The only job I want you to offer me is that of adoring husband. Will you marry me?'

'Not today,' said Beverley, but although she spoke primly, she could feel her heart swelling with excitement. Life with Luke could be a lot of fun, and perhaps they would be able to achieve something worthwhile together. So, not today, but perhaps tomorrow. 'But yes to the first question. I am offering you a job. To help me run the charity I was telling you about. Would that interest you?'

'There's nothing nicer than giving away other people's money.' Luke made a brave but not entirely successful attempt to hide his disappointment at being forced to

277

change the subject. 'If you insist on evading my proposal, tell me about the charity.'

Beverley described what she had in mind. 'So the manager would have to look after almost everything to start with,' she said. 'Organise the paperwork, keep the accounts, think of ways to make the opportunities known, help to evaluate the applications, and explore ways of providing help.'

'Sounds a delightful variety. One important question, though. What precisely would you be doing?'

'The Helping Hand is my personal baby,' she told him. 'It was my idea and I'm the one who's going to make sure it works. I shall call myself the president, because that sort of title will sound impressive when I'm fund-raising. But if you take the manager's job you'll have to surrender a desk in your office and be prepared for me to drop in at any time. As well as licking the stamps, or whatever, I shall make the final decisions on whatever candidates or schemes you put up to me. In fact, I shall interfere in everything. Could you put up with that?'

'When can I start?' asked Luke, half-rising from his chair, but almost at once he became serious again and for a second time reached out to take her hand. 'You do realise, don't you, that I should regard it as an apprenticeship? Putting up with Beverley Jamieson during an eight-hour day as a means of persuading her to put up with me for a lifetime. It would be a little cruel of you to accept my indentures if you weren't prepared to look favourably in a general way, shall we say, on the prospect of granting me my Master's certificate in the end. If you see what I mean.'

Beverley saw what he meant, and happiness made her honest, if only obliquely. 'When can you start?' she asked in reply.

Luke began to laugh, and Beverley laughed with him. Only after that did the conversation become more practical. It was possible, he pointed out, that the professor who had promised to employ him might actually be hoping for some research help.

'I'll report in to him tomorrow. I'm sure he won't need

me full-time, if at all, so I can give you at least a share of my precious time. And I'd better sign myself up for some evening classes in bookkeeping, to make sure that I keep the accounts in a proper form.'

'No need to bother with classes. One of my father's accountants will give you a crash course. You'll have access to the computer too, so you may need familiarisation sessions.'

'I may well. All a little different from my great-grandfather's handwritten registers and file cards.' He shook his head in surprise. 'Odd that I should find myself in the same line of country as old Mr Chisholm. Odd that in a sense I've been preparing for it since I was fourteen. And particularly odd that you shouldn't hold against me what the Orphans' New Life Society did to your grandfather.'

'I thought a lot about that when I was in London,' she told him. 'By the time I'd sorted out what happened in 1910 I reckoned that Malcolm McEwan was an out-and-out villain. I can't think of a single good thing to be said for him. His lawyer, Gordon Blair was perhaps nothing more sinister than a cold fish. No feelings. Doing what he was ordered to do and thinking that absolved him from blame. Even if he didn't commit any actual crime, he must have seen what distress he was causing and wondered about the ethics of it. I've no love for him either.'

'But you see Great-grandfather as being different?'

'He probably did believe that he was doing the best thing for his orphans. Even the system of separating siblings, which seems so terrible now – in those days some people sincerely thought it would make it easier for a child to settle down in a new life if the whole of the old one was left behind. I'm doing my best to act as Prisoner's Friend, you see. However hard the kids' lives were in the colonies, they might have had an even harder time if they'd been left to fend for themselves in the city slums.'

'That's on the assumption that they were all genuinely destitute.'

'Right,' agreed Beverley. 'Not many of them were diddled out of castles, I don't suppose. There was injustice in my grandfather's case because he ought not to have been destitute. That letter you found showed that Mr Chisholm owed Mr Blair a favour – not personally, but on behalf of his charity. He must have realised that he was being expected to repay it by not asking questions when Mairi and Jamie were brought in and registered under different names. But he would have been confronted with two small, dirty children who were undeniably orphans. So in his case I can just about bring myself to be forgiving. That's all old history, anyway, and I'm not interested in history any more.'

'I rather am. I ought to confess to you that I still have the urge to write your grandfather's biography. I even tried the idea out on my grandmother as a reason for coming to Australia. She was so pleased by my interest in one of her father's boys that she went straight into town and changed her will. One of these days I shall inherit the entire contents of the sanctum. Not to mention the house which contains it. So when you're considering me as a prospective husband, I hope you'll take into account the fact that I have Expectations. House prices in North Oxford will astonish you! But seriously, reverting to your grandfather, will you show me a photograph of him sometime?'

'I can do better than that. If you've finished your drink, we'll go across the road to eat. I thought the club would be the cosiest place to meet, but our table's at the Top of the Tower. To dazzle you with the most magnificent view of Sydney, from the tower which my grandfather built to remind him of his childhood. On the land which he was given by Harry the Hat. Free meals at The Castle are one of the family perks.'

She led the way outside and pointed to the shining skyscraper. Luke looked up only briefly before returning his gaze to ground level. Clearly he was trying to put himself into the shoes of the eighteen-year-old country boy who had stared at a patch of scrub and seen a vision.

But he made no comment before following her across the road and into the hotel's huge reception area.

'There you are.' She pointed to a large painting which occupied the place of honour between the curves of a double staircase. It was a portrait of a large, sandy-haired man in his fifties, relaxing in an arm chair. 'Wee Jamie Jamieson.'

'Wee Jamie!' Luke laughed, as everyone laughed who first heard the adjective applied to such a big man. 'He has your eyes.'

'You could say I have his.' But her attention was distracted by the touch of a hand on her shoulder. Jock Jamieson had been moving towards the portrait in the company of a workman when he caught sight of her.

'Hi, Bev.'

'Hi, Dad! Can I introduce a friend of mine? Luke Dancy, just arrived from England. He's supposed to be doing research for some professor. But he's going to take on all the hard work of running the charity for me. And he wants to write a biography of Gramps as well.'

'Is that all?' her father asked her jokingly as he shook hands with Luke.

Isn't that enough? What else should there be? Struggling to choose between phrases, she found herself unable to say any of them. As the ridiculous silence lengthened she was aware of the two men turning to look at her. Her father's eyes sparkled with amusement and Luke's with delight. If they could both read her thoughts with such ease, she might as well answer truthfully.

'That's all for the moment,' she said, and hurried to change the subject. 'What's going on here?'

'There was a plaque attached to your grandfather's portrait, if you remember. I've had it brought up to date.'

The carpenter was fixing it at that moment. Beverley waited until it was in place before stepping closer to look at it.

'Didn't see why I should pay a lawyer to prove what my daughter's discovered for free,' said Jock. 'The truth's the truth, right?'

'Right,' agreed Luke. Beverley was conscious of his arm moving to encircle her waist as together they read the new inscription.

JAMES McEWAN JAMIESON

'Wee Jamie'

1906 – 1987

Founder of the Castle Hotel Group

and

Laird of Lochandar